Rendezvous with Death

by

Suzanne Rossi

Rendezvous with Death

Cover Art by *Kim Mendoza*

The Wild Rose Press, Inc.
PO Box 708
Adams Basin, NY 14410-0708
Visit us at www.thewildrosepress.com

Publishing History
First Crimson Rose Edition, 2015
Print ISBN 978-1-5092-0252-2
Digital ISBN 978-1-5092-0253-9

Published in the United States of America

"Thank you for lunch, Mr. Mallory. I hope you have a safe trip home."

He also stood. "I'm sticking around for a while. See what the police uncover. I want Marc's killer caught and brought to trial."

"We all do."

On the sidewalk, I offered my hand. "Goodbye, Mr. Mallory, and thank you again."

He smiled, grasping my hand firmly. My arms broke out in goosebumps while a small thrill zipped up my arm and traveled to the pit of my stomach. Oh, no! Not *that*!

"Don't make it goodbye. We'll be seeing each other again. I'll be in touch."

He turned and walked away. I stood in the middle of the crowded sidewalk, examining my skin for singe marks. An attractive man who sucked that kind of a reaction out of me was dangerous in more ways than one.

He disappeared, swallowed up by strolling tourists and bustling businessmen. Yes—very dangerous. I didn't want to admit he intimidated the hell out of me.

Praise for Suzanne Rossi

"What a GREAT book this is! I absolutely adored several things about *DEATH IS THE PITS*, first of which is the murder mystery/whodunit storyline. The pace was quick and the wit was sharp and Ms. Rossi kept the twists and turns going. Every 5 minutes I could see another character being the culprit, and though I thought I figured out the real story, the truth kept me guessing until the very end."

~*Delta, TheRomanceReviews.com*
~*~

"Ms Rossi kept me intrigued in this mysterious murder mystery. The pace of this [*THE REUNION*] is good and the storyline flowed well. The characters were well developed and the emotions of the characters were so real. I loved how one of the characters was the drama queen of the bunch, and I especially loved how she was retelling what had happened."

~*CozyReader, TheRomanceReviews.com*
~*~

"Suzanne Rossi writes fabulous romantic suspense…I am such a suspicious person when reading romantic suspense but [the hero] got through my defenses very quickly…If you are looking for a mystery reminiscent of the classics with a touch of heat then [*DEADLY INHERITANCE*] is a fabulous choice. I admit I enjoyed the look into the lives of the uber-wealthy and as always am looking forward to the next story by this author because she never disappoints."

~*Night Owl Reviews*

Dedication

This is my eleventh book, and one of the things I love to do is a dedication to those special people who helped guide me along the path to publication. However, dedications can also be the hardest things to write. I found that to be true for this book.

In desperation, I threw out the question of "who" on Facebook and received some interesting replies from friends and relatives. All had merit, but my husband, Bruce Peek, came up with the winner.

So, with no apologies to The Mamas and the Papas, this book is "dedicated to the ones I love," which includes a lot of people.

With that in mind, I hope you all enjoy *Rendezvous with Death*.

Chapter One

The mist drifted into the alley, its damp tendrils wrapping around my legs and obscuring my feet. A streetlight from across the road sent a diffused glow into the yawning darkness. Further up the alley, a back door light added its feeble beam to the area.

Fog is not a regular visitor to Port Royale in South Florida, and I was uneasy that, tonight of all nights, it had chosen to make an appearance. In spite of the faint illuminations, I shivered.

Mist should smell clean and fresh, but this stank with the dank odors of garbage, damp pavement, and something worse—something metallic and menacing. I stood rigid, my throat dry, then swallowed hard, shivering again. The thickening fog muffled the normal sounds of the night. The eerie silence tortured my ears.

A stray breeze parted the surrounding gray curtain long enough to reveal shadows of movement scurrying behind a dumpster. Rats. I suppressed a scream and balled my fists in the pockets of my trench coat, clutching the smooth folds of the satiny lining between cold fingers. *Get a grip, Shelley. You can do this. And where the hell is Marc?*

I glanced up and down the alley. What was I doing here? Why the hell had I agreed to meet Marc Chambers in this clichéd location under such melodramatic circumstances? If he had information

1

regarding the allegations of city corruption my boss was investigating for our newspaper, the South Florida Standard, he should have come to my office in the morning like any other civic-minded citizen. And what kind of information did he have? He wasn't an informant, even though he worked for the company suspected of handing out bribes. I hadn't spoken to him in months.

The fog thinned, allowing the shadows to take shape. Boxes and garbage bags littered the narrow space. If Marc didn't show in another minute, I was out of here.

Or perhaps he's already left. I'd been twenty minutes late.

I pulled my cell phone from my pocket, intending to call him, and peered up the alleyway. In the dim light, something new attracted my attention. My heartbeats accelerated and my knees went weak. No, surely not…it couldn't be. My eyes had to be listening to my imagination and messing with my mind.

I sucked in a startled breath, dropped my phone back into my pocket, and walked ten feet down the alley toward the back light, my reporter's curiosity stronger than my fear.

This was no garbage bag. It was Marc. He laid face up, one arm to his side, the other over his head. I stooped, feeling for a pulse, but found none. Three large, dark stains on his shirt front verified I'd never talk to my friend again. His skin was still warm to the touch. He hadn't been dead long. My mind screamed, "Run," but my legs refused to obey. I rose, stumbling to the opposite side of the alley, and threw up.

Clapping a hand over my mouth, I whirled, took

three steps, and then stopped. Marc said he had vital information that would prove my newspaper's allegations, sending a lot of people to jail, including high-profile city officials. Should I look for it?

A shudder rolled over me from head to toe. Oh God! Search a *dead* man? I was very much alone. What if the killer still lurked in the mist and shadows? No, surely not or I'd be dead already.

I looked back at Marc, stiffened my shoulders, and my resolve. The mist had crept in again. It would shield me from prying eyes.

I stooped beside my friend, the metallic smell making my stomach cramp, and thrust shaking fingers into the pockets of his raincoat and slacks. Nothing. I didn't even know what I sought. An envelope? A computer printout? A CD? I had no clue.

A car raced past in the street. The tires hissing on the wet pavement reminded me that if I had found Marc, so could someone else. They'd also find me. I needed to get out of here.

I rose, whispering, "Goodbye, Marc. Rest in peace."

I started to leave when I noticed his shoes—the kind serious joggers wear with a zippered hideaway for ID. Marc had never jogged a day in his life.

I crouched tugging at the zipper on his right foot. It slid open, and I shoved my finger inside. A metal object scraped my fingertip. I wiggled it free and held up a key, noting the short shank and circular head, and then realized what I held.

"A post office box," I said out loud.

I rezipped the compartment in his shoe, and then used the hem of my trench coat to wipe the little zipper pull clean. No use in leaving behind fingerprints. With any luck no one would think to check for DNA inside the damned thing.

A clanging noise from the far end of the alley brought me to my feet, my heart pounding in my ears. Clutching the key in a tight fist, adrenaline gave me a kick in the ass. I raced back to the street, high-tailing it around the corner to where I'd parked my car. I threw myself inside, locking the doors behind me.

Now cocooned in the relative safety of my Honda Civic, the reality of what I'd experienced broke over me like a tsunami. My chest tightened, squeezing the breath from my lungs. I gripped the steering wheel, and rested my forehead on my hands, struggling to breathe, before finally drawing in a breath only to expel it in a heavy sob.

Oh, God! The riddled corpse lying back there was Marc, my friend, a man I'd dated, kissed, and almost slept with. The suppressed emotions of the last few minutes erupted. I cried, gasping and choking. Tears spilled down my cheeks and onto my clenched hands. When the storm passed, I raised my head, wiping the wetness from my face.

I couldn't leave Marc in that rat infested alley, I just couldn't. He'd trusted me, and by being late, I had let him down.

Trembling, I fumbled for my cell phone to dial 9-1-1, and then stopped. My caller ID would show up. I didn't want anyone to know I had found Marc or why I'd been in that alley. His murder *had* to be connected to the investigation.

I tucked the key into my bra. I'd find a pay phone and call it in anonymously. Two blocks later that's what

I did from outside a convenience store.

"Nine-one-one emergency."

"I want to report shots fired from an alley between Lake and Johnson Streets on Northwest Thirty-fifth Avenue."

"Your name?"

I hung up, jumped back into my car, and fled. My hands shook so badly, I had trouble gripping the steering wheel, but my mind worked just fine.

Where is this post office box?

****

I arrived home sometime after two o'clock and crawled into bed. Sleep was impossible. I couldn't erase the sight of Marc or the smell of the alley from my mind. Tossing and turning, I caught little catnaps only to jerk awake convinced the killer lurked in my bedroom.

I abandoned sleep at seven o'clock, showered, dressed, and was in the process of once again hiding the key in my bra when something I should have noticed last night but didn't, stopped me with my fingers between my boobs.

Keys! Where were Marc's keys?

Even if he'd taken a cab, his house keys should have been on him. Had the killer stolen them?

"Of course the killer took them, dumb ass," I said out loud. "Who else?"

The murderer had probably tossed the place, but why should that stop me? Maybe *he* didn't know what to look for either. I'd go to Marc's and earn my journalistic pay by snooping. As an accountant, he always had a backup for everything, including house keys. Being mildly anal had its uses. But maybe a key wasn't necessary. *Would the killer really re-lock the door after ransacking the joint?*

I hurried into the bathroom and grimaced at the image in the mirror. My shoulder length auburn hair was tangled worse than a ball of string after cat play, and the dark circles under my hazel eyes did nothing for me.

I wielded a comb, slapped on some make up, and charged out to my car. Life-sustaining coffee could wait a bit longer. I'd be into the office late, but who cared? The lead reporter on the investigation and my boss, Bill Mathias, wouldn't raise a stink when I told him why. Tracking down information qualified as a good excuse. I just wouldn't tell him the complete truth.

Marc lived in a fashionable section of Port Royale, not far from the trendy Riverside shopping district. I parked two blocks away and walked. If anyone suspicious loitered near the townhouse, I'd keep on walking.

No one suspicious lurked. Instead, cops swarmed around the entrance. A sizable crowd of curious onlookers had gathered. I wiggled my way to the front until stopped by yellow crime scene tape strung between two light poles and the front stoop. Uniformed and plainclothes cops came and went.

"What happened?" I asked a man in jogging clothes. I guessed this was more interesting than pulse rates.

"Beats me."

A woman next to him said, "I heard them talking, and the guy who lived here was found murdered last night."

"No kidding? In this neighborhood?" I asked. She

looked like the kind of person who'd make it her business to know everything.

"I know the superintendent, and he said they found his body in an alley near the flea market. The cops rousted the super out at four in the morning. He let them in and guess what?"

"What?" the jogger said.

"The place was torn apart. Books tossed on the floor, upholstery slashed, drawers overturned, the whole nine yards. I wonder what he was into. Think he may have been a drug dealer? I'll bet that's it. Why else would he be in an alley in that part of town? He was a drug dealer, and this was a deal gone sour—just like on TV."

The woman's avid imagination made me want to smack her. Marc had been the most conventional, law-abiding person I'd ever met. I opened my mouth to set her straight, and then closed it again.

Shut up, Shelley. Don't draw attention to yourself.

I moved away and sidled up to another group of people, asking the same questions. When they couldn't add anything I continued on. No one had any information. I needed to find the superintendent.

Then a familiar face popped out of Marc's front door, Detective Frank Whitten. I ducked my head and turned away.

Swell, the one person I didn't need to see.

I had interviewed him a few months ago on a piece about the murder of a homeless man. He'd been uncooperative and I'd reciprocated by being less than flattering in my article. Rumor had it he was about to retire complete with a gold watch and a plaque thanking him for thirty-five years on the force.

I shoved my way through the crowd and retraced my steps down the block. It wouldn't do for Whitten to know I'd been a friend of Marc's. My presence at the townhouse would lead to a seat in an interrogation room.

Back in my car, I paused to think. Where would Marc have rented a post office box? Close to home? His office? Was it in a branch or one of those mail drop places in a strip mall? Would he rent under his name or use an alias?

My brain refused to work, so I drove to the nearest coffee house for caffeine and ordered a second double shot to go.

I staggered into the office at nine-thirty, a good hour and a half late, bumped against the nameplate on the outside cubicle wall knocking it to the carpeted floor. I set the container on my cluttered desk, retrieved the nameplate, stuck it back in place, and then dumped my purse on the floor before sinking into my chair. It had been a helluva night. The morning hadn't started any better.

I turned on my computer and jerked the lid off the container, spilling some on my desk.

"Shit," I mumbled, mopping up the mess with a tissue.

"Well, look who decided to come to work. The great Shelley Jackson finally appears," a voice sounded from my cubicle doorway.

Doug Elliott, a staff reporter who had coveted my job when it became available last summer, leaned against the doorway. Fortunately, my boss's opinion of Elliott mirrored mine—an ass-kissing toady who owed his job to an aunt who owned a fair amount of stock in the paper.

"Yeah, I got special dispensation from the Pope to sleep in today. What was your excuse last Thursday?" I tossed the sopping tissues into my wastepaper basket.

He ignored the question and sat on the corner of my desk. His rear end took up considerable space. He stood a couple of inches short of six feet. His lack of exercise and love of good food showed.

"Maybe you should go back home and try again. You look like you hit every bar on South Street," he said with a smirk, naming the local nightclub district.

"Maybe you should get your fat ass off my desk. I've got work to do."

Doug picked up a sheet of paper and read it. "I hear Mathias has you doing legwork on this bribery scandal thing. Find out anything yet?"

I snatched the paper from his hand. "Nothing you need to know. Don't you have an obit to write or a political profile to update?"

I made a mental note to either lock my desk or take important papers home. After last night, I trusted no one.

"Aw, come on, don't be like that. What have you got?"

"Nothing, and get outta here."

I rolled my chair back several inches when he leaned in close, his pale blue eyes sharp and gleaming.

"I've got a friend in the police department," he said, his voice barely above a whisper. "He told me an accountant from Shay and Holmes was found dead in an alley early this morning. Kinda suspicious, don't you think? We could work together on this."

"Drop dead."

Bill Mathias walked up behind Doug. "Elliott, don't you have work to do?"

He jumped off my desk and shot my boss an ingratiating smile. "Yes, sir. I was just telling Shelley a friend of mine on the force called a while ago. He said a Shay and Holmes accountant was murdered last night. I thought there might be a connection to this bribery thing. If you'd like, I'll follow up on it."

"You think I don't have connections in the police department?" Bill asked.

"No, sir, that is, I'm sure you do, but I was just trying to be helpful." Doug slid past Bill, smoothing his sandy hair with a well-manicured hand. "Well, I'll talk to you later, Shelley. I've got a deadline." He hurried away.

A sneer curled Bill's lip. "What a worm. My contact called at six this morning with the information. He just called again. The dead guy's name is Marc Chambers and his townhouse has been tossed. Poke around and see what you can find."

I suppressed a shudder. *I've already poked and found enough.*

"I'm interviewing Councilwoman Anne Hodges at eleven, and then have to meet with Dave Brooks for a late lunch."

"Dave Brooks, the general contractor? Didn't he get outbid on the River Towers Condo project by Shay and Holmes?" I asked.

"And he's still madder than hell about it. He may be able to shed some light on S and H." Bill paused, shifting his gaze to me. "Get started, and try to be on time tomorrow, okay?" He walked toward his office.

Bill Mathias was an all right guy, but twenty years'

experience had given him a certain amount of arrogance. He took on the more glamorous stories while I did his legwork. He said I had to earn my dues. Of course, his byline would be above my work.

I gulped the espresso. The key in my bra pressed against my breast. This story about Marc could be *my* ticket to a byline. I could write it up and turn it into the editor on my own, bypassing Bill. What difference would it make? He'd still have his bribery scandal. Maybe I should scan the Yellow Pages for possible mailbox sites. I had an obligation to Marc. He was my friend. He'd trusted me, and now he was dead.

I finished the coffee, tossed the cup into the trash, and got online, pulling up the phone book.

****

Privacy was hard to achieve in the office. Doug found a dozen reasons to pass my cubicle, slowing his step and cocking his head to pick up any stray conversation. At the moment, he lounged on a desk talking to of one of the secretaries. His eyes frequently swiveled in my direction.

Volunteering to teach the miserable prick a lesson, I accessed the Port Royale phone book, and found the address I sought.

Whipping out my cell as if it had rung, I slapped it against my ear. Dougie straightened and ambled back my way. I turned from the cubicle entry. In the reflection of my desktop monitor, I saw him stop and went into my spiel.

"Of course, you can trust me…I swear I'll be alone…They look suspicious to us, too. That's why the paper's investigating…You name the place." I scribbled the address I'd looked up on a pad of paper.

"The Haven? I can be there by twelve-thirty. How will I know you…You're joking, right? I'm supposed to walk up to a six-foot-two-inch, two-hundred-pound stranger and a say 'What's new, pussycat?' That's ridiculous…A code is not necessary. Neither of us is James Bond…All right, all right, I didn't mean to offend. I'll do it your way."

I hung up, and Doug turned pretending to read something in his hand. Rising, I headed for the ladies' room, leaving the note on my desk. Once inside, I opened the door a crack and peeked through. Doug slithered into my cubicle like a snake and snatched the notepad. He jotted the address on the back of the envelope he carried, grinned, and hurried out.

Back at my desk, I chuckled. The Haven was a gay biker bar in a seedier part of town. There had to be at least one six-foot-two-inch guy bellied up to the bar.

"Have a ball, Dougie," I murmured to myself. "I hope you like white wine and know how to waltz."

****

I hung up in frustration. I'd called four mail drops and none of them would give me an answer on whether Marc had rented a box. Not revealing names must have topped the list of commandments.

I'd have to find Marc's post office box the old-fashioned way—on foot. I left a message for Bill saying I was out gathering information, and then headed for my car. Behind the wheel, I retrieved the key from my bra and examined it again.

Last night I'd been too shocked and scared to do much more than toss it on my nightstand. This morning I'd given it just a quick glance. In the limited light of the garage, I squinted at the number imprinted on the head—four-one-two.

A car started and Doug pulled out of a spot near the door to the stairwell. The clock on my dash read eleven-thirty. I chuckled, sorry to miss the fun at The Haven.

****

I circled the parking lot at my sixth mail drop several times until finding a space. The closest post office branches were located several miles from both Marc's work and home, but next on my list if I struck out here.

My search began near the Shay and Holmes offices on the theory Marc would rent a box close to work where he could walk on his lunch hour. Now, ten blocks separated me from S and H. Marc wouldn't walk this far any more than he'd jog.

I entered the store and discovered the mailboxes lived behind a locked screened gate. I tried the key. Nothing happened.

"May I help you?" a woman's voice sounded in my ear.

I stepped back. "Hi, I'm here to pick up some mail for a friend, but I can't seem to get the key to work."

"That's because it's not the gate key."

"This is the only key I have. Could you let me in?"

"What's your friend's name? I'll check our records."

"Marc Chambers. Box four-one-two. He had to go out of town and was expecting a package."

The woman returned to the front desk and entered Marc's name into her computer.

"Sorry, but we have no one by that name renting here."

I wasn't about to give up. "But, I'm sure this is the place. Maybe you remember him—tall, six-one, blond hair, blue eyes, kind of a stocky build?"

"Doesn't ring a bell."

"Do you have a number four-twelve?"

"Yes, we do."

"He gave me the key several days ago. Last night he called and said he urgently needed the contents. Could I please take a look?"

I tried to look earnest, but she didn't buy it.

"I'm sorry, but it's against policy to let anyone other than a registered renter behind the gate."

"But, it's important."

"No can do. Now, unless you plan on mailing something, I'll have to ask you to leave," she replied.

I gave up and walked out.

Sitting in line at a fast food drive-thru, I mapped strategy. Shay and Holmes was located in Sunnyside Beach, a northern suburb of Port Royale. Marc lived in the city, so I would now concentrate on the area around his home.

I scarfed my burrito and chugged iced tea while driving through traffic. It was February, high season in South Florida. The snowbirds had arrived making parking a nightmare. I found a space and walked. Three hours later, I had nothing to show for my efforts except sore feet.

I stumbled back to my car and waited for the air conditioning to cool me off. An impatient horn from a car wanting my spot blared behind me. I ignored the noise and examined the key again.

"Okay, Marc, what's going on? You didn't use a mailbox close to either your work or your home. So, where is it, and what did you get yourself into?"

The car moved on, its driver leaning on his horn and making a rude gesture. This being South Florida, second only to New York for attitude, I reciprocated with an even ruder one, and then resumed my thoughts.

Turning the key over in my hand, I rubbed the imprint with my finger. It was well-worn, but with the bright light streaming into my car, I noticed something I'd neglected to see earlier. A fourth number, barely legible, showed up behind the "two"—another "one"— making it forty-one-twenty-one, not four-twelve.

"Aw, shit!" I'd wasted an entire day.

I called myself every kind of stupid, and then stopped in mid-mental tirade. None of the places I'd been would have a number this high.

Of course! Marc said he didn't trust anyone other than me. If he suspected he was being followed, logic demanded he'd rent a box in the biggest post office with the heaviest flow of traffic.

Safety in numbers, right, Marc? Why didn't I think of this earlier?

I jammed the car into gear and headed for the main post office on Hunter Boulevard.

****

With Marc's key clutched in my hand, I entered the building. It took several minutes to find the boxes and several more to find four-one-two-one. Taking a deep breath, I inserted the key and turned. It opened.

I thrust my hand inside withdrawing a small padded package. A square casing like a CD was traceable through the bulk. I shoved it into my purse along with the key and left. Whatever the CD contained had cost Marc his life.

A wave of cold rolled over me, and I shivered in the hot car, but no one in the parking lot aroused my suspicions. Nevertheless, I drove a roundabout route home, in case anyone followed.

If someone tailed me, I couldn't tell. My sweaty hands slipped on the steering wheel as I turned into my driveway where I breathed a sigh of relief.

I hurried to my front door. Footsteps thudded on the walk behind me. I whirled and screamed.

Chapter Two

Detective Frank Whitten advanced up the walk. I didn't know whether to cry or curse and hugged my purse closer to my body. My heart hammered and my knees shook as he approached. Whitten—of all the damned luck.

"Miss Jackson? I'm sorry, I didn't mean to frighten you."

"You scared the crap out of me."

"Why?"

"I wasn't expecting anyone to come sneaking up my walk. What can I do for you?"

"Mind if we go inside? And I wasn't sneaking."

I didn't want to let him in, but saw no graceful way out of it. I unlocked the door, and he followed me to the living room where I nonchalantly dumped my purse on the coffee table.

"What's this all about?" I asked.

Whitten's sharp blue gaze swept the room before returning to me. His iron gray hair bristled in a quasi-military cut, and God help any crime victim if Whitten had to chase down a perpetrator. Years of donut shops had taken its toll. Still, I'd hate to underestimate him.

"How well did you know Marc Chambers?"

"Who?"

"Miss Jackson, I don't have time for games. Mr. Chambers was murdered last night. Your cell was the last number he called. We also found your name in his agenda, and early this morning I saw you walking away from his place. Care to explain?"

Damn. I didn't want to explain anything at the moment, not until I had a chance to view that CD. If I told him the truth, the CD would end up in police hands. I can think on my feet when necessary, and this looked like a good time.

"Marc called last night and asked me to meet him in a coffee shop on Riverside this morning. When he didn't show, I went to his place. I saw all the activity and left."

"A hot shot reporter like you sees police activity complete with crime scene tape surrounding the home of the guy she's supposed to meet for breakfast and doesn't stick around to even ask what happened? Let's try this again."

Double damn. I was botching this.

"All right, I talked to some people in the crowd, and they told me what happened. Then I saw you come out and knew my chances of getting anything except the brush off were slim, so I left. I called in a few markers and got what I needed." I knew the explanation sounded cold and uncaring, but I had no choice.

"Like what?"

I shrugged. "Marc was found in an alley near the flea market. Whoever killed him must have tossed his place."

Whitten stared at me through narrowed eyes. "Uh-huh. What else?"

"That's it. Swear to God."

I stared back. I didn't know how much information had been released to the public. To say any more might give away I had found the body.

"You don't sound all that broken up about it. How well did you know Chambers?"

"We dated a couple of years ago—nothing serious—and still saw each other once in a while."

"When did you last see him?"

"I'm not sure. Four or five months ago. We had dinner on Riverside, and then a little late night fun on South Street. No big deal."

I remembered that night. Not much of a drinker, Marc had slammed back scotch and water like tomorrow would never come. His gaze scanned the crowd every few minutes as if watching for someone.

"Marc, what's wrong?"

"Wrong?" he said, finishing yet another drink. He held the glass high to signal a refill.

"Marc, you're antsy as hell and drinking like a condemned man. Now, what's going on?"

"Maybe I just want to get a little tight—throw caution to the wind."

"You?" I laughed. "You're the most cautious person I've ever met."

"Which means you think I'm boring. That's why you broke up with me, isn't it?"

Surprised by the anger in his voice I reached across the table and clutched his wrist.

"Marc, I never thought any such thing. God Almighty, you are in a state. Come on, you can tell me."

The waiter brought his drink and he took a giant gulp.

"I can't talk about it. It involves work. I promised someone I wouldn't say anything. I'm not good at

keeping secrets. The stress is getting to me." He shoved the half-empty glass back. "Come on, let's go to The Wild Dog before I get too drunk to enjoy the show. I hear it's a blast."

We'd hit every nightspot on South Street. I ended up driving him home at three-thirty in the morning. The following afternoon, he called with a huge hangover and sincere apologies.

"I'm so sorry, Shell. How did you get home?"

"I called a cab from your place. Are you all right?"

"Other than the mother of all hangovers—yeah."

"Marc, if you have a problem or just want to talk, I'll be glad to listen."

He was silent for a moment. "Thanks, but I'm fine. We're going through an audit at work and I've been busy, that's all. Sorry, if I spoiled your evening. I'll call you in a couple of weeks and we'll try again. Okay?"

Only he'd never called. I meant to pick up the phone and check on him, but I'm ashamed to admit, out of sight, out of mind. I forgot.

At the time the paper hadn't been investigating Shay and Holmes, so I thought he may have been involved with a married woman. I didn't make the connection later because Marc worked in finance. He had nothing to do with contracts or construction.

Whitten's voice jerked me out of my thoughts. "He called at eleven forty-five. Kind of late to be making a date for the following morning. Did he say why he wanted to see you?" His glacial stare had sharpened at my prolonged hesitation.

"No. Just that it had been a while and he wanted to get together."

"Where were you supposed to meet?"

"At The Wake Up Call Café on Riverside."

"What time?"

"Around eight, eight-fifteen."

"How far's that café from his place?"

"I don't know. Eight or ten blocks."

"So, why jump in your car and drive to his apartment? He could have been on his way. Why not phone?"

"Because I forgot to charge my cell. It was dead."

"Pay phones still exist."

I shrugged. "I didn't think about it." That was a typical South Florida answer. Get in the car, burn polluting fossil fuels, and by all means, don't stop to think.

"Anyone see you there?"

"Lots of people. The place was packed." I spoke the truth, only an hour later than when I told him.

"Chambers worked for Shay and Holmes Development and Construction. Your paper is investigating them, and you didn't ask why he wanted to see you?"

"Look, Whitten, he was a friend. If he wanted to discuss why the sky is blue that was fine with me. Now, if you're finished, I'd like you to leave. I've had a busy day, and I'm tired."

He rubbed his nose and turned, pausing at the front door. "The nine-one-one call on Chambers was made by a woman from a pay phone at a convenience store on Armstrong Boulevard at one thirty-three in the morning. Where were you at one thirty-three this morning, Miss Jackson?"

"In bed, sound asleep."

"Alone?"

"Go to hell, Whitten."

His lips curved in a humorless smile. "We're pulling surveillance tape from the store now. It'll probably be grainy and hard to see, but we might get lucky. I wonder if your voice matches the one on the emergency tape."

"Good *night*, Detective."

He left. I bolted the door behind him and sagged against it, then turned and gazed through the peephole. I was in deep trouble.

Whitten turned to stare at the closed door, then got into his car and drove away. How much did the surveillance tape reveal? Would he really do a voice comparison? It was a possibility.

I shivered, pushing Detective Whitten and his suspicions into the back of my mind. I'd deal with them if and when they re-appeared.

His questions and my reminiscences brought a sharp jab of guilt to my conscience. I knew something had bothered Marc and should have insisted he tell me. If I'd pushed hard enough he would have done so. In hindsight, I should also have realized this had nothing to do with an office affair. Marc would never become involved with a married woman. He had a strong moral streak.

I shook my head. I had a CD to view. Convinced his death and that night months ago had a connection, I owed it to Marc to find his killer. I chided myself again. *If only I hadn't been late.*

Grabbing the disc from my purse, I hurried to my desk, fired up my laptop, and slid the CD in. Within seconds the contents popped up onscreen.

I don't know what I expected, but a list of recipes was not it. The air rushed out of my lungs in a gasp of disappointment. My shoulders slumped, and I stared at the ingredients for pound cake in disbelief.

"What the hell is this?" I asked out loud.

Why would Marc send this to a post office box and hide the key in a shoe? It didn't make sense. Then I remembered Marc's slightly paranoid, anal tendencies. I read through the CD.

Recipes for everything from spareribs to soup and how to make ketchup, rolled by before a large blank space appeared. What followed had me more confused than the recipes.

A series of numbers and letters scrolled up. I counted over sixty in the group. I kept going in the hope Marc would have left a few notes or comments as an explanation, but the CD ended with nothing more.

I spent the next six hours trying to unravel the code taking only a short break to shove a sandwich in my mouth. There had to be an explanation—a solution. Logic problems and cryptograms had never been my forte. Numbers confused me, which explained why balancing my checkbook was an exercise in frustration.

I finally gave up. I'd explore codes on the Internet tomorrow and try again. Popping the disc out, I held it for a moment. I needed a secure hiding place. That eliminated my office.

"Too much traffic and too many curious eyes," I muttered, thinking of Doug Elliott.

I could cart it around in my purse, but one purse snatching and I'd be out of luck. My house, a two-bedroom, two-bath rental in the southeast section of the city near Port Royale Medical Center? A quiet neighborhood wasn't always a detriment to crime. I was getting as paranoid as Marc. He died because of this CD and whatever information it contained.

Then I had an idea. I'd take it back to the post office box. At least it would be safe there.

I shut off the computer and went to bed with the disc under my pillow. Sleep eluded me. In my mind, I saw letters, numbers, and dead bodies in dark alleys.

****

I dashed into work at the absurd hour of seven-thirty in the morning to make up for yesterday's tardiness. The deserted place gave me the creeps. My gaze probed the corners and shadows. Satisfied no one lurked, I turned on my computer.

While waiting for it to boot up, I gulped half of my cooling double shot in an effort to pry my eyes open. A super hit of caffeine was essential to get my heart pumping and allow rational thought.

I flinched at the musical tones of my computer program opening. Quiet at home was good, but the office should bubble with voices, phones ringing, and the occasional swearing by our editor, Calvin Randolph, as he chewed out some reporter. I'd been called on the carpet once. He looked like my grandfather with a mane of white hair, blue eyes, and a husky voice.

The resemblance ended there. His words could rip the hide off a rhinoceros. The blue eyes blazed fire and the voice reverberated like thunder. He refused to shut the door to his office, so the entire news room got to hear every humiliating word. It was not an experience I cared to repeat.

I stuffed my purse containing the CD in a desk

drawer, and then locked it, taking no chances. I'd decided renting a post office box closer to my home made more sense. Easier to retrieve and deposit.

The temptation to view it again now was strong, but I refused to take the chance of someone else, like Doug Elliott, getting an unauthorized peek. I had no intention of sharing, and cracking the code would send my stock skyrocketing with both my boss and Cal. I'd work on it again tonight.

I finished my coffee, snapping on the radio to break the silence, and then hunkered down in front of my keyboard to write about Marc, trying to keep emotions out of it. I didn't want to divulge our friendship yet. The police knew, of course, and I still worried Whitten would match my voice and face to the 9-1-1 and surveillance tapes.

I was deep into Marc's bio, totally focused, and had no concept of time passing.

"Making up for yesterday's lost time?" Bill asked from behind me.

I jerked, emitting a squeak.

"Good Lord, you're jumpy."

"Sorry, I didn't hear you. This place is creepy with no one in it." That statement was no longer true. While I'd worked, the room had filled with employees.

"What are you writing?"

"My notes about Marc Chambers. You asked me to check him out."

"Anything I should know about?"

"Not too much. He was quiet, kind of shy, and worked in the accounting department at Shay and Holmes."

"What was he doing in an alley off of Northwest

Thirty-Fifth Avenue?" Bill asked coming in to read over my shoulder.

"Nobody can explain that."

"Maybe he was into drugs."

"No, not Marc...uh, not this guy. From what I was told, he was a straight arrow."

Bill eyebrows rose. "Marc?"

"I feel like I know him," I said, covering my slip. I tried to divert his attention before he could ask another question or give me that penetrating stare he gave people when he knew they were lying. "How did your interviews go? Did you get anything good we can use on Shay and Holmes?"

"I'm not sure yet. Anne Hodges was just elected to the City Council last year. She's already frustrated with how things are run. As a political newcomer, the woman doesn't have the cynicism of the rest. She still believes in truth, justice, and the American way."

"A lot of people do. It's a nice thing to believe in. Why is she frustrated?"

"Says she campaigned on a platform of less development, as did several other council members, yet they end up approving new development all over the city."

"Welcome to the real world. What did the Shay and Holmes competitor have to say?"

"Dave Brooks is frustrated, too. He knows his bids for city work aren't the lowest, yet he swears S and H can't competently do the jobs for what they bid," Bill replied.

"So, they overrun on costs or skimp on quality. Wouldn't it make sense to go with the company whose bid may be higher, but who may also come in on, or even under, budget and who would produce a good product?"

"It would, but remember who we're dealing with. A billion here, a billion there and pretty soon you're talking real money."

The quote was from some old-time politician. I laughed, knowing from past experience he expected it.

"He said one of his sub-contractors recently hired some guys who worked on Shay and Holmes projects. They didn't have a lot of nice things to say. Dave told me the crew is on a job in Orlando this week, but should be back by Monday. Maybe I'll go have a chat with them."

He had a perplexed expression on his face.

"You look like you're working on a puzzle."

He frowned. "In a way I am. Anne Hodges and Dave Brooks have similar frustrations. It all centers on Shay and Holmes Development. Neither one would say it, but I think they believe S and H *is* handing out big bucks to certain people."

"As in bribes and kickbacks?"

"I don't have the proof yet, but I'm sure more than one city employee is on the take."

Proof—oh my God. Money, finance, accounting. Marc? But would an accountant have access to that kind of information? Maybe he ran across something by accident and decided to investigate. He'd had a natural curiosity and loved solving those damned puzzles that confound me. Did someone know? My breath caught in my throat, and I forced myself to breathe. I had to crack that code.

Bill turned to go, and then said, "Good God, what happened to you?"

I swung around in my chair and gazed at Doug Elliott glaring from my cubicle entry. He sported a multi-hued shiner surrounding his left eye. I'd forgotten about his excursion of the day before and suppressed a laugh.

"Wow, Doug, what's the other guy look like?" I ventured, trying to keep a straight face.

"You know damned well. You set me up." Doug curled his lip into a snarl.

"I have no idea what you're talking about." Bubbling laughter threatened to burst from my chest.

"You deliberately sent me up to that bar knowing full well what it was."

"What bar?" Bill asked, shooting me a funny look.

"You said you were meeting an informant at The Haven." Doug drew his lips further back over his teeth and clenched his fists by his side.

I drew back, certain he wanted to deck me.

"The Haven? That's a gay biker bar. I didn't know you swung that way, Elliott," Bill said, his lips twitching.

"I don't!" Doug's dark red face contrasted well with the black eye.

"Who were you going to see?" Bill asked me.

"I never got a name. The guy called back and cancelled. I'm curious how you knew about my meeting, Doug. I never told anyone."

"You set me up, damn it, and I'll get even if it's the last thing I do." He strutted off, his back rigid.

"Leave it to Doug Elliott to exit on a tired cliché," Bill said.

I no longer held back and sputtered with laughter.

"What the hell did you do?"

I told him, and his laughter joined mine.

"Kid, that was terrific. You got great instincts. Maybe it'll teach the little bastard something, but I doubt it." Bill started out the doorway. "Tell you what—make that piece you're doing on Chambers into a little thousand word human interest story. His death might be a slice of a bigger pie. I'll see Cal runs it under your byline."

He left and my laughter died. I turned back to the computer not wanting to write a human interest story on Marc. He was far too human and had already become a slice of the pie—along with me.

****

"Let us pray."

I bowed my head as the minister wound down Marc's funeral service. He'd had a modest turnout and other than Detective Whitten, I recognized no one. Marc had been a nice guy. He didn't deserve to die in a filthy alley. I walked by the casket with the rest of the assemblage murmuring a soft farewell. The pallbearers stood off to the side waiting to carry Marc to his final resting place.

Avoiding Whitten, I hurried to my car for the funeral procession. The sky boasted a few white, fluffy clouds, the kind pictured on postcards tourists loved to send back home. When my time came, I wouldn't mind a sunny day.

I flipped on the air-conditioning wondering how many people present were Shay and Holmes employees. I'd never met either principal, but hoped one of them had the decency to attend. People not in their cars stood in little knots talking, smoking, and glancing at their watches. I saw one woman wiping her eyes. The rest of the crowd didn't appear all that upset. Then, I realized my eyes were dry.

Sadness choked me. I would truly miss Marc. A memory arose in my mind—his first gift.

We'd been out to dinner when he handed me a rectangular shaped box. Expecting jewelry, I'd been puzzled by the hammer-like instrument inside.

"What is it?"

"An escape hammer," he'd replied in a serious tone. "See the pointed ends on the head? If your car ever goes into a canal, just whack the window with this. It'll shatter and you won't drown."

I'd thanked him, but didn't mention I wasn't stupid enough to drive into a canal. Later, I'd dropped the thing into my console and forgotten it.

I blinked tears from my eyes as more mourners wandered toward their cars. It had been such a Marc type of gift—so practical.

The funeral director pointed me to my place in line. A dignified, blonde lady dressed in black walked out escorted by a gray-haired man in a navy blue suit. Marc's parents? A younger dark-haired man wearing a gray suit accompanied them. He'd been one of the pallbearers. I wondered at his identity and if he and Marc were related, but Marc had never talked much about his family. I only knew his parents had been divorced when he was very young, and he'd gone to boarding school.

The cortège wound its way through the streets of Port Royale until arriving at the cemetery. One row of chairs had been provided by the gravesite. I hung back as the man and woman were seated along with several other men. Shay and Holmes? I didn't know. I stepped to the back of the crowd. When the service ended, I'd leave and have a good stiff drink.

The pallbearers, including the man in the gray suit, brought the casket to the gravesite. My eyes smarted with unshed tears, and I bowed my head for the last prayer. Then it was over. I daubed my eyes with a tissue and headed across the well-tended grass to my car. Would anyone here today remember to visit the grave? Probably not, including me. Such is life, but I felt guilty all the same.

"Miss Jackson," a voice called out. "Miss Jackson, please wait."

I stopped and turned. The man in gray strode toward me.

"You *are* Shelley Jackson, aren't you?" he asked.

"Yes."

"I'm Jason Mallory, Marc Chambers' step-brother. Could I speak with you for a few moments?"

Mallory spoke in a clipped authoritative tone. He may have asked a question, but his manner told me it was more of a demand.

"Marc told me he was an only child," I said. It was the only thing I could think to say.

"Technically, he was. I guess he didn't want to bore you with family details."

I know a reprimand when I hear it and his words put my back up. Instant dislike formed. He had an aura that said he could be trouble for anyone who dared cross him. He stood six feet tall, and while I'm lousy at judging weight, I put him at around one-eighty-five. Aviator sunglasses shielded his eyes, but a straight nose and thin lips were set in a determined face.

"What did you want to speak to me about, Mr...?"

"Mallory. I'd like to ask you some questions regarding Marc." He gazed at the mourners leaving. "This isn't the right time or place. Please, allow me to buy you lunch. My car is at the funeral home, but if you name the restaurant I'll find it."

I didn't want to have lunch with him or anyone else, and I certainly didn't want to discuss Marc.

"I'm sorry, Mr. Mallory, but I have to get back to the office. I doubt if I can tell you much. I hadn't seen Marc in several months."

"Four to be exact, and I think you either saw or talked to him the night he was killed."

An icy chill washed over me in spite of the noontime sun beating down on my head. "I have no idea what you're talking about."

"I think you do, and it had nothing to do with a breakfast meeting, did it?"

I broke out in a sweat. He'd obviously talked to Whitten and to Marc. Marc's last phone call jumped into my mind with startling clarity.

"Shell, it's Marc."

"Marc, how's it going?"

"Not so good, Shell. I need to talk to you. Tonight." His hushed voice trembled.

"What's wrong, Marc?"

"I've got a problem. You're the only one I trust."

"What kind of a problem?"

"I can't explain over the phone, but I have proof of the bribery you're investigating. It'll put a lot of city officials in jail, but I think I'm being watched."

"By whom?"

"Not over the phone," he repeated.

"Marc, call the police."

"No! I can't do that—not yet. Shell, please, meet me in the alley between Lake and Johnson Streets off Northwest Thirty-fifth Avenue. It's near the big flea market."

"What! Are you crazy? No way."

"An hour from now. Please, it's important."

He'd hung up, leaving me with no option and my reporter's sense of curiosity aroused.

"Miss Jackson, are you going to give me an answer?"

Mallory's sharp question jerked me back to the present. A few yards away, Detective Whitten stared. In another moment, he'd join us.

"The Tavern," I said. "It's on Riverside. I'll get us a table."

I whirled and walked to my car on shaking legs. What had Marc gotten me into and how much did Mallory know?

Chapter Three

I sat at a table in The Tavern nursing vodka on the rocks, hoping to calm my nerves. Mallory knew way too much, and step-brother or not, I didn't trust him. Even with just a brief conversation, I could tell he was a smooth character—one accustomed to calling the shots. The man came directly to the point. He'd want answers before paying the check. I expected a few answers of my own.

I glanced at my watch, took another sip of vodka, and fiddled with the olive pick. He was late. Maybe he couldn't locate a parking spot or find the restaurant.

Or maybe it's deliberate. Maybe he just wants to make me sweat.

Whatever—it worked. I lifted the drink again and tried to ignore my trembling fingers. I stared over the rim of the glass as he entered. He spoke to the hostess who pointed in my direction. Mallory nodded, and then glided like a sleek jungle cat between the tables. The symbolism made me shiver.

"Miss Jackson, I apologize for taking so long," he said, sitting down. "I had a few things to discuss with the funeral director."

"No problem."

"Thank you for agreeing to meet me."

He removed his sunglasses, and I got the shock of my life. I'd expected a match to his dark hair, but instead found myself gazing into a pair of the most penetrating gray eyes I'd ever seen. His stare skewered me to the seat. I drained my glass to cover my uneasiness.

Act normal. Show no fear.

A waiter appeared, asking, "May I get you something from the bar, sir?"

"Ketel One martini, straight up."

"And another Grey Goose on the rocks for you, ma'am?"

I nodded, pushing the glass to the edge of the table where the man scooped it up and left.

Mallory stared with a look on his face that stated no compromises. Then he smiled, and while I could admit he was damned good-looking, the smile did not reach those steely eyes. Something told me he used charm to coerce concessions from business rivals—or lovers. I had no intention of falling into either category.

He cleared his throat. "This is awkward, isn't it? I'm sorry if I seemed to come on strong at the cemetery, but I need to talk with you. I don't like being brushed off."

Amazing. He sounded both sincere and threatening in the same sentence.

"It wasn't a brush off. I have to get back to work."

His eyes narrowed slightly, and his gaze sharpened. "Miss Jackson, exactly what was your relationship with my step-brother?"

The waiter brought our drinks. I used the distraction to do some fast thinking. I'd already deduced he had talked with Detective Whitten. All I had to do was follow my story.

The waiter left and I sipped, savoring the ice cold

liquor as it moistened my parched throat. "We dated for a while a few years ago and still got together every now and then."

"When did you last see him?"

"About four or five months ago. You know, you can get these answers from Detective Whitten."

"Who's he?"

"Mr. Mallory, you're the step-brother of a murdered man. Are you trying to tell me the lead detective on the case hasn't knocked on your door or you on his? Besides, you mentioned I was supposed to meet Marc for coffee. Only Whitten knew that."

He sipped his martini and smiled again. "You're right, I spoke with him, but I was already aware you knew Marc."

Heat suffused my body and sweat dampened my palms. I'd been an idiot to agree to this meeting. I should have put it off until I could find out more about him.

"Oh?"

"Marc told me. About four months ago, I got a call. He was nursing a mighty hangover and sounded strange. He told me he'd been out on the town with a friend and mentioned your name."

"Strange how?"

"I thought maybe you could tell me."

"Sorry. We had a typical night on South Street. Lots of bars. That's the last time I saw him."

"No, but you heard from him the night he was murdered, didn't you?"

"Why do you say that?"

Shrugging, he took another sip, those disturbing eyes never leaving my face. He looked cool and composed, whereas my heart thumped loud enough to be heard over the conversational babble in the crowded restaurant.

"Score one for you. Detective Whitten told me. I'd like to know why he called you that late at night."

"I didn't realize we were keeping score, Mr. Mallory." I gave him the same story I'd given Whitten.

"That's what the police told me."

"Well, if you got it from them, why ask me?"

"Sometimes people don't always tell everything to the police."

The waiter reappeared and we ordered—a salad for me and steak for him. My appetite had fled, but I'd eat if it killed me. The interruption gave me a chance to compose myself. He didn't know as much as I'd feared, but no doubt suspected I withheld information.

"What can you tell me about his employers, Shay and Holmes Development and Construction?" he asked.

"Not much. They've been in South Florida for over thirty years and became involved in the development game six or seven years ago. They moved up to the major leagues a few years after that landing some big city contracts."

"Yet, your newspaper is investigating them. I believe there's been mention of bribery and city corruption."

"And you know this how?"

He smiled that cold smile again. "As you said— I'm the step-brother of a murdered man. I asked questions."

I'd won a small victory by making him answer.

"Mr. Mallory, I'm just a small potatoes reporter. Bill Mathias is working that story."

"I see. I met Kenneth Shay and Bradley Holmes today."

"Then you're one up on me. I've never met either man."

I took another swig of vodka. My hands had ceased sweating and my throat no longer felt like the Sahara. It was time to take control. After all, I *was* the reporter.

"I was surprised to learn you were Marc's step-brother. He never mentioned any siblings."

"My father and his mother were married for five years. I was seven years older, and he looked up to me. He was okay as far as step-brothers went. After our parents divorced, he kept in touch. I helped him get a job when he graduated from college."

"I remember him telling me his first job was for an architect."

"Yes, for my firm in Los Angeles. He worked in accounting and was damned good with numbers."

Numbers? As in codes? If he could probe, so could I. "I'll bet he was a whiz at those logic problems and cryptograms. I remember seeing one of those magazines like for crossword puzzles in his place once."

Mallory actually laughed. It rumbled from deep inside and a chill danced up my spine—not of fear, but of awareness. In spite of his menacing gaze and questions, this guy was drop dead sexy.

"He loved them. He used to sign his letters and later e-mails to me with a cryptogram. We had a bet going. If I solved it, he owed me a buck. If I couldn't, I owed him." He sobered and finished his drink. "I'm going to miss my brother."

I had the impression that for the first time today, he

meant what he said. It made him human. I didn't want him human. Not with all those chills racing up and down my body. I polished off my drink, too.

"I'm sure everyone who knew Marc will miss him. He was a nice guy, and there aren't too many of them around. I take it the lady with you at the funeral was his mother?"

"Yes. Marc's father passed away eight or nine years ago. The gentleman today is her latest husband. They were married a few months ago. "

"She must be devastated."

"She and Marc weren't close—too many step-fathers and boarding schools for that—but yes, Marlene is torn up."

I thought his tone sounded cold, uncaring. "Maternal instinct is never lost."

Our food arrived, and we spent the next few minutes concentrating on steak and Cobb Salad. My instincts told me our conversation had been designed for pulling information out of me. I'd dodged well, but expected another invitation for either lunch or dinner soon.

I barely tasted my food, preferring to watch Jason Mallory. When he had first arrived, I'd noticed not only did he move with grace and precision, but with authority as well. Anyone in his path automatically moved aside. I would not want him as an enemy.

As a reporter it was sometimes my job to take the measure of the person being interviewed. I couldn't help noticing the broad shoulders. His long legs had eaten up the distance between the door and our table. Not blessed with X-ray vision, I had no idea of the condition of that lean body, but would be astonished at anything other than, shall we say, well-kept.

He had great taste in clothes. The suit was conservatively cut and undoubtedly custom made, which also meant it had a four-figure price tag. The splash of color from his maroon tie contrasted against his white silk shirt. I hadn't paid any attention to his shoes, but bet they were Italian.

I'd paid two hundred dollars for the navy blue suit I wore and another hundred for my shoes, yet felt like I'd raided a thrift store.

Regardless of his impeccable taste and good looks, I still didn't trust him.

"What's your story?" he asked. "Are you native to Florida?"

We were halfway through our meal. I wondered if he had spent the time analyzing me, too, and if he was impressed.

"No, I'm originally from Chicago, but have been here three years. Marc was one of the first people I met."

"Where was that?"

"A co-worker took me to a nightclub on the beach. Marc sat next to us with a friend. We hooked up, dated for a few months, decided there was no romantic spark, but continued to see each other off and on."

"I'm glad to hear he had friends. He was shy and not an aggressive sort. He wouldn't push himself on others."

Unlike you.

I nudged the bowl away. I'd had enough of food, drink, and Jason Mallory. I wanted to get back to the office and research the man.

"I don't think he went out much," I said.

"Other than you, did he date anybody?"

"You're asking me about his love life?"

"I thought he might have confided something, since he trusted you."

"Sorry. If he was seeing anyone, he didn't tell me."

Mallory finished his steak. The waiter timed the end of the meal perfectly, appearing within seconds of Mallory's fork hitting his empty plate.

"May I get you some dessert? Coffee?"

My dining companion looked at me and when I shook my head, said, "Just the check." When the man left, he turned his gaze to me. "Thank you for being Marc's friend."

What an odd thing to say. It made me uncomfortable, because I'd often gone months without thinking about him. I mumbled a reply. "Like I said, he was a nice guy."

The waiter presented the check. Mallory extracted a slim alligator wallet from the inside of his suit coat, and laid three twenties on the tray. "Keep the change."

A sixty-dollar lunch. I was impressed, which was no doubt his intention. My instincts had been right. This guy demanded and would pay for the best of anything. Not wanting to prolong this uncomfortable meal, I shoved my chair back and rose.

"Thank you for lunch, Mr. Mallory. I hope you have a safe trip home."

He also stood. "I'm sticking around for a while. See what the police uncover. I want Marc's killer caught and brought to trial."

"We all do."

On the sidewalk, I offered my hand. "Goodbye, Mr. Mallory, and thank you again."

He smiled, grasping my hand firmly. My arms broke out in goosebumps while a small thrill zipped up my arm and traveled to the pit of my stomach. Oh, no! Not *that*!

"Don't make it goodbye. We'll be seeing each other again. I'll be in touch."

He turned and walked away. I stood in the middle of the crowded sidewalk, examining my skin for singe marks. An attractive man who sucked that kind of a reaction out of me was dangerous in more ways than one.

He disappeared, swallowed up by strolling tourists and bustling businessmen. Yes—very dangerous. I didn't want to admit he intimidated the hell out of me.

****

I took my time returning to the office. *The Standard* is located three blocks from Riverside, so I had parked in the garage and walked to the restaurant. With two vodkas in me, I needed time to get the fuzzy feeling out of my head, not to mention my unsettling reaction to his touch.

Everything about the man un-nerved me, including the nagging suspicion he had said something I should have questioned. At the moment it eluded me, and I brushed it aside. Right now, my mission was to find out more about Jason Mallory.

I breezed past Doug Elliott's desk without a second glance. The colors in his black eye had intensified over the last couple of days. That must have been a hardship for a self-proclaimed Lothario like him.

Biting back the urge to laugh, I entered my cubicle and pushed the clutter from my desk, then sat down to get on the Internet, pulling up Google. I typed in "Jason

Mallory, Architect, Los Angeles" and waited a few seconds for the information. I clicked on his bio first.

Jason Thomas Mallory was the sole owner of Mallory Architectural Associates, employing over sixty people of varying skills. Upon his father's death, he'd inherited Mallory Construction Company and incorporated it into his business. Over the last five years, he'd bought out small electrical and mechanical contractors.

Three years ago, he'd opened a branch office in Houston, Texas, and was slowly adding other companies under its umbrella.

Mallory Architectural and its owner had garnered a whole slew of awards over the last eight years, making it—and Jason Thomas Mallory—one of the most sought after architects in the country. It had also made him a very rich man. He was unmarried, which didn't surprise me in the least.

The article went on to list all of his numerous accomplishments, including the fact he sat on the boards of several businesses.

There was more, but I stopped reading. His unmarried status held more interest at the moment, so I delved into the archives of a Los Angeles newspaper where I was bombarded with seventy-two articles mentioning Mr. Mallory in the past year.

He never missed an opportunity to be seen with a beautiful woman. Blonde, brunette, redhead, all shapes and sizes—it didn't matter. And never did the same woman show up in a photo more than twice. Most of the pictures and stories concerned charities. A few were of political fundraisers for candidates from all parties. He spread his wealth around.

"Who's that?"

I jumped and swiveled my chair around to face Doug. "Damn you, Elliott. Hasn't anyone told you it's polite to knock before entering?"

"There's no door," he said, trying to look over my shoulder.

I moved to block his view. I knew I'd taken a chance of someone seeing my online investigation here at the office, but my cell phone data plan gouged my budget. "Then try coughing. You are such a weasel."

"Nice looking broad," he commented, side-stepping for a better look. "Who is she, and why are you so interested?"

I minimized the screen and glared. "I'm doing preliminary research on political fundraising, if you must know."

"Political fundraising? What the hell for?"

"Bill asked me."

"I didn't know he was working on fundraising."

"Why should you know everything Bill or anybody else around here does? Now, get out. I'm busy."

He grinned, reaching out to stroke my hair. I slapped his hand away.

"Don't touch me. Get out. Now!"

"Aw, don't be that way. We could make a good team." He leaned forward and ran a fingertip down the lapel of my suit stopping just short of the "V" between my breasts.

Disgusted, I wanted to plant my fist in his face. I'd always considered him a jerk and a pain in the ass, but this was creepy.

I picked up his finger and removed his hand from my chest. "Beat it, asshole, before I report you for sexual harassment."

He straightened and strolled to the entryway. "I'd be careful if I were you. There may come a time when you'll beg for my attention."

He left, and I resisted the urge to grab a can of spray disinfectant from the storage room. It was probably his idea of getting even with me for The Haven. I turned to my computer, bringing the screen back into full view, and then switched back to the bio.

I read the article on Mallory until calming down—not an easy task. Doug had set my teeth on edge, and I skimmed the information.

"Mallory is considered by many to be on par with Frank Lloyd Wright and I. M. Pei with bold, innovative designs…"

Slimy little twerp. Does he think he can touch me and get away with it just because his aunt owns stock in the paper?

"…in Los Angeles and Houston. Rumor has it he is also thinking of expanding further into the South, including the Miami area…"

Next time I won't send him to The Haven, I'll ship his ass to that place down in Sunset Beach where gangbangers hang out.

That article ended. I clicked on another more personal one. I gritted my teeth as Elliot continued to occupy my mind.

Yeah, gangbangers sounds like a good start. He'll get more than a black eye from them.

"…latest dinner partner, model and actress, Caroline Denham. Does this signal the end of his high-profile relationship with Lady Patricia Ravenswood? When asked, Mallory stated, 'Lady Patricia and I are good friends. She left for her home in England last month.' He has great taste not only in clothes, but in women…"

Wonder how many other women Elliott's harassed. Maybe I should say something to Cal. No, he's old school. Believes if women want equality in the workplace, they have to roll with the punches.

I didn't want to read any more about Jason Mallory's taste in clothes or women. I pulled up a professional article on him.

"Mr. Mallory sits on the boards of Mercy Hospital, The Cancer Foundation along with those of several businesses, including Graves Publishing, Tower Data Systems, and Shay and Holmes Development and Construction, one of the hottest development companies in South Florida."

Much to my annoyance, my mind still wandered. *I don't mind paying my dues or rolling with the punches, but that doesn't include having to be pawed or manhandled by…*

I yanked my mind from Doug Elliott back to the last few lines of the paragraph. I re-read the sentence in astonishment.

Shay and Holmes? He sits on the board of directors of *Shay and Holmes*? And he told me today was the first time he'd ever met Kenneth Shay or Bradley Holmes. He'd even asked me for information on the company.

The lying bastard.

Now, I remembered what he'd said earlier—the comment that had nagged, but eluded my memory. Something about Marc trusting me. How would he know *that*?

I sat back in my chair. What the hell was going on? I didn't have time to answer the question. The phone on my desk rang, its strident tone cutting through my astonishment.

"Shelley Jackson here."

"Miss Jackson, my name is Kenneth Shay. I'm the Executive Vice-President and Chief Operating Officer of Shay and Holmes Development and Construction."

How many more surprises were coming my way today? "Yes, Mr. Shay, how may I help you?"

"Miss Jackson, I need to talk to you about Marc Chambers. Would you please meet me at The Marina Boatyard on Seventeenth Street this evening—say at five-thirty?"

"And why should I do that?"

"I don't want to talk about it over the phone."

"Why would you want to meet with me? I'm not the reporter investigating your company. And what does Marc have to do with it?"

"I'd like to talk with you about that, too. Please, it really is important."

The pleading tone in his voice didn't reflect his VP and COO positions. Most people didn't introduce themselves to total strangers by announcing their professional status. A simple, "I'm with Shay and Holmes" would have sufficed.

However, it didn't matter how officious he sounded, the fact he had called *me* sent my antennae skyward.

"All right, Mr. Shay. The Marina Boatyard at five-thirty."

"And this is off the record," he said, hanging up.

Okay, he had my attention. Maybe I could pump

him about a certain board member.

I peeked over the cubicle partitions to Bill's office. The door was closed and the window dark, telling me he had left for the day. I glanced at my watch—four o'clock.

I read a few more articles on Jason Mallory, then logged off and shut down, but not before changing my password. The encounter with Doug made me cautious.

Since Bill had left, I also called it a day. Besides, I needed to stop at the post office to retrieve the CD. If I didn't crack the code by tomorrow morning, I'd make a copy for Bill and see what he could do with it. He'd be pissed I hadn't given it to him immediately, but I didn't like admitting defeat.

Once again, I peered over the top of my cubicle wall, this time looking for Doug, finally spying him across the room talking with a sports writer. I hurried to the elevator and pressed the button. The little slime's earlier actions had me more spooked than I cared to admit, and the thought of being trapped in a confined space with him for even a few minutes made my stomach turn.

Forget Doug Elliott. I have something more important than perverts to worry about.

Like why the hell would Kenneth Shay want to see me?

****

I arrived at The Marina Boatyard, took a seat at the bar, and ordered white wine. The restaurant catered to a well-heeled clientele many of whom were boaters, if that was the proper term for the owners of the eighty-foot-plus yachts docked behind it. I gazed at the crowd. They brought the phrase "casual elegance" to a whole new level, although I'd never thought of Armani and Gucci as casual.

The bartender set the wine in front of me while I fished in my purse for my tape recorder. I made sure it worked and put it on top for easy access. Kenneth Shay might not want to be on the record, but I sure as hell did. I only used my recordings as reference anyway.

I raised the glass to my lips with a shaky hand. I'd been in journalism for eight years, and this was the first time I played in the big game. If I wormed information out of Shay for Bill, I might get to do a few pieces of my own on the investigation.

Why not? I'm as ambitious as the next guy.

"Miss Jackson?"

Even though I expected him, Kenneth Shay's appearance startled me. I remembered having seen him at the funeral.

"Yes. Mr. Shay?"

He nodded. "Thank you for agreeing to meet me." He slid onto a stool.

I took the opportunity to set my open purse on the bar between us, then casually reached in and pressed the record button when he ordered a drink.

"Johnny Walker Blue on the rocks," he told the bartender, before turning to me. "Would you like to get a table?"

"I'm fine, Mr. Shay. What's this all about?"

"In a minute. I need a drink. It's been a long day."

I took a few seconds to observe him. He stood about six-one, but a fleshy build suggested he liked the finer things in life. The drink choice confirmed it. His expensive suit strained a tad across the shoulders. He styled his light brown hair on the long side, had a pugnacious jaw, and exuded arrogance. Tanned skin indicated an outdoorsman, a damned good tanning salon, or someone who vacationed on St. Barts. I bet on the islands. He didn't look like the outdoorsman or tanning salon type to me. The requested drink arrived.

"I understand from the police you were a friend of Marc Chambers," he said, taking a long swallow of very expensive scotch.

"Marc and I were friends." I followed his example with my wine. I'd ordered Chardonnay and for the price charged, it was ordinary.

"When was the last time you saw Marc?"

I wanted to ask "Alive?", but refrained. "A few months ago."

"Not since?"

"Mr. Shay, exactly what is this all about and why do you want to see me?"

He frowned and drained his glass, signaling the bartender for another. "Miss Jackson, there are files missing from our offices. We suspect Marc was feeding information to your boss. I was going to fire him."

Marc? I suppose it made sense. The original tip regarding bribery had come to Bill via an e-mail.

"Information?"

"We can't find sensitive files of an accounting nature and wonder if Marc had given or sent them to you."

"Why would he do that? I have nothing." Accounting nature? What the hell did that mean?

His second drink in five minutes came, and Shay gulped half of it. "These files contain tax information and payments to various lobbyists in the county and state. It's confidential and not the kind of thing we'd like to see in the hands of a reporter."

"Payments?"

His jaw clenched and his eyes narrowed. "Miss Jackson, Shay and Holmes has done nothing wrong. It is not illegal or in any way unethical to obtain the services of a lobbyist. I suggest that if you're in possession of these files or *any* Shay and Holmes files, you return them immediately or face the consequences."

His voice had a threatening tone, and while I wasn't afraid, I *w*as uneasy.

"Consequences?"

"It's our property. We'll sue to get it back and slap an injunction on *The Standard* from making any information they contain public." He downed the rest of his drink in one long, smooth motion, and then leaned close to me. "And don't forget, Marc Chambers is dead."

On those chilling words, he slipped off the barstool and left. I fumbled to shut off the tape recorder, swallowing hard. I was out of my league. Not only had the son of a bitch stuck me with the bill, but I'd never had a chance to ask him any questions concerning Jason Mallory.

****

"Bill, can I talk to you for a moment?" I asked the next morning, closing his office door behind me.

"Sure," he said, raising his eyebrows.

I'd been up until two in the morning trying to break Marc's code and came to the conclusion it would take someone smarter than me.

"You're going to be madder than hell, but here it is."

I told him most of the story, leaving out the part about discovering Marc's body. I wasn't ready to confess *that* yet. I said the CD had been mailed to me.

Madder than hell was mild. "A murdered man sends you a CD and you haven't told anyone? Jesus, Shelley, the man was killed for crissakes. What's on it?"

"I haven't got a clue. It's in some kind of code."

"Let me see."

I handed him a copy of the disc. The original remained in my post office box.

He shoved it into his computer, and for the next twenty minutes tried to decipher what we saw. He finally sat back with a sigh.

"I'm not good with this kind of stuff either, although the recipe for Spiced Rum Punch sounded interesting." He shook his head. "FL4-30BOC720866922-2114-20—what the hell does that mean?"

"I don't know. Some of the numbers repeat themselves. For instance, the BOC720866922 is in several sequences, but the FL4-30 and the numbers on the end aren't."

"And here's an FL5-15TCB35470-2177-10." Bill tapped his fingers on the arm of his chair. "I'll keep this and work on it."

"There's something else." I told him about my meeting with Kenneth Shay and played the tape.

"All that crap about injunctions is nonsense, but I don't like the threat. He probably said it to scare you. He's a blustering fool with expensive tastes. I'm not surprised he wanted to see you rather than me. I'd have asked pertinent questions. You should have let me know the instant he called."

"You weren't here. I wanted to help."

"Well, you didn't," he snapped. "Anything else I should know about?"

I told him about Jason Mallory's relationship to Marc and with Shay and Holmes.

"I knew he sat on the board, but not about being the murdered man's step-brother. Mallory is an architectural genius with the reputation of being a ruthless businessman." Bill frowned. "I'd like an interview with him. If something's smelly at Shay and Holmes, he might know and be willing to help, provided he's not in on it."

"I don't picture Jason Mallory as a crook, Bill."

"Doesn't matter. Keep your distance. The guy is hard as nails and twice as smart as the smartest person you know. Don't trust him, Shelley—not one inch."

Chapter Four

My punishment for withholding information and botching the Shay interview was banishment to the archive room in the basement. Bill had me researching Shay and Holmes from the first day they opened. Many of the details he wanted were too old or obscure to be online, so I sneezed my way through back issues not on microfilm.

Bill had snagged an interview with Jason Mallory at three o'clock, which meant he'd be unable to keep his appointment with the former S and H construction crew in Boca Raton at two. I got that assignment.

I found the construction site and thought being only ten minutes late wasn't bad. The foreman for Brooks Construction met me at the door of the office trailer.

"Sorry I'm late," I apologized. "But you know South Florida traffic."

"Yeah, I know. My name's Harry Benson. What happened to Bill Mathias?"

"Shelley Jackson. Bill apologizes. He got tied up and rather than postpone, he sent me. Hope that's all right."

"Doesn't matter to me. I won't be doing the talking. Follow me. I'd better warn you, a couple of the guys don't speak much English."

"I'll be all right provided someone translates the

harder parts."

He shrugged and led me out the door to another trailer. Seated around a small conference table were four men all of whom bore uneasy expressions.

After introducing me, Benson left. I rummaged in my purse for a pen, pad of paper, and the tape recorder. One of the men eyed it suspiciously and spoke in rapid fire Spanish.

A weather-beaten man sitting next to him translated. "Carlos doesn't like the tape recorder."

"I only use it to keep my facts straight. No one else will hear it. I promise."

He nodded and spoke in low tones to two of the men. They looked at each other, and then jerked their heads in acceptance.

"I'll need your names, but if you don't want them printed, tell me now." It was unanimous—no publication of names. I switched on the recorder and turned my gaze to the man on my left. "What is your name and how long did you work for Shay and Holmes?"

"My name is John Smith—no really, it is," he said when I made a sound. "I was with S and H for close to fifteen years. Worked my way up to supervisor."

"Why did you leave?"

"Got fired," he said in a bitter tone.

"Why?"

"I refused to sign off on some of the construction. My supervisor came to me and said I could either sign off or take a hike. I told him to shove it, and he fired me."

"Why and what did you refuse to sign?"

John scratched his head and glanced at the other

three men. "I didn't like the way we was cutting corners. We worked on a small project in Sunshine Beach—a motel," he said, naming a small suburb of Port Royale. "Now when you use cement block and poured concrete, you gotta have rebar all the way to the top of the walls and spaced every few feet. It's code for hurricanes. Well, we didn't. The third floor had no rebar and the second story had it spaced out real wide. Code also demands that every roof truss be tied down with metal ties. Didn't happen. Only about every third truss was done."

"So, in a big blow what would happen?"

"A category three storm, maybe only a two, would probably tear the roof off. The third floor walls would bear the brunt and be destroyed."

"Why would the building inspector pass something like that?"

"My supervisor said the building department had okayed the changes and not to worry. He also dismissed the notion of a category four or five storm ever ripping through this area." He snorted. "How quickly they forget."

"Forget what?" I asked.

"Hurricane Andrew, 1992. The building department down in Miami-Dade got fat in the seventies and eighties and was lenient about enforcing codes. You're a reporter. Go look at the pictures of the damage done to something that ain't up to code."

"I'm a roofer," the man on my right added. "S and H skimped on roofing, too."

"And you are…"

"Fred Simms. I worked for them greedy bastards for seven years. Fired me, too, about a year ago."

"Did you work on the Sunshine Beach motel?"

"No, but I watched them cutting corners at other job sites. They charged top dollar to the owners, then gave 'em cheap shit. There's a restaurant in Palmetto Gardens whose roof is probably leaking like a sieve. The tiles were too thin, cracked easily, and the sheathing not done proper."

Palmetto Gardens was another western suburb, more upscale than Sunshine Beach. Then something he'd said caught my attention.

"Whoa, wait a minute, back up. Owners? I thought Shay and Holmes were developers. This wasn't their property?"

Smith shook his head. "Not at that time. The development part of the name was added about six or so years ago, but they didn't get around to actually developing anything on their own until four years ago. They still do outside construction work."

"They didn't own the motel either?" I asked Smith.

"Nope."

"Mr. Simms, I take it you complained and were told the same as Mr. Smith," I said, writing fast.

"I was overheard tellin' some of the guys what I thought. Next day I got canned."

The two Spanish speaking men now spoke in staccato tones using lots of facial expressions and gestures. Their words were too rapid fire for me to follow. Smith translated.

"Carlos says he and Juan were on another job in Port Royale when they bit the big one."

"What are Carlos' and Juan's last names?"

"Montoya and Ramirez."

"What happened?"

The two men talked for a solid five minutes without interruption before Smith turned to me.

"Carlos and Juan worked with concrete. Carlos mixed and Juan smoothed it after pouring. Carlos told his supervisor the mixture had too much sand, but the reply was to shut up and do as he was told. Juan explained the poured concrete was several inches short of the right depth. When he brought it to his supervisor's attention, he received the same warning. Both men informed the building inspector when he showed up. That evening, they were fired."

"What project was this?"

"The River Tower Condos on Riverside by the Seminole River," Smith replied.

A chill swept over me. "Are you telling me, The River Tower Condos, finished last year and now sold out, is unsafe?"

"That's the gist of it," Fred Simms stated. "And that *is* an S and H project. They owned it. I talked to a couple of buddies a few months ago. They said the place is a disaster waiting to happen. In a big blow, the facades will peel off, the windows will pop out, and the roof may take off for Oz. The whole shebang could go down like a house of cards."

"Might not even take a hurricane for some of that to happen," Smith said. "Just exposure to the salt air can rot inferior concrete. Once that starts happening, windows get loose, and even a gusty day will rip one or two out."

Visions of the World Trade Center flashed through my head. "But if things were so bad, how did it pass inspection?"

"How do ya think?" Fred snorted rubbing his

thumb and finger together.

"Bribes," I stated.

"How else?"

"Of course, we can't prove a damned thing. Never saw money actually change hands. You only have our word for all of this, but logic tells you somebody was paid off. On our dismissal records, it says we were fired with cause for insubordination. That's why we don't want our names used. We'll come off sounding like disgruntled employees," Smith said, the bitterness back in his voice.

They *were* disgruntled employees, but that didn't make them wrong. "Yet you were hired by Brooks Construction."

"Dave Brooks is an okay guy. Actually comes out on the site to see how we're doing and shows up when the inspectors are due," Fred replied.

"Used to be that way at S and H. When the kids took over, things went downhill real fast," Smith said.

"The kids?" I knew who he meant, but wanted it on the record anyway.

Smith curled his lip. "Brad Holmes and Ken Shay. Brad oozes around political circles getting his name and picture in the papers. Ken Shay is a worm. From what I've heard, he struts into the office at noon and leaves at four-thirty for another round of night clubs on South Street. Bob and Tim must be rolling in their graves."

"Bob and Tim?"

"Their fathers, the original Shay and Holmes."

"Is the company in financial trouble?"

"From what I hear, they're making money hand over fist." Fred snorted and shook his head. "You mark my words, it'll all come back to bite 'em in the ass."

The door opened, and Benson popped his head in. "Mr. Brooks is here and would like a brief word with you, Miss Jackson. Is this about to wind up? The men have to get back to work."

"Yes," I replied, turning off the recorder and slipping it into my purse. "Thank you all very much. You've been a tremendous help."

After the men filed out, I traipsed back to the operations trailer where Dave Brooks waited.

He introduced himself, and then asked, "Did you get the information?"

"Yes, thank you. Your men were very helpful. Are you aware of what they had to tell me?"

He nodded. "Yeah, I know. That's why I set Bill Mathias up for the interview. He left a voicemail earlier to say he'd been delayed and had sent you."

"If I may ask—how come you didn't tell anyone about the shenanigans at the River Tower Condos project? According to your men, the place is a hazard. Why didn't you contact the building commission or the city council?"

"Miss Jackson, corruption is like termite damage. Everything looks fine on the outside, but dig deep enough and the wood's riddled with holes and tunnels. If I complain to the wrong person, I may never get a permit in the city again. I can't afford to do that, so I play by the rules and hope that sooner or later honest people win. Do I think bribery is rampant from S and H? Hell, yes. Can I prove it? Hell, no. That's why I called Bill when I learned what the boys had to say."

He was caught in a corner with no clear path to the door, but I wondered how he'd feel if, God forbid, something happened with the condos. I asked the question.

Brooks gazed out the window for a moment, a grim expression on his face. "Miss Jackson, let's hope I never have to face that."

Driving back to the office, I passed the River Tower Condos and pulled over, looking up its twenty-seven story north face. A woman was watering plants on her balcony about half-way up. I shivered. How long would it be before the shoddy concrete would crumble and send her hurtling to her death?

****

It was after four when I entered my cubicle. Bill was still out, and while it was tempting to write up the story myself, I refrained.

"And where have you been all afternoon?" Doug said from my entryway.

"Take a hike, Elliott. I don't have to answer to you."

"I heard you've been buried in the archives as punishment. What did you do?"

The smugness in his voice made me want to black his other eye. "Punishment had nothing to do with it. I was researching something for Bill."

"Oh, yeah? What? More fundraising bullshit?"

"Why don't you ask Bill? If he wants an obit writer to know, I'm sure he'll tell you all about it. Now, get your perverted self out of here. I have work to do."

He scowled, but left. I turned to my computer as my phone rang.

"Shelley Jackson."

"Miss Jackson, Jason Mallory here."

My stomach cramped and my nerves jumped. "Mr. Mallory, what can I do for you?"

"I'm glad you put it that way, Miss Jackson. I'd like to invite you to dinner tonight."

Bill's warning popped into my mind. "I'm sorry, Mr. Mallory, but I'm not available. Perhaps, some other time. Goodbye."

"Please, don't hang up. I want to talk to you about Marc—not his death, his life. His mother is distraught and anything I can tell her would help. I came on strong yesterday. I apologize. I'm used to conducting business and arguing with engineers. I'm afraid I'm often abrasive. Let me make it up to you."

I weakened. "I don't know…did you talk with my boss, Bill Mathias today?"

"Yes. That's why I'm calling. I feel badly."

Bullshit. I doubted Jason Mallory felt sorry concerning anything, but my curiosity about the interview overrode any warnings. Besides, his presence and the simple touch of a handshake had activated my hormones. It was my one great vulnerability. I often gave in to those hormones.

"Very well, Mr. Mallory."

"Good. I'm staying at The Waterfront Hotel on Seventeenth Street. There's an Italian restaurant in the shopping center attached to it. Would you mind meeting me there at say, eight o'clock?"

I knew the place. It was called Leonardo's and located a stone's throw from The Marina Boatyard where I'd met with Shay.

"Eight o'clock is fine."

"Thank you, Miss Jackson."

For the next hour, my mind jumped from visions of crumbling condos to Jason Mallory to Kenneth Shay. I couldn't concentrate and finally gave up. Bill had not returned, but that didn't surprise me. Sometimes when writing up a good interview, he did it from home. I'd catch him tomorrow. And maybe this time I wouldn't be banished to archive purgatory.

*****

I deliberately arrived at Leonardo's fifteen minutes late. Let him cool *his* heels for a while. It would do him good.

The maitre d' led me toward the far corner where I spotted Jason Mallory sipping a martini, his long legs crossed, the crease in his navy slacks sharp. I had to admit, the light blue shirt with the sleeves rolled up to reveal strong forearms and the top two buttons undone to show a tantalizing glimpse of dark chest hair, gave the casual look a heavy wallop of sexy. Emotion should never play a part in business, but damn, he cranked up my heat factor. He also didn't look in the least concerned by my late arrival and smiled as I approached, rising to pull out my chair.

"Sorry, I'm late. I had a few unexpected things come up at the office," I said, settling myself as he reclaimed his seat.

"No problem. You look lovely. Those colors suit you."

"Thank you."

He knew how to play the game. I appreciated the comment anyway, having spent the better part of two hours trying on and discarding clothes before choosing the chocolate skirt and yellow, long-sleeved jersey top. The clinging fabric molded to my breasts and emphasized my waist. I also wore my brown snakeskin stilettos. I love stilettos and wear them whenever possible, even to work upon occasion. My feet would forgive me provided I didn't have to walk any further than from the restaurant to my car.

The waiter appeared. I ordered a martini, and then picked up the menu with shaky fingers. The man unsettled me, and I didn't like it. Okay, I did like it, but my relationships frequently ended up in the dump. To cover my confusion, I skimmed the selections. Attracted, yet uneasy in his presence, I now regretted accepting his invitation.

My drink arrived. I sipped, letting the cold vodka slide down my throat to warm my stomach. With my nerves steadied, I allowed my gaze to contact his.

He smiled, the right corner of his mouth curling up further than the left. "I won't eat you. There's no reason to be nervous."

Damn, he saw too much. "What makes you think I'm nervous?"

He didn't answer my question. "Tell me about Marc."

"Mr. Mallory…"

"Jason. Call me Jason."

"All right, Jason. I'm Shelley. We covered this at lunch. Tell me the real reason you've asked me out."

He stared for a second, and then sipped his drink. Everything this man did was precise and ordered.

"All right. Bill Mathias told me Marc had sent you a CD in some kind of code. I want that CD."

"Thank you very much for the drink, *Mr. Mallory*."

I tossed my napkin on the table and started to rise. Swift as a snake's tongue, his hand whipped out and grasped my arm.

"Forgive me. I put that badly."

"You have a habit of doing that."

"What I meant was I understand codes. Marc and I used to dabble in them. I mentioned that already. I may be able to decipher it."

I resettled in the chair. "Kind of forgot to tell me you sit on the board of directors of Shay and Holmes, didn't you? How convenient that Marc also worked there."

"I admit I got him the job."

"Why? He liked working at J. R. Lennox. He was a CPA. Why take a lowly accounting job at a development company? It doesn't make sense."

"I want to find out who killed my brother. If what's on that CD is the key, then I have a right to know."

He danced around my question, but I saw his point.

"Bill has it. Come by the office tomorrow morning and we'll let you take a crack at it." The CD was not up for discussion, so I got back to what I wanted to know. "What did you and Bill talk about?"

"Mostly about Shay and Holmes and me. He told me he's investigating a city corruption scandal. What's that all about?"

"Didn't Bill tell you?"

"He said an anonymous e-mailer contacted him about two months ago saying S and H was bribing building inspectors to pass work that should be rejected. Are they?"

I shrugged, taking another sip of my drink. "In my opinion, yes. A second e-mail arrived blowing the whistle about shoddy construction."

"Both from the same person?"

"Bill didn't say."

"So, it's possible two different people contacted him. What's your connection?"

"I do some of his research while he conducts interviews. Bill's been closed mouthed about things the last few weeks. I do know, however, that his scrutiny has veered in a different direction."

"What kind of direction?"

"He wouldn't tell me."

Jason finished his drink and ordered another. I followed his lead vowing to sip this one slowly. The man had elicited information from me without half trying, and so far, I hadn't learned a damned thing.

He must have read my mind. "Let's not talk business tonight. How did you get into the journalism game?"

This time his smile reached his eyes and my breath stopped somewhere between my lungs and my throat. A long, slow shiver started at the base of my spine and crawled to the nape of my neck. Good Lord, this man was gorgeous. *Probably knows it, too, and uses it to his advantage.*

"My mother was a writer. I guess some of the genes must have been passed on."

"Was she a reporter?"

"No, fiction. She wrote mysteries. They were good, too."

The waiter appeared with our drinks and we ordered, including a bottle of wine.

"Does she still write?" he asked when the man left.

"No, she died when I was fourteen—automobile accident."

"That's a rough age to lose a parent. What about your father?"

"Daddy's a doctor in Oak Park, just outside Chicago."

"Have you ever tried to write a mystery?"

"God, no, I'd be awful at it. I just don't have the imagination for fiction. What about you? Did you always want to be an architect?"

He laughed. "I was the kid who glued his building blocks together so they couldn't be knocked down."

I laughed with him. "Was that a family trait?"

"In a way; my father owned a construction company in Los Angeles. I worked there during my summer breaks from college."

"How did Marc fit in?"

"His mother was my father's third wife."

"Third?"

"Dad loved being married. He just had trouble staying that way."

He sipped his martini, and I changed the subject.

"You started your own company at an early age."

"I worked for an architectural firm after I graduated from USC. I hated taking orders from people who never put an original idea on the drawing board. So, I borrowed money from Dad and opened my own business. I'll admit I got lucky. I hired Mallory Construction to do the work. Dad charged the minimum. I started out with houses and renovations before working my way up."

"And now you do high rises and win awards."

"Isn't Google a wonderful thing?"

I had to laugh again. It was true. For all I knew, he'd Googled me.

Our food arrived and for the next several minutes savoring the meal replaced conversation. I'd ordered Veal Parmesan. The perfect blend of flavors exploded in my mouth and sent a tingle all the way down to my toes. I'm a sucker for Italian food.

Jason apparently had no problem with his Chicken Marsala either for he also concentrated on the food.

"How do you like Port Royale?" he asked when we resumed talking. "Marc said South Florida was more artificial than Southern California."

"This is New York with palm trees. The people are rude, the traffic horrendous, and the salaries small. However, I do appreciate it at this time of year. I never did like snow."

"You plan on staying?"

"Maybe. I don't know. If I don't get a byline soon, I may move on."

"Is a byline important to you?"

"Of course. I want to waltz into the White House press room, plant my rear-end in Helen Thomas's front row seat, and watch the President of the United States smile, then call on me by name."

Jason whistled softly. "That's ambitious. But didn't Helen Thomas pass away not too long ago?"

I waved a hand in dismissal. "Doesn't matter. I still want the seat. And I want it before the age of forty."

"No husband or family in your future?"

"Only if they can accept my career comes first."

The waiter cleared our empty dishes and presented the bill. Jason laid a credit card on the tray, and the man whisked it away.

"Shelley, about that CD. Bill has a copy, doesn't he?"

"Bill tell you that?"

"Let's just say I don't think either of you would take a chance on having the original get lost or stolen."

I drained my wine glass. He had it figured out. I

should have known.

"It's in a safe place."

"Would you bring it to my hotel room in the morning?"

Would I? I didn't completely trust him, yet at the same time, I didn't think he'd do anything physical to get the CD, especially if I announced myself at the front desk first.

He smiled as though reading my mind. "I promise I'm not a closet molester. I just really want to see that CD."

Maybe it was the smile. Maybe it was the martinis and the wine. *Maybe* it was my own desire to see him again that prompted me to nod. "I guess I can do that."

"Good enough. I need a favor. I want to pack some of Marc's things tonight. His place isn't far from here. Would you like to help?"

Me pass up a chance to look inside Marc's home? No way. "Sure."

He smiled, and his fingers grazed the back of my hand making my nerves hum. I was suddenly very glad I'd come and was eager to spend more time with Jason Mallory.

****

We were several blocks from Marc's when I pulled over to let a fire engine, siren blaring, roar past. A minute later I repeated my actions when fire truck number two flashed by. Ahead, a reddish-yellow glow lit up the sky.

"Looks like a big one," Jason commented from the passenger seat.

I resumed driving, and the closer we got to Marc's the harder my heart pounded. The fire was damned close to his townhouse.

I turned the corner and jammed on my brakes, staring at the sight before me. Marc's home was fully involved. Flames shot through the roof of the narrow three story structure while thick, black smoke billowed from the front windows. Every few seconds a yellow tongue of blazing heat flicked out like the angry snap of a carriage whip.

"Shit!" Jason leaped from my car and ran.

I parked and tried to follow, cursing the stilettos. The firemen had numerous hoses trained on the conflagration. I'd never seen a big fire up close and couldn't get over the noise. The crackling of the raging flames, the whoosh of the water leaving the hoses and hissing as it hit hot embers, along with the shouts of the people all melded into a scene from Dante's *Inferno*. The smell of burning wood, wet ashes, and smoke turned my stomach, and my eyes stung bringing tears.

A sizable crowd had gathered. I was sure it included evacuated neighbors. I caught up with Jason at the police barrier.

"I don't care who you are, mister. You ain't getting any closer. Now, you try getting past this barrier again and I'll arrest you for hindering a fireman. Got that?"

"Jason, there's nothing you can do," I said, grasping his arm. "It's gone. I'm sorry. Did Marc have much left in there for his mother?"

"Some, but I was more interested in finding clues to his murder. I thought maybe he'd left a key to the code he used on the CD."

He continued staring at the fire. The firefighters had the upper hand, so I scanned the crowd.

"Wait here. Don't move. I'll be back in a couple of

minutes," I told him. He nodded never taking his eyes off Marc's burning home.

Weaving my way through the crowd, I found a woman sobbing into a cell phone. When she finished the call, I sidled up, placing my arm around her shoulders in a comforting gesture.

"I'm so sorry. Are you a neighbor?"

She nodded, sniffling and wiping her eyes with a tissue. "Yes. I live right next door. Oh, I hope they can put this out before it spreads to my house. There's a firewall, but I worry about the roof. I guess the water and smoke damage will be bad."

"Be happy you got out in time." I tried to soothe her before asking more questions.

"The poor man's dead, you know. I mean the owner," she said.

"Someone died in the fire?"

"No, no—at least, I don't think so. But the man who owned the place died last week. He was murdered."

"How awful. Maybe the fire was set by kids or a burglar knowing it was empty. Do you know how it started?"

She shook her head and wiped more tears from her face. "I was watching TV when all of a sudden there was this loud boom. It rattled pictures on the wall and the china in my hutch. A few minutes later, I smelled smoke and called the fire department. By the time they arrived there were flames everywhere."

A man rushed up. "Marilyn, are you all right?"

The woman sobbed into his chest, and I eased away until spotting a man talking with a policeman. When he finished, I sauntered up.

"Wow, this is awful. What happened?" I asked.

"Don't know. I live across the street. I was ready to take my dog for a walk when there was an explosion."

I faked a horrified gasp. "You mean like a bomb? What did the policeman say?"

"Not much," he answered and looked at me with a frown. "Do you live around here?"

"Up the block. I just got home."

He turned his attention back to the dying fire.

I talked with a couple of other people, but got the same story—a big boom, then fire. I made my way back to Jason. He hadn't moved. In the flashing emergency lights of the fire trucks and police cars, I easily read the fury on his face.

I told him what the neighbors had to say about how the fire started. "Maybe there was a gas leak," I said.

"Maybe, but I don't think this was an accident."

I tugged at his arm. "Come on. Let's get you back to the hotel. You won't be able to do anything until morning. The police and the firemen will be here all night."

He finally turned to look at me. I shivered at the cold look in his eyes.

"No, you go on home. I'll call a cab later."

Arguing with him was fruitless. He'd stay, asking questions until he got answers. I wouldn't mind hearing those answers myself.

"I'll stay with you."

"No, I don't think so." He grasped my arm and walked me back to the car.

"Hey, wait a minute. I have just as much right to be here as you do."

"No, you don't. Marc was my brother and this was

his home. It's none of your business."

"It is if it's arson."

He opened the car door and shoved me in. "Then I should be the first to know, not a reporter. Go home. If you don't, I'll tell everyone what you do for a living. They'll see you as a vulture picking at their misfortune, which you are. I'll see you in the morning."

He slammed the door and stalked back to the barriers to resume his watch. I twisted the key with a vicious motion and jerked the car into gear.

"'I'll see you in the morning,'" I mimicked. "Like hell, buster."

Jason Mallory could whistle up a drainpipe. I'd be damned if I let him see Marc's CD now.

****

I pulled into my driveway still muttering epithets about Jason, unlocked the front door, dumped my evening bag on the hall table, and strode to the living room where I snapped on a light. My heart gave a sickening lurch and my whole body trembled at the sight in front of me. I clapped a shaking hand over my mouth.

The place had been ransacked—furniture overturned, books and papers strewn all over the floor, rugs tossed aside. Even the blades of my ceiling fan, now hanging by only the wires, lay in a splintered heap.

My bedroom looked the same, as did my office. The dining room didn't have much to vandalize, but the chair seats had been cut to ribbons.

Shocked, I stared. I'd never been a crime victim before. I felt violated and exposed.

In spite of the mess, I couldn't find anything missing. My TV, stereo, and jewelry were still here. I ran back into my office. My laptop was gone. Who would take a computer, but not a plasma TV or a Bose stereo system? And how had they gotten in?

I hurried into the kitchen to check the back door and stopped dead with my hand over my nose. I had only one gas appliance—my water heater located in the laundry room off the kitchen. The stench of escaping gas scared the hell out of me.

I raced for the back door.

Chapter Five

I had a tiny back yard, which provided no cover from an explosion. Kicking off those damned shoes, I dashed around the house and across the street before it dawned on me my cell phone was inside. I ran to the front door of a house and pounded. A glaring man opened up.

"Please, call nine-one-one," I said, gasping. "My house has been burglarized and I smell gas. Hurry!"

He grabbed my arm, pulling me inside. "Angie, grab the kids and get the hell out."

His wife didn't argue, but disappeared toward the back of the home. I followed, scooping up a slow moving toddler on the way. We ran to the end of the block while the man alerted neighbors.

Within minutes, fire engines and cop cars raced past, stopping in front of my place. The men crashed through the front door and ran inside. I held my breath, moving closer when several firemen and two cops went in, and then came back out. No one was in a hurry. The fact nothing had blown up gave me hope. Weaving my way through the spectators, I walked up to them.

"Did you get it turned off?" I asked.

"Who are you?" one of the policemen said.

"Shelley Jackson. I live here."

"What happened?"

"I came home, saw the mess, smelled gas, and ran

75

for my life. A neighbor called."

"You did the right thing," a fireman told me. "Whoever broke in disconnected the gas line after shutting off the pilot. A lighted candle was on top of the refrigerator."

"Why not leave the pilot light on? It would be quicker."

"Too quick. Gas is heavier than air. The pilot may have ignited things before the vandals escaped. And relying on a light switch or thermostat might take too long. This method is old, but reliable. By the time the fumes reached the candle, the vandals would be long gone."

And I flipped on a light switch in the living room. Thank God, I left the light on over the sink. I shivered at the thought of what could have happened if I'd done the same in the kitchen.

The flames eating through the roof of Marc's townhouse and neighbors describing an explosion hammered in my mind. This was no coincidence.

"How did they get in?" I asked the cop.

"Jimmied the back door," he said, writing in a notebook.

I'd been so scared I never noticed on my wild dash to safety. "May I go in?"

The fireman nodded. "If it's okay with the police. We turned off the gas."

The cop shrugged. Taking that to mean yes, I hurried through the front door. The other policemen were in the living room and stopped me.

"I'm sorry, ma'am, but you'll have to leave. This is a crime scene."

"But I live here. Besides, I already walked through

it when I got home."

"Is anything missing?"

"Just my laptop. I can't think why they didn't snatch the plasma and the stereo."

"Maybe they parked too far away. Carrying a laptop might not arouse suspicion, but a plasma TV would."

I thought he credited the bastards with too much intelligence. Then I remembered what was on my laptop. A cold chill slithered up my spine. I had burned the CD for Bill on it. Even though encrypted, the information was on my hard drive.

"If it's all right with you, I'd like to grab some clothes. Obviously, I can't stay here tonight."

"Sure, but first, I'd like to ask you a few questions. Where were you tonight? What time did you leave the house?"

I spent the next hour answering questions. They finally released me, and after retrieving my purse from the hall table, I lugged a small overnight bag to my car. Detective Frank Whitten strolled up.

"Hear you had some trouble," he said.

"Yeah, I'm just another crime statistic."

"Kind of strange, you and Marc Chambers' place getting hit tonight. You were lucky. His house burned to the ground."

"That's a shame," I replied heaving my bag into the car. "Any idea what started the fire?"

"Not yet. Arson squad arrived as I was leaving. How well do you know Jason Mallory?"

"Not very."

"But well enough to have dinner with him?"

I shrugged. "Why not? He's Marc's step-brother.

He wanted to know how Marc was getting along down here."

"Don't suppose you were with him this afternoon at Chambers' house, were you?"

Jason had already been to Marc's today? I'd been under the impression he had wanted to pack things tonight. Why not do it this afternoon?

"Nope. I was in the office until four-thirty. Why?"

"Just curious. Someone tossed Chambers' place just after he was killed. Now, his house burns a few hours after Mallory leaves. Your home is tossed, and if you'd been a half an hour later, you'd be sifting through ashes, too."

"Well, Jason Mallory certainly didn't do it. I left home at six o'clock this evening. He was with me until I left the fire scene."

"Never said he did. Where are you going to stay?"

"I haven't decided yet."

"Keep in touch."

Whitten nodded and sauntered toward the front door. I quickly drove away, turned the corner, and pulled over to think.

Did Whitten seriously believe Jason Mallory had set his brother's house on fire? For what reason? The detective's suspicions activated my own. Jason wouldn't get his hands dirty. He'd hire someone, and then make sure I was out of the way, so they could ransack my place. What better way than to ask me to dinner? He kept me in my seat with mention of the CD.

And why return to Marc's tonight? Because he knew what we'd find, and I'd be the perfect alibi? Or could it have been another delaying tactic to make sure I was nowhere near my house when it blew sky high?

Then another thought flashed through my mind—one I should have picked up on immediately. Why the hell would Bill mention the CD to Jason Mallory, especially after telling me not to trust him? Once again I'd let a good-looking man dull my reporter's senses.

"Damn," I muttered to myself. I was in over my head and for the first time since finding Marc's body, scared. And I was just a minor player. Who else was being victimized?

"Oh, my God—Bill," I said out loud. I should warn him.

I fumbled in my purse for my cell phone. Due to the late hour, I called his cell first, but got no answer. The same results occurred with his home phone. I even called his direct office line with the hope he'd gone there to finish his article. No luck. I left the same message on all three phones.

"Bill, its Shelley. If you're there, please, pick up. This is urgent." I received no response. "Call me as soon as you can."

A prickle of uneasiness crawled over my scalp. Bill was rarely incommunicado, even on a hot date.

I glanced at my watch. Not quite midnight. In any event, he would eventually get my messages and call.

Tossing my phone onto the seat, I tried to ignore the trickle of something not quite fear, but more than worry nagging at the back of my mind.

I drove aimlessly for a while, my eyes glued on my rearview mirror until I was sure no one followed. Speeding down Hanover Street and across the bridge over the Intracoastal, I finally turned into a hotel on the beach. A room would cost a fortune in February, but they had valet parking. My car would be tucked out of sight, not exposed in a motel parking lot.

I tossed and turned, sitting up at the smallest noise. I finally dropped into a fitful doze and awoke at seven-thirty. Eating a quick breakfast, I checked out and drove to the post office where I retrieved the CD. I wanted answers from Marc's step-brother.

****

I paused in front of Jason Mallory's hotel suite torn between knocking and running away. My suspicions of his motives for asking me out last night still hadn't disappeared. I cursed Whitten for planting them.

I didn't want to show him the CD, but had thrown in the towel on trying to decipher the code. Since Mallory knew of its existence, I decided to play his game. How did he know about the CD? Certainly Bill hadn't said anything. I was determined to pry the answer out of him. Plus, I needed to squirm out of Bill's doghouse.

My concern about Bill increased. He hadn't called, and when I tried his various phones again this morning, I had come up dry.

Whether I liked it or not, Marc's step-brother might be my last hope of trying to discover what the numbers on the CD meant.

Come on, dummy. Knock and get it over with. You'll get arrested loitering in the hallway like this.

Hoping I wasn't making a huge mistake, I knocked and waited for what seemed an eternity before Jason opened the door.

Casually dressed in tan slacks and a light blue polo, he held a cup of steaming coffee. Over his shoulder, I spied a room service tray sitting on a small dining table in the sitting room.

"Shelley, I'm glad you came. I'm sorry I was so rude last night. My only excuse is I was furious about Marc's place. Would you like some breakfast?" He moved aside so I could enter.

I slipped past him. He sounded sincere, but I imagined he could sound damned sincere when he wanted. "I've already eaten, but you go ahead. I wouldn't refuse a cup of coffee, though."

"You, too, huh," he said, laughing. "Sometimes I think I have caffeine in my veins instead of blood."

Small attempts at humor didn't cut it. I sat opposite him and blew on the hot liquid before taking a sip. "What time did you leave last night?"

"About four. I followed the arson squad around like a reporter." He tossed me a smile.

"Very funny. Did they find anything?"

"Too soon to tell. They'll go back this morning, but the preliminary opinion is the fire was deliberately set."

"Let me guess. Someone disconnected the gas line and set a burning candle on top of the refrigerator."

He stopped chewing his scrambled eggs and bacon, inspecting me with narrowed eyes. "Something like that. How did you know?"

I told him of my adventure after leaving him.

"Anything on your laptop?"

"Plenty. I'm pissed about losing Bejeweled Blitz. My record is seven hundred fifty-two thousand points." I enjoyed needling him. Besides, an internet game is never lost.

"That's not what I mean and you know it. Was there anything relating to Marc or the investigation your boss is working on?"

I hesitated. Should I trust him? The CD held the

key. If I wanted the code broken, I had no choice.

"Some and, of course, what was on this," I replied taking the CD out of my purse.

"Damn. If they know what Marc was doing, they'll cover their tracks fast."

"And just what was Marc doing?"

"I don't know. That's why I need to see this CD."

He gulped his coffee and took the CD over to his laptop on the desk where he pulled up the information. I followed, gazing over his shoulder.

"What the hell is this? Recipes? I don't need recipes. Where's the code?"

"Keep going. The recipes are a dodge. And by the way, if whoever stole my laptop breaks the password, that's how it'll show up in my document file—Mom's Recipes. If I hadn't received the CD the way I did, I'd have brushed it off and never scrolled further than halfway."

"Marc, you sly devil, you," Jason commented as he zipped past the ingredients for lasagna and rhubarb pie. He came to the gap between tuna casserole and the first set of numbers. "Got it."

I poured another cup of coffee and finished off the last piece of toast while he muttered and scribbled on a pad of paper. The urge to pace or hang over his shoulder again was strong, but I forced myself to stand by the window, gazing at the street below. He sat back and sighed.

"Figure it out?" I asked, joining him. A series of numbers was displayed.

"Not completely. It's not a cryptograph. I have no idea what the FL, WK, AD or BOW followed by numbers means nor do I understand the last six numbers in the sequences, but I think I may have the middle section knocked."

"Plan on sharing?" I asked when he didn't continue.

"Sorry, I was thinking. The letters and numbers in the middle may be bank accounts—offshore would be my guess."

"But where?"

"Could be anywhere. Look," he said, pointing to a sequence beginning with BOW. "NBP could represent the name of the bank and the 67335 the account number. BOC, TCB, CBB all appear on a regular basis even though the numbers change, which means we could be dealing with multiple accounts. I'd bet the first set of letters refers to the owners."

I stared at the screen mentally separating the numbers and letters at the beginning.

"Look at FL. The numbers after the letters go up from 430 to 515 to 629 then drop back down to 106." I quickly scanned for the same pattern. "It does the same with others. Jason, if the first letters are account owners could the first set of numbers be dates?"

"And you said you were bad with codes."

"It was just a thought. You separated the sequence. But what year? I mean, the last entry could reference ten years ago for all we know."

"True. I'll keep this and work on it some more tonight," he said. "What's your agenda for the day?"

I slid my hand into my purse and handed him a blank CD. "Number one on my agenda is taking the original CD back to its home in the post office. Make a copy." I couldn't keep the hard edge from my voice.

He stared for a moment, but did as asked, returning

the original. "You don't trust me, do you? Why?"

"I find our dinner last night to have been very convenient. And your desire to drive to Marc's even more so. Why go back when you'd been there in the afternoon?"

"I see you've talked to Detective Whitten. I returned last night for the reason I told you. I wanted to finish the packing and not be interrupted by a dozen business calls."

"And the longer I stayed with you, the more time someone had to blow up my house, too."

"What are you insinuating? That I had Marc's house set on fire and yours ransacked?"

I don't know how he did it, but his eyes had the look of cold steel and shot sparks at the same time. His face was set in stone, and his lips hardened into a thin line.

"How do I know? After all, you sit on the board of directors of Shay and Holmes, and Marc was your *step*-brother. And you haven't been real forthcoming. Exactly what were you and Marc doing? For all I know, his townhouse contained incriminating evidence about Shay and Holmes you don't want known. And while we're at it, how the hell did you know about the CD?"

Even as I spoke, my assumptions didn't make sense. If something incriminating was there, why not just remove it? No need to burn the place to a crisp.

He launched himself out of the chair and stood over me. I couldn't help but to back up a couple of steps.

"Marc was the only one of my many step and half-siblings I felt any affection for. And while we're on the subject, you haven't been a fountain of truth yourself."

I swallowed hard. "Well, I wasn't about to announce the CD to just anyone. I don't believe Bill said a damned thing to you about it."

"He didn't. Marc did."

"What!"

"Marc called me the night he died. I was out and had my cell turned off. He left a message, saying he had information I needed to know, but thought he was being watched. He told me he was leaving a CD with a good friend, a girl he used to date."

"How did you know it was me?" I could barely croak the words out of a tight throat.

"I put two and two together. Marc was nuts about you, would do anything you asked. Whenever we talked, he'd rave about how wonderful you were—right up until you dumped him for being a nice guy."

Jason spat the words out and balled his fists as though he wanted to slug me. He'd known from the beginning I had the disc. I backed up another step and couldn't answer.

"Marc was too smart to just pop the CD into his pocket and stroll out to meet you in an alley. The minute I saw Marc's shoes and the zipper, I understood. You know what I think? I think you either met Marc in that alley and he gave you whatever was hidden, or you took it after he was dead. I can't make up my mind if you killed him or not."

My frozen voice finally thawed. "God, no! I swear I didn't kill him. I was late getting to the alley. I found his body, but had no idea what he had for me. I knew the shoes were out of character, opened the zipper, and found a key. Turned out it belonged to a post office box. If you only knew how scared I was. Damn you, I liked Marc. I didn't break up with him because he was a nice guy. Oh, shit!"

I broke down and cried. My tears were therapeutic, washing away the fright of the past few days. I stumbled to the sofa and sat down, burying my face in my hands. A few seconds later, the cushion next to me sagged and a handkerchief was pressed between my fingers.

"Here," a calmer Jason Mallory said. "I'm sorry, but I had to know. I don't really think you killed Marc. Tell me what happened."

"God, it was awful."

I wiped my tears and blew my nose while I told him the whole story.

"And you saw or heard no one in the alley?"

I shook my head. "No, it was quiet, except for the rats. I had trouble finding the place and was about twenty minutes late. Maybe, if I had been on time…" I let the sentence trail off.

"Then you'd both be dead." Jason rose. "It's after nine, and I want to get to Marc's. Then I'll spend some time at Shay and Holmes making a pest of myself asking questions."

"Questions?"

"About Marc, his personal life, and what he did in accounting. Someone knows something." The grim lines returned to his face.

"Be careful. You may ask the wrong person questions."

"I'm the grieving brother. It's my right." He smiled. "I take it you no longer think I have ulterior motives about last night."

"No. I think its Whitten's way of getting even with

me for an unflattering story I wrote several months ago. He's retiring soon and coasting."

"Come back here tonight. We'll order room service and take another crack at those numbers. Which tip came first to Mathias—Shay and Holmes cutting corners or city corruption?"

"I'm not sure. Bill didn't say, but it may have been the shoddy construction, then S and H bribing inspectors."

"Ask Mathias to come, too. He may share information if I can be his inside man."

"I will if I can find him."

Jason shot me a startled look. "What do you mean?"

"I tried to call last night to warn him. He has a copy of the CD, too, although I don't think anyone knows that. He hasn't answered yet."

"Is that unusual?"

"When Bill's on the trail of a good lead, he doesn't let anything distract him, but his phone is always on. He may have seen me on caller ID and is ignoring it until he's finished with what he's doing."

"And you're sure nobody else knows Bill has a copy?"

"I'm not certain. I don't know who he'd tell other than our editor, Cal Randolph. Bill and I viewed it in his office with the door closed. I don't see how..." I stopped in mid-sentence and bit my lip.

"What?"

I shrugged. "Oh, it's just—there's this nasty little, sexual-harassing snoop in the office named Doug Elliott. His aunt owns stock in the paper, and he thinks he should be the editor. He wanted my job and when he didn't get it, made himself obnoxious."

"Do you think he knows anything?"

I thought for a moment before replying. "No, I doubt it. He may have seen us through the window and been curious, but knows better than to question Bill. I had an ugly run in with him yesterday. He touched me, and I took exception. Called him a few choice names."

Jason's eyebrows rose. "Want me to buy out his aunt?"

I laughed and stood. "Not yet. I can handle him." I started for the door. "What time do you want me here?"

"Meet me in the bar at six. We'll have a drink, and then come up here. If Mathias checks in, urge him to come."

I nodded and left. In the elevator, images of the fire, the mess in my house, and the horror of the alley flitted through my mind. Then Bill's face flashed in front of my eyes.

Damn it, Bill. Why don't you call?

****

I called work, telling them about the burglary and that I would be in after lunch, asking the receptionist if she'd seen Bill. She hadn't. I tried calling his numbers again, but received no answer.

After replacing the CD in the post office box, I went home and spent the rest of the morning trying to salvage what I could. Luckily, it was a matter of just picking up. Other than my ceiling fan and dining room chairs nothing had been destroyed. The fan puzzled me until I realized a CD taped to the top of a blade was a great hiding place. The vandals must have figured the fire would take care of everything else.

Bill's office was still dark, the door closed and

locked. I entered my cubicle, firing up my computer to check for e-mail. I also checked my voicemail, but found nothing. Nobody had seen or heard from him since he left yesterday afternoon to interview Jason Mallory, and Jason admitted talking to him. Six hours ago, I'd have found that suspicious.

The phone on my desk rang and I answered it, hoping it was Bill.

"Jackson, you all right?" Calvin Randolph's voice grumbled in my ear.

"I'm fine. There wasn't much damage, just a mess," I replied, disappointed at the voice's owner.

"Come in here. I need to talk to you."

I hung up, biting my lip. Now what? I didn't think I'd done anything wrong—lately. Maybe he was pissed about my time away from the office. His door was open, and I walked in.

"Close it behind you," he said.

Well, I couldn't be in too much trouble. He left it open for ass-chewings.

"Sit down." He rested his elbows on the desk and frowned at me. "Want to tell me what's going on?"

"About what?"

"Shay and Holmes, the investigation, step-brothers of murdered accountants who just happen to sit on the S and H board, dinners, fires, burglaries—take your pick. And do you have any idea where Bill Mathias is?"

"None. I tried calling him last night and again this morning. I'm worried."

"So am I. Bill called yesterday afternoon around four. He brought me up to date on Jason Mallory and his relationship to this Marc Chambers. He also told me the murdered man was a friend of yours."

"That's true." I had no idea if Bill had mentioned the CD to Cal. I doubted it.

Cal stared out of the window at the high-rise going up across the street.

"Bill thought he was on to something, but didn't say what. He sounded excited. I suppose he could be holed up somewhere writing, but I don't like him being out of touch like this."

I shifted uncomfortably on my chair. I didn't like it either. "How did you know I was with Jason Mallory last night and about the fire at Marc's?"

"When you called in this morning, I contacted a friend at the police station. He told me." He frowned and fiddled with a pencil. "I want you to write a story about the fire. Then write another story about how it feels to be a crime victim. Have them on my desk by tomorrow morning."

I left his office comforted by his concern about Bill and excited the top dog gave me an assignment. I wrote the crime victim story first since it was freshest in my mind and e-mailed it to Cal for final approval. I wrote about the fire at Marc's, next trying to keep my involvement out of it. I was two-thirds of the way through when I felt "the presence."

"Hit the road, Elliott. I'm busy."

"Jesus, you grow eyes in the back of your head?"

"Where you're concerned, yes."

"Rumor has it Bill's missing. Is it true?"

I heard the avid curiosity in his voice, and resisted the urge to throw my coffee mug at him. Sickened, I ignored his attempt to elicit information.

"Well, is it?" he persisted.

"Bill is off somewhere doing his job and just

because you haven't seen him, doesn't mean he's missing. Now, get the hell out of my cubicle."

"Maybe I can help. Just tell me what you have, where he was going, and who he was going to see. I'll do your leg work. Cal won't mind."

I swiveled my chair sharply to face him. "I'm telling you for the last time—fuck off. If Bill or Cal thought you capable of helping with anything other than cleaning the johns, they'd have said so."

Doug's face darkened and he glared malevolently. The weasel looked ready to stroke out. "Sooner or later, you'll have to deal with me. My aunt owns a chunk of this rag, and I expect to be in a position of authority in the future. Watch who you insult."

"You'll be old and gray by the time you reach any level of responsibility on *The Standard*, and I long gone. Now, get out, or do I have to call security?"

He sucked in a breath, thrust his chin out, and strutted away. I strode into the break room for a bottle of cold water. The sad part was the little shit was right. He'd inherit the stock and set himself up as editor. Maybe it was time to move on.

I returned to my cubicle, trying to concentrate on my article, but my attention wandered. Bill still hadn't put in an appearance and as much as I hated to admit it, Doug's word "missing" made me uneasy.

I saved my story and switched off the computer. It was after five-thirty, and I wanted to change clothes before I met Jason. I was a step from the cubicle entry when my desk phone rang. Bill? I leaped to answer.

"Shelley, come to my office." It was Cal and he sounded grim.

My heart knocked against my ribs. He'd called me

by my first name, something he rarely did. I was "Jackson."

"Sure, what's up?"

"Just come and don't talk to anyone along the way."

I hung up and hurried to his office. Cal sat at his desk, an expression I couldn't begin to describe on his face. His lips had compressed, the wrinkles around his mouth forming deep grooves. Two uniformed policemen and another man stood to one side.

"Shelley, sit down."

I obeyed. "What's going on?" My first thought was that something had happened at my house—like it blew up.

"Shelley, this is Detective Sorenson of the Port Royale police. A couple of maintenance men were clearing out some overgrowth in Wildwood Park." He closed his eyes. "They found Bill's body. He'd been shot in the head."

Chapter Six

Cold numbness prickled my scalp. My vision blurred and darkened. By the grace of God, I didn't faint. I wanted to, but didn't. I rocked back and forth unable to say a word, my hands gripping the seat of the chair like a lifeline.

Then my stomach clenched in a vise-like cramp. A burning sourness rose in the back of my throat. I leapt to my feet, gagged, and clapped a hand over my mouth. Without waiting for permission from anybody, I jerked open the door racing for the ladies' room where I threw up. I knelt in front of the toilet, grasping my hot cheeks with cold trembling hands and sobbed.

Wildwood Park. Three acres of prime real estate in the heart of the city. Hailed by environmentalists, it paid homage to native trees and bushes. Nature, however, took its course and soon the place resembled a jungle. Occasionally, the city cleared things out. In recent years, it had become a hangout for the homeless.

I rose, rinsed out my mouth, and made my way back to Cal's office, ignoring several pairs of staring eyes. I closed the door behind me and resumed my seat.

"I'm sorry, but I couldn't help it."

"Are you all right?" Cal asked. Worry and sorrow clouded his eyes.

"I will be," I replied, placing a shaking hand on my tummy. "The shock…"

"We understand," Detective Sorenson said. "Are you up to answering a few questions?"

I nodded and sniffed.

"When did you last see Mr. Mathias?"

"Yesterday. I spent most of the morning down in the archives doing research. After lunch, I had an interview scheduled in Boca. Bill set it up."

"Who with?" Sorenson asked.

"Some members of a construction crew who used to work for Shay and Holmes."

"That's right, he wrote a column insinuating bribery, didn't he?" the cop said to Cal.

"Yes, Bill was lead investigator—a damned good one, too. He was also my friend. Any chance his death can be linked to it?" Cal replied.

"Too soon to tell, but it looks random. His wallet, minus cash and credit cards, was found in a trash can twenty feet from the body. We're checking for fingerprints now. Did he carry a cell phone?"

Cal nodded, his face set in harsh lines.

"That's what I thought. We didn't find one. His car was parked in a slot over on Second Avenue just west of South Street."

South Street? What was Bill doing there? If he wanted to party, he did it on Riverside or at the beach. He'd been a regular at The Corner Bar. The South Street nightclub district made no sense. And why would he be in that god-awful park? Unless he intended to meet someone.

"His keys, however, are also missing. Neighbors said his alarm system went off early this morning, around two o'clock. By the time our guys got there, it had turned itself off. Everything was quiet. After we identified the body, we went back. The place had been searched."

Sorenson's words chilled my blood. Damn, first Marc, then me, and now Bill. Somebody wanted something real bad—like a CD? God, what had Bill done with his copy? The urge to cooperate with the police and my instincts as a reporter fought a good fight. Instinct won—at least for now.

"Mr. Randolph, we'd like to get a look at Mr. Mathias's notes and computer. His office door is locked. Could you let us in?"

Cal frowned. "Sorry, don't have the key. I want to check with our lawyers before handing anything over to you. There could be confidential sources in his files and as a newspaperman I'd hate to violate the first amendment."

"May I remind you a murder has been committed?"

"I understand, but if it's a random killing, then it doesn't matter what's on his computer."

"And if it's not random, but connected to your investigation?"

"Then maybe you'd better get a court order."

I only half listened to Cal and Sorenson. If Bill's keys were missing and the killer wanted the CD, why hadn't he come to the office first? Then I remembered. Anyone entering the building after eight o'clock in the evening had to sign in with security and show a photo ID. And for obvious reasons, day time was out of the question.

My stomach rolled and I swallowed to fight the nausea. I'd had enough. "Detective Sorenson, do you need me for anything else? I'm not feeling so hot."

"Not at the moment, Miss Jackson." He snapped

his notebook shut. "In fact, it looks as if most of your employees are gone for the evening. We'll be back tomorrow. Just one more question, Mr. Randolph…"

I didn't wait to hear it, but rose and left, closing the door behind me. My legs, still unsteady and weak, managed to carry me to my cubicle. I paused in the doorway and gazed around the office. Sorenson was right. Most of my co-workers had already called it a night, including I was relieved to note, Doug Elliott.

I sank into my chair holding my head in my hands. *Bill, what on earth happened? Why South Street?*

Maybe he met someone claiming knowledge of bribery. But would he have met an informant in Wildwood Park at night? Perhaps, especially if he didn't feel threatened. I doubt if he'd be afraid if a frightened woman had called—or someone he'd trusted. Did he know his killer?

I didn't want to think any more. I needed to get out of here and go home. I wanted a good, stiff drink—several, in fact.

My head came up with a jerk. Drinks—oh crap. I'd forgotten about meeting Jason Mallory. It was six-fifteen. I didn't have his cell number, and could have reached him through the hotel, but suddenly wanted to see him. Everyone who'd seen that CD ended up dead. Were we next on the list?

****

I hurried into the hotel over a half an hour late. Jason sat at the bar, sipping a martini, a frown on his face. I slid onto a vacant stool next to him.

"Do you own a watch?" he asked in a testy voice.

"Bill's dead—murdered last night. They found the body this afternoon and notified the paper just as I was leaving." I ordered vodka on the rocks.

"Good God, what happened?"

"He was shot in the head. I assume at close range. Cops didn't say. They think it was random, but I'm not so sure."

I told him what I knew, gulping half my drink when it came. It burned all the way down my throat, exploding in my stomach. The heat helped warm my cold, shaking fingers.

"Did they mention what caliber bullet killed him?" he asked. "Marc was shot with a thirty-eight."

"They didn't say, at least not while I was there. I spent several minutes in the restroom throwing up. What I can't understand is why he was in the South Street district. He didn't like it. And on a week night, too. Not the usual time to party."

Jason finished his drink. Sounded like a great idea. I did the same. He signaled for refills.

"When Bill interviewed me yesterday afternoon, he asked a lot of questions about Shay and Holmes and the board of directors. He wanted to know if the others knew about Marc's and my relationship."

"Did they?"

He didn't answer my question. "He left a little before four. I saw him on his cell in the reception lobby."

"Wait a minute, where did you two talk? At Shay and Holmes?"

Jason nodded. "Yeah, Bradley Holmes is letting me use a small office there until I can clear out Marc's things."

"But where did Bill conduct the interview?" I persisted. "In your office?"

"Yes. What are you getting at?"

"Then anybody at S and H, if they were real ambitious or suspicious, could have planted a bug. Have you checked?"

"The thought never crossed my mind, but I'll look first thing in the morning. And someone could have just as easily overheard him talking on his phone. The receptionist sits a few feet away."

We each drank from our glasses. I could see Bill getting a perverse kick out of conducting an interview with the brother of a murdered man in the offices of the corporation he was investigating.

"I wonder what Mathias uncovered in his investigation. Did he tell you?" he asked.

"Not really. Bill could play his cards very close to the vest. He didn't write a story until he verified the facts, which is why follow-up articles were sometimes printed a couple of weeks after the original."

"In other words, he'd space them out to prolong interest."

"I don't know if it was deliberate or just his style, but yes—the first couple of stories would result in a lot of letters to the editor. He brought the problem to people's attention, and then when the hubbub died down, he'd revive the issue."

I swallowed the rest of my vodka, shaking my head to clear it of the buzz the liquor created. I turned my gaze to Jason's frowning face. "I'd like to know what Bill did, too. I have an idea. Before I get too drunk, why don't we go back to the office and see what we can find?"

"Can you get in?"

"Bill gave me the key to his office quite a while

ago in case I needed something while he was out. I also know his computer password."

Jason's eyebrows rose. "He trusted you with that?"

"Yeah. He was on a fishing trip in a remote area of Northern Canada last summer and lost his flight itinerary. Apparently, the place he stayed didn't have WiFi or a cell tower nearby. He called on a landline from the lodge lobby. I had to print it out and fax it to him."

"He hasn't changed the password in the last few months?"

I shrugged. "I don't know, but I suggest we find out."

"Will the office be empty? It's almost seven. I'd just as soon no one saw us snooping. Check, please," he said to the bartender.

"It's possible someone will be working late, but if we wait until after eight, we'll have to sign in and show ID to go upstairs. *I'd* rather not do that."

"Then let's go."

We left the hotel and drove to *The Standard*. I parked in the space closest to the elevators.

"An awful lot of cars here," Jason remarked.

"Press room and night desk employees. They'll be getting things ready to print in a couple of hours. The reporters manning the night desk are on the other side of the building from our offices. Are you ready?"

He nodded and opened the door. We rode the elevator up to the fifth floor in silence. Exiting, I noticed two or three cubicles had lights on. Someone talked on the phone. Jason and I walked softly through the maze of half walls, ducking low when necessary, until stopping at my cubicle to retrieve the key from the desk drawer, and then continued on to Bill's office.

"Damn," I muttered, seeing the bright yellow crime scene tape on the door. It had probably been placed there as a deterrent to anyone entering until the question of confidentiality had been answered.

Jason carefully pried it off one side. "Open it."

I wiped my sweaty palms down the sides of my slacks and threw one last glance over my shoulder. No one in the cubicles emerged. I slid the key in and turned it. The click of the latch unlocking sounded like a gunshot. My heart thumped hard, and once again I looked around. Jason had no such fears. He turned the knob and opened the door, shoving me through.

"Close the blinds," he ordered, moving toward the desk.

I did as he asked and joined him. He turned on the desk lamp.

Alarmed, I lowered my voice to a whisper. "Should we have a light on? Someone might see."

"Do you have a flashlight?"

"Of course I don't."

"Well, we can't search in the dark. Fire up his computer while I check the file drawers."

Some spy I'd make. I couldn't even remember to bring a flashlight. I hoped no light showed around the edge of the blinds causing a late worker to investigate.

I flipped on the computer, crossed my fingers, then typed in MURROW and held my breath. The screen flashed several times. The icons popped up. I was in.

Bill had a lot of files, but I concentrated on the last couple of months. Rather than take the time to read them now, I rummaged in his desk drawer until I found a CD and copied as many as I could.

"How are you doing?" Jason asked from the other side of the room.

"Fine, I'm making copies. How about you?"

"Nothing of any use. Mostly old articles and contacts." He closed a drawer and moved to the desk where he flipped through Bill's Rolodex. "Could this be of any use?"

"I doubt it. He'd keep confidential sources on the computer or on his cell, probably encrypted. You know, the cops will be on your doorstep when they find out Bill interviewed you. What are you going to tell them?"

He paused for a moment. "The truth. Are you about finished? I want to get out of here before eight o'clock."

"Another ten minutes should do it."

Jason paced. With every step, my nerves tightened. He barked out orders like a drill sergeant, and I wasn't sure I approved of his interest in Bill's files. Until I'd told him, Bill had had no knowledge that Marc Chambers or his death could be important to the investigation. What had Jason expected to find? Mr. Calm-Cool-and-Collected acted very nervous.

"Will you stop? You're driving me crazy," I snapped.

"Can't help it. What's taking so long?"

"There are a lot of files and I'm not sure what's what. If the police get a court order, they may confiscate the computer. I want to make sure I have everything. If I want to be an investigative reporter, I might as well start out on the right foot with all the information I can."

While the last few files downloaded, I asked, "Did Bill use his digital recorder during your interview?"

"Yes, why?"

"Because I don't think the police found it on him and if he was meeting someone who had information about the bribery scandal in the nightclub district, he'd have that recorder with him. So, that means either the killer took it or it's here. If he returned to the office to perhaps change memory discs, it would have been after hours. Not likely anyone would have seen him."

I opened the desk drawers, but found nothing, including the CD. However, I did find several small diskettes. I scooped them into my purse as the computer beeped signaling it had finished with the copies. I slid the CD out of the slot, put it in a protective sleeve, and then hesitated. With a quick move of the mouse, I deleted the files I'd copied. The fewer people who knew about them the better.

I rose and my foot bumped into something under the desk. Reaching down, I touched Bill's laptop neatly secured in its carrying case. He usually used it when working from home. He'd often polish the final article there before e-mailing it to Cal.

"Are you ready yet?" Jason asked, peering through a slit in the blinds.

"Just finishing."

I wondered if Bill had used his laptop lately. Maybe he'd put the CD in there, intending to view it later. I grasped the case and slung the strap over my shoulder. What the hell. I needed a laptop, at least until I could get a new one. Leaning over the desk, I snapped off the lamp plunging the room into darkness.

Jason helped me to the door. We stopped dead in our tracks at the sound of footsteps approaching. His hand tightened on my arm, and my heart ratcheted up several beats per second. I held my breath, standing still as a statue. The walker paused, and then moved on.

"Oh, thank God," I said with a gasp, my body slumping into his.

"Give him a few minutes to leave, and then see if the coast is clear."

I counted to fifty and peeked through the blinds, but saw no movement. I nodded to Jason who eased the door open. We slipped out, hurrying to the elevators, but Jason steered me toward the staircase.

"Use the stairs. They're quicker and we aren't as likely to be seen."

Neither of us spoke until we got back in the car.

"I thought I'd die when that guy walked past. How could we have explained being there?" I said, gulping in huge breaths of air.

"You're a reporter. I'm sure you would have thought of something. I'd like to see what's on that CD."

"You will as soon as I sort out what's relevant. You don't need to see confidential sources."

"A confidential source could have killed my brother and Bill or might have information as to who did."

I didn't answer, but started the car and pulled out. The dashboard clock read eight-oh-five. The whole operation had taken less than an hour. I wanted nothing more than to go home, look at Bill's files, and fall into bed, but Jason's insistence on viewing the CD made me suspicious.

"Let's have dinner," I suggested. I had a few questions for Jason Mallory.

I chose a small, intimate restaurant called Reggie's

not far from the paper. Now that the rush of breaking the law had passed, I remembered why we had been in Bill's office. My appetite fled, but Bill's warning about Jason Mallory hung in my memory. I didn't exactly distrust the man, but neither did I believe everything he said. My wimpy waffling irritated me. It was time to settle everything once and for all.

We ordered drinks, wine for me and a martini for Jason. When the waiter returned with the drinks, I looked my companion in the eye.

"A little while ago, you said you wondered if I had killed Marc. Well, I could say the same regarding you and Bill. You saw him last. I only have your word about what was said and that he was on the phone. You could have easily arranged to meet him later on South Street, lured him into the park, killed him, and taken his cell and recorder to make it look like a robbery gone bad."

"You're not serious," he replied with a hard gleam in his steel gray eyes. "Why would I do that?"

"I don't know. If there is something funny going on at Shay and Holmes, you could be in on it. You sit on the board of directors. Maybe Marc discovered something amiss and reported it to the wrong person—his step-brother. I also only have your word that the relationship between the two of you was friendly. And Marc *never* mentioned you."

"And if I'm not mistaken, I was with you last night," he challenged.

"South Street doesn't get rolling until after ten o'clock. You marched me to the car before then. You could have left."

A flush darkened Jason's face and his eyes turned

an even darker shade of gray. His lips tightened while his fingers clenching the stem of his martini glass threatened to snap it like a toothpick. I braced myself for a verbal shot to the jaw.

Instead, he leaned back and said, "If you were a man, I'd invite you outside, but since you're not, I can only say that I want Marc's killer brought to justice. And rest assured, *Miss Jackson*, I will do everything in my power to make it happen, including breaking the law if I have to."

Besides angry, he also sounded sincere, but then he always sounded that way. Bill's voice rang in my mind.

"Bill warned me not to trust you, and you seem to have more than just a passing interest in his work. I think there's a lot you're not telling me, especially about Marc. Why would he call you about a CD or bring my name into it? Marc is dead. I can attest it was not a pleasant death. He had three huge holes in his chest and died on a bed of garbage in a stinking alley. I threw up then, too. Death upsets me. Now, are you going to tell me what was going on?" I leaned forward. "Mr. Mallory, I want some answers before I cooperate with you further on anything."

I glared, determined to get an answer. I meant every word I'd said. Jason stared into the depths of his glass for several long seconds.

"It's my fault," he said at last, still in a hard, anger-filled voice. "I killed Marc."

Chapter Seven

My breath stopped, and my heart thudded in slow, heavy beats. I struggled to breathe. I was having drinks with a *killer*? We sat in a corner of the restaurant—a very dark and isolated corner.

His head came up and his gaze made contact with mine. I read blazing anger mixed with grief.

"Get that look off your face. I don't mean I pulled the trigger. Marc was doing me a favor, and he's dead because of it."

"What are you talking about?" I croaked, taking a drink of wine to clear my throat.

He finished his martini, signaled the waiter for another, and continued. "My father sat on the board of directors of Shay and Holmes. When he died three and a half years ago, out of respect for him, I was asked to take his place. I knew something about the business, and having my name on the website didn't do their image any harm either."

So, not only did he feel guilty about Marc, but his own ego was on the line.

He continued. "I met the rest of the board, including Bradley Holmes and Kenneth Shay, sons of the original owners. Brad worked well with people, but Ken struck me as a weak link, as did Board Chairman, Dexter Marshall."

"I've met Ken Shay. He's a dick."

He nodded. "My opinion exactly. Anyway, since I was the new kid on the block I asked for monthly and year-end financial statements, but living in California meant I didn't often attend meetings. I voted by phone or proxy."

The waiter returned with our drinks and asked if we wanted to order. Jason looked at me with raised eyebrows. I nodded. Any more booze without eating, no matter how interesting his story, I'd fall face down on the table.

Jason resumed when the waiter left. "About two years ago, the financial reports began arriving later and later. I called Brad. He apologized and said they were short-handed in accounting." He took a sip of his drink and frowned. "On the surface the reports looked fine. The company was making money—lots of it."

"How was that suspicious?"

"Every company has its ups and downs. Sometimes it's a seasonal thing or the local economy takes a dip, but at S and H, the rise was meteoric. I know seasons don't affect the construction business in South Florida, and the economy at the time was recovering, but still something didn't ring true. I investigated other construction and development corporations in the area. I found those peaks and valleys."

"S and H cooked the books?"

"I wasn't sure, but trying to find out anything long distance was a pain in the ass."

"Enter Marc," I said.

He nodded. "Enter Marc. That's one reason why I agreed to sit on the board. He worked in Port Royale, and I could see him every once in a while. I needed eyes and ears. I got to know the head of Human

Resources on my few trips here. I called and asked her if accounting was shorthanded. When she confirmed it was, I suggested that as a favor to me she hire Marc. I then called Marc asking him to quit his job and apply for a new one at Shay and Holmes. I'd reimburse him any difference in salary."

Our salads arrived. I don't know if it was Jason's story or the wine, but my appetite had returned.

"So, he got hired with no trouble?"

"According to my friend in HR, the head of accounting jumped all over Marc's resume."

"And they had no idea you were related?"

"None."

"And they didn't question why a CPA would leave a good-paying job to take what amounted to a demotion and pay cut?"

"We used the excuse that the stress of his former job was getting to him and he wanted a slower pace with less responsibility." He frowned as though deep in thought before continuing "Marc used the first couple of months getting acquainted with his co-workers. He worked in accounts payable and sent me regular reports via e-mail from his laptop. At first, everything seemed on the up and up. I thought I'd made a mistake. Then Marc called. He had gotten into the files and seen a month-end statement from several months earlier. He sent a copy to me. The figures didn't match."

"So they were playing fast and loose with the balance sheets like Enron?"

"Big payments were going out to consulting firms, but didn't always have invoices to back them up."

"Were the consultants fronts for bribes?"

"Marc suspected so and documented as much as

possible. He took to coming in early and leaving late in order to investigate. Then a couple of months ago, he had the feeling he was being watched."

Jason stared at his untouched salad as though surprised to see it there, then picked up his fork and stabbed several pieces of lettuce.

"I should have pulled him out then, but Marc insisted he could get into the main files of both the head of accounting and the CFO. I should have followed my instincts and never allowed him to stay."

He stared at the greens on his utensil, then dropped it into the bowl and shoved the salad away uneaten.

"You can't blame yourself. You had no idea it would turn violent."

Our salad bowls were whisked away and replaced by the entrees. My Chicken Cordon Bleu smelled delicious. I cut off a portion and popped it into my mouth. The taste lived up to the smell. Jason stared at his steak, then gulped the remainder of his martini and ordered another. We ate in silence until it arrived.

"Marc left a message on my cell the night of the murder to say he had everything, and it was worse than we thought. He told me he'd put the information onto a CD, but to be on the safe side, he was giving a key to a friend, someone he trusted. I thought he meant a house key. That's why I was at the house."

"And you thought I was the friend."

"Not at that time. I was more concerned with the fact he suspected someone was watching him. I didn't like it and told him to get out of town—immediately. Marc had described you once, so when I saw you at the cemetery, I made the connection. I hoped you were the friend."

"He arranged to meet me and met a killer instead."

Jason pushed his half-eaten steak away. I pushed the plate back.

"Eat. You've been drinking and need food."

For the first time tonight, his lips curled into a half-smile, but he cut another piece.

"The police called the next afternoon. The ransacking of his home and the fire tells me someone at Shay and Holmes killed him. I want that someone."

"It doesn't have to be an inside job. If the consulting firms were fronts, it could be one of them. And don't forget, city officials are involved, too."

"That's true. Once corruption gets started it's hard to stop. A lot of reputations are on the line and some people will kill to maintain a reputation. I also suspected Marc had a backup in case something happened to the original CD. That's why I was in his place yesterday afternoon. I was looking for his laptop. I couldn't find it anywhere."

"Don't look at me. I don't have it," I said. "Maybe the thieves found it the night he was murdered."

"If they had it, they'd have torched the place then. I think they missed it and were afraid I'd find it." He shoved his plate away with three-quarters of his meal eaten. "I've spent the past week feeling guilty as hell. I always will."

"Guilt is a strong emotion. If I hadn't been late…" my voice trailed off for a moment before resuming. The image of Marc's body would never be erased from my memory. "…if only I hadn't been late."

He signaled the waiter. "Let's get out of here." He flipped out his credit card and our server vanished with it. "I have a proposition. Let's work together. I plan to research as much about S and H projects over the last five or six years as I can. I want to know how long this rot has been going on. I'll work the inside. I have an office at ground zero and can ask questions of a lot of people. You can work the outside and dig up information that's a matter of public record—permits, inspections, things of that sort."

"Be careful who you question," I warned. "Bodies are popping up fast."

"Which is why I feel safe. One more even remotely connected to S and H could make for some very unwanted police attention."

The waiter returned, and Jason signed the receipt. I dropped him off at his hotel where he poked his head back in the car window before I drove away.

"Is it a deal? Do we work together on this?"

"It's a deal. I'll let you know about Bill's files as soon as I separate them."

"Fine. I'll call you tomorrow." He handed me a business card. "Here's my cell number."

I reciprocated. He disappeared into the hotel, and I headed for home no longer considering him the enemy. He, too, had something to lose. If S and H was playing fast and loose with finances, Jason Mallory's reputation, along with that of his late father, would be tarnished. And then, of course, there was Marc's death.

The first thing I did upon arriving home was check out the laptop case, and found the CD copy nestled in a zippered compartment. It would join the original in the post office box.

I jammed the CD I'd made in Bill's office into the laptop and opened several files. My research into S and H would be helped along by my boss's efforts. He'd been reviewing them, too, but his information only included the last two years. I finally went to bed, dreading going into work tomorrow.

****

Somber was a severe understatement to describe the office mood the following morning. Shock and disbelief showed on everybody's faces from the receptionist Carol Lee to food editor Edith Groves. Many of my co-workers stopped by to offer comments.

"Honey, I knew something bad had happened the minute I saw you run from Cal's office," Maizie Calhoun, one of our staff reporters said. "I thought you got fired or something."

"Shelley, did the police give you any details?" asked another reporter.

"I can't believe it. He was such a nice man. He always remembered to smile when he passed my desk," a secretary added.

Not wanting to be here, I tried to answer the questions as briefly as possible and accepted the kind words. I wanted to be at home with Bill's notes and files.

"Shelley, I'm so sorry to hear about Bill," another well-wisher said, poking his head in my cubicle. "He was a great guy. We'll all miss him."

"Yes, we will. He taught me a lot." I wished they'd all shut up and go away.

I finished the story I'd started before hearing the news about Bill when a familiar voice drawled from the doorway.

"So, I guess old Bill's gone to that great press room in the sky. Are you going to get his job and his office?"

I resisted the urge to plant my size eight, blunt-toed, platform Stuart Weitzman square in Doug Elliott's crotch.

"You fucking worm. How can you bring that up at a time like this? Bill's not even cold, you ghoul."

Doug shrugged. "I'm just being practical. Someone will have to take over soon, and the race is to the swift."

"What's that supposed to mean?"

"It's a plum job and my guess is Cal's already had people from other papers in the area calling to politely inquire." He smiled a nasty little smile. "Don't get left out in the cold, sweetie."

"Get out of here!"

"Have the cops talked to you yet?"

"I was informed of Bill's death last night before I left. I've already talked to them."

"They're questioning everyone this morning in the conference room. I've taken my turn."

Before I could reply my desk phone rang. "Jackson, come into my office," Cal ordered. "I need to talk to you."

I pushed Doug aside on my way out and stalked to the editor's office.

"Close the door. What can you tell me about Jason Mallory?"

"Jason Mallory? In what respect?"

"You had dinner with him the night Bill died, and I'm sure he was the last person other than the killer to see Bill alive."

"He couldn't have had anything to do with it," I protested, forgetting my own suspicions of the night before. "He was with me until after ten o'clock."

"I'm not accusing him of being a killer," Cal said impatiently. "I just want to know more about him."

I gave my editor a condensed biography, which he waved away with a flick of his hand.

"Yes, I have all that. I can use Google. How did you hook up with him?"

"I was an acquaintance of his brother."

"That would be the Shay and Holmes accountant murdered last week?"

"Yes. We met at the funeral and he asked me out to dinner. He wanted to know about Marc's life in Port Royale."

"I see. Why didn't you tell me you knew the victim?"

"I was upset. He was a friend. I *did* tell Bill."

"Anything else you neglected to tell me? Is Mallory moving here?"

"No. He's going back to L. A. soon."

Cal sat back and tapped a pencil on his desk blotter. I could see the wheels of his mind meshing gears.

"Write an article on Bill from a colleague's point of view. Have it on my desk by three today. I'm going to do an editorial eulogizing him. Both will run tomorrow." He leaned forward. "I don't believe Bill's death was a simple mugging, and I don't think you do either. Don't go off and play the crusading reporter, solving the murder, and being the heroine. You don't have the experience. Is that clear?"

I nodded. He saw way too much, but I decided to ignore his sage advice. Finding Marc's body had thrown me head first into this whole mess. I intended to find out who was responsible. Doug's words about someone having to do Bill's job echoed in my mind. It might as well be me.

Writing the article on Bill Mathias proved easy. The words flowed because I meant what I wrote. Or maybe Bill was standing beside me guiding my hands on the keyboard. I only knew the words pouring out were heart felt.

I was about halfway through the assignment when one of the secretaries stuck her head around the cubicle wall.

"Miss Jackson? Detective Sorenson would like to see you in the conference room."

"Right now? I'm in the middle of something."

"He said now."

I sighed with irritation, saved the article, and made my way to the conference room off the reception lobby.

"Miss Jackson, thank you for coming. Please be seated."

I did as he asked. "Will this take long? I'm in the middle of an article. Besides, I can't think of anything else I could tell you."

"We have Mr. Mathias's agenda. It shows he met with Jason Mallory yesterday at three o'clock. We've spoken with Mr. Mallory, and he says he was with you the night your boss died. Is that true?"

Thanks a lot, Jason. "Yes, it's true. We were having dinner."

Sorenson twirled a pencil between his fingers like a miniature baton. He was pretty good at it. "And were you with him last night?"

Damn. Jason and I should have thought to concoct a story. It never occurred to me they'd ask about *last* night. I took a chance that since Sorenson had asked, Jason had told the truth.

"Yes, we had drinks, and then dinner. I was upset

about Bill."

"And where did all this take place?"

"Drinks were at his hotel and dinner at Reggie's."

"That's just a couple of blocks from here, isn't it?"

"Yes." I squirmed in my chair keeping my answer short, not sure where this line of questioning was headed.

"Did you come back to Mr. Mathias's office?"

Shit. Had someone seen us?

"No. Why should I?" The minute the lie left my mouth I knew I was in trouble. Of course, someone had seen us—why else would he ask?

He flipped through his notebook. "You tell me. When we arrived this morning, we found someone had tampered with the crime scene tape. An employee, Harry Swenson, says he noticed it when he left last night at eight o'clock. Carrie Parsons remembers hearing the elevator indicator ding a couple of times, but admits she didn't pay much attention. And when we left yesterday evening, the office was locked, but was unlocked this morning. Do you have a key?"

Damn, we forgot to lock the door? Of all the stupid...

"No, I don't." Couldn't they hear my pounding heart or see the quivering of my hands?

"Sure you don't have one hiding in your desk?"

"Search it if you want, but you won't find one."

On this I told the truth. It still lay snug in a zippered compartment of my purse. I hadn't gotten around to replacing it yet.

"I'm sure that won't be necessary." The detective smiled. "I just got real curious about who wanted into Mr. Mathias's office, so I checked the security desk downstairs. No one came in after hours. So, I had a look at the video tape from the parking garage security cameras. Guess what I saw?"

Oh, shit! The cameras—I saw them every day and never paid any attention. Damn.

Sorenson answered for me. "We saw a car pull into the slot nearest the elevator at seven-seventeen. You and Jason Mallory emerged from the vehicle and got into the elevator. You exited via the stairwell, returned to the car at eight-oh-four and left. Would you care to explain those forty-seven minutes?"

I thought fast. Jason and I hadn't been seen except by the camera, and I wasn't about to admit to anything.

"I was upset about Bill and forgot some files I'd planned to work on from home. While we were here I noticed I had a few voicemails and listened to them. Then I decided to do the same with my e-mails. I even opened some of my regular mail. Yesterday was hectic what with my home practically firebombed the night before, and I wasn't in my cubicle until late."

"I see. Why didn't you tell me that when I asked?"

"You referred to Bill's office. I was nowhere near it."

"Mr. Swenson says he doesn't remember seeing lights on in any other cubicle."

I shrugged. "Then he just didn't notice. Maybe we'd already gone by the time he walked past."

"Then how did he beat you down to the garage? The cameras show him leaving at seven-fifty-two."

"We stopped in the restrooms."

"One last question, did Mr. Mathias have a laptop?"

"Yes." I didn't mention the object of his curiosity

was hidden in a box marked "jumper cables" in the trunk of my car.

"Any idea where it might be?"

"None." I kept my answers brief. The less I said, the less I could give away.

"Did he keep it here or at home?" Sorenson persisted.

"Sometimes it was here, sometimes not."

"Seen it lately?"

"No." With every lie I dug a deeper hole, but I was in too far to quit now.

He snapped the notebook shut and rose. "Thank you for your cooperation, Miss Jackson."

I stood on shaky legs and tried to walk with confidence to the door. Once through, I paused before fully closing it.

"She's lying through her teeth," a voice said.

"I know," Sorenson replied. "She and Mallory wanted something in Mathias's office. Keep an eye on them."

I shivered, hurried to my desk, and thought. I'd lose the key at lunch, but first had to warn Jason. I whipped out my cell phone, and then thought twice. If the cops checked phone records, my call coming a few minutes after my interrogation would look suspicious. I walked across the room to an unused cubicle and called the number on the card he'd given me. I got his voice mail.

"Jason, call me on my cell as soon as you can. It's important. Do not talk to the cops again before talking to me."

I forced the interview with the police into the back of my mind and finished my article on Bill. I reread what I'd written, made a few changes, and then e-mailed it to Cal. It was a good piece. Bill would have been happy with the contents—not syrupy or sweet, but respectful as one colleague to another.

Too early for lunch, I researched Shay and Holmes projects beginning with the public records of Sunshine Beach where I found three permits pulled in the last six years, including one for The Leisure Time Motel. The original permit had been issued four years ago, but construction had languished for a year. Then things had shot forward like a rocket. The three-story structure had been completed in less than six months, passing all inspections. I also noted a permit issued last week for the same address. I jotted down the phone number of the original owner.

I moved on to Palmetto Gardens and discovered two permits in the last four years with a restaurant called Iguanawana being the first. It, too, had risen in record time after an initial slow start.

I counted four apartment buildings, several small condo complexes, and of course, The River Tower Condos just a few blocks from where I sat—all in Port Royale. The city accounted for over half of the permits pulled by S and H in the last four years with eighty percent in the past two. Most of the permits were for condominiums.

"Busy, busy, busy," I muttered transferring files to my jump drive before logging off. The documentation looked in order, yet something had sent up a red flag to both Bill and Marc.

A call to the owner of the former Leisure Time Motel had him agreeing to meet me at four o'clock.

I glanced at my watch. I'd visit Iguanawana after a

quick lunch and use the concerns of the workmen interviewed as the basis for my questions.

"Heard you had another session with the police. Are you a suspect?" Doug asked from my doorway, his voice startling me.

"Certainly not! They just wanted more information about Bill." I stood and glared at the slug. "Now, if you'll excuse me, I'm going to lunch."

"I'll join you. We can discuss Bill's bribery story."

"I'd rather eat with a sewer rat."

"Aw, come on, baby, don't be that way. Maybe you should cooperate with me a little more. It could be beneficial to both of us."

"Drop dead, and get out of my way."

He let his gaze wander up and down my body, and then leered at my chest. Before I could react, Cal walked up.

"Nice article, Jackson. I made a few minor changes, but that's all," he said. "I think Bill would have approved."

"Article? What article?" Doug asked, narrowing his eyes. "You wrote an article on Bill, too?"

"What do you mean, 'too'?" I said.

"Cal, did you get the obit I did?" he said with an ingratiating smile at the editor.

"Yeah, all two paragraphs of it. Bill was a valuable member of *The South Florida Standard* and a respected journalist. He deserves more than two paragraphs, Elliott."

"I…I didn't have any more information," Doug stammered. "I'm not sure where he came from or went to school."

"Then find out," Cal barked, his voice carrying

halfway across the room. "That's what reporters do. I suggest you do research instead of loitering."

Cal stalked back to his office. A distinct snicker emanated from a nearby cubicle. Doug's face turned an interesting shade of puce. I couldn't help getting in one final dig.

"Better take a bottle of water with you. Those archives are dusty. Excuse me, but I'm hungry." I breezed past him and headed for the lobby.

Jason returned my call as I ate. "What's up?"

I told him about my interview with Sorenson and what I'd overheard.

"You told him we were in the restrooms?"

"Hey, it's the best I could come up with given the circumstances. You're lucky I didn't confess. Have they contacted you yet?"

"I talked with them this morning. They called again about an hour or so ago. I'm meeting Sorenson in the hotel coffee shop at three. I'll stick with your version, although I would have used something more believable."

Like a spot of heavy breathing in the elevator?

My unexpected thoughts caused a flutter in my tummy and a rush of heat from head to toe. I damned near dropped the phone in the remains of my salad.

I shook off the disturbing reaction and answered, "Just tell him we went to the john—and don't forget to say how upset I was."

"All right, but it sounds silly. By the way, I thought you might be interested in knowing Shay and Holmes is hosting a fundraiser for several politicos tomorrow night. I've been invited. Would you like to go? The mayor and a lot of other bigwigs will be there. You can get a chance to see how they and S and H employees interact."

"That sounds *very* interesting. I'd love to go."

"How goes your research?"

"Good. Why don't you come to my place for dinner and we'll go over what I've uncovered so far."

"What time?"

"Seven o'clock."

We hung up, and I picked at the rest of my salad. Inviting him over might not be the most sensible thing to do, but I had confidence in my ability to stay focused on other things. I'd begin now.

I shoved a forkful of lettuce into my mouth. The fundraiser would give me an opportunity to talk to Marc's co-workers and city politicians. A social setting complete with liquor and a large crowd could loosen otherwise tight tongues. One booze-induced slip of the lip and I could come away with ammunition for Bill's bribery theory.

I finished eating, paid the check, and stopped in the ladies room where I wrapped Bill's office key in a used paper towel, tossing it into the trash. Mission accomplished.

I walked back to the office with a light step, my mind in the clouds. I'd write a terrific story using Bill's information as a springboard. It could make my career.

But first, I had to snoop in Sunshine Beach and Palmetto Gardens.

Chapter Eight

I pulled into the parking lot of the Iguanawana restaurant and stopped, my spirits plummeting.

Iguanawana no longer existed. The sign over the entrance read The Beer Wagon, but beer hadn't flowed in a long time.

The roof was covered in a blue tarp, which in Florida usually proclaimed major hurricane damage. Plywood covered the windows. Huge hunks of stucco had been gouged from the exterior by flying debris. I read the faded orange sign attached to the front door. It was a condemnation notice. That didn't surprise me. The place looked ready to fall down.

I noted the phone number on the notice and called. It took a while, but eventually I located the owner, Mason Detwiler, a CPA whose office was ten blocks away. He agreed to see me in spite of his heavy appointment schedule.

I walked into his small, rather depressing business. The carpet in the tiny reception area showed the footsteps of years' worth of clients. The receptionist sat in the corner at a desk not much bigger than a card table. Her computer looked at least ten years old.

"Hello," she greeted with a smile. "May I help you?"

"My name is Shelley Jackson. I'm with *The South Florida Standard*. Mr. Detwiler is expecting me."

She lifted the phone, announced me, and then requested I have a seat. The brown, simulated leather chair crackled as I sat, and I pressed my finger to the armrest. It was sticky with untold filth. I pulled my arms close to my body and picked up a magazine from the plastic cube table, scanning events that had occurred six months ago. This guy was worse than my dentist.

The phone buzzed. The receptionist answered, hung up, and smiled again. "You may go in, Miss Jackson. Mr. Detwiler's office is the furthest one back on the left."

I thanked her and strode down the hallway, passing accountants entering data into their computers. Detwiler's door stood open. I knocked and he rose from his seat behind the desk.

"Mr. Detwiler, thank you for agreeing to see me on such short notice. I know this is a frantic time of year for you."

He reached across, shaking hands. His brown eyes looked sharp and his salt-and-pepper hair was neatly cut. Short and rotund, he stood only a few inches taller than me. I appreciated the firm handshake.

"Believe me, the pleasure is all mine. Please be seated. If I can give you any information about those bastards at Shay and Holmes or the city of Palmetto Gardens, I'll be glad to help." He closed the door.

I sat, hauling out my notepad and recorder. To my astonishment, he did the same.

"I hope you don't mind if I record," he said. "I want to make sure I'm not misquoted."

This was a first. "Uh, no, not at all. Mr. Detwiler, you were one of the original owners of what was then Iguanawana, is that correct?"

"Yes. I put up most of the money—close to five hundred thousand dollars."

"When was that, and who were your partners?"

"My partner was Jim Donohue. He was a chef, and I ate on a regular basis at the place he worked. Over the years, we became friends. His wife and mine still keep in touch. Jim died last year. The doctors said it was a heart attack, but I think Shay and Holmes are to blame."

"How so?"

"He put his heart and soul into that restaurant. When it went under after only six months, a part of him died with it."

I wrote quickly, and then asked, "Mr. Detwiler, why don't you tell me what happened from the beginning? How did you come to invest?"

"Jim came to me with the proposition. A prime piece of property was on the market in a great location. A couple of small houses had been leveled and the owners would build to suit. He showed me a business plan. It was solid, so I investigated the owners, Shay and Holmes Development and Construction. They had an excellent reputation."

"When did you find out differently?"

"It didn't take long. Bradley Holmes said he would take care of all the permitting and dealing with the city. That alone should have told me to beware. A CEO's job wouldn't include dealing with the permits. When four months passed and not so much as a thimbleful of dirt had been moved, I demanded to know why. The answer was that city bureaucracy runs slowly, and I needed to be patient. It was almost eight months before we saw any progress. By that time, costs had risen, necessitating more money. We needed other investors and I contacted relatives and several clients. Most of them came on board." Detwiler spoke in a bitter tone.

"How much did they put up?"

"Altogether, another hundred grand, but the costs kept escalating. I pulled money from my retirement and sold part interest in my CPA firm to cover everything. Then one day, Ken Shay called saying he needed another fifty grand. Jim and I cashed in part of our kids' college funds."

"If you had a contract, how could S and H keep demanding more money? It's usually the contractor who takes it on the chin."

"There was a clause, hidden in the middle of a paragraph, stating the contractee would guarantee half of the overages if we changed the plans," he replied, an expression of embarrassment on his face.

"I take it you did."

He nodded. "The original plans were inadequate for our needs. Jim tried to tell me, but I didn't understand the restaurant business. Jim didn't understand accounting and let me make the decisions."

"Didn't you have a lawyer go over the contract?" I asked in amazement.

"My brother-in-law checked it out. My mistake. I tried to save a few bucks. Ernie deals in tax litigation."

"I take it *you* never dealt in this kind of thing before either." I couldn't think of another explanation. Detwiler didn't look stupid.

He shook his head. "But opening night made up for all the delays and extra money. The place was packed, and we got good reviews in the paper. Based on those first few months, I figured I'd make back my investment in three years. Then the roof fell in—

literally."

"How?" I remembered the roofing man's comments from the other day and had a pretty good idea.

"A heavy thunderstorm tore off some tiles and the next thing we knew a chunk of ceiling fell. Luckily, it fell in a storeroom, but we had to shell out to have it repaired. The contractor we hired told us the entire roof was improperly sealed and should be replaced. I thought it was a scam. Should have listened."

"How many times did your roof fall in?"

"Twice. At the same time plumbing problems surfaced in the kitchen and restrooms, plus circuit breakers blew like crazy. The board of health paid a visit and shut us down until we fixed the problems. By the time we did, the damage was done. That Board of Health notice tacked on the front door scared customers away. We closed a few months later."

"And what did Shay and Holmes say?"

"They blamed the subcontractors. We sued, but the lawyers stalled until we finally had to drop it. We ran out of money." He sighed and sat back, a look of pain on his face. "I sold my business in order to reimburse the investors. I also had to pay off my attorney. I started over with four loyal employees. I'm still struggling to keep my head above water."

I turned off the recorder and put away my notepad. I didn't know what to say. It was a sad story, but for a man who made his living with numbers, he'd been less than observant regarding his own investments.

"Mr. Detwiler, thank you for taking the time to speak with me," I said, rising.

"Is this going to be in the paper soon? I want the

entire county to know Shay and Holmes are a bunch of crooks."

"This is preliminary research. Did you read Bill Mathias's article a few weeks ago regarding Shay and Holmes? He suspected substandard work and possible bribery of city officials to see inspections passed."

He walked me to the door. "Yes, and I wouldn't be surprised. Sorry to hear about his death."

I thanked him again and left, making a mental note to find out the names of the inspectors of Iguanawana.

****

Carl Bresloff, the owner of the Sunshine Beach motel site, had requested I meet him in the parking lot of a fast food joint on Oceanview Boulevard. I pulled in, parked, and rolled down my window. A man standing next to his car straightened.

"Miss Jackson?"

"Yes. I take it you're Mr. Bresloff."

"Guilty." The man smiled as I exited the car. He was in his mid-fifties, on the tall side, with gray hair and a mustache. Sunglasses blocked his eyes, but his manner appeared laid back.

"Shall we go in?" I asked.

"Let's take a little walk. I have something to show you a couple of blocks away."

He cupped my elbow and we crossed the busy street. The traffic noise made conversation impossible until arriving at a vacant lot.

"This is The Leisure Time Motel," he said, pointing to the empty space. He nodded toward a bench where we sat under the shade of two ravaged palm trees.

I brought out my recorder and notebook. "What

happened?"

"Hurricane Isabelle last September, but demolition was well on its way before that."

"You're tearing it down after only a couple of years?"

"Not intentionally."

"Start at the beginning," I suggested, pushing the record button on the recorder.

"My family has owned the property for years. I inherited from my father. As you can see, it's a big piece of real estate. It was a small strip mall containing a convenience store, a couple of souvenir shops, the usual kind of touristy places. I got a good income from the rents, but time had taken its toll. The building looked rundown."

He sighed and crossed his legs, clasping his hands over his knee. "I realized the potential for something nicer. So, I got the bright idea of building a motel for families on a budget. The location is perfect—on the beach and close to decent restaurants and shopping. I found an architect who recommended a general contractor."

"Shay and Holmes Development and Construction?"

"They were the lowest bid. The architect had used them several years ago, so I went with them on his recommendation."

"Records show that almost two years passed between the first permit to the final inspection."

"They demolished the old building and poured the foundations for the new when work came to a screeching halt. The foundation failed inspection, not once, but three times. It was the same with the masonry.

129

A month here, a month there, and the next thing I knew I was in a financial bind. I needed the income the property could produce. I hadn't expected it to take so long."

"Did you complain to S and H?"

He ripped off the sunglasses, squinting tired blue eyes at the ocean waves breaking and tumbling up the beach before being sucked back out to sea.

"I complained. Ken Shay said the inspectors were inconsistent with their opinions, and that he was frustrated, too. He asked me to be patient. Patience I had. It was money I was short on."

"So you went through a period of almost no activity for—what, a year?"

"About."

I nodded and wrote. Shay and Holmes had a pattern of halting construction until about two years ago when the situation improved.

"I was called out of town on a family thing. When I returned, I was delighted to see progress. I was told the problems had been resolved and work would continue. Six months later, I had a motel."

"I take it there were issues with the quality."

Bresloff laughed. "I'll say. Leisure Time passed final inspection, but the minute the ink was dry on my check, it was one thing after another."

"Like what?" I persisted.

"I had electrical concerns. Power surges, lights dimming and flickering, circuit breakers tripping. That sort of thing occurred on a regular basis. I called S and H and was told they were tied up on other jobs, but would send someone out in a couple of weeks. I waited a month, and then called again."

"How long before someone showed?"

He snorted clapping his sunglasses back on. "The sons-of-bitches gave me the run around for over three months. I finally called in my own electrician. He told me the wiring was inadequate for my needs and would have to be redone unless I wanted to run the risk of fire. So, I had it rewired."

"What did Shay and Holmes have to say?"

"Blamed the sub-contractor who was now conveniently out of business. Then I noticed a crack in the asphalt in the parking lot. It was an inch wide and I saw sand underneath it. Cracks also developed in the exterior walls, and I had windows popping out after every thunderstorm."

"And Shay and Holmes took no responsibility?"

He shrugged. "According to them, it passed inspection. If I had a beef, it should be with the city of Sunshine Beach. The city claimed inspection reports showed everything conforming to code."

"How long did you struggle?"

"Over a year. Then last summer Hurricane Isabelle put me under. A lousy category one storm left gaping holes in the roof and blew out what were supposed to be hurricane resistant windows. A portion of the ocean side exterior wall caved in making the entire structure unsafe."

He rose and picked up a piece of coral, then flung it toward the sea. It fell where I assumed the front lobby must have been.

"I'm still arguing with the insurance company. I had the place bulldozed two months ago. When I did, I had an independent inspector look at things. It was damn near all sub-standard construction. I'll rebuild, but this time I'll make sure the general contractor is not Shay and Holmes, and I plan to be present at every goddamned inspection."

Bresloff turned to me. His lips were set and his hands fisted on his hips. "Two weeks ago I filed a lawsuit naming both the city of Sunshine Beach *and* Shay and Holmes Construction as litigants. I'm accusing the city of negligence in regards to inspections, and Shay and Holmes of shoddy construction or whatever the legal terms are."

I turned off the recorder and returned it to my purse, then rose. "At least you managed to hang on to your property. Others haven't. Good luck with your lawsuit. I imagine Shay and Holmes will tie it up for years if they can."

We walked back to where we'd parked. "Let 'em. When I'm pissed, I'm tenacious."

We returned to our cars. He waved as I swung out of the parking lot, into the evening traffic. Shay and Holmes had pulled a lot of permits in the last two years. I worried about the people living in those apartments and condos.

****

I arranged the lemon pepper chicken breasts artfully on a couple of plates and slid them into the warmed oven hoping the rice pilaf wouldn't dry out. Next I dumped the container of new peas with chives and herb sauce in a casserole dish before popping it into the microwave. I'd warm it up when Jason arrived. He'd never know I'd placed an order with Chef Rene's Take Home Kitchen.

Cooking was not high on my list of priorities. My areas of expertise were limited, making me a big zero in the culinary department. The only item on tonight's menu I'd made was the salad, which any doofus can do.

I paced the living room while waiting for Jason, stopping occasionally to move an object on a table a couple of inches.

"This is ridiculous," I muttered to myself. "It's not like you're trying to impress him or something."

Of course, if that were the case, I'd be giving him canned spaghetti for dinner. *Lighten up, Jackson. This is business—nothing more.*

The doorbell rang and, giving my appearance a final check in the foyer mirror, opened the door.

"Something smells good," Jason commented, entering.

"Dinner will be ready in a few minutes. Have a seat," I said, directing him toward the living room. "Would you like a drink before we eat?"

"Martini is fine."

"Would you do the honors?"

He mixed the drinks and gazed around the room. "This is nice—comfortable and cozy."

"Thanks," I replied, accepting a glass. "It's close to downtown and the beach. I like the urban atmosphere, yet the neighborhood is quiet."

"Except when you're getting vandalized and set up for arson," he replied in a dry tone.

"Touché. Other than the dining room chairs, most of it was just stuff tossed around. Luckily, I was able to replace the chairs."

I sipped the martini and sighed. He had a few other skills besides architecture.

"So, what's it going to be—dinner, and then business, or business first?" he asked, setting his half-empty glass on the coffee table.

"Why don't we eat? I have an excellent bottle of wine chilling in the fridge. If we discuss business first the chicken will be inedible."

He laughed and rose, following me into the dining room where he took a seat. I brought the wine and corkscrew, letting him deal with the cork.

Chef Rene was damned good. The perfectly seasoned chicken hit the spot and the pilaf had not dried out as I'd feared. Our dinner conversation was about favorite vacation spots and fantasy trips—safe, general topics.

When we finished, I cleared the table. "We can work here if you like."

"Sounds fine. How did your day go?"

I brought him my recorder along with four discs. "Listen to this while I clean up. The first session contains my interview with the work crew up in Boca last week. The second and third are my interviews this afternoon with Mason Detwiler and Carl Bresloff. The last one is Bill's interviews with City Councilwoman Anne Hodges and general contractor Dave Brooks."

"Did you find my interview?"

"No."

"Did you get a chance to look at Bill's laptop?"

"Not really. We can do that tonight."

Jason nodded, inserted a disc, and punched the play button. A pang of sadness stabbed at me when I heard Bill's voice. I would miss his wisecracks, pithy humor, and advice.

Clean-up didn't take long. Chef Rene also provided disposable cooking containers. I brought out another bottle of wine and joined Jason.

While he finished the last interview, I removed Bill's laptop from my office and set it in front of him.

"Anne Hodges sounds frustrated as hell," he remarked.

"That's what Bill said. He also thought she was clean as far as any bribery goes."

"She noticed Shay and Holmes projects are passed with barely a ripple of city council opposition."

"Except for her and Jose Cortez's votes. She was elected on an anti-development platform. I don't have her record in front of me, but I doubt if she'd vote yes to any kind of new building, especially in sensitive areas like the beach and the river front."

"Dave Brooks sounds just as frustrated."

"He is." I slid the new wine bottle toward Jason who opened it and refilled his glass. "I talked with him briefly up in Boca. He's walking a thin line. If he complains too much, he could have trouble obtaining *any* permit from the city of Port Royale. What did you think of my interviews?"

"Interesting. Detwiler was an idiot not to have done his homework on the contract. With a project that had the potential to make millions over time, he chose to go cheap and have his brother-in-law review it."

"I know. Remind me to never have him do my taxes."

"Bresloff was also careless in not supervising the construction closer. My father always had a supervisor or manager present during inspections. I'll look into the lawsuit tomorrow." He swirled the wine in his glass and frowned into its depths. "The construction crew's comments concern me. If what they're saying is true, then there are a lot of projects around this city in danger. I see more than one lawsuit down the road." He reached for the laptop. "Let's have a look at this. Do you know the password?"

"Try Murrow."

"Murrow?"

"As in 'Edward R'."

A few seconds later Jason reported, "Murrow worked."

I pulled up a chair and read over his shoulder. Most of the folders contained the rough drafts of future stories, including the Ann Hodges and Dave Brooks interviews. Bill had also been trying to track down the second e-mail sender who had alerted him to possible misconduct at Shay and Holmes. It had been sent at twelve fifty-three from a library four blocks away from the Shay and Holmes offices.

"An employee on his or her lunch hour?" I questioned.

"Maybe."

"Could it have been Marc?"

"I don't know, but I'd think he'd clear it with me first unless…"

"Unless he felt the need to have someone else be the center of attention—someone like a reporter."

"That's a possibility."

He frowned again, his brow knitting into furrows. We read several more files, none of which were pertinent to the Shay and Holmes scandal. Jason finally turned the computer off.

"There's nothing else. Have you looked at the CD from the office computer yet?"

"Just a little. I'll do it tomorrow or over the weekend. I do have other assignments, you know."

"Sorry. Didn't mean to suggest otherwise."

We left the dining area for the comfort of the living room and another glass of wine. Seated on opposite ends of the sofa, I gazed at him from behind my lowered lashes as I sipped. He looked totally relaxed, his hands clasped in back of his head, and legs crossed. He wore jeans tonight along with a light blue knit shirt.

He caught me staring and smiled. "So, tell me more about yourself. I know you're from Chicago, your mother was a writer, and your father's a doctor. What else? Where did you go to college?"

"I was a hometown girl. I stayed at home and went to Northwestern University where I got my degree in Journalism. I thought I had the world by the tail."

"Most college grads do until reality sets in. Where and what was your first job?"

I took another sip of wine. "The Rockford, Illinois, *Register* hired me for a ridiculously low salary. I did the usual things a cub reporter does. I wrote obituaries, updated profiles of city and state officials, and occasionally covered a women's club meeting. I stood it for a whole year before moving on to St. Louis. I was a staff reporter covering a wide range of topics."

Jason grinned and refilled his glass. "How long did you last in The Gateway to the West?"

"Three years. When a position as assistant to the top dog investigative reporter opened up, I applied, but was turned down. Not enough experience, so I quit and ended up in Biloxi, Mississippi."

"Biloxi, Mississippi!"

I had to laugh. "I know—small town, small newspaper, but I also thought advancement might be easier."

"Big fish, small pond."

"Something like that. I liked Biloxi in spite of its split personality. It has a small town mentality, but is still a resort area with casinos."

"And did you advance?"

"Yes. A series I did on the homeless in the midst of all the money on casino row got me this job."

"Why didn't you stay in Biloxi?"

"I loved my boss, Harry McAlister, but he was the brother-in-law of the publisher and firmly ensconced in the job. I'd gone about as far as I could, so I traded magnolias for sunshine. That's about all. What's your story?"

Jason shrugged and drank more wine. "You already know most of it. You Googled me, remember?"

"I also nosed around in the archives of the L. A. papers. You have one hell of a social life."

"It comes with the territory. I have to attend social functions, and I dislike going alone."

My investigative antennae were on red alert. "You haven't said much about your family other than Marc. Do you have other siblings?"

"So many, I can't remember all their names."

He answered in a light tone, but I sensed resentment in his words.

"That's right; you mentioned your father had been married several times."

Jason finished his wine and poured another glass. "My father made the trip down the aisle six times. My mother managed to do it four."

My jaw dropped. "That's a lot of weddings."

"It certainly is. That's why I decided a long time ago never to marry or have children. It just wasn't worth the pain and suffering."

"Yet, you're hardly a recluse."

"I love women and their companionship, but that doesn't mean I have to get married to attain it. I am not the marrying kind. What about you? Any long-term relationships?"

"Nothing serious. I dated Marc for several months. That seems to be about the usual time frame."

"What about girlfriends?"

"Girlfriends?"

"You know, the opposite of boyfriends. Don't you ever have a girl's night out?"

I sipped my wine, contemplating his question. I hadn't had a real girlfriend since the age of fourteen.

"I like a trip to the mall as well as the next person, but lunching with a bunch of other women, listening to them bitch and moan about the men in their lives doesn't appeal. I prefer work. I'd think you'd understand. How many times do you go out with the guys?"

Jason frowned. "I see your point. People who are driven to succeed often sacrifice their personal lives. We have a lot in common."

I twirled the stem of my wine glass between my thumb and forefinger. I didn't like talking about my personal life. "How did your father end up on the board of directors at Shay and Holmes?"

Jason looked at his watch. "Let's save that for another time, shall we?" He set his glass on the table and rose. "Thanks for dinner. Can you call in sick tomorrow? I'd like to pay a visit to a few more Shay and Holmes building sites. Afterwards, we can go to the fundraiser."

"Bill's funeral is tomorrow morning, but I should be free by noon."

Nodding, Jason said, "You can drive. You know your way around the city."

"All right," I replied, moving to the front door.

He opened it and peered out into the night. A palm tree filtered the light from the street through its fronds.

"Good night, Shelley."

He leaned down and covered my lips with his. Instant heat swamped my body like a blaze roaring out of an open furnace door. My ears buzzed. Before I knew it my arms clasped around his neck. He clamped me to his body and deepened the kiss into a mind-blowing spectacle. Multi-colored lights flashed behind my closed eyelids. I reveled in the taste of him—a mixture of lemon chicken, wine, and his own uniqueness.

I groaned, kissing him back. My leg curled around his. His excitement pressed against me, hard and growing harder. I uncurled my leg and made a move back inside. Jason's hands grasped my shoulders, separating us.

I stood dazed, waiting for my vision and hearing to clear and my heart rate to slow. "Oh, my."

He dragged in a deep breath. His breathing was a little on the short side, too. He stepped back. "Yeah. I'd better get out of here before we both end up doing something we'll regret."

Regret? I didn't think I'd regret a goddamned thing.

"Good night, Shelley."

He turned and walked down the steps to his car.

"G…good night."

I closed the door and leaned against it. I hadn't had a jolt of pure sexual desire like that in a long time. If I wasn't careful, Jason Mallory could mean a lot more to me than just Marc Chambers' step-brother.

Chapter Nine

"I am the resurrection and the life…"

At my second funeral in as many weeks, I was trapped in the front row at the mortuary, half-listening to the eulogies and the minister.

I didn't pray, but shifted my gaze toward the front. Bill's family had chosen a closed casket. A photo taken several years ago when he'd won a local journalism award graced the lid.

I sat between Cal Randolph and Miriam Noble, the owner of *The Standard*. I had arrived late, hoping to avoid sitting up front, but Cal insisted.

Shifting uncomfortably, I crossed my legs. Cal sat with his arms folded over his chest, a stern expression on his face. Miriam simply sat, here for appearances only. Not attending the funeral of a valued employee, especially one who'd been murdered, wouldn't have endeared the old witch to anybody. Inheriting the paper from her late husband, she rarely put in an appearance, but had no problem phoning in demands about content.

Every seat in the room was taken. Late-comers stood along the back wall. Cal informed me reporters from all over Florida and the East Coast attended. I wouldn't know. Being Bill's assistant, I hadn't met anyone from out of town. Bill worked in Philadelphia before coming south, and I never realized how solid his reputation was.

"Doug, dear, hold my sweater. It's way too warm in here. They should do something with the air-conditioning," a voice whispered behind me.

I didn't need to turn around to identify the parties. It was Doug Elliott and his aunt. I'd had the dubious honor of being introduced as I'd walked through the door.

The organist cranked up an old hymn. The mourners filed past the coffin. I rose, joining the procession, and then hurried outside into the sunlight. No graveside services were planned. Bill's final resting place would be in his New Jersey hometown.

A hand touched my elbow and I turned. "Miss Jackson, may I offer my condolences?"

It was Dave Brooks, the general contractor. "Thank you, Mr. Brooks. It was kind of you to come."

"Bill was a nice guy and a damned good reporter. Have you got a minute? There's something I'd like to talk about. Could I buy you a cup of coffee?"

I glanced at my watch, needing to go home, change clothes, and pick up Jason. I opened my mouth to refuse when out of the corner of my eye I saw Doug and his aunt emerge from the funeral home and look our way. I had the impression he was about to approach us.

"I'd love a cup of coffee, Mr. Brooks. There's a place called Java the Hut on Casey Avenue near the hospital. I'll meet you there."

He nodded and we went our separate ways. I slid into my car, cranked the engine, and set the air conditioner on high.

I beat Dave Brooks to the coffee shop, ordered two cups of regular French Roast, and waited. He walked in the door a minute later.

"Thanks for agreeing to meet," he said, sitting and sipping the strong, hot liquid.

"What is it you wanted to tell me?" I also drank. It was coffee and not worth the three-fifty I'd paid.

"After Bill and I talked last week, we had a couple of beers. He told me he wanted to interview Sharon Ireland, but wondered if I could smooth the way. I went to school with Sharon and see her once every blue moon."

"Who's Sharon Ireland?"

"Sharon's the daughter of Doris Hancock, the original owner of the property where The River Tower Condos were built."

"Why would Bill want to interview her?"

"I don't know all the ins and outs of it, but he'd heard rumors that the city literally stole the property—something about a park ending up as condos."

I sat back tapping a finger against my lips. I had no idea what he was talking about. Bill had never mentioned nor asked me to do research on either Sharon Ireland or Doris Hancock.

"You say they owned the property? How did the city get a hold of it?"

"I'm not sure. Like I said, I know Sharon, but not well enough to know something like that." Dave took another sip of coffee and frowned. "I also talked to my crew, the guys you interviewed. They're all nervous as cats. Fred swears someone is following him, and Immigration showed up yesterday checking Juan and Carlos's status."

"They're legal, aren't they?"

"Absolutely. Their green cards are in order," he declared. "Smith says he's had several hang up calls in the last few days, too. Do you think Bill's death was random?"

"Not a chance in hell. He hated the nightclub district. If he was there, it had to be important." I finished the mediocre coffee.

"Do you think his murder is related to the Shay and Holmes investigation?"

"God, I hope not." I sat back and chewed my lip for a second. "Maybe I should interview this lady. How can I reach her?"

Dave drained his cup. "Let me see if she's willing to talk. I'll call you."

"Thank you. I'd appreciate it." I handed him my business card. "Use my cell phone. I'd rather we keep this private."

He nodded and tucked the card into his shirt pocket before handing me his.

"Was the River Towers project the first you'd lost to Shay and Holmes?"

"No, but I made a decent bid and could have brought it in under budget. The Shay and Holmes bid was too low to be believed. I warned the city there would be overruns."

"Were there?"

"Of course, but at the time, that slimy bastard, Bradley Holmes, just smiled and made a crack about S and H being a better run organization."

If Bradley Holmes was anything like Ken Shay, I was prepared to hate his guts. I glanced at my watch and rose. "I've got to run. I have to be someplace at noon. Thank you for everything, Dave."

He smiled and also stood. "No problem, Shelley. I'll be in touch."

We left Java the Hut, and I waved as he drove from the parking lot. I sat for a minute, hands resting on the steering wheel.

This was a new wrinkle. I'd never considered how the city had obtained the land for the condos. I was very interested in what Sharon Ireland had to say.

****

I dashed home, changed into jeans and a blouse, and arrived at Jason's hotel only a few minutes late.

"Are you ever on time?" he asked, sliding into the passenger seat.

"Sorry, but nobody in South Florida is on time. Besides, I have a good excuse." I told him about my conversation with Dave.

"He thinks the city stole the property? How could they do that?" he asked.

"Eminent domain? The Supreme Court ruling a few years ago opened the door for greedy cities and developers."

"I was under the impression the River Tower Condos land was sold before eminent domain became synonymous with theft."

"I hope Dave convinces Sharon to agree to an interview."

I had turned west and now stopped at a light. Gas stations sat on two of the four corners. A liquor store occupied the third, while the fourth contained a boarded up building. Strange how a neighborhood could change within just a few blocks.

"Where are we going?" I asked.

Jason pulled a list from his pocket. "The Garden Acres Apartments are on Creekside next to The Big Bend Golf Course."

"That's not too far. It won't take ten minutes."

In spite of the noon hour, I was correct on my time. I drove to the leasing office and parked. So far, I wasn't impressed. Most of the parking slots were empty and the faded paint on the front doors of the units gave off an air of depression.

"How are we going to play this? I don't think just barging in and asking questions is going to work."

"Especially since Shay and Holmes still owns the place," Jason said. "It's a cash cow. Exorbitant rent for what you get and lousy maintenance make for good profit. I see most of the roof of one building is under a blue tarp."

"Hurricane damage. Why should they be any different?" I opened my door, but Jason's hand stopped me.

"I'll begin, then you do the talking. Keep the manager distracted while I check for problems in the unit we're shown. I wish we could talk to a few of the residents."

"Let me think on it. I'll find a way."

We exited the car and strolled to the office. Jason grabbed my hand in a firm grasp. I shot him a look, but he smiled and winked.

"Just for show," he murmured, opening the office door.

Too bad. His warm hand sent chills up and down my spine, and I remembered the kiss from last night. I heaved a sigh and blew it out. Now was not the time to get turned on.

A receptionist sat at a desk filing her nails. "May I help you?" She didn't bother to look up.

Jason grinned like the Cheshire cat. "You sure can,

miss. My fiancée and I want to rent an apartment and we'd like a tour of this place. Is the manager available?"

"Just a moment." She lifted the phone and talked to someone on the other end, then hung up. "Mr. Hamilton will be out in a moment. Have a seat." She examined her nails and resumed scraping the emery board over a forefinger.

A few seconds later a door opened and a thickset man with dark, greasy, slicked-back hair appeared. He beamed from ear to ear.

"Welcome to Garden Acres. I hear you and the little woman-to-be are looking for a place to call home." He shook Jason's hand like a pump handle.

Little woman! This clown was asking for it. As though sensing my indignation, Jason threw his arm around my shoulders pulling me close to his side.

"That's right. We're tying the knot in a couple of weeks. Happened to be passing by and thought we'd stop in."

"Garden Acres is just the place for newlyweds. My congratulations, ma'am."

"Thanks," I tried to sound happy.

"You got anything in a two-bedroom, two-bath available?"

"Sure do, Mr…"

"King, Stephen King."

I wanted to groan. Using the name of a famous novelist was pushing our luck. I worried unnecessarily.

"Well, now, Mr. King, my name is Bert Hamilton. I'll be glad to show you an apartment. Let me get the keys. Don't worry about the blue tarps. The roofers should be here and finished in a couple of weeks."

Hamilton drove us around the complex in a golf cart, gushing away at the natural beauty and how we shouldn't be concerned because the landscapers, window repairmen, pool guy—fill in the blank—would be on the scene in a week or two.

Yeah, right. I refrained from saying it out loud.

Stopping in front of an end unit, Hamilton led us up to a second floor apartment.

The walls hadn't been painted in years and the carpet was filthy. I wore sandals and hoped nothing catching crept between my toes. Judging from the crud accumulated on the stove, I doubted it had ever been cleaned. I can't begin to describe the bathrooms. Back in the living room, I gazed out of the dirty windows and admired the view of the side yard with the street a mere twenty feet away. A passing truck rattled the glass.

"Of course, the previous tenants just moved out the other day. We haven't had a chance to clean it yet, but it's the layout that counts," Hamilton oozed in my ear.

Jason wandered around in an aimless fashion. Distraction time had arrived.

"Oh, and this *is* a wonderful layout," I oozed right back. "Would you have any objections to changing the wall color? I'm thinking a nice soft beige."

"No problem at all, Miss…"

"Dickinson, Emily Dickinson." If Jason, now out of sight in the kitchen, could play literary games, so could I. "And plants…I just love plants." I eyed the dozens of holes in the walls where nails had been ripped out. "Do you mind if I hang some supports for my plants?"

"Of course not, you decorate any way you like."

"The draperies look a little worse for wear. Would

you mind cleaning them?"

I shook the limp fabric hanging from a sagging rod. Dust billowed, and I sneezed several times in succession. Hamilton was a consummate liar. The dump had been empty for months.

I tried to look apologetic. "Oh, dear. Please excuse me. Allergies, you know."

Jason strolled out of the kitchen heading down the hall to the bedrooms and baths.

"Sure." The manager looked over his shoulder. "Where's Mr. King?"

"Taking a second look. He'll be back in a moment. I want to ask you about the locks. I notice you don't have deadbolts or security rods for the sliding glass doors. Is the complex patrolled by guards?"

Hamilton swallowed and smiled, though not as jovially as before. "Of course, especially at night."

I pulled the sliding door open and stepped onto the balcony. Old Bert did not follow. I held my breath. The weathered wood was cracked and several spindles on the railing missing.

"Don't worry about that. Repairman is due to fix it in a…"

"…couple of weeks," I finished for him.

The manager smiled weakly and nodded.

I quickly returned inside just as Jason rejoined us.

"Well, sweet thing, have you seen enough?"

"Sure have, dumpling," I cooed back. Did people really talk this way?

"Well, let's head for the barn. I'll tell you all about the rent and the rest of the amenities." Bert had a relieved smile plastered on his face.

We piled into the cart and Hamilton drove past a

swimming pool with a *No Swimming* sign tacked onto the rusting wrought iron fence around it. I understood why. Algae clung to the sides and floated on the surface turning the water an interesting shade of green. He parked and ushered us into his office.

"I want to thank you for showing us around, Mr. Hamilton," Jason began when I interrupted.

"Honey, I'm just dying for a smoke. Why don't you and Mr. Hamilton take care of business? I don't understand all this money stuff anyway." With a little luck, I'd find a couple of tenants out and about.

Quick-witted Jason caught on, nodding. "You go ahead."

I dashed past the receptionist—now reading a magazine—and out the front door. I hurried around a corner to the parking lot, but saw no one. Then a noise from the side of a building had me turning in that direction. A woman had just dumped a bag of garbage into the overfilled dumpster. I rushed over.

"Excuse me, ma'am, could I speak with you a moment?"

"You sellin' something?"

"Heavens, no. My fiancé and I are thinking about renting. Do you like living here?"

The woman snorted. "You gotta be kidding. Don't waste your money. The place is a dump. The garbage bins are always overflowing and the rats are bigger than my Aunt Sadie's cats. And forget maintenance. I waited three weeks for someone to repair my shower. The walls are paper thin, and everyone's been burglarized at least once. If I could afford to move, I would."

She turned, stomped up the cracked sidewalk and into her apartment. Across the way, I saw an elderly man carrying a grocery sack. I asked the same question, getting much the same answer.

I'd been gone maybe fifteen minutes—time to rescue Jason and get out of here before we ended up with an apartment. A sign I'd overlooked earlier by the front door gave us a reason to leave.

I sauntered back in, and Jason rose to his feet.

"We'll be in touch, Mr. Hamilton," he said.

"Did you ask him about Fred and Ethel, dear?"

Jason gave me a strange look. "Uh, no, can't say that I did."

"Who're Fred and Ethel?" Hamilton asked.

"My dogs. I have a St. Bernard and a German Shepherd. They're no trouble at all and almost housebroken," I replied. "And the barking won't be an issue once I take them to obedience school."

Hamilton's shoulders slumped. "I'm sorry, but we don't allow pets. It says so on the sign out front."

"Oh, what a shame." I hoped I looked disappointed.

"Well, thanks anyway," Jason said, steering me out of the office and to the car. We managed to hold our laughter in until I pulled out of the driveway.

"Fred and Ethel?" he said with a chuckle.

"What about Stephen King, for crying out loud?"

"I swear I don't know where it came from."

"That's all right. I told him my name was Emily Dickinson. Luckily, he's illiterate. What did you see?"

"Cheap, shoddy construction, loose outlets, corroded window frames—the list is endless."

"At least you didn't go out on the balcony. The damned thing almost swayed in the breeze."

"Did you have a chance to talk to anybody while

Hamilton bent my ear?"

I gave him the list of complaints from the two tenants, and then asked, "Where to next?"

"The Strathmore Condos on Hayward Avenue. They also do rentals. The map shows them being just off Gateway Boulevard."

We stayed with the same game plan getting the same results—shoddy construction and low maintenance.

The Westside Shopping Mall was of the strip variety, and we had no trouble eliciting a plethora of problems from the shop owners.

When we finished, I drove Jason back to his hotel. "Tomorrow I'll check on who the inspectors were for these properties. There must be a pattern. All the inspectors can't be on the take."

"Tomorrow's Saturday. I'll go into the office and see if I can find the records on the buildings we saw today." He got out of the car and leaned back in the open door. "I'll pick you up for the fundraiser at seven-thirty."

I nodded and drove away. Tonight was going to be very interesting.

****

The babble of conversation hit me like a physical blow when Jason and I entered the ballroom of The Quiet Palms Hotel. Good thing I had taken the time to choose my dress carefully. There had to be over three hundred people taking advantage of contributing a whopping one thousand dollars each for the privilege of rubbing elbows with local celebrities and politicians.

We threaded our way through the crowd and waited in line at the bar to order. "Two vodka martinis,"

153

Jason told the harried bartender when we finally pushed our way to the front.

With our drinks in hand, we carefully retraced our steps until a woman stopped us.

"Jason, how nice of you to come."

"Thank you, Lynnette. May I introduce Shelley Jackson? Shelly, this is Lynnette Palmer, the CFO of Shay and Holmes."

Short and on the dumpy side, the woman wore an unflattering, long out of style suit made from some kind of shiny fabric. The shoulder pads convinced me she played football—in the nineteen-eighties. Both the skirt and the jacket were too long. The gray color did nothing for her pale complexion. The mousy hair was styled in a weird updo that reminded me of a beehive. Her make-up was heavy and her jewelry excessive. As a professional image, it sucked.

"How do you do, Ms. Palmer? It's a pleasure to meet you." I stretched out my free hand.

She hesitated a moment, and then shook it with slightly cold, clammy hands. "Thank you for coming to our reception, Miss Jackson. What a lovely dress."

I wore a bright green halter dress, a pair of gold sandals, and carried a gold evening bag over my shoulder.

"Thank you." What else could I say?

"It looks like you have a great turnout," Jason said.

Lynnette looked around as though surprised to see other people. "Yes, I guess it is. I'm sure Congressman Hayes will be pleased."

So that's who this shindig was for, I thought. Congressman Peter Hayes, a mediocre house member who retained his seat because the district he represented voted over twenty-to-one for his party. Donald Duck could run under the party banner and get elected.

Lynnette turned to me, smiled, showing lots of teeth, and asked, "What do you do for a living, Miss Jackson?"

I dug in my heels and lifted my chin. "I'm a reporter for *The South Florida Standard.*"

Jason's hand tightened on my waist and Lynnette Palmer almost choked on her drink.

"Oh, oh I see. That…that must be interesting."

"It can be," I replied.

"Will you excuse me for a moment? Someone I need to see just came in. A pleasure meeting you."

She fled from my presence like I carried the plague. I took a sip of my martini. "Well, that was fun. Who's next?"

"Did you have to mention you're a reporter?"

"Why not? Besides, she asked. Was I supposed to lie? It might shake up a few of the S and H people to know I'm here."

He swallowed a huge gulp of his drink. "Then let's meet some more."

He grabbed my hand and led me around groups of contributors before stopping in front of a portly gray-haired man obviously uncomfortable in a tux. His voice boomed when he saw Jason.

"Mallory, good to see you, good to see you. Glad you could make it. And who is this vision of loveliness?" he said, turning in my direction.

"Dexter, this is Shelley Jackson. Shelley, this is Dexter Marshall, Chairman of the Board of Directors of Shay and Holmes."

"My dear, Miss Jackson, it is a pleasure to make

your acquaintance," he said, bowing over my hand and casting his eyes down the front of my dress.

Chairman or not, I wanted to push my hand hard into his nose. Instead, I chose to be civil. "I'm very glad to meet you, Mr. Marshall."

"No, no, the pleasure is all mine."

He straightened smiling fatuously, his eyes not quite focusing. The man had obviously found a home at the bar. Another man joined us before the conversation could continue.

"Ah, there you are, Dexter. Nice to see you, Mallory. Dexter, Councilman Russell would like a word with you."

"What a shame. Duty calls. Please excuse me."

He left, and I couldn't tell if his weaving gait was due to the necessity of avoiding knots of party-goers or from an overload of bourbon.

"Dennis, I'd like to introduce you to Shelley Jackson. Shelley, this is Dennis Birdsong, the head of accounting at Shay and Holmes."

And Marc's immediate boss. My interest picked up. He shook my hand and dropped it in record time. I surreptitiously wiped my palm on my drink napkin.

Birdsong was sweating like a laborer in the hot sun. His expression screamed that he'd rather be in hell than here. His every move had a jerky, nervous quality. His suit hung on his tall, thin body like a shroud.

Before I could engage in any conversation, he said, "I'm pleased to meet you. Forgive me, but I must find my wife. I'm sure I'll speak to you later." Without so much as a goodbye, he turned and left.

"Well, that was abrupt," I said to Jason.

"He's been a nervous wreck ever since he found

out I was Marc's step-brother. I saw him talking to Lynnette a few minutes ago. I don't know whose presence scares him more—yours or mine."

"Jason, good of you to come," a voice said from behind me. I turned to face Ken Shay and another man.

"Brad, Ken, I wouldn't miss it for the world."

So this was Bradley Holmes. He stood a couple of inches under six feet with a medium build. His brown hair was styled in a conservative manner and his blue eyes looked sharp. The rest of his features were average—the kind that would blend in and never stand out.

Ken Shay's eyes popped wide and he stared at me with barely concealed astonishment. Jason introduced me to both men.

"A pleasure, Mr. Holmes. Nice to see you again, Mr. Shay." I was pleased to note the unease in Shay's eyes.

"You've met before?" Holmes said with raised eyebrows.

"Yes, about a week ago, wasn't it? Did you ever find those missing files?"

Holmes turned to his partner and spoke in an ice cold voice. "What missing files?"

Next to me, Jason tensed.

"Oh, some of Marc's files turned up missing and I asked Miss Jackson if perhaps Marc, having been her close friend, may have seen them. Luckily, it was all a mix up. We found them."

Holmes sent a hard glare at Shay who responded with a weak smile. He wiped a drop of perspiration from his temple and drained his drink in one long swallow.

Holmes swiveled back to me with a smile. "Well, I'm pleased that was cleared up. I understand you're a reporter, Miss Jackson."

"Yes, for *The South Florida Standard.* I was Bill Mathias's assistant."

"My condolences. He was a fine reporter, although way off base with his suppositions in his last series of articles. What a shame we never connected on a time and place to present the Shay and Holmes side of things."

He'd left the door wide open. I blasted through like a rocket leaving the launch pad.

"That can still be arranged. Would you agree to let me do the interview?"

Ken Shay made a choking sound, but Brad Holmes's smile never wavered. "That's an excellent idea, Miss Jackson. The sooner the better for all concerned, don't you think?"

"Absolutely, Mr. Holmes. When would you like to meet?"

"How about Monday afternoon—say about two o'clock at our offices?"

I hesitated about meeting on their turf. On the other hand what could happen in a bustling office in broad daylight?

"That sounds fine. I'll see both of you then."

I nodded to them. Jason grasped my elbow leading me in the opposite direction and spoke in a low voice. "He contacted you about missing files? Why?"

I told Jason about our encounter at The Marina Boatyard.

"He threatened you and you didn't tell anyone?"

"I told Bill, who was furious. To tell the truth, after

158

all that's happened, it seemed unimportant."

We wandered from group to group, chatting and sipping. I met a couple of city council members, but my profession did not come up until the mayor sidled into a conversation we were having with one of his underlings. Out of politeness the man had to introduce us.

Mayor Martin Cosworth had held his position for close to twenty years. Charismatic and warm, he gave the impression he cared. Carefully styled and unashamedly dyed hair was a signature trademark. His blue eyes crinkled with what appeared to be sincere happiness to meet me. He was, however, nobody's fool.

"Mr. Mallory, please accept my condolences on the loss of your brother. Brad mentioned you were staying in town to clear up his affairs."

Cosworth had done his homework on the internationally known, award-winning architect brother of a murdered man.

"Yes. I should be finished in a few more days, and then it's back to L. A."

"And I understand you worked with the late Bill Mathias," the mayor said, shaking his head and turning toward me. "What a tragedy. I told the city council security in the South Street nightclub district had to be beefed up during season. It's a major tourist destination, and I'd hate to see it go under because of crime."

An outrageous idea popped into my head and out of my mouth before I had a chance to think.

"I agree, Mr. Mayor. Bill was a close friend and mentor. Would you consider giving me an interview on the subject of security? A lot of local people, including me, enjoy clubbing."

He raised his eyebrows as though I had caught him off guard, but recovered quickly. "I think that can be arranged, Miss Jackson." He turned to the silent man standing next to him. "Howard, please give Miss Jackson your card so she can call. Mr. Whitman makes all my appointments. If he gets sick, I don't know where to go or who to see. It was a pleasure meeting you, Mr. Mallory."

He nodded and left. Howard handed me his card.

"Please call on Monday morning. I'll see if I can fit you in sometime this week." Then he, too, melted into the crowd.

"Well, you didn't let any grass grow under your feet," Jason commented in a dry tone.

"It may have been pushy, but who knows when I'd ever get another chance to ask?"

The dimming of the lights signaled the end of the cocktail party. Jason and I filed out of the room toward the dining area with the rest of the throng.

A sense of elation and accomplishment burbled inside me. I had interviews pending with Bradley Holmes, Kenneth Shay, *and* with the Mayor of Port Royale. Bill would have been proud. Visions of bylines and the front row at the White House danced in my head.

Chapter Ten

The elevator doors slid open, yet I hesitated before finally stepping into the busy hallway, then stopped in the middle of the corridor and gazed at the glass portals to *The Standard's* offices. The funeral had hammered home the fact Bill was gone. For the first time since being hired, I didn't want to enter. Nothing would be the same without him. The thought of a new boss didn't sit well. Bill taught me a lot, and once said I had "moxie"—an old-fashioned term for guts, I think.

A man hurrying through the hall bumped into me. "Lady, do you have to stop and admire the view? Come on, one way or another."

"Sorry," I muttered, moving forward and shoving open the doors to the reception lobby.

Inside my cubicle, I flipped the computer on before escaping to the break room for a cup of coffee.

I'd spent most of the weekend trying to sort out the material downloaded onto the CD. It had been tough concentrating. Jason Mallory hadn't called, but Dave Brooks did on Sunday evening.

"Shelley, Dave Brooks here."

"Hello, Dave. Did you get a hold of Miss Ireland?"

"Yeah. She said to give her a call Tuesday morning. She's tied up tomorrow."

I scribbled the number on a loose sheet of paper.

"Dave, you are the best. Thanks."

"No problem. All I ask is that you keep me up to date on what's happening. If you and The Standard *can take down Shay and Holmes, I'll personally buy you the biggest steak South Florida has to offer."*

"I never turn down a free meal."

I sighed, and then jerked with surprise spilling hot coffee on my slacks when my desk phone rang. Swearing, I grabbed a tissue with one hand and the phone with the other.

"Yes," I barked, daubing at the stain.

"Jackson, come into my office for a moment," Cal ordered.

I hadn't bothered to call in on Friday and assumed I was about to be reamed out for the whole office to hear.

I was wrong. Detective Sorenson lounged in a chair in front of Cal's desk. *Shit. Now what?*

"Come in, Jackson. Close the door behind you. Detective Sorenson has some things he needs to clear up."

Without being asked I sat in the other chair and crossed my legs. A hot gush of adrenaline surged through me as Sorenson's narrowed gaze homed in. I didn't think I was going to like what he asked.

"How can I help you, Detective?"

"I'm glad you put it that way, Miss Jackson. Your corporate lawyers agreed to let the police have a peek at Bill Mathias's computer last Friday and guess what?"

"What?" I answered. My voice sounded cool considering my heart rate had just jumped several levels.

"Our experts say a lot of his files were deleted last

Wednesday night at about the same time we caught you and Jason Mallory on tape in the parking garage. Care to go over your story regarding that night again?"

"Why should I? I didn't mess with Bill's computer." A nervous tremor spiraled from the pit of my stomach.

"There's something else." He leaned forward and picked up a TV remote from Cal's desk, then punched a button. The TV/VCR flashed on. The surveillance tape showed Jason and I swing into the parking spot, the date and the time clearly displayed in the bottom right hand corner.

"I've already admitted I was here," I said.

"Let me speed this up." Sorenson pushed another button and the tape fast forwarded to when we left. He froze the frame as I stepped clear of the elevator.

"Miss Jackson, what is that slung over your shoulder?"

"It's called a purse, Detective Sorenson."

Soon my internal trembling would reach my extremities. I clenched the arms of the chair. A trickle of cold sweat crept down my spine. I knew he didn't mean my purse. He meant Bill's laptop case.

"I'm referring to the bulky item in the black carrying case—the thing under your purse. Could that be a laptop?"

"As a matter of fact, it is."

"You know, we can't find Mr. Mathias's laptop anywhere." Sorenson turned off the TV and leaned in closer. "I think you and Mallory were in the office that night. We retrieved lots of fingerprints, many not as yet identified. I'm sure you and Mr. Mallory won't mind coming down to the station and getting printed, will you?"

My fingerprints could be explained. Jason's couldn't. "I have no problem with doing that, and I wasn't anywhere near Bill's office."

Sorenson ignored me. "You messed with the computer and stole the laptop. That, Miss Jackson, is hindering a police investigation. What was on Mathias's computer, and where is the laptop?"

The tape didn't lie, but I sure did. "Bill kept confidential files on his computer along with a lot of other things. I have no clue where his laptop is. I borrowed the one in the tape from a friend after mine was stolen. I forgot to take it with me when I left the office earlier that evening. The news about Bill pushed everything from my mind."

"What's the name of this friend?"

"Joanna Campbell." I made a mental note to call Jo and have her cover for me as soon as this ghastly interview ended. I gave him her home number. At this time of day, Jo would be at work.

"I'd also like to know why you left so many urgent messages for your boss the night he was killed. What was so important?"

"My house had been burglarized and my laptop stolen. I was trying to warn him sensitive information might be compromised."

"Care to change your story? It won't take long to identify those fingerprints in Mathias's office."

I shrugged. Since he hadn't pulled out his handcuffs, the spiraling shakes had diminished. "A lot of people came and went in Bill's office, including me. You'll find my prints on his phone and his computer. I often looked things up for him when he was out of the office."

"Then you knew his password," Sorenson said.

"He changed it every couple of weeks. He'd tell me what it was when he'd call."

Cal's eyebrows rose. He knew Bill was secretive as hell about his files and refused to change his password because he could never remember it.

"Detective Sorenson, if there isn't anything else, could we wind this up? Miss Jackson has work to do," Cal said, shooting me a glance.

Sorenson rose and headed for the door. "One more thing. We got the ballistics report on the bullet that killed Mr. Mathias. It was fired from the same gun that killed Marc Chambers."

On that cheerful news, he left. Now I did tremble and sweat. The two deaths were connected just as Jason and I suspected.

Cal glared. "All right, Shelley, I want the truth. Don't try to bullshit me. What's going on? Why did you delete Bill's files, and don't try to tell me you didn't."

I could have lied, but I wanted to cover my ass as much as possible. I only lied a little.

"I didn't want Bill's files to fall into police hands. He had the names of several of his contacts and informants stored on his computer. Some are cops. Don't worry. I copied them onto a CD. He never kept anything like that on his laptop, so I borrowed it until I can replace mine."

Cal's glare softened, but his voice was still tough.

"I'll cover you as much as I can, but you're in way over your head. I take it Mallory was also in the office."

"He checked the file cabinet. I'm sure he can come

up with some kind of explanation."

"He's on his own. I'm not covering his ass, too." He ran an agitated hand through his hair. "Aw, hell, the police experts will get the files off the hard drive anyway. Anything else I should know?"

I told him about my pending interviews with Brad Holmes and Ken Shay and the one with the Mayor.

Cal pursed his lips and whistled softly, then leaned back in his chair. "Okay, kid, you've got a tiger by the tail. Just be careful how hard you twist. I don't want anything to happen to you, too. And get me that CD of Bill's files."

I nodded and escaped to my cubicle where I sat and shivered for a few minutes before calling Jo's cell from a nearby empty cubicle, then breathed a sigh of relief when she agreed to say she loaned me a laptop. I also left a message in Jason's voicemail, giving him a heads up on the fingerprints and Sorenson's suspicions.

My coffee was cold, and I returned to the break room for another cup. My shaking hands didn't help my aim and coffee slopped onto the countertop. I gripped the edge of the scarred Formica sucking in deep breaths.

Marc and Bill had been killed with the same gun and both had connections to Shay and Holmes. I raised the cup to my lips with trembling hands. I was due in the lion's den at two o'clock this afternoon. I hoped I came out alive at three.

****

I smoothed the skirt of my navy blue suit nervously while waiting in the reception area at Shay and Holmes. I'd taken my lunch hour to go home and change from the coffee-stained slacks to a more professional appearance.

Jason was here, but the receptionist said he didn't answer his office phone nor had he returned my call from earlier. I wanted to tell him about the ballistics report, and find out what, if anything, he'd discovered about the properties we'd seen on Friday.

"Miss Jackson, it's good to see you again," Brad Holmes said, entering the area from a door to my left. "Mr. Shay will join us in a few minutes. Shall we go into the conference room?" He indicated an ornate door to my right. "It's quiet and we won't be disturbed."

"That's fine. I won't take up much of your time. I know you're busy."

CFO, Lynnette Palmer breezed through the doors, skidded to a stop, and stared with an anxious look on her face. Her attire today consisted of a lavender tweed suit, a yellow blouse, and pastel pink pumps. Was the woman color blind?

"Miss Jackson, what are you doing here?" she asked in a high squeaky tone.

"Mr. Holmes and Mr. Shay have consented to an interview."

Her amazed and frightened glance shot to Brad Holmes. "You have?"

"Yes. I think it's a good idea to clear up any misconceptions the late Mr. Mathias may have had concerning the company. Don't you agree, Lynnette?"

She licked her lips and gave me a tight smile. "Yes, of course. A very good idea. Well, if you'll excuse me, I have work to do."

She nodded and continued through the reception area.

"Please, follow me, Miss Jackson." Holmes led me

through the door on the right.

The room was like most conference rooms, with a large mahogany table surrounded by upholstered chairs. A small kitchenette complete with a microwave, coffee urn, and a mini-fridge, nestled in the far corner. A sideboard stood next to it.

I took a seat and set up my recorder, then brought out my notepad. Holmes pulled three bottles of water from the fridge. He offered me one and cracked the top on another for himself before sitting opposite me.

"I'm glad we're getting this opportunity to chat, Miss Jackson. We've been very upset about the accusations and now that Mr. Mathias is dead, we feared our side of the story would never be told."

"In that case, I'm happy I was able to attend your party the other night and meet you."

"I didn't know you were acquainted with Jason Mallory." He took a swig and smiled.

"We met at Marc's funeral."

"A terrible shame about Marc. We had no idea he was related to Jason."

Brad Holmes was slick. He sat shaking his head while trying to suck information out of me. I refused to play the game his way. Glancing at my watch, I said, "Shall we begin?"

"If you'd like. Ken will be along shortly. He was on the phone with a client."

He settled back while I started the recorder. "Mr. Holmes, can you address the allegations of bribery of building inspectors brought forth by the late Bill Mathias?"

"We deny anything of the sort. Shay and Holmes has been in business for thirty years and our reputation has never been questioned."

"And yet, I understand there are serious concerns by some former employees regarding the quality of workmanship and materials used in recent years. Would you care to comment?"

Holmes took another drink and sighed, a classic stalling tactic. "Miss Jackson, let's call it what it is—disgruntled employees. For various reasons we had to let people go, especially with some workers whose documentation appeared shaky. We also discovered one man had a drinking problem. We'd warned him, but he showed up drunk one morning and was fired on the spot." He frowned and shook his head. "Another man had an attitude his supervisors could no longer deal with, so he was let go."

He obviously spoke about the work crew I'd interviewed in Boca Raton.

"I saw what used to be the Iguanawana restaurant in Palmetto Gardens. The former owner claims the construction was sub-par from day one."

"I remember that building. The owner was a cheapskate who constantly urged us to use cheaper subcontractors and less expensive materials. He also changed the building plans every few weeks. We tried to explain the costs to him, but he wouldn't listen and has only himself to blame."

"He says the contract had a clause hidden in it saying he'd bear half the cost of overruns. Kind of a strange clause, isn't it, Mr. Holmes?"

"The clause wasn't hidden and he signed the contract. Not our fault if he didn't read it."

For the first time, his voice sharpened. I don't think he realized I'd talked to Detwiler.

"And the Leisure Time Motel?"

"A hurricane did major damage, Miss Jackson. We cannot be held responsible for an act of nature. Any problems prior to that can be laid at the doorstep of poor maintenance. The building passed all inspections."

The door opened. Ken Shay walked in snatching the last bottle of water from the table and slouching into the seat next to Holmes.

"Sorry I'm late, but I just couldn't get off the phone. You know how it is. Have I missed much?"

"We were just talking about The Leisure Time Motel in Sunshine Beach," I answered.

"I remember that one. The owner's trying to sue us. Ridiculous, of course."

Shay opened the bottle and drank half of it. He smiled, but his eyes had a distinct reddish tinge and his hands shook. He was hung over as hell.

"I believe you mentioned inspections, Mr. Holmes, which once again brings up the bribery angle."

"The word bribery was first used by a rival contractor we successfully outbid on numerous projects. I'm afraid whatever he tells you is nothing more than sour grapes. He's barely keeping his head above water and has to blame someone, I suppose."

"Besides," Shay chimed in, "we have a very good relationship with the city council. They know and respect our work. Every one of them was at the party."

"I see. So, it's advantageous to work closely with the powers that be," I said.

Shay finished his water and laughed lightly. "I don't deal with the political end of it. That's Brad's job."

Holmes smiled. "As CEO of the company, I do

most of the schmoozing and make the political contacts. It never hurts to have the city government familiar with your company and its record. Ken is better suited to the day-to-day operations of the company. Our respective fathers held the same positions for thirty years. It worked for them and it's working for us."

The two of them spent the next half an hour detailing the successful projects of the past five or six years with the River Tower Condos heading the list.

I listened with only half an ear. They'd given the usual stock answers. Hearing any more wasted my time. I let them talk a while before turning off the recorder.

"Thank you very much, gentlemen. It's been an enlightening interview. I can't tell you when it will be printed, but I'm sure it will be sometime in the next couple of weeks."

I stood and shook hands, then walked out the door. Both men had smiled, but the look in their eyes warned me to watch my back. I shivered. Marc and Bill were dead. Was I next?

****

"There! Done," I muttered, hitting the save button. My interview notes were transcribed and transferred to my JumpDrive so I could work at home.

A glance at my computer clock told me it was quitting time. Most of the employees had already called it a day. I half stood, craning my neck, unable to prevent my gaze from automatically seeking Bill's darkened office. The crime scene tape had been removed, and I wondered if it was too soon to apply for the job. Cal's office door was closed, but through the window I saw him inside talking to someone out of my line of sight.

My cell phone rang, and I read Jason's ID. "I thought you'd never call. Did you get my message?"

"I got it. Sorenson left one, too, but I haven't returned it yet. I'll dodge getting fingerprinted. I've never been printed before—no military service or brushes with the law for them to compare."

"What did you find out about the places we visited?"

"Not much we didn't already know. Why don't you have dinner with me in my room? We can compare notes."

"Give me fifteen minutes." I shut down for the night and drove to the hotel.

Jason opened the door, waving me inside. "Martini?"

Nodding, I dumped my purse and laptop on a chair. "What did you find out?"

"I snooped around on Saturday and finally found the contracts on the properties in a file room. No matter how many technical advances are made, people still have to keep a written copy."

"And?"

He shrugged, handing me a drink. I sipped, almost purring—ice cold and warming at the same time—perfect.

"The Iguanawana contract had the infamous clause in the middle of a very long paragraph. It was definitely hidden. How did your interview go with Shay and Holmes?"

"They're a couple of smooth operators—Holmes more so than Shay. Where were you? I could have used a little moral support."

"I thought it might be better if we didn't have any

contact. They're keeping a polite eye on me. I was over in Human Resources and Finance being charming to secretaries. Secretaries and receptionists know everything."

"Well, they don't know this." I told him about the ballistics report.

He drained his glass, his face set in a stony expression. "I didn't really think Bill's death was random. Now we know—someone at Shay and Holmes is a killer."

"Not necessarily. If bribes were paid, it could be a building inspector. Don't forget them."

"I'll stall Sorenson as long as I can. If I do get printed, I can always say I went to Bill's office before he died."

"You may get away with it. The surveillance tapes are on a twenty-four hour loop. Found that out a few months ago when some thief disguised as a food delivery person made his way into one of the offices on the second floor."

"Good. I'll make it sound convincing."

"He knows it was us anyway. I think he views us as a couple of amateur sleuths. If he didn't, we'd be locked up by now."

Jason mixed another drink. "Did you get an interview with the Mayor?"

"Yes. I called this morning and have an appointment for Wednesday at nine. It should be interesting."

"Shall we order?"

"Nothing fancy for me. A burger and fries will do. Do you happen to know if Shay and Holmes still owns the River Towers Condos?"

He called down our order before answering. "Funny you should ask. I saw a paper in one of the files today showing they sold the last three units five months ago. The deeds were transferred to the condo association a week later. I also took a look at their current projects. All of them are being subcontracted by legitimate, reputable companies."

"How current?"

"The permits were pulled in the past four months."

"Just after they unloaded The River Towers. They're covering their asses for a while."

"It's also about the same time Marc discovered the discrepancies."

Jason read the files I'd found on Bill's computer referring to the scandal along with my notes on the interview while we waited for room service. To my amazement, dinner arrived in less than thirty minutes.

"Award-winning architect gets preferential treatment," I murmured, taking a seat.

"Award-winning architect paying eight hundred dollars a night for a suite gets preferential treatment," he corrected with a smile.

We concentrated on eating and talking about the similarities between Los Angeles and South Florida until the conversation drifted toward Marc.

"What I can't understand is why my brother was in an alley," Jason said, cleaning up the last of his fries.

"And why that alley? There are plenty of alleys close to his home."

"Why an alley at all? What's wrong with a bar or a restaurant, or even the mall?"

"Could Marc have had a mole in the company?" I asked.

"You mean someone gathering information, and then passing it along to him?" Jason shrugged with a thoughtful expression on his face. "Possibly. It would look suspicious for him to work late every night or even a couple of nights a week."

I finished my burger before dipping a fry into the ketchup. "Maybe Marc wanted to meet me there because it was familiar territory, like he'd used it before."

"But why there? It's miles from his home."

"And why all the cloak and dagger? Why a key? Why not just hand me the CD?" I paused. "Maybe that alley was convenient for the mole. Maybe he or she lived close by."

"Who? A secretary?" Jason wondered.

"A secretary would only have access to files in the department where she worked, not the entire company. And aren't most offices locked at night?" I stiffened as a thought came to me. "I wonder…"

"You wonder what?"

"Who is the one person who *has* to have keys to all the offices?"

"I don't know—security, the building supervisor, maintenance, jani…" He stopped, his eyes opening wide.

My heart rate accelerated. Had we stumbled onto the answer? "The cleaning service has to have access to all the offices. It would be simple to pay one or more of the crew to rifle the files for the information, slip into the copy room for a minute, and then replace the material. When the mole was finished, he'd call Marc and they'd meet, exchanging money for papers. But what about security cameras?"

He rose and paced a few steps. "The building has one in the hallway outside the office, and S and H has one in the reception foyer. I haven't noticed any others, but obviously the parking garage has one somewhere."

"Marc tells the mole which files to pull and copy. He or she either takes the copies home or leaves them on Marc's desk or in some accessible spot and that's it. Done in less than five minutes."

"And very few of the file drawers are locked because offices are. Shelley, you're a genius."

He laughed and pulled me from my chair, kissed me lightly, then ceased laughing. His eyes narrowed and my heart thumped harder. With a small groan, his lips covered mine.

In an instant replay of the other night, the heat gushed through my body, and I gave in to whatever would occur.

Jason's tongue danced with mine and when his hand unbuttoned my blouse, my nipples tightened into hard buds. He shoved the garment down my arms and made fast work of my bra. I struggled out of the straps tossing the clothing onto the floor, and then tugged his polo shirt over his head. It joined the growing pile at our feet.

I ran my fingers through the mat of dark hair on his chest before reaching down to unbuckle his belt, no easy task with his erection straining against his fly. I wasted no time lowering the zipper and plunging my hand inside to surround and stroke the swollen shaft.

He groaned, bent me back over his arm, and clamped his mouth over my breast. A tremendous throb from my core reminded me how long it had been since I'd felt this good.

His nimble fingers had my skirt undone when my cell phone rang.

"Damn," I muttered, breathless.

"Ignore it," he replied, his voice raspy.

"I can't. I'm supposed to be available."

I stepped back and clutched my loosened skirt, then scrambled for the phone, tripping over the pile of clothing we'd discarded. It was after nine o'clock. Who'd be calling me now? Caller ID showed it to be the office. "Hello?"

"Miss Jackson, this is Sam McAfee on the night desk. I caught something interesting on the police and fire scanners. Bill gave us a list of Shay and Holmes properties with instructions to monitor and call if anything came up. The Century Arms, a condo complex for seniors is burning like a torch. They've just called in the third alarm."

Chapter Eleven

My heart lurched. This was what I'd feared. Shitty construction endangering innocent people. *Oh God, please let everyone get out all right.*

"Where are they located?"

"In Port Royale, on Grayson just north of Balfour."

"I know where it is. Thanks, McAfee, I'll get right on it."

I hung up and turned to Jason. "A condo built by Shay and Holmes is going up in flames."

He grabbed his shirt. "Let's go."

We dressed, then raced from the hotel room to the elevator and hauled ass through the lobby. I had a fleeting image of the desk clerk frowning as we passed on the run. Lounge patrons gave us strange looks. We ignored them and barreled out the front door.

"Please tell me you didn't valet park," Jason commented. We paused to let a car drive past.

"Of course not," I said leading the way across the entry pavement. "I parked illegally in the restaurant parking lot."

I slung the laptop into the trunk, and then slid behind the wheel. Jason was still fastening his seat belt when I peeled onto the street. I dodged around traffic taking the shortest route.

Finding a three-alarm fire was easy. The angry red glow in the sky led us straight to The Century Condos. I screeched to a stop, and the two of us ran until the police stopped us.

The blaze had taken control, engulfing one of the five two-story buildings composing the complex. Shouting firefighters worked to save adjacent structures from igniting. Greedy flames shot through the roof and out of every window. Cascades of water arched in the air and plunged into the conflagration with diabolic hissing. Then the center portion of the roof collapsed spewing a shower of red hot embers into the smoky night sky. Screams and a few sobs erupted from the bystanders. The stench gagged me, and I was reminded of the night Marc's townhouse had burned. The end of another building fifty feet away smoldered, and the firemen trained their hoses on it.

"What kind of construction is it?" I asked.

"Cheap," Jason replied, a grim expression on his face. In the light of the fire, it gave him a satanic look— all angles and shadows. In spite of the heat being generated, I shivered. I'd seen enough. It was time to ask questions. I hurried to the nearest policeman.

"Please, officer, what happened?"

"Step back, lady."

"But you don't understand. My elderly uncle lives here. His name is Stephen King, and I think the building going up is his. I can't remember his unit number."

The cop jerked his chin toward a knot of people standing behind one of the fire trucks. "We got all the residents out. Check over there."

Silently thanking God no one was injured, I grabbed Jason's arm and led him to the fire rescue truck where most of the survivors congregated. A man stood alone on the fringe of the crowd. I headed in his direction.

"Excuse me, but I'm looking for my uncle. I think he lives in the building. His name is King."

The man gazed back with a dazed expression and for a moment, I didn't think he understood.

"Sorry, but I don't know anyone by that name—not here." He turned his attention back to the fire.

"Do you live in the building? What happened? How did it start?"

An elderly woman standing a few feet away answered. "It started in my apartment," she said, clutching a cat in her arms. "I live in one of the middle units downstairs. I was watching TV when suddenly I smelled something funny and heard crackling from behind the walls. I got up and touched the wall. It was red hot. Then smoke drifted out from under the baseboards and the outlets. I ran into the kitchen to call nine-one-one. When I finished, flames were crawling up the walls and across the ceiling."

"Good heavens, it certainly spread fast," I probed when she stopped for breath.

"You have no idea. I grabbed my cat and ran for my life. George here," she indicated the dazed man, "was just pulling into his parking space. He pounded on people's doors to alert them."

A paramedic approached the woman. I steered Jason to another couple. Tears slid down both of their faces.

We got basically the same story from them. By the time the first fire truck had arrived the entire building of ten units was fully involved.

"Sounds electrical," I said to Jason, backing away

to a less crowded location.

He looked at the remaining buildings. "These aren't that old. And my guess is there was no firewall between any of the units. Whatever the cause it's probably present in the other buildings, too. Come on, we can't help these people. Let's go back to the hotel. Are you going to write an article about this?"

"As soon as I get home. I'll e-mail it to Cal, so he can see it first thing in the morning."

As we drove away, I wondered if this was the first disaster of many. How many other ticking bombs existed courtesy of Shay and Holmes?

I dropped Jason off at the hotel, returned home, showered the stink of smoke from my hair and body, and wrote the article, then sent it off to Cal before stumbling into bed. Sleep, however, proved elusive. My mind kept swinging between the fire and the equally hot kisses Jason and I exchanged. If McAfee hadn't called when he did...I burrowed my head deeper into the pillow.

It had been an eventful night—on all levels.

****

I stepped into my cubicle the following morning invigorated and ready to bring down Shay and Holmes. I turned on the computer when the desk phone rang.

"Shelley, would you please come to my office?"

Shelley again—not Jackson. I sensed something serious coming and didn't think it was good news. I strode into his office with a confident step anyway.

"You wanted to see me? Did you get my article?"

"Yes. It's excellent. I made a couple of changes and sent it on with approval. Close the door."

I did as he asked and took a seat in front of his

desk. "What's wrong? You look like you've got bad news. Please don't tell me somebody else has died."

Cal shook his head. "Look, Shelley, you're a good reporter. According to Bill, you can become great. What you lack in experience, you make up for with instinct. By all rights, you should have Bill's job. I think Bill would have wanted it that way."

I held my breath and tried not to let my elation show. I'd be in charge. I'd have my own byline.

"But you're not going to get it."

Shit! "Why not?" Heat radiated from my face.

Cal's gaze refused to meet mine. For the first time since I'd known him, I sensed embarrassment.

"Is it because I'm a woman?" I couldn't keep the angry tone out of my voice.

"No!" he barked, finally looking at me. "No, I have to give it to someone else."

"Who?" Okay, I could *try* and work with an outsider, especially if he or she was on the ball.

He shifted in his seat and said, "Doug Elliott."

Shock rippled through me. I stared in disbelief. Then the shock gave way, replaced by a bubble of anger that grew in my chest until erupting.

"You've got to be fucking kidding!" I leaped to my feet and slammed my fist on his desk. "He's no more qualified than a roof rat. I will not work for him. Consider *this* my resignation."

I grabbed a book from his desk and hurled it against the wall missing his head by inches. Cal had the good sense to duck.

"Shelley, simmer down. I had no choice in the matter. His aunt talked to Miriam Noble at the funeral and convinced the old bat to give her 'up and coming *and* highly talented' nephew the job."

"Highly talented! The fucking moron can't even write an accurate obituary. Plus, the little bastard is a pervert. He can't keep his hands to himself."

"I know, I know, but *my* hands are tied—at least for now."

"What do you mean?"

"I told Miriam Elliott was unqualified for the position, but she insisted. I also told her that I could not in all good conscience compromise the integrity of *The Standard* by placing him in charge when he's not ready. I hit her where she lives—in the purse, explaining that if the quality takes a dive, so do her profits."

I fisted my hands on my hips and glared. "And?"

"I asked her to make the promotion conditional for six months. If he proves he can handle the job, it's his. If not, I have the discretion to replace him. She finally agreed."

"Well, don't expect me to carry his ass. I'll sabotage the little cretin at every opportunity, and I don't care if you fire *me*."

Cal leaned back and smiled. "Do whatever you think is best."

I absorbed the implication and my anger drained away. "You want me to screw him over?"

"I want you to continue investigating Shay and Holmes. Write your articles and send them directly to me. If he gives you any grief, tell him those are my orders."

"All right, but if he so much as lays one hand on me, I'll file for sexual harassment."

Cal winced. "Try not to do that. It would be bad for the paper's image. Handle it yourself." Cal leaned forward and smiled. "We both know how it's going to end."

"Does he know about this yet?"

"Not from me, but I'm sure his aunt has clued him in. Now, go pretend we haven't had this conversation and for crying out loud, don't let him have Bill's notes."

****

I was back in my cubicle writing a follow-up on the fire when Doug walked in.

"I guess you've heard the news. I'm your boss."

"Yeah, Cal told me this morning. Congratulations."

"I'm moving into Bill's office. As soon as I'm settled I want all of his notes on this bribery thing on my desk."

"No can do," I replied continuing to type and not bothering to raise my head from the keyboard or even turn around. I'd once heard some cultures considered presenting your back to a foe as the ultimate insult.

"And why not?" Doug's voice took on an arrogant tone.

"Because I don't have them."

"Of course, you have them. Quit stonewalling. Whether you like it or not, I'm your boss and if you want to continue working here, you'll do what I tell you."

"I gave everything back to Bill the afternoon before he died. I assume they're on his computer."

The police had returned Bill's desktop a day or two earlier. I typed another sentence listening to Doug's breathing accelerate.

"I can't get into his computer. I don't have the password."

"Oh, really? Try 'Murrow' or 'Cronkite.' Those were his two favorite newsmen, but I wouldn't hold my breath. The police have already scanned the computer and said Bill must have deleted his files."

"Why would he do that?"

I shrugged and adjusted a comma. "I have no idea. Maybe he transferred everything to his laptop."

"I can't find that either. And where's his recorder and the discs he kept?"

"Maybe whoever killed him stole them."

"Then how am I going to investigate?"

Doug was too stupid to call our IT department. They'd have the hard drive out in no time and the files recovered. I'd looked at most of them. They contained nothing screaming the killer's name.

"Well, I guess you'll just have to work for a change."

Doug strode behind me and jerked my chair around. His face was mottled red with temper. He held me in place with his hands on the chair's arms.

"You know, Shelley, it would be in your best interests not to fight me. A little more cooperation would do wonders for your career."

He leaned down and let his fleshy lips hover an inch from mine. Disgusted, I raised my hands and shoved him hard in the chest. My action loosened his grip and sent him staggering back a couple of feet.

"Don't touch me. If you do or even look like you will, I'll file sexual harassment charges," I said with a hiss.

"You bitch. I'll have you fired if you do."

"Try it, and see just how nasty my lawyer can be. I'll end up owning this place and can *your* ass."

Doug straightened, ran his hand down the front of his shirt, and took a couple of deep breaths.

"I demand respect and cooperation. I have an assignment for you. There's a bar called The Bad Ass Dog on West Highland Boulevard. A friend of mine told me the owner is trying to soften the biker image. Go out there at noon and get the details. I want the story on my desk by five tonight." He turned on his heel and disappeared.

The Bad Ass Dog? It was more than just a biker bar. Drug sales and gang activity were centered from the place. The cops could count on being called out to break up fights and investigate gunfire on a regular basis. Who was Doug kidding? I wanted to laugh. The poor jerk didn't even have the imagination to set me up with a decent payback assignment for The Haven.

I immediately logged in to the archives and gleaned a few scraps of information about the bar, then wrote the most ridiculous article I could. I gave a song and dance about new décor and security guards. I finished it off with a description of new landscaping. I'd send it about four o'clock and wait for the explosion sure to follow. If nothing else, I would be guaranteed a laugh and a long lunch hour.

I enjoyed a leisurely lunch on Riverside where I contacted Sharon Ireland, whose family had once owned the land the River Tower Condos now occupied, to set up an interview for the next day. She sounded like a nice woman who had more than a bit of resentment bottled up toward the city of Port Royale. She now lived in the town of Westover and invited me for lunch.

It was after two-thirty when I strolled back into the newsroom. Doug was ensconced in Bill's office like a king working on the computer, no doubt trying to unlock its mysteries. A second computer, his I guessed, sat on a side table. I chuckled and entered my cubicle, then finished the follow-up fire story, which I sent directly to Cal. With time on my hands, I called Jason, leaving a message to join me at my place for dinner. Then I called Chef Rene for an order of salmon pinwheels with all the accompaniments.

An hour later, I was sitting in the break room with my feet propped up on a chair reading a magazine when Doug walked in, scowling.

"What are you doing here? Do you have the article I assigned?"

I looked up and shrugged one shoulder before gazing back at the magazine.

"Sure, I just finished it. I'm taking a little break."

"So, how did it go? Did you get a good reception?" The gleam in his eyes told me he hoped I'd been roughed up and fondled.

"No problem. I borrowed a friend's Harley and drove right up. I met the owner, Bad John Rankovich. We compared tattoos—I've got a great one on my ass—and he answered my questions. He even asked me out. I may take him up on the offer. I don't know yet."

Anyone in their right mind would know bullshit when they stepped in it, but not Doug Elliott. He may have suspected I exaggerated, but still bought it.

"Fine," he snapped. "Have it on my desk immediately."

I tossed the magazine onto the table and rose. "Sure, I'll e-mail it to you now. Oh, by the way, I have a doctor's appointment, so I have to leave by four-thirty."

I sauntered into my cubicle and sent the article. I doubted he'd bother to read it, but was certain his name would replace mine. Cal, of course, would reject it.

Ten minutes later that's what happened. Cal called Doug in and the whole office heard it. I left before the fireworks ended.

****

Jason arrived on time at seven-thirty carrying two bottles of wine—one red and one white.

"I'm covering all bases," he said with a smile when I accepted them.

I laughed. "We're dining on salmon tonight, so I guess that means both."

"How was your day?"

I told him of the developments at the paper while he mixed the martinis. He followed me into the kitchen and sat at the table before I could remove the take home bag from Chef Rene's. He picked it up, laughing.

"Chef Rene's Take Home Kitchen?"

Busted! I gave him a look and confessed. "Okay, cooking's not my strong suit." To prove my point, I rescued the cooking instructions from the trash and tossed them onto the counter. Following the directions, I slid the salmon into the oven.

"Do you want to impress me that much?" he asked, taking a sip of his drink.

I strolled over, removed the glass from his hand, and set it on the table. Then I planted myself on his lap, wound my arms around his neck, and kissed the hell out of him.

"Hmm, consider me impressed," he murmured.

"With my cooking?"

"You have so many talents, my dear Miss Jackson.

I'm impressed with all of them."

He ran his hand up my rib cage and over my breast. His fingers tightened sending a jolt of electricity to every extremity I possessed. A timer dinged reminding me to microwave the green beans.

"Oh, no you don't, buster. Not yet. I refuse to have dinner spoiled—not at Chef Rene's prices."

I slid off his lap, his chuckle following me across the kitchen before he sobered. "So, you have a new boss who's a moron and both you and your editor are sabotaging him from the get-go."

"It's no way to run a business, but then Miriam Noble is no businesswoman. She inherited the paper and hasn't got a clue." I set the timer for the beans and slipped the new potatoes with garlic and parsley into a bowl.

"Be careful or you'll both end up unemployment statistics."

"Miriam may be dumb about some things, but she knows Calvin Randolph is one of the best editors going. Without him, the paper would suffer and Miriam likes the profits. With readership declining for print media nationwide, he's safe as judges."

"Are you?"

"Who knows? How did your day go?" I joined him at the table, sipping my martini.

"Very productive. I spent a large portion of the morning with the head of human resources, Helen Goddard. She's been with Shay and Holmes for over twenty-five years. She knew my father and after some careful probing, told me she can't wait to retire next year."

"Complete with a gold watch and a plaque

thanking her for her service?"

"She wouldn't take a damned thing from either Brad Holmes or Kenneth Shay. She hates their guts. According to Helen, the past three years has seen a marked downward spiral of benefits even though the company is making huge profits. Health insurance is minimal. She also gave me the name of the janitorial service and the man to contact. I called and left a message. He's on vacation, but due back next week."

"Good work. If you ever get tired of architecture you can be a reporter."

The microwave timer dinged. I stirred the vegetables and resumed my seat, pushing the corkscrew and the red wine in Jason's direction. "Dinner will be ready in a few minutes."

"Terrific. I'm hungry." He opened the wine, releasing the cork with a satisfying pop. "I also snooped in finance."

"Talk about being careful."

"I chose to do it while most of the bigwigs were in an internal affairs meeting. I struck up a conversation with a guy who worked with Marc in Accounts Payable. He says there are problems."

"What kind of problems?" I rose to set the table.

"I was asking about the construction on the recent permits pulled. The guy said there have been massive cost overruns and work stoppages due to several failed inspections."

"You mean they're relying on honest building inspectors? That seems out of character," I said, setting the silverware on the placemats.

Jason shrugged. "Maybe Bill's article or Marc's activities scared them. They could be biting the bullet until the dust settles. The fire last night also got me to thinking about insurance, so I asked a few questions in that department, too."

"Why would Shay and Holmes need insurance on The Century Arms?"

"They wouldn't, but they still own a lot of property like Garden Acres and the strip mall we visited."

All of my timers went off and the conversation ceased while I served up the meal. Chef Rene had done it again. The pinwheels were perfect and the crabmeat stuffing seasoned just right. The potatoes and the green beans complemented the fish and I wondered if Chef Rene would consider moving in. I sipped the wine, and brought the talk back to business.

"We were discussing insurance. Are the apartments and the shopping center insured?"

"To the hilt along with more properties scattered throughout the county. And get this; each policy is with a different carrier. Sometimes the same property with a *couple* of different companies. The payoffs in case of fire are enormous."

"More than the structures are worth?"

He nodded and sipped his wine. "Way over insured."

"Would they deliberately put people's lives in danger by setting a fire?" The specter of arson and Marc's townhouse, not to mention my own home, flashed through my mind.

"I honestly don't know, but if S and H needed quick cash that would be the way to get it, even if they had to negotiate with the insurance company—or companies—for a lower payoff."

We ate in silence for a few more minutes when I

brought up a subject that had bugged me since the fundraiser.

"Jason, what can you tell me about the people in the finance department? If a CEO or COO is going to cook the books, wouldn't they have to have the cooperation of the CFO or at least a couple of accountants?"

"Definitely." He wiped his lips with a napkin, drank the rest of his wine, and refilled the glass. "Ken Shay was appointed Chief Operating Officer a few days after his father died. About a year later, Dad told me he and Brad performed a major overhaul of the finance department. The Chief Financial Officer and the Head of Accounting, both longtime employees, bit the big one. Lynnette Palmer moved into the office with a majority of the votes from the Board of Directors."

"Majority?"

"Dad voted no. She didn't have the credentials."

"Which were?" I asked, finishing, and then refilling my wine glass.

"She had worked as an accountant in a large CPA firm up in Boca for close to fifteen years."

"Wait a minute. She went from accountant to CFO? Skipped a few steps along the way, didn't she? What kind of idiots sit on the board? No offense to your father."

"None taken. Most of the board members are retired. They'll agree to anything as long as they can get on the golf course by noon. Her abilities were highly touted by Ken Shay."

"She does what she's told with no questions asked."

"That's my guess. And while we're on the subject,

Dennis Birdsong, the Head of Accounting, moved up from an accountant's position at the same time."

"Setting the stage for massive fraud."

I told him about my encounter with her prior to my interview, including her nervous attitude.

"I'm not surprised. The woman is in way over her head," he replied.

I picked up our empty plates and Jason helped with the brief clean up. Afterward, we settled onto the sofa in the living room with the last of the wine.

"Who was the drunk at the party? The one who ogled my boobs."

He grinned and slid along the cushions, hooked a finger into the top of my shirt, pulling it away from my neck, and cast his gaze downward.

"That would be me." He kissed the pulse point in my neck, sending an instant shot of heat shimmering along my nerves. "Or perhaps you're referring to Dexter Marshall?"

"Marshall, you idiot," I said, trying to stay focused on the conversation, no mean task. His hand had slipped under my top and his quick fingers released the front catch of my bra. He shoved the material aside and palmed my breast, his thumb circling the nipple with a gentle touch.

"Hmm, you smell good. Dexter Marshall is Chairman of the Board and an old drinking buddy of Tim Shay's. He does what he's told, too."

His answer had been whispered in my ear and now he took the opportunity to nibble on it. I didn't give a rat's ass about the board of directors of Shay and Holmes. The familiar fire in my belly had been stoked from a warm glow to a burning urgency I had no intention of ignoring. I managed to find the coffee table with my glass, then grasped Jason's head and proceeded to put a sloppy, wet lip lock on him.

When we came up for air, he hauled me to my feet and slung me over his shoulder like a caveman with a prize.

"Where's the bedroom?"

"Through there," I pointed down the hallway.

Jason covered the distance with long strides and unceremoniously dumped me on the bed. "We were interrupted last night. Let's hope we aren't tonight. I want to take it slow."

The promise of slow left me breathless and dizzy. He pulled his shirt over his head and I stroked his hard muscled chest.

I helped him remove my top and bra. He straddled my hips and captured my hands with his, holding them above my head while he kissed and licked first one breast then the other. When he suckled the sensitive tips, several deep throbbing contractions rippled through my core.

I gasped and cried out. My God, he'd brought me to orgasm with barely a touch. I wiggled my hips wanting more. He released my hands, laughing against my skin, and unbuttoned my jeans, slowly sliding them and my panties down my legs. He tossed both on the floor. Beginning at my ankles he kissed and nipped his way back up my body until he stopped at the junction of my thighs. Jason spread my legs wide and found the throbbing little bud with his tongue.

I cried out again. Clutching the bedspread with my fists, I dug my heels into the mattress and lifted my hips. I had no rational thought, but begged him not to stop.

He didn't, and within seconds I climaxed again hard, the raw pleasure washing back and forth through my body like waves on the shore. I know I screamed, twisting and writhing to get everything possible from the ecstasy.

Jason swung off the bed and quickly shed the rest of his clothing. Taking a packet from his pocket, he sheathed himself, and returned to my still wide open thighs, plunging inside and stroking slowly. My hands loosened their grip on the linens to caress his shoulders and back, the muscles bunching and relaxing with every move. I buried my face in his neck inhaling the musky, male scent.

He increased the pace. The bed creaked and groaned under our pounding bodies, adding another sound to the room besides our labored breathing and hoarse cries of pleasure.

"Oh, God! Yes!" I shrieked.

I locked my ankles around his waist and pumped my hips to his rhythm. Fire licked along every nerve, the coiled spring within me winding tighter until it reached the point of no return. I erupted like Mt. Vesuvius, screaming and sobbing. Jason followed within seconds, shouting and lunging even deeper.

Finished, he collapsed and lay beside me. My heart hammered in my ears and my lungs demanded air. Next to me, his breath rasped in and out. Neither of us spoke.

Jason picked up my hand, kissing the palm. I turned my head. He was still hard. My gaze traveled to his face. He smiled and squeezed my hand. "Give me a couple of minutes to catch my breath."

"You've got to be kidding." I never remembered

experiencing multiple orgasms in my life. Now he was suggesting more?

"Lady, there are some things I never kid about."

He reached for me again, and the night swirled away in a whirlpool of pleasure.

Chapter Twelve

I smoothed my skirt and entered the Mayor's office for my interview at precisely nine o'clock. A woman in her mid-forties with a no-nonsense expression clearly stating, "No appointment, no access" greeted me. She checked a book on her desk before indicating I have a seat while she picked up the phone. A minute later, Howard Whitman emerged from an inner office.

"Nice of you to be on time, Miss Jackson," he said, leading me across the spacious waiting room to a heavy oak door. "You have exactly thirty minutes. Mayor Cosworth is due at a meeting in Preston Lakes at ten."

"I understand."

He opened the door, announcing, "Miss Jackson of *The South Florida Standard* to see you, Mr. Mayor."

He stepped aside. The Mayor rose from behind his desk and advanced to shake hands, a welcoming smile on his face.

"Miss Jackson, I'm glad we're getting an opportunity to talk. Please, be seated."

He resumed his seat while I sat in an armchair in front of his desk, set up my recorder, and fired the first question.

"Mr. Mayor, as you know, the South Street nightclub and Riverside districts attract a lot of tourists. The recent spate of muggings and a murder in the area have some business owners nervous. Could you please comment on that?"

He launched into an impassioned speech about how the area was a mecca not only for tourists, but for residents as well.

"I've instructed the police department to step up patrols in both areas and along the beach. Our economy depends on people having a good time. Those areas are dining and nightlife destinations. The recent residential construction has also provided new life to a tired downtown area. We can't allow the criminal element to take control."

He left the door wide open, and I stepped through. "There have been a huge number of high rise condominiums going up all over Port Royale. Some people claim they're being bought by speculators."

"Speculators pay taxes, just like the rest of us."

"Yes, but the Seminole River is lined with condos and the beachfront is going the same way. Parking lots are disappearing and locals fear they're being squeezed out of beach activities. It seems excessive in an over-expanded and now depressed real estate market."

"Progress is measured in dollars and cents, Miss Jackson. Port Royale can't afford to be left behind," the Mayor stated, steepling his hands under his chin. "I have faith the markets will return to normal levels soon. Empty units will be sold."

"I understand the land The River Tower Condos now occupies was some kind of legacy to the city. I was under the impression it was to be used for a park."

A frown marred his brow, and he shifted in his chair. My comment must have caught him off guard.

"Yes, that's true, but in the end we decided a park was unnecessary. There are several other parks nearby, all of which are on the river."

"Plus, the city was having a financial crisis at the time," I added.

"I wouldn't refer to it as a crisis. We needed to budget carefully, yes. That's why we elected not to build another park. Parks must be maintained, and we had cut down on municipal staff."

"I've heard it said the city had a shortfall because too much money was put into pension and other retirement programs for city workers, including the council and their staffs."

The frown turned into a scowl. "That's a lie. The city survived two hurricanes in as many years. We took care of our citizens and the infrastructure. The money from selling the land helped."

"And you sold it to Shay and Holmes for—let me check my notes. Ah, yes, here it is—thirty-five million dollars?"

"I believe that was the final number. I thought you were here to discuss crime, Miss Jackson."

"Shay and Holmes seems to be the preferred developer and contractor of the city, Mayor Cosworth," I continued, ignoring his complaint.

"The city has always been proud of our relationship with Shay and Holmes. It goes back many years."

"But weren't you distressed at the size of The River Tower Condos and the severe lack of parking for the upscale retail establishments on the ground floor?"

"Once the land was sold, the city was no longer involved. And there's plenty of parking available."

"At ten dollars a pop. There are rumors to the effect Shay and Holmes cut corners on construction."

With lips thinned into a stern line and flared nostrils, his eyes widened ever so slightly. I knew only years of public relations and political experience kept his temper from exploding.

"I wouldn't know anything about that. As mayor, I can honestly say the city has no comment on rumors." He looked at his watch and rose. "I'm sorry, but your time is up. Thank you so much for coming."

According to my watch, I had plenty of time left, but decided not to push it. Besides, I wasn't going to get any more out of him.

I scrambled to stow my equipment in my purse and he escorted me to the door. I had barely stepped through when it closed behind me with a polite, but controlled thud, telling me not to call for another interview.

I nodded to the receptionist and took my leave. As I walked down the hall to the elevators, a bubble of satisfaction grew inside me at the thought Bill and I had been right. I wondered how many city council members sat snug and secure in Shay and Holmes's pocket. And was the mayor one of them?

****

I found the nearest coffee house with WiFi access and set up shop in a corner. Avoiding the office and Doug, I decided to write the story while it was fresh in my mind. The recording provided verbal accuracy, but my brain remembered the facial expressions.

I ordered breakfast and wrote the piece, using quotes as often as possible with the end result being a good article. I double checked my facts, and then e-mailed it to Cal.

Next, I surfed the web searching for the phone

numbers and contact names of city council members. I'd try to set up interviews with each of them, too. Their responses would be interesting.

Sooner or later, I'd have to return to the office. That might be the best time to catch a break with the political powers-that-be. I picked later—after my interview with Sharon Ireland.

I turned my attention to the cities of Sunshine Beach and Palmetto Gardens. It took a while, but I finally found the names of the inspectors of The Leisure Time Motel and Iguanawana in public records.

By and large building inspectors are overworked and underpaid. Still, I was surprised to see that all major inspections—with the exception of electrical— had been done by the same inspector in each municipality. Normally, it didn't work that way, but if the building department was small or short-handed, I could see it happening.

On a hunch, I called the building inspector's offices in Palmetto Gardens.

"Inspections Office, how may I help you?" The person answering the phone sounded harried. Voices babbled in the background.

"Hello. Could I please speak with Joseph Sawyer? He's an inspector."

"Joseph Sawyer?" The woman on the other end paused. "I'm sorry, ma'am, but no one by that name works here."

"Are you sure? I need an inspection done and was told he's one of the best. I'd like him to come out and give me a final on my house addition."

"That's not the way we do it, ma'am. This is not a radio station. We don't take requests. You take whoever is next on the list. Now, if you'll give me your name, address, and permit number, I'll have someone out in a couple of days."

"But Joseph Sawyer does work there, doesn't he?"

"Just a minute," she said with an exaggerated sigh. Not bothering to cover the mouthpiece she hollered, "Hey, anyone here know a Joseph Sawyer...Yeah? Well, talk to this woman, would you?"

A second later, a man came on the line. "Joseph Sawyer no longer works here."

"Do you know where I can find him?"

"He up and retired a couple of years ago. Came into an inheritance and scrammed. He went to live near his kids in Texas somewhere."

"Oh, I see. How about Randall Cashman?" I asked naming the electrical inspector.

"Quit a few months ago and moved. Don't know where."

Dead end. "Okay, thanks."

I hung up. An inheritance? *Yeah, right, and I'm Miss America.*

I tried Sunshine Beach next with much the same results. Bart Winters had "won" a hunk of cash in the lottery and relocated "somewhere in the Caribbean." His good fortune occurred about the same time the motel was finished. The electrical inspector on that project was also no longer in the area.

All of them had the good sense to take the money and run. I wondered how many Port Royale inspectors had opted for early retirement in the last couple of years.

I had time to kill, and needing a break, ordered another cup of coffee. While I sipped, staring into space, and reliving last night's action packed moments with Jason. God, he was fantastic—a sexual dynamo who managed to pull me along in his wake. Just when I thought I couldn't possibly come again, I had—more times than I'd thought possible.

Hope I haven't used up my lifetime quota of orgasms. The woman who finally nails him down in holy matrimony will be guaranteed a never-ending smile on her face. Wonder if it could be me?

Surprised at the directions of my thoughts, I sat back to analyze them. *Why shouldn't it be me?*

Number one, we were great in bed—enough said. Number two, Jason was as tough and career oriented as me. He understood my passion for work, and while the distance thing could present problems, I had no doubts we could work it out. One of the articles I'd read said he might open another office in the Miami area.

And lastly, I liked his take charge attitude. He was always in control, a quality I desired in a man, provided it didn't mean relinquishing any of *my* control. So far, that hadn't been a problem. I mentally shrugged. *Worry about it later.*

I couldn't believe I was thinking along these lines. Me and marriage? With Jason Mallory? Oh, crap, we were made for each other. Okay, it was a cliché, but clichés were sometimes true. I shivered, but whether in fear or excitement, I wasn't sure. Marriage meant commitment. *Am I ready for that? I'm a big girl. I don't need a piece of paper or a ring on my finger for great sex. Yet I like the thought of him being bound to me and only me.* I shook my head. *Think about that later, too.*

I put Jason Mallory out of my mind for the

moment, finished my coffee, and packed up my gear. The next stop was Westover and my luncheon interview with Sharon Ireland. If I got lucky and Cal was in a good mood, I might have both interviews published next to one another in tomorrow's edition.

I left the café with a spring in my step only to stop when the creepy sensation I was being watched tickled the back of my neck. I turned and surveyed the sidewalk. Just people walking—some fast, others with cell phones pressed against their ears. I shrugged. Imagination in overdrive.

****

"Miss Jackson? Won't you come in?" Sharon Ireland said, opening the front door to her palatial home.

"Thank you, Ms. Ireland. I appreciate your agreeing to the interview."

I stepped into a large foyer. Directly ahead was a great room with the emphasis on "great." It looked to be thirty feet square and the furnishings, though casual, were expensive. Beyond the wall-to-wall French doors, I glimpsed the shimmering water of an opulent swimming pool.

"Please, call me Sharon. You're Shelley, right?"

"Yes."

She turned, leading me through the great room into a well-appointed kitchen and eating area. "I was surprised to hear from Dave you wanted to interview me. I thought that business between the family and the city was old news."

"Well, you know the saying, 'Everything old is new again.' I guess it applies here. Have you read any of the articles lately regarding Shay and Holmes?"

"Not really. Once the property was sold and we lost the lawsuit, I didn't pay much attention to what happened." She opened another pair of French doors leading onto a screened lanai. "I thought we'd eat first, if that's all right with you."

"Fine," I replied, sitting at a round patio table already set. A buffet along the wall held a pitcher of iced tea and a bowl of fruit.

"I'll be right back," she said.

Her absence gave me the opportunity to inspect the back yard. The house bordered a lake, its waters ruffled by a breeze. A small sailboat lazily bobbed its way down the far shore and nearby, ducks swam.

Sharon returned with a large tray bearing salads. She set one in front of me and filled two glasses with tea. She was about my height and slim. Her dark hair was styled in a short gamin cut. Blue eyes gazed at me in a forthright manner. I had the feeling this woman would not mince either her words or opinions.

"If you need refills on anything, just help yourself."

"What a lovely view. Have you lived here long?" I asked, spearing a piece of lettuce.

"In this house, about three years. My husband and I built it in protest. I refused to give one more dime in taxes to the city of Port Royale."

"I take it you're a native."

"Oh, yes, my father was Ephraim Hancock. Are you familiar with the name?"

"Can't say that I am."

"In that case, I'll give you a brief family history. My great-great-grandfather Noah Hancock came to the area in the last years of the nineteenth century. He built the first inn for travelers, developed a ferry service across the river, and lived above his hardware store."

"So he was one of the first settlers?"

She nodded. "My great-grandfather, grandfather, and father carried on the merchant tradition. The piece of property in question was the last bit remaining of a once very large landholding. I'll get to that later. Tell me about yourself."

I spent the next twenty minutes giving her the life history of Shelley Jackson. The food was delicious and a change of pace from the usual sandwiches. When we finished, I brought out my recorder and notepad. Refreshing my iced tea, I probed further into her family history.

"What can you tell me about the land the River Tower Condos now occupies?"

"It was the site of Noah's first business establishment and the last remaining parcel of many throughout the city. Riverside has always been a center for retail stores, but over the years it had fallen on hard times like most downtown areas. When the city revealed plans to revitalize the area, my father was thrilled. Daddy died twelve years ago and Mother continued to collect rent from our tenants in the shops situated on the property."

"How did the city come to own the land?"

"My mother passed away six years ago. In her will, she suggested donating the land to the city in return for building a park to honor the Hancock name."

"And you and your family weren't angry? That must have represented a lot of your inheritance. The land is worth a fortune."

Sharon waved a hand and gulped iced tea. "The

money didn't matter. We had plenty of it. But the thought of honoring our ancestors tickled our fancies or egos, if you prefer."

"So, how come there are condos and no park?"

Her eyes darkened and her jaw set. "The bastards accepted, and then reneged. At first they told us they had to wait for the tenants' leases to expire. A couple of them were long-term, but finally the buildings were empty and demolished within a few months."

"Did you have any contact with city officials or lawyers during this time?"

"Not really," she said shaking her head. "We had signed all the necessary papers when the city agreed to the transfer. Call us stupid or naïve, but we honestly expected a park to be built."

"What happened?"

"The property sat for a long time with no action. When I called, I was told certain budget restraints were in the way, but not to worry, progress would soon be made. Progress my ass," she spat out, rising to refill her glass.

I followed suit and when we were seated again, she continued.

"I often shopped on Riverside and one day I drove past the site and saw a sign bearing the likeness of a soaring tower of concrete and glass with the words, 'Future home of The River Tower Condominiums by Shay and Holmes Development and Construction.' I hit the roof. I called the city and was told the land had been sold. Then I called my lawyer."

"I take it they had covered their asses?"

"With circus tents," Sharon replied, her tone bitter. "The court decided the language in Mother's will was 'ambiguous' as they put it. 'In the hope of establishing' was not considered binding. If you look closely today, you can see a small plaque embedded in cement at the base of a palm tree off to the far side of the property. It states this is the site of the first inn built in Port Royale by Noah Hancock. That's it." She gulped her entire glass of tea. "Bastards had the gall to invite me to the dedication ceremonies when the condos were done. I told them to go to hell."

"Which bastards?"

She laughed. "All of them—the developers and the politicians."

"So, you're boycotting the city of Port Royale?"

"As much as I can. If they charged a one cent toll to drive through, I'd drive a hundred miles out of my way to avoid paying it."

"What was the reaction from the public at the usurping of your mother's wishes?" I made a mental note to check our archives for past editorials and letters to the editor.

"A lot of people supported us, but in the end it didn't matter. The fucking condos were built, Shay and Holmes made money, the city made money, and my family got a shitty plaque hidden from view."

I turned off the recorder, putting it and my pad of paper away, giving Sharon a few moments to collect herself.

I rose and held out my hand. "I can't thank you enough for agreeing to see me and for a delicious lunch. It's been a long time since I've had such a lovely interview."

She grasped my hand. "No, the pleasure is all mine. It won't make any difference, but I love to needle the city however I can."

Her comment about the city and S and H making money tightened the bond between the two entities. I was convinced they were hand in glove concerning other activities as well.

I pulled out of her gated community and headed back to the office checking my rearview mirror as I made lane changes. I noticed a black sedan with tinted windows several car lengths behind me. Some gut instinct made me suspicious. It was always there, never getting closer or falling back.

I turned right at the next stoplight. So did it. I turned left a couple of blocks later. It followed.

My heart pounded and I gripped the steering wheel hard. I made more turns, but the sedan stayed with me. In spite of the air-conditioning a trickle of sweat ran between my breasts. I had no idea what to do. Stay on surface streets? Head for the interstate? Pull in somewhere? The faces of Marc and Bill flashed through my head.

Then ahead of me I spotted a police car. I sped up and blew past it twenty miles an hour over the limit. The lights came on and I pulled over. The black sedan passed by, turning left at the next corner. Had it been following me or was my imagination in high gear?

The cop walked up to my window. "Driver's license, registration, and proof of insurance, please, ma'am. Do you know how fast you were going?"

"Not a clue," I answered, handing him the items. "But I do have an excuse. I think that black sedan was following me."

"Black sedan? What black sedan?"

"The one that was following me. It went on and

turned left at the corner."

"Uh-huh. That's one of the better excuses I've heard in a while. Almost as good as the old I-have-to-go-to-the-bathroom routine."

"But it's true!"

"Sit tight while I run this."

He strutted back to the squad car while I fumed. *Damn all cops to hell.* On the other hand, the black car was gone and not likely to resume surveillance, if indeed it ever had been tailing me. The driver would have no idea what I told the cop or if my story would be believed. The smart thing to do was take off.

I accepted the ticket and drove back to the office, keeping a close eye on my rearview mirror. No black car with tinted windows appeared.

****

Back at the paper, I didn't see Doug anywhere and hurried to Cal's office. He motioned me in with a gesture to close the door while cradling the phone against his cheek and shoulder. I took a seat.

"Did you get my interview with the Mayor?" I asked when he hung up.

"Yeah, good stuff. It could stoke a few old embers. If I remember correctly, the park-condo thing was editorial and letters-to-the-editor fodder for months. A dozen different lawsuits were filed by everybody from the family to preservationists and environmentalists, but they all got squashed."

"I just came from Sharon Ireland's house. Give me an hour or so and I'll have her story, too. Where's Doug? I half expected him to leap all over me for being AWOL."

"He stomped in here demanding I dock you pay for

being late. I told him you were on assignment for me. I also told him that before he could give orders, he had to prove to me he could conduct an interview and write a decent article. I sent him down to the flea market with orders to talk to vendors. It should keep him busy for a while." Cal leaned back and fiddled with a pencil. "Shelley, in spite of my misgivings about your lack of experience, I'm going to let you continue investigating. Do you have anything new?"

I brought Cal up to speed on my suspicions about the building inspectors in Sunshine Beach and Palmetto Gardens, and told him I would check into those in Port Royale. I also told him Bill's files hadn't revealed anything we didn't already know. I didn't tell him about the black sedan. Now that I thought about it, I had no evidence the driver was following me.

"All right, but be careful *and* discreet. Bill wasn't much for subtlety and look where it got him. Even the most experienced reporters can find themselves in trouble. Keep your eyes open and your ass covered. Play it smart."

I was kind of touched by his concern. He must have seen something on my face for his manner changed back to curmudgeon. He quit twirling the pencil and grabbed a stack of papers.

"Go on, get the hell out of here, Jackson. You've got a story to write."

Back in my cubicle, I spent the next hour going over my notes and listening to the recordings. By the time I finished, the city *and* Shay and Holmes would look like the Grinch stealing the Who's roast beast.

I'd just gotten down to business when my cell rang. I answered with an absent minded, "Hello?"

"Shelley, Dave Brooks here."

I perked up. "Dave, good to hear from you. I just got back from my interview with Sharon Ireland. What a terrific lady. She's also madder than hell. Gave me a lot of details. I can't thank you enough for running interference."

"No problem. I'm glad I could help," he said in a subdued voice.

"Dave, is anything wrong? You sound funny."

"Shelley, last night on my way home, a car almost ran me off the road. Given the drivers in South Florida, I didn't pay much attention. I went directly to another job site this morning and arrived back in my office a couple of minutes ago. I had a message on my answering machine. The caller stated that if I didn't stop stirring up trouble with wild accusations and talking to reporters, I'd regret it. I can take care of myself, but thought I'd warn you."

My heart plummeted and a sick, queasy sensation in my stomach had me looking over my shoulder. *The car!*

"What color was the car?"

"Not sure. A dark SUV—maybe blue. It was dusk and I couldn't tell."

"And this happened before you got the message?"

"Yes. But I'm not sure the two are related."

"Thanks, Dave. I appreciate the heads up. Take care."

I hung up and swallowed hard. Crap. Now what? Fear trickled down my spine and I bit my lip to suppress it. Dave said the car following him was an SUV. The car following *me* was a sedan. Not the same. Not even close. And given the idiot drivers in South

Florida, the fact he'd almost been run off the road didn't surprise me.

My unopened mail sat in my inbox. I flipped through it, but saw nothing I couldn't identify. Then I opened my e-mail. A reporter's e-mail address is available at the bottom of any article they write. It was standard procedure. I had twelve messages. The fourth was it.

"Stop your vendetta against Shay and Holmes. If you don't, what's one more dead reporter?"

I forwarded the threat to Cal, marched into his office, and told him in a tight voice, "Check your e-mail."

"Why?"

"There's something you should see."

He twirled his chair to the table behind him and read, then swiveled back. "Congratulations, Jackson, you've just joined an elite group. Most good reporters receive hate mail and threats. I'll call Sorenson and forward this to him. Most of these things are garbage sent by assholes who want to feel important. Don't let it get you down. Any idea who the sender is?"

"Not a clue. The e-mail addy is probably a dummy account anyway." I told him about the black car.

Cal stared and frowned. "I don't like this, Shelley. Are you sure you were being followed?"

"No. It could have been a coincidence. Nobody knew I was going to Sharon's."

"For God's sake, be careful. You okay?"

"Yeah, I can handle it." I hoped it was true.

I returned to my desk, my focus fractured. It was four-thirty before I finished the article. I sent it to Cal and turned off the computer. It had been a long day. My cell phone ringing damn near scared me to death.

"Hey, beautiful," Jason said when I answered. "How was your day?"

"Some good, some bad."

"Oh? How about a late dinner tonight? I have a conference call to L. A. at seven our time, but should be finished by eight or eight-thirty. How does Leonardo's sound?"

"Sounds good. I'm tired, but we can talk over dinner. I'll meet you there."

"Okay. Maybe good Italian food, wine, and a brilliant dinner companion are just what the doctor ordered."

"I'll see you later, Dr. Mallory."

I was on my feet when my desk phone rang. I reached for the receiver, and then stopped with my hand six inches away. *Maybe I should let it go into voice mail.* The hesitant action irked me. *Damn it, why let some jerk-off keep me from answering my own phone? Don't be intimidated.*

I snatched the receiver and snapped, "Shelley Jackson."

A moment of silence sent my heart rate up several notches, and I clenched the phone in a sweat dampened palm. On the other end someone breathed raggedly. My own breathing increased.

"Is anybody there?" I disliked the sharp tone and the undercurrent of fear in my voice.

"Ah, yes…yes, I'm sorry. Is this Shelley Jackson?" a timid female voice inquired.

Hadn't I just said that? Then I relaxed and sat down. "Yes, this is Shelley Jackson. How may I help you?"

"Miss Jackson, my name is…oh, dear, I don't know if I should be doing this." Fear throbbed in the woman's voice and she sounded ready to cry.

"Please, don't hang up. Is something wrong? Can I be of any help?"

"I…I…yes, yes you can," she said in a rush. "My name is Peggy Wyatt and Marc Chambers said I could trust you."

I froze at the mention of Marc's name. I'd never heard of Peggy Wyatt.

"Do I know you, Miss Wyatt?"

"No. But Marc said if I ever felt afraid or worried, I should get a hold of you if he wasn't available. And…he's not available." She finished with a sob.

"Miss Wyatt, please tell me what's wrong. *Are* you afraid or worried about something?"

"Oh, God, yes. I work at Shay and Holmes. I'm Lynnette Palmer's secretary. Marc and I were dating and…and now I'm scared. I don't know what to do."

"About what, Miss Wyatt?"

"I…I was questioned this afternoon by my boss and Ken Shay. I didn't tell them anything, but I still don't know what to do with it."

I had no idea what the woman was talking about, but Peggy Wyatt knew something. "What didn't you tell them, and what is 'it'?"

"I didn't tell them about what Marc and I did or how he asked me to keep it."

Pulling information out of the woman was like trying to remove a railroad spike with tweezers.

"Keep what?" I asked as patiently as possible.

She rambled on. "I promised him I'd keep it safe. I have Marc's laptop."

Chapter Thirteen

I couldn't move. I sat glued to my chair in shock. Marc's laptop! *She* had it? The killer hadn't stolen it nor had it been incinerated in the fire.

"Hello? Hello, are you still there?" Peggy asked in an anxious tone. "Miss Jackson?"

I gathered my wits. "Yes, I am. Sorry, but your news shocked me. I thought it had been lost or stolen."

"After Marc died, I didn't quite know what to do, so I just held onto it."

"Have you opened any of the files? Have you read them?"

"No. I—Just a minute, somebody's coming."

She covered the mouthpiece and spoke to someone, then a few seconds later, came back on.

"Sorry, but another secretary stopped by."

"Where are you?"

"At the office."

Oh, God, no. She was calling me from Shay and Holmes. I hoped they didn't keep a log of outgoing calls.

"Peggy, we can't talk over the phone. Meet me tonight at the Waterfront Hotel on Seventeenth Street at eight-thirty, room ten-sixteen. Bring the laptop with you."

"All right, but can't you just come to my house and pick it up?"

"No. I don't think we should be seen together."

"Do you think I'm being followed like Marc?" she asked, her trembling voice lowering to a whisper.

Soothing words weren't my forte, but I tried. "No, I doubt it. If you're worried, call a cab or use valet parking at the hotel."

"Okay. I'll see you at eight-thirty."

She hung up and I called Jason, leaving a message to cancel dinner and order in sandwiches for three. I told him what had happened.

Any thoughts about leaving work early vanished. Enthusiasm surged. I'd call every city council member and ask for an interview. By now, at least some of them must have heard about my talk with the mayor.

I started with Gerald Talman. His secretary claimed he wasn't in the office, so I left a message to call me back.

Bennett Russell was next on the list. He flatly refused an interview. His secretary relayed the message, "Councilman Russell has no comment and will not discuss rumors or unfounded allegations."

Word *did* get around fast. I wasn't surprised.

My next call went to Jose Cortez. He'd been elected two years ago and his voting record was a mixture of pro and anti-development. Tough as nails and with a sharp manner, he didn't always endear himself to other politicians or those seeking to curry favor. To my amazement, he answered the phone.

"Jose Cortez, how may I help you?"

"Mr. Cortez, my name is Shelley Jackson. I'm a reporter for *The South Florida Standard*."

"I kind of wondered if you'd be calling. I heard about your little chat with the mayor this morning. He wasn't too thrilled with you."

"Is the mayor's office ordering city council members not to talk to me?"

"Nothing that blatant, but it was suggested we politely refuse all invitations to the dance."

"I see. I was hoping you liked to tango, Mr. Cortez."

He chuckled. "Miss Jackson, I don't like being told—or having someone suggest—who I can and cannot talk to."

Finally, a man with a backbone. "In that case, would it be possible to ask you a few questions regarding Shay and Holmes Development and Construction?"

"It would, but I'm going to be out of town for a couple of days. In fact, I'm leaving for the airport in ten minutes. Why don't you come to my office at eleven o'clock next Monday morning?"

"Thank you very much, Councilman Cortez."

"No problem. If there's something dirty going on, I want to know about it."

I hung up and marked my calendar, then dialed Eleanor White. I'd never met the woman, but legend had it she was hell on wheels when it came to pushing her personal projects through city council meetings. On the council for five terms, she had a reputation as a back-stabbing bitch. Word on the political street was never cross her.

I expected to be turned down, so it surprised me when she came on the line.

"Miss Jackson, is it?"

"Yes, Councilwoman White." I came straight to the point. "I wondered if I could set up an interview with you regarding the allegations of bribery in connection with Shay and Holmes Construction and Development."

"I haven't got time to sit and chat, but I can give you five minutes right now," she said in a firm voice. "I try to cooperate with the press. By the way, my condolences on the loss of your boss."

"Thank you, Ms. White. What can you tell me about the land the River Tower Condos occupies? I understand it was given to the city to be used as a park."

"That's quite true, but things sometimes don't work out the way we want. At the time, the city needed money. We evaluated our priorities and found a park not to be in the best interests of the citizens. Two other parks were available just a few blocks away. We sold the land and refilled the bank accounts. You see? There was nothing devious about the deal."

"In spite of the donating family's objections?" Silence followed.

"Is there anything else?" she finally asked.

Since she ignored my question, I plowed on. "Which brings me to Shay and Holmes. They seem to be the preferred developers and general contractors of the city over the past two or three years. Can you comment?"

So far her little speech had parroted the mayor's answer this morning. She talked, but said nothing.

"They've come in with the most competitive bids and we always try to save the people money whenever possible."

"What about the cost overruns and the rumors of sub-quality construction?" I persisted.

"All construction companies have cost overruns. And I've seen no problems with quality. In any case, those rumors can be traced back to a rival contractor who was outbid on several projects."

"And yet, I have seen some of the Shay and Holmes properties. They're in poor condition for being less than six or seven years old."

"Miss Jackson, bad maintenance would make the Taj Mahal look like a dump. Once the contractor or developer is finished, they can't be held responsible for the upkeep or lack thereof, by the owners. Is there anything else?"

Her answers were not likely to change. I couldn't see continuing the discussion. She wasn't going to tell me anything I hadn't heard before.

"Thank you for your time, Councilwoman White. Have a good evening."

I hung up and organized my notes, then sat back and drummed my fingers on the arm of my chair. I bet if Talman and Russell had talked to me the words would have been the same. The settlers had circled the wagons.

****

I met the room service waiter leaving Jason's suite as I entered and closed the door behind me. Jason was on the phone with what I assumed to be his conference call.

Dumping my purse and Bill's laptop case on the sofa, I sauntered over to the cart, which held an assortment of sandwiches, side dishes, a huge pot of coffee, and a pitcher of iced tea. I helped myself to turkey on wheat along with a glass of tea, and then sat down to eat while waiting for Jason to finish. When he did, he didn't waste time with chitchat.

"How did this secretary get a hold of Marc's laptop?"

"I'm not sure. I didn't press her on details," I replied, talking with my mouth full. I hadn't eaten since lunch at Sharon's and was starved.

"What do you mean you didn't press her? Why not?"

"She was calling from her office. I thought it best not to ask questions, so I told her to come here. Do you know her?"

Jason reached for a roast beef sandwich and poured a cup of coffee. I snatched another turkey concoction.

"I remember seeing her, but that's all. Tell me exactly what she said."

"Not much other than she was scared, had Marc's laptop, and was questioned by her boss, Lynnette Palmer, and Ken Shay."

"About what?" he asked taking a bite.

"About her relationship with Marc, I suppose. Ask her when she gets here."

I had barely uttered the words when a light knock sounded on the door. I jumped to my feet. "Let me get it. She's expecting to see me."

I hurried to open the door and gazed at a woman in her late twenties, standing maybe five-feet, two-inches with short blonde hair and blue eyes. At the moment, her head darted from side to side, her wide-eyed gaze scanning the hallway. She clutched a laptop case to her chest, her fingers nervously opening and closing.

"Miss Wyatt? I'm Shelley Jackson. Please come in."

I stepped back. She practically ran into the room,

and then halted abruptly when she saw Jason.

"Mr. Mallory? I...I didn't know you were going to be here."

"This is my suite. Shelley thought you'd be more comfortable here. Is this Marc's laptop?" he asked, reaching for it.

Peggy backed away several steps, her eyes wary. "Marc said I should give it to Miss Jackson."

"It's okay," I said. "Jason can be trusted, too."

"Mrs. Palmer said Mr. Mallory was only here to pack up Marc's things."

"I decided to stay a while longer. I want to see Marc's killer brought to justice." Jason threw Peggy a smile guaranteed to charm. "I know you do, too. Maybe whatever is on his laptop can help. May I look?"

Licking her lips, Peggy glanced at me. I nodded and she handed the case over to Jason who took it to the desk. I recognized her now. She had been the woman crying at Marc's funeral.

"Would you like a sandwich, Miss Wyatt?" I steered her toward the meal cart.

"I'm not sure I can eat anything."

"Have you had dinner?" She shook her head. "Then have something to eat."

She selected a tuna sandwich and some potato salad while I poured her a glass of tea. Settling on the sofa, I gently questioned her.

"Miss Wyatt..."

"Please, call me Peggy."

"Thank you. I'm Shelley and he's Jason. Tell me how you met Marc."

"At work. We met in the elevator one night. He was like me—kind of shy and quiet. The next thing I knew, we were meeting in the break room for coffee, and then for lunch. Sometimes we'd brown bag it, sometimes we'd go to a little café down the street. Before long we were dating. It wasn't any big deal—a quiet meal somewhere, a movie, the theatre, good conversation. We discovered we liked the same things." Her eyes misted over with tears and her chin trembled.

"Were you in love with him?"

Her face screwed up, the tears overflowing. She wiped them with her napkin and nodded. "I think so. I looked forward to seeing him and enjoyed his company."

I let her eat and regain her composure before continuing. "Over the phone, you mentioned you and Marc had done something. What did you mean?"

She worried her lower lip for a moment. "We were going through an audit about four months ago. Marc had already told me he thought my boss, Lynnette Palmer, was unqualified for her position, and he was concerned because he had some conflicting numbers in his accounts. He also admitted he was doing undercover work for someone who believed the company books didn't jibe with the truth. He asked me if I'd come with him to the office at night and access files not available to him."

I threw a glance toward Jason. He had Marc's computer up and running, and while he didn't appear to be paying attention to us, I knew he listened. I also figured if he wanted to join the conversation, he would.

"Didn't you think that rather odd?"

"Not really. You see, I knew Mrs. Palmer had no idea what she was doing. I mean, her cousin was in at least once a day giving her instructions on something or the other."

"Her cousin?"

"Ken Shay—he's her cousin."

My back straightened. Her cousin? I looked at Jason who turned, gazing with a lifted eyebrow. So, this was news to him, too.

"I had no idea. Could you hear what kind of instructions he gave her?"

Peggy nodded again. "They didn't always close the door and I'd hear Mr. Shay tell her to open special files for certain checks and budget items."

"What kind of checks and budget items?"

"Things like payments to lobbyists, consultants, and other corporations. Mr. Shay said they needed to be kept separate for easy access."

Easy access, my ass. He meant easy deletion if an outside audit ever came about. Jason had been right to suspect S and H of cooking the books.

"So, you returned to the office and looked through the files. What did you find? Did Marc download them onto his laptop?"

"No, we tried, but Mrs. Palmer had changed her password. That's routine at Shay and Holmes. Every couple of months, passwords have to be changed. Mrs. Palmer had trouble remembering hers from one change to the next, so she usually gave it to me in case she forgot, but hadn't gotten around to it yet. We had to make do with hard copies of bank statements and cancelled checks."

"What did you find?"

"Well, we found a whole bunch of checks made out to consulting firms and lobbyists on a regular basis over the past three or four years. I made copies, but it took forever. A few days later my boss gave me her password. Marc and I came back and this time he made a CD of everything he could find. I guess it's on the laptop. He was going to call the state to see who the principals were in those firms."

"Okay, Peggy, let's skip ahead to how you got the laptop. Why did Marc give it to you?"

Her eyes teared up again. "We had lunch out the day before he died. He'd been jittery and jumpy for the past week or so. He told me he thought he was being followed. Marc said his research with the state had turned up some interesting facts, but he wouldn't tell me what. He just said he wanted me to keep his laptop for a while, and if I felt scared or was worried, I could contact you at *The Standard*. You were trustworthy."

Guilt and shame clawed in my chest. I hadn't bothered to talk to Marc, even though I knew he'd been worried when I last saw him. If I had, he might not have ended up in that alley. Trustworthy? My conscience gave me a mighty kick in the ass.

"He told me the laptop was under the desk in the empty cubicle next to him. That night, I stayed late, and when most of the people had left, walked in bold as brass and got it. It's been behind my sofa ever since."

Jason left his search and joined us. "Why did Lynnette Palmer and Ken Shay question you?"

"I guess they must have finally heard I had been dating Marc. We didn't keep our relationship a secret." She sniffled and daubed her eyes.

I patted her arm. "Marc was too honest for secrecy. What did they ask?"

"Things like how long had we been dating. Did Marc seem secretive? Did he ask me to do something I shouldn't in regards to my job? Did he give me any files or something to keep for him? My heart was racing, and I was so nervous I almost passed out. I lied, babbling about how much I missed him, and then started crying. I guess they put my reaction down to the murder."

Jason smiled and took her hand in his. "That was good, Peggy. I was very fond of my step-brother. He was a nice guy, and you sound like the kind of woman he could have married. I'm sorry. Tell me, who contacted Bill Mathias?"

With a sheepish expression on her face, she smiled at Jason and said, "I did. After we had accessed the files, I was afraid Marc might be in over his head. I'd read Mr. Mathias's articles over the years. He had a way of finding out the truth about things, so I went to the library on my lunch hour and sent him an e-mail using a second account—you know, so my name wouldn't appear as the sender."

"That's what I thought," Jason said. "You were trying to help, and I appreciate it."

"I guess I didn't help enough." Peggy's gaze switched between me and Jason, and then she said in a hushed tone, "There's something else."

"What?" Jason still held her hand.

"Marc never said so, but I had the feeling he asked for my help because someone else couldn't or wouldn't."

"You mean another person in the office?" I asked.

"Maybe, I don't know. It could be he was receiving information from someone no longer with the firm. I always meant to check the personnel files to see who may have left the company about that time, but never got around to it."

The mole Jason and I had discussed a few days ago? Could be.

Jason dropped her hand and walked back to the cart where he poured a fresh cup of coffee. "Let me do it. I'm on good terms with the head of human resources. You've already stuck your neck out for Marc. And by the way, I was the person he was working for. Coffee?"

"No, thank you, Mr. Mallory. When I found out you were Marc's brother, I kind of suspected that." She rose. "I should be going. I hope you find something useful on the computer."

I walked her to the door. "Can I call you a cab or did you drive?"

"I drove and valet parked."

"Let me have your ticket," Jason said. She handed it over, and he picked up the phone. "Valet parking, please...Yes, this is Jason Mallory in suite ten-sixteen. Please have the car with ticket number six, nine, three, three, eight, one brought down immediately." He finished by saying, "Put the charges on my bill and add twenty percent for yourself. Thank you."

He hung up, faced Peggy again and smiled. "Your car should be waiting when you get downstairs. I'll walk you down."

"Thank you, Mr. Mallory."

Jason and Peggy left. He returned a few minutes later.

"So, what's on Marc's computer?" I asked, unable to contain myself.

"Not as much as I had hoped. I found one file with ten or twelve consulting firms listed, and another file of cancelled checks corresponding to the firms."

"Did you recognize any of the names?"

"Not a one. Nor did I find any of his research on those firms. Detective Whitten told me the police would check the calls in and out on Marc's cell phone. I'll call tomorrow and get a list of the numbers." He turned the laptop off and closed the lid. "If Marc was checking these firms out with the state, he wouldn't be doing it from work."

"And he couldn't do it after work because the state offices in Tallahassee would be closed," I added. "He may have contacted the state through private e-mail."

"I doubt it. E-mails sometime have a habit of showing up again on one end or the other. So, that leaves his cell phone on his lunch hour. And I'll tell you something else—if Lynnette Palmer and Ken Shay *are* keeping two sets of books, then Dennis Birdsong has to be in on it. As head of accounting, he'd have to see the real files and any audit would show the doctored ones. If he were honest, he'd spot it right away."

"Then Birdsong is getting a slice of the pie, too." I shook my head. "I wonder how deep the corruption runs. Was Marc the only honest man in accounting?"

"Birdsong joined the company seven or eight years ago. He's in on it all right. He's made no secret that he's married to Bradley Holmes's older sister. Thinks it gives him importance." Jason grabbed another sandwich and lounged back on the sofa.

"Just one big happy family," I muttered. "I guess the family that cheats together, prospers together."

"If Peggy is right about Marc having another source of information, it could have been one of the cleaning crew. The owner is supposed to call on Monday. I'll use some excuse to ask if any of their employees who may live near the alley have left in the last two or three months." He finished the sandwich and drained a glass of iced tea, then patted the cushion next to him. "Come, sit with me."

I obeyed, and he immediately swung me onto his lap.

"What say you spend the night?" he murmured, his nose and lips nuzzling my neck.

His actions propelled a delicious vibration along my nerve endings setting fires in all the right places. I captured his lips in a long, wet kiss, our tongues lunging and thrusting like dueling swords. His fingers slid through my hair and tightened—almost painfully, but I didn't care. I burned hotter and unbuttoned his shirt, then slipped my hand inside to caress his chest.

With a groan, he rose and carried me into the bedroom.

****

"Are you sure you won't stay the night?" Jason asked in a drowsy, satisfied voice.

He lay amongst the rumpled bedclothes, propped up on his elbow, a smile on his lips, and looking sexy as hell.

"I'm sure." I was pretty satisfied myself. "I have a busy day tomorrow. I'm on a roll and want to try and snag an interview with the Building Department Administrator. I also want to do research on how many inspectors have taken early retirement in the past couple of years."

I finished fastening my skirt and fished my shoes out from under the bed.

"I'm amazed more women don't break their ankles in those silly heels," he commented.

"Stilettos are incredibly sexy."

"Don't your feet hurt at the end of the day?"

"Sometimes, but the pain is worth it."

Jason chuckled, threw back the covers, rose, and pulled on his slacks. He put his arms around me as I slipped my shoes on, and then nibbled on my ear.

I groaned, stepping away. "Behave yourself. Are you a satyr or something?"

"Could be. Maybe you just bring out the beast in me."

I laughed. "I'll talk to you tomorrow. Dinner? My place? Seven-thirty?" He kissed me again, nibbling on my lower lip this time. I shoved him playfully in the chest.

He laughed, grabbed a T-shirt, escorted me downstairs, and across the hotel entry drive to my car parked in the restaurant lot.

The drive home took only a few minutes and I walked in to a ringing phone. Dumping my stuff on the sofa, I ran to answer my landline.

"Hello?"

"Miss Jackson?" a man's voice asked.

"Yes, this is Shelley Jackson. Who's this?"

"My name is Roland Starke. I work at Shay and Holmes in the construction office." He spoke in a low tone.

"Yes, Mr. Starke, what can I do for you?"

"I order the materials and have information you may find interesting."

My interest piqued in spite of his slightly slurred speech. I tried to keep my tone neutral. "Such as?"

"Not over the phone, Miss Jackson. I know this is an imposition, but could you meet me tonight?"

"Tonight?" I glanced at my watch. It was after eleven.

"I have documents, and don't want them in my possession any longer than necessary. I live in Springdale. There's a twenty-four hour diner called Jack's in a strip mall just off Springdale Road and Dolphin Street. We can meet there in—say half an hour. I'll give them to you, and no one will be the wiser."

"Why are you doing this?" Given Marc and Bill's murders, the black sedan possibly following me, and my threatening e-mail this afternoon, I couldn't help being suspicious. On the other hand, he *had* identified himself as an S and H employee, and if I ended up dead, he'd have no assurances whether or not I'd passed the information along to a third party.

"The fire the other night scared me, Miss Jackson. The sub-contractor used on that job was not licensed. My name is on the contract and a lot of purchase orders. It's not the first time Shay and Holmes has done this. Sooner or later, someone's going to get hurt. I don't want to be the one to take the fall."

"So, you're blowing the whistle?"

"Yeah, I guess I am."

"Why don't you contact the city and tell them?"

He laughed softly. "And talk to whom?"

I got his drift. "Then why not the police?"

"And incriminate myself? No thanks. I want this anonymous—no names."

"Mr. Starke, why don't you come to my office tomorrow morning or better yet, I'll meet you at The Wake Up Café on Riverside at seven?"

"No! It's tonight or not at all. I drank half a bottle

of scotch just to screw up the nerve to call you. I may not be able to do it again if I wait. I'm also tired of not sleeping at night."

I thought quickly. The fear in his voice sounded genuine. At this time of night, Springdale, a northern suburb, would be a fifteen minute trip—twenty at the most. My curiosity and my reporter's instincts spun in high gear. If a reporter didn't take chances once in a while, they had no business calling themselves reporters, I rationalized. I chose to ignore the consequences of Bill's having taken chances and of Cal's warnings. The front row seat in the White House briefing room swam into focus.

"Okay, I'll meet you. Give me directions."

He breathed a loud sigh and gave the detailed instructions. I hung up and called Jason to see if he wanted to come. His phone rang with no answer, so I left a message in his voice mail.

"Jason, this is Shelley. I got a call from a man named Starke at Shay and Holmes who says he has papers proving the use of unlicensed subcontractors. I'm meeting him at a place called Jack's Diner in Springdale in half an hour. Come join me if you want."

I ran to my car elated at the thought of yet another link to shoddy construction courtesy of Shay and Holmes.

****

"This can't be right," I muttered out loud, turning into an industrial complex. I stopped under a light in the parking lot and reread the directions. Had I made a wrong turn somewhere? A dark, silent warehouse stood to my left. The parking lot stretched to my right. Straight ahead the inky expanse of a lake glowed in the lamplight. The musty swamp smells of the Everglades less than a mile away drifted through the window, clogging my nostrils. I hit the door locks and raised the windows.

Uneasiness tightened my throat. Something was wrong—very wrong. I'd been an idiot to come out here.

Cursing, I spun the steering wheel and exited left onto a narrow two lane road. I was lost and wondered if Starke still waited at the diner. I was half an hour late.

My heartbeats hammered in my chest. I decided to follow my instincts and beat it.

"Screw Starke," I muttered again. "I'm outta here."

I retraced my way by turning left at the next intersection and concentrated on where I was going. This part of Springdale had just begun to develop, and the road was dark.

I hadn't driven far when headlights closed fast in my rearview mirror. The driver flipped his lights onto high beam and accelerated.

Sucking in a startled breath, Dave Brooks' voice boomed in my mind. He'd been run off the road. Maybe I had been followed from Sharon's after all. Bill had been shot in the head. And Marc had taken three bullets to the chest.

My heart slammed against my ribs. My breaths rasped in my throat. I'd been set up, and cursed myself for ignoring the obvious. Ambition had trumped common sense. I'd been beyond stupid and didn't want to pay for my lack of judgment with my life.

I jammed my foot on the accelerator, flooring it. The car kept coming and I braced for the impact. It was a big SUV, black or dark in color, and the bumper slammed into me like a battering ram. The car lurched, and I screamed. My Honda fishtailed. I fought to maintain control.

I didn't take time to call myself every type of stupid. That would come later if at all. Now, I concentrated on staying alive.

The SUV backed off, and then roared forward again. This time the jolt was hard enough to send the car sliding broadside down the road. I frantically turned the wheel until it straightened.

A glance in my mirrors confirmed I was about to be hit again. Ahead, a T-intersection loomed, the gleam of a guardrail reflecting back at me. Beyond laid total darkness. It took a moment to understand I stared at a canal.

The intersection rushed at me as did the SUV. If I braked, I'd be rear-ended again. If I didn't, I'd never make the turn. I waited, then hit the brakes and turned at the same time.

The tires screeched and skidded. The guardrail banged into my door. The SUV hit me in the right rear quarter panel. I never had a chance. The airbag deployed as the car ripped through the guardrail, spun around, and tumbled down a steep embankment to land with a splash right side up in the canal. On the road above, my pursuer stopped, and then took off.

I still grasped the steering wheel in a death grip. My heart pounded in my ears, and I panted with fear. I batted the airbag out of the way. Then my scalp prickled at the slow gurgling sound.

My feet were cold and covered with water. Unable to move, I stared as the trickle become a stream, and then the stream a flood. The car was sinking.

Chapter Fourteen

Panic is not pretty. I'd never experienced panic before, but now it shredded whatever rational thought I had left. My heart galloped. I couldn't breathe. I felt lightheaded and shook from head to toe. I wanted to throw up. My body refused to move.

Oddly enough, I was not in total darkness. The headlights of my car still burned, stabbing through the inky water, creating a ghastly green glow. The cold water crept up my legs and the inertia gripping me vanished.

I hit the door locks, fumbled for the handle, and wrenched, but the door refused to budge. My heart raced faster when the car tilted nose down.

The electric windows were out of commission, but I jammed hard at the button anyway. Nothing. I surrendered that last piece of calm. I unfastened the seat belt and knelt on the seat screaming and beating at the window with my fists. It was no use. I was trapped, unable to move. The outside water steadily marched up the windshield.

Something poked me in the rear end. I reached back and grasped my shoe. Wrenching it off, I held it in both hands and pounded the heel on the window. It refused to break. The rubberized tip bounced off the glass. With a sob, I grasped the end and pulled. It remained in place. I tried to wedge my fingernails between the rubber and the leather. Two of them broke.

Oh, God, please don't let me die. Not this way. Not in some slime infested canal where my body may not be found for months.

I sobbed and continued to scream as the putrid water rose. I thought of my father, Bill, Marc, and Jason. I didn't want to die. I was only thirty-two. *I'm not prepared for this!*

The car was now two-thirds submerged. Then through my fear, I remembered. Marc! That silly hammer he'd given me! I clawed at my console. Jerking it open, I frantically felt in the bottom of the compartment. My grasping fingertips touched metal. I pulled it free.

The water lapped around my hips. Another sickening nose down lurch told me I needed to act now. With a hard swing, I hit the window. The glass crackled into a multi-lined star shape. I whacked it again. A hole appeared. I hit it hard a third time. The hole enlarged. Taking a deep breath, I pushed against the glass. It popped out. I wormed my body through, the remaining jagged edges ripping my clothes. I wasted no time, kicked off my other shoe, and swam for the bank five feet away.

Gasping and choking, I clutched at anything that would help propel me upward and away from the terror of that liquid abyss. My bare feet slipped in the mud sending me back toward the water. I dug in with my toes and fingers.

"Here! Take my hand!" a male voice shouted.

I looked up at a shadowy figure and grasped his outstretched hand. He pulled me to the top of the embankment where I lay on my back, gazing at the stars overhead and panting. I rolled over, struggled to my hands and knees, and then puked.

My savior knelt beside me. I realized he was speaking and had been for some time.

"Lady, lady, answer me! Are you alone? Is there anyone else in the car?"

I sat up and sobbed. "No. I—I was a—alone."

My teeth chattered. My body was numb and no matter how hard I tried, I couldn't stop shaking.

The man ran to a pick-up at the side of the road and returned a minute later with a blanket. He draped it over my shoulders and flipped open a cell phone.

While he called 9-1-1, I stared at the water ten feet below me. My car hung perpendicular three-quarters submerged. Air rushed out in a froth of bubbles before it disappeared under the greasy surface. For a couple of seconds the taillights remained visible before they blinked out of existence.

The man knelt beside me again. "Come on, lady, lie down. You're in shock."

I did as he ordered and clutched the edges of the blanket together, quivering as though in the grips of a high fever.

"Th—thank you. I—I thought I was dead."

"You damn near were."

Sirens screamed in the distance. The man ran to the side of the road waving his arms. Cops and paramedics arrived at the same time.

The ambulance crew worked on me first, sticking an IV into my arm and slicing my sodden clothes off except for my underwear. They slapped me on a gurney, and then covered me with what looked like an aluminum foil sheet. Warmth permeated my skin.

My rescuer talked with the police. "Yeah, I was heading home when suddenly this dark SUV comes barreling around a curve doing about ninety. The son of a bitch had his brights on—damn near blinded me. I swerved and missed sideswiping him by inches. Past the curve, I noticed the ground was all chewed up and the guardrail smashed. I saw lights in the water, pulled over, and went down to help."

"Thank God, you did," I said. "I owe you my life."

"Glad I could help."

I was loaded into the ambulance and my last view of my savior was him getting back behind the wheel of his truck.

The paramedics did the usual medical things. At the hospital, I was wheeled into a treatment room where more staff hovered. They drew blood for what I assumed would be a blood alcohol test to make sure I hadn't been drunk on my ass.

"Is there anyone you'd like us to call?" a woman with a clipboard asked.

I shook my head, and then changed my mind. I wanted Jason. I wanted his warm arms around me, holding me close, protecting me.

"Yes! Please get in touch with Jason Mallory in room ten-sixteen at the Waterfront Hotel on Seventeenth Street in Port Royale."

She exited as a doctor appeared and wrote on a chart. A policeman stepped up. "Can she talk, doc?"

"Yes. She's still a little shocky, but she can answer your questions."

I looked into the smiling face of a young officer who asked, "How are you feeling?"

"Better."

"You had one hell of a ride, Miss Jackson."

"Tell me about it." I would feel that cold water creeping up my body for years to come.

"Can you tell me what happened?"

"Someone had tried to kill me." Suddenly, I was scared all over again. I told him the whole story of how I came to be in Springdale at midnight and the consequences.

"Wasn't another reporter killed last week?"

"Yes. Bill Mathias, my boss."

He snapped his notebook shut. "Miss Jackson, no story is worth your life. Forgive me, but what you did wasn't very smart."

"Don't I know it!" I shivered, thinking of the water again.

"We'll contact the Port Royale police and send them a report, but if we find the SUV, my bet is it'll come back as stolen."

I was too tired and scared to argue. "I'm sure you're right, officer."

"We'll pull the car out of the canal, but you'll have to tell us where to send it."

"I'll call tomorrow. Okay?"

He nodded and left.

I pulled the covers up to my chin and closed my eyes. Weariness washed over me. To my surprise I drifted into a light doze. When I awoke, Jason stood next to the bed. An instant sense of relief that everything would be all right flooded through me.

He leaned over kissing my forehead. "Are you all right?"

"Yeah, but I'm still scared.

"I spoke with the doctor. He wants you to stay

overnight for observation."

"No way. I'm not injured and the shock is almost gone. I want my own bed."

He smiled and kissed me again, this time on the lips. The sense of security deepened.

"That's what I thought you'd say. I'll go see they get the papers together."

"Thanks. Oh!"

"What?"

"I just remembered. They cut off my clothes. I don't have anything to wear."

He tossed a plastic bag on my tummy. "You do now. When I discovered your condition wasn't life threatening, I figured you'd need dry clothes, so I stopped at a twenty-four hour drug store and bought a few necessities."

He left the room as I opened the bag and peeked inside. Drug stores down here carry everything a tourist could want, including T-shirts, shorts, and flip-flops. For the first time in several hours, I chuckled.

The T-shirt was large, hot pink and emblazoned with garish blue and purple dolphins surrounded by a turquoise sea. A few lime green palms trees added to the nauseating color scheme.

The shorts were lemon yellow and a size too small, while the flip-flops matched the pink shirt and sported sequins. They were a size too big, but who was I to argue? At least I had clothes.

Jason and the doctor returned. "Please, sign this waiver, Miss Jackson. Even though your vital signs are normal, I advise you to stay overnight."

The doctor handed me a clipboard and a pen. I scribbled my name and returned it.

"No, thanks. If all my vitals are normal, I'll be fine. I just want to go home. Thank you for everything."

He accepted the papers back with a shake of his head.

When he left, I held up the T-shirt for Jason to see. "Couldn't you have found something more colorful?"

He grinned and reached for one of the flip-flops. "Hey, I'm fond of the shoes. I grabbed the first items I saw. Don't get picky on me. I'll go settle the bill while you dress. Since your insurance card and ID are gone, the hospital wants to be paid."

When he'd gone, I slipped out of bed and dressed. I couldn't decide if I looked like I'd been attacked by a crazed artist with a full palette or was impersonating a hooker. Maybe people would think I just had bad taste.

An orderly pushed a wheelchair out to the car where he helped me in. Jason slid behind the wheel. Neither of us spoke again until he turned onto the street and headed east.

"Okay, tell me what happened." The jocularity of the ER vanished. His voice turned hard.

I sighed and gave him a blow by blow description. "I should have remembered Dave Brooks's warning, the car, and the e-mail."

"What warning, car, and e-mail?"

Damn. My brain still wasn't working. I hadn't intended to tell him anything, but did so now.

"What the hell were you thinking! After all that, you still went out alone to talk to a supposed informant? God, how stupid can you get?"

"Hey, I called you, but you didn't answer, so I left a message."

"I stopped in the bar for a nightcap. When I got

back to the room, I showered and went to bed. Never thought to check my voicemail."

"Look, I know what I did wasn't smart, but if a reporter didn't take chances once in a while, nothing would get reported."

"Your boss is doing a good job of reporting now, isn't he? I could have told you Shay and Holmes has nobody in the office named Starke and materials are ordered directly by the contractors. Don't ever do something like this again."

"I'm sorry, but the guy sounded legit."

I'd seen and heard Jason angry before, but this time his voice had an edge of fear in it. I liked the idea the fear was for me.

"Damn. How do you think I felt when the hospital called and told me you'd been in an automobile accident in Springdale? When I heard you'd gone into the water, I almost had a heart attack. Marc told me how cars and drivers disappear into canals." He slapped his hand on the steering wheel. "Damn!"

"It's thanks to Marc that I'm alive." I told him about the hammer.

"Marc was a logical man."

"I know, and I'm sorry."

I appreciated Jason was here for me, but right now, I couldn't deal with any more criticism or listen to one more word about what an idiot I'd been. I knew I'd been dumber than a box of rocks. I leaned my head back, closing my eyes. Jason took the hint and the rest of the ride to my house was silent.

With my keys still in the ignition of my car, I extracted my emergency house key from under a flower pot on the front porch. Jason opened the door and made me stand in the foyer until he'd checked the whole place.

"Okay, it's empty." He stood with his hands in his pockets. "Would you like me to stay the night?"

I opened my mouth to say no, and then changed my mind. "I'd like that."

Taking charge, he lifted and carried me down the hall to the bedroom. I kicked off my sandals, pulled down the covers, and then headed for the shower where I scrubbed the miasma of the canal and near death from my body. When I finished, I donned a less gaudy T-shirt and slid beneath the covers.

"I'll be right back," Jason said. He returned carrying two glasses. "Here, drink this. It'll help you sleep."

I obeyed and let the vodka slide down my throat. It burned all the way to my stomach sending instant heat throughout my body. I downed the rest in a single gulp.

"Thanks. It's a cliché, but I needed that."

I handed the glass back. He bolted his, set both glasses on the nightstand, shed his clothes, and crawled into the bed. His arm grasped my waist and pulled me close.

Never had I appreciated a man more. I snuggled into his body, grateful for the warmth and the comfort. It would be nice to do this on a regular basis.

I closed my eyes, wondering if I, of all people, was falling in love.

****

In spite of the vodka and Jason's warm body, I couldn't sleep. Every time I drifted off, the smell and feel of the cold water encasing my body jerked me awake. Jason would tighten his arm and murmur soothing words in my ear. After four hours of trying, I gave up. I lay quietly listening to Jason's slow even breathing. The canal smell still clung to my skin. Another shower was in order. When I tried to ease out of bed, he opened his eyes.

"Are you okay?" he asked.

"I'm fine, but I can't sleep any more. I think I'll get up, have some breakfast, and then go into work."

"Are you sure? Maybe you should take the day off."

"No. I have to tell Cal what happened, and then I want to write a story about it. I'll try to tie it in to everything else."

Jason threw back the covers and sat on the edge of the bed, a frown on his stubble-covered face.

"You were damn near killed last night and all you want to do is make sure you have a sensational story with your byline on the front page?"

I pulled my robe on and slipped the sequined flip-flops on my feet.

"It's news, and if my experience can help the investigation, then I need to write it now while I can still inject all of the horror. I also plan to attend the City Council meeting tonight."

"Why?"

"To see if someone is surprised I'm alive."

I made my way into the bathroom. When I returned, Jason was gone. I sniffed the eye-opening aromas of coffee and frying bacon, dressed, and joined him.

"That smells wonderful." I inhaled deeply in culinary anticipation.

"It tastes wonderful, too." He poured me a mug of

coffee. "Sit down. Scrambled eggs all right with you?"

"Fine."

I sat and sipped, my elbows propped on the table. Jason stood at the stove with his back toward me. I stared in appreciation at his rear end in the tight jeans and loved the way the muscles on his back moved under the equally snug T-shirt. Canal dunking or not, my libido wasn't damaged one iota. I spent the next several minutes admiring the view and letting my imagination run wild.

"Would you like some toast?"

His voice brought me back to the real world. "Toast is fine."

I gulped more coffee and tried to keep my mind on the day ahead of me. I had a ton of phone calls to make regarding insurance, a rental car, a new driver's license, and credit cards. A new cell phone was also in order. I carried my day-timer in the computer case, which thank God, I'd left on the sofa.

Jason set my breakfast in front of me and I dug in needing the fuel. Today shaped up to be hell. I couldn't wait to see Cal's reaction.

****

It was close to ten o'clock when I dumped my gear in my cubicle and marched to Cal's office.

"You're late," he snapped. "It's getting to be a habit."

I closed the door and stood front of him with my arms crossed over my chest. "Someone tried to kill me last night."

He stopped what he was doing and leaned back, his expression inscrutable and his eyebrows raised. "Tell me."

I told him everything from the time Peggy Wyatt had called to my release from the hospital, omitting Jason's part. Cal didn't need to know he'd spent the night.

"And here I credited you with some intelligence. What on earth possessed you to track down this informant alone? Didn't I tell you just yesterday to be careful? Didn't this call coupled with Dave Brooks's warning and the anonymous e-mail send up a red flag? Jesus, Jackson, people and cars disappear in those canals and aren't found for years."

He shouted, but at least the door was closed.

"Look, I already know it was a stupid thing to do and you can believe I won't do it again, but I *can* write a story about the experience. Maybe the publicity will stop the person or persons behind the killings."

Cal shook his head and ran his hand through his hair. He looked worried.

"Maybe, but I wouldn't count on it. Someone is getting desperate. Go write your story, and then take the rest of the day off." He reached for the phone as I left the office.

The story practically wrote itself. I sent it on to Cal a little before noon and got down to personal stuff.

My first order of business was to call the Springdale Police Department and tell them where to take my car. They replied it was being fished out of the canal now. I skipped lunch and spent most of the afternoon on the phone dealing with all the nit-picking things necessary when a person's life is turned upside down. I needed information in my purse. One of our messengers offered to drive north and get it. An hour later I opened the slimy leather bag. My wallet was ruined, but the driver's license and credit cards remained intact. The same couldn't be said for my cell. The waterlogged circuits had bitten the big one.

It was after four when Cal poked his head out of his office door and hollered, "Elliott, get in here."

Doug bounded out of Bill's office like a spooked kangaroo and scurried to obey. Cal left the door open.

"Do you call this a story?" Cal's reprimands always started out loud and progressed to louder.

"What's wrong with it?"

"It stinks. I send you out for a human interest feature about vendors at the flea market, and you hand me an essay on gold jewelry and some woman with big tits. Did you even bother to go to the place or did you write this sitting on your ass at home enjoying a cold one and watching TV?"

"No—no, sir," Doug stammered. "I walked my feet off at that dump. I thought I captured the atmosphere."

"Look at this paragraph. It contains exactly five sentences. Three begin with the words 'the flea market' and two with the pronoun 'it.' There are no quotes anywhere in the article, and the only vendor you describe is this woman." The disgust in Cal's voice came through loud and clear. "A fourth grader could do better than this. You have a lot to learn, Elliott, if you expect to fill Bill Mathias's shoes."

"May I remind you that my aunt—"

"I don't give a flying fuck about your aunt or that toad Miriam Noble. Neither of them knows newspapers or how to write. Now take this, throw it away, and tomorrow morning I want a one-thousand-word article on the traffic you encounter on the way home tonight."

Doug emerged from Cal's office. The arrogant

sneer had disappeared from his face and as he passed the cubicles, grinning heads previously buried in pretend work, popped up like prairie dogs. That silly arcade game Whack-a-Mole came to mind.

With the amusement over for the day, I continued with my phone calls. The city council meeting was due to begin at seven. I hoped the rental agency would have a car here before I had to leave.

Much to my relief, the guy showed up a little after five. I signed the papers and accepted the keys to a cheap shoebox on wheels. At least it was transportation.

I'd had a bitch of a day and decided to treat myself to dinner before the city council meeting. I turned off my computer when Doug stepped into my cubicle. He held an open folder and had a frown on his face.

"Shelley, I found several files hidden in the bottom drawer of Bill's desk."

"Hidden?"

"Yeah, I was rearranging some things and found them under a ream of copy paper. I didn't pay much attention at first because they were labeled 'old letters.'" He extended the folder to me. "Who are these people?"

I took the file remembering the ream of paper, but never thinking to check under it the other night Jason and I had poked around. Now, I gazed at a photo of several people taken at some social event.

"The man on the left is Bradley Holmes. The guy next to him is City Councilman Bennett Russell, and next to him is City Manager, Ron Zimmerman. The clown on the end with the silly grin on his face and his arm draped over Zimmerman's shoulder is Kenneth Shay."

"And the woman in the background?"

I stared hard at the image just over Shay's shoulder.

"I think it might be Councilwoman Eleanor White, but I'm not sure. She's not facing the camera. Any idea when this picture was taken?" I asked, handing the file back to him.

"The notation on the back says March of last year. Who's the guy with her?"

"I have no idea."

"Thanks," he said, the frown on his face deepening.

Doug walked back to Bill's office, and I slumped into my chair. I'd lied. Eleanor White may not have faced the camera, but the man with her sipping a martini did—Jason Mallory.

Am I sleeping with the enemy?

****

On the drive to the city council meeting, I couldn't keep the photo of Jason and Eleanor White out of my mind. Why had he lied to me? Exactly how well did he know city council members?

The urge to demand immediate answers was strong, but I knew I'd have to take it slow and be diplomatic. There might be a reasonable explanation for his presence. I couldn't bear to think otherwise.

I contacted my cell provider, relieved to hear I could go to the nearest store and get a new one with the same number. Replacing all the information it contained, however, was another story. A quick trip to the mall had produced a new phone. I'd reprogrammed some of my contacts, but would have to finish later. I kept a Rolodex at the office.

I parked and hurried toward the doors of City Hall

where a small group of people with picket signs milled around. One of the signs read, "More Parks, Less Condos." I put on the brakes and turned to the nearest woman.

"Are you going to the meeting?"

"We tried, but they took one look at our signs and tossed us out. Claimed protest signs were not allowed."

"Then deep six the signs and go on in."

One of her companions pointed to the doors. "See that big bruiser of a security guard standing there? We did that and he told us we weren't allowed to attend."

"That's bullshit. This meeting is open to the public. Come on." I led them up to the doors.

"Sorry, ma'am, but you're not allowed in here."

"My name is Shelley Jackson. I'm a reporter for *The South Florida Standard*." To ram my point home, I showed him my press credentials. They were still damp, but legible. "I think the city council would rather deal with a few concerned citizens now than my story in tomorrow morning's paper about how they were denied access to a public forum. It's called the Sunshine Law."

The guard looked over his shoulder, but found no help. He must have decided seven or eight protestors was better than bad press and waved us by.

The mayor saw me first and leaned over whispering to the Vice-Mayor, Eleanor White. Her gaze swung to me. She in turn whispered to the man sitting next to her, Gerald Talman. Within seconds, the entire dais knew of my presence.

Mayor Cosworth banged a gavel bringing the crowd of sixty or so people to order. The room was jammed.

"If everybody's here, let's begin the meeting. We

have a short agenda tonight."

The following hour was taken up with old business and I took the time to scrutinize the panel. At some point during the proceedings, all of them cast guarded glances at me. If one of them tried to kill me, he or she did a great job hiding it. They looked innocent as babes—or as politicians with something to hide.

Finally, they got to the discussion of new business.

"The Council is going to hear a presentation by Rogers Development regarding a three-story, twenty-four-unit condominium to be built on the corner of Schultz Street and Northeast Second Avenue," the Mayor announced.

I guessed Shay and Holmes had passed on this one. The neighborhood was marginal and trying to make a comeback. The developer described the proposed condos as "affordable," which meant inexpensive and not overly profitable.

The builder stood, giving his spiel, and then sat down.

Cosworth asked, "Is there any discussion?"

The woman I'd met outside jumped to her feet. "My name is Joan Hollister and I have a question. What is the problem with you people? Are we going to let this city become more of a concrete jungle than it already is? The river is a canyon of steel and plate glass, and the beachfront is losing all its personality to development. Our green space is disappearing for the sake of a few dollars citizens will never see. For God's sakes, the area in question could use a park. If you want to attract families, add a place for their children to play without fear of drug peddlers."

"In order for the families to move, the housing

must come first. There are plans in the works for a small neighborhood park in the future," Councilman Russell said.

"That's the promise the people of the Pelican Glen neighborhood heard three years ago. They have no park and the last two acres of land was sold three weeks ago to a developer for a strip mall. I can't figure out how the fuck you people keep getting re-elected," the lady fumed.

The gavel banged. "Watch your language," Mayor Cosworth barked. "You've had your say, now is there anyone else who has a constructive comment?"

A man two rows in front of me rose. "I do. My name is Hiram Butler, and I live in Pelican Glen. I want to know why you didn't keep your promise to build us a park. A park makes more sense than a strip mall or another condo complex. The housing market *and* the economy still suck. Who's going to buy?"

The gavel banged again, harder this time. "That is not the subject up for discussion. Consider this your first and final warning. One more outburst disrupting legitimate business and you'll be ejected. Is that clear? Now, if there are no more comments, shall we get on with our vote?"

I rose looking him straight in the eye. "Shelley Jackson of the *South Florida Standard*. I'd like to know why you won't answer the man's question."

The mayor's face turned red. "You're out of order. I haven't recognized you."

The room erupted with people jumping to their feet and angry voices filling the air. The yelling continued for a several minutes with the gavel banging away like a sledge hammer until the police came in and escorted the protestors from the room. They started with me.

"Hey, let go," I said as a cop grasped my arm to lead me away. "I'm a reporter and have every right to be here."

"Come quietly or I'll run you in for inciting a riot."

"What riot?" Joan, also in the grasp of a policeman, asked. "We are peacefully exercising our rights as citizens. I'll sue."

About fifteen or twenty of us were dragged through the lobby and shoved out the front doors.

"You have five minutes to disperse. If you don't, we'll arrest you for loitering," one of the cops told us, then slammed the door and locked it. He strutted out of sight.

"Well, we tried," Joan said.

"You did more than try. You just gave me a great story. It may not make tomorrow's edition, but I bet it will the next one."

Plus, city council meetings were taped, and I wondered how long it would take for one of the TV stations to get their hands on a copy. Maybe a phone call to Channel 8 would be a nice touch, assuming the tapes didn't mysteriously disappear or get erased as soon as the meeting ended. I called immediately.

I spent a few minutes recording names and neighborhoods of the protestors along with complaints, then waved goodbye and walked toward the parking garage.

As entertainment, the evening had been better than a night at the movies. The City Council would need to do serious damage control.

Chapter Fifteen

I spent most of the next morning at home on the phone. The insurance adjuster viewed my car, declared it a total loss, and had it towed—at my expense—to the junkyard. He also advised me my premiums would rise.

I headed to the office after a quick lunch where I found Cal not in the best of moods.

"Jackson, get in here," he yelled.

Now what? I wasn't in the world's greatest mood either. I entered his office. The door remained open.

"I'm so glad you were able to make time in your busy schedule to actually appear this morning," he said, glancing at his watch. "Oh, excuse me, this afternoon. Do you suppose you can make the effort to show up for a full eight hours just once in a while?"

"I had a few personal things to do. I want to tell you about last night. I went to the…"

"I know where you went," he interrupted. "I had a call early this morning from Councilman Russell saying you and a bunch of—how did he put it—'screwball, anti-development whackos,' disrupted the city council meeting and had to be escorted from the building. I don't like getting irate phone calls from city councilmen before I've had my coffee. What the hell were you doing?"

"That is not quite how it went down. I ran into some concerned citizens who were refused entrance to the meeting. A public discussion on development was being held. Those people had every right to be there."

I told him about the events of the previous night and by the time I finished, he had calmed down.

"Okay, write the story, but steer clear of the council meetings for a while. And for crying out loud, try getting to work on time for a change. Your paycheck says you work from eight to five with an hour's lunch. You're a bad influence on others."

"What others?"

Cal sat back. "Close the door."

I did as he asked and plunked myself in the chair in front of his desk.

"What others?" I repeated.

"Doug. He hasn't put in an appearance today either. I gave him a bullshit assignment yesterday with orders to have it on my desk this morning. I've tried calling, but he isn't answering either his home or cell phones."

I shrugged. "So what? If he's not here, he can't give us any grief. I wouldn't be surprised if he's taking a crash course on how to write."

"Or he's whining to his aunt, who'll call Miriam and whine to her. Then *that* hag will call me. I'm in no mood for it today."

"Why don't you just tell them Doug is unsuitable for the job?"

"Because, like it or not, Miriam signs my paycheck just like she does yours." Cal sighed and shook his head. "Hell, the little worm will come strolling in soon. Get back to work. Write the story about the meeting last night and don't make it too long or self-righteous. I can't promise it will be in tomorrow's paper, but I'll try."

I nodded and rose to leave when he stopped me.

"By the way, your articles have generated a lot of letters to the editor. Shay and Holmes built more than a couple of shitty condos and apartments."

"Any pro Shay and Holmes?"

"Yeah, one written by Shay, one by Holmes, and another written by their lawyers threatening to sue for defamation of character. Keep the pressure on."

Back in my cubicle, I sorted through my mail—mostly good—and read my e-mail, also on the positive side. Then I started on my voicemail. Most of the messages were from people who lived or had lived in Shay and Holmes projects. I listened with half an ear, my mind busy arranging the details of last night's encounter, but a message from Doug had me paying attention.

I listened, replayed it, and then replayed it again before calling Cal.

"You gotta hear this. It's Doug and he left a strange message in my voicemail."

In less than thirty seconds my boss stood next to me listening to the drunken slur on my speaker phone.

"Hey, Jackson, I just wanted to tell you that you and that son of a bitch Randolph are gonna be sorry for the way you've treated me. I have the scoop of a lifetime. I'm gonna bring home the story you and Bill couldn't. Have a nice night."

"What the hell? What's that noise in the background?"

I listened again, this time concentrating on what wasn't being said. "He's in a bar. From the music and stomping going on, not to mention the cheering, I'd have to say he was calling from The Wild Dog on South Street."

Cal curled his lip. "The little SOB, he's sleeping one off. What's this nonsense about bringing home the story? You have any idea?"

"None. He stopped in late yesterday with a picture of some councilmen with Brad Holmes and Ken Shay. It looked like it had been taken at a cocktail party."

"What picture? Where did he find it?"

"He said he found several files in the bottom of one of the drawers in Bill's office."

Cal frowned and strode out of my cubicle for Bill's. I followed. He entered the unlocked office and flipped on the light, then headed straight to the desk where he opened every drawer. I checked the file cabinets. No folder appeared.

"Well, he either filed them somewhere else or took them home. As soon as he shows his face, I want to see him. Aunt and publisher be damned, his days are numbered."

I returned to my cubicle and tried to work on my article, but Doug's expression of yesterday afternoon kept intruding. He'd looked serious and puzzled. Yeah, that was it—puzzled as though trying to sort out a complicated math problem. His expression didn't jibe with the semi-drunken rant of later. He must have solved whatever bothered him and called to gloat.

I had written only a few paragraphs when my phone rang. I answered with a crisp, "Shelley Jackson."

"How are you feeling today?" Jason asked.

"Better. How are things at Shay and Holmes?"

"Shay and Holmes avoid me and hint that I've outstayed my welcome. I've been told the office I'm in has been allotted to a new employee who starts on Monday. After this weekend, I'll be homeless."

"Your presence there *is* rather daunting considering your relationship to Marc."

"Which brings me to why I've called. I have most of Marc's belongings I saved from the house and the things from his office in boxes. How about coming by the hotel tonight and helping me go through them. We'll order room service and sort things."

My spirits lifted. "What time?"

"Any time after work is fine. We'll have cocktails, eat, and then go through Marc's stuff."

"I'll go home, change clothes, and see you around six. Okay?"

"Six o'clock. I'll have the martinis poured."

I hung up, and *then* remembered the photo.

****

I used the valet parking at Jason's hotel this time. The weather today had been unseasonably warm and humid. Now, dark clouds gathered offshore and toward the south promising thunderstorms later in the evening. I walked through the lobby pulling my blouse away from my sweaty back and blessed the air-conditioning cooling my overheated skin.

Jason opened the door, smiled, and presented me with a martini glass. I accepted and curved my lips over the icy rim. Hmm, fire and ice—the perfect combination—slid down my throat.

I walked in and stared at the stacks of boxes strewn around the room. "I thought most of Marc's stuff was destroyed in the fire."

"I'd already had some removed to a storage facility. I want to make sure there's nothing that should go to Marc's mother before I give things away to charity. I hauled out four boxes from the office this afternoon. I guess one of the secretaries packed it away. I haven't looked through any of those yet."

I skirted past a couple of cartons and settled into a corner of the sofa. Jason filled a martini glass for himself and joined me. I hadn't forgotten the photo, but decided to wait until after eating to ask questions.

"I took the liberty of ordering dinner. I hope you like filet mignon and lobster tails."

"Who doesn't? I suppose there's champagne included."

"But, of course."

He took a long, slow swallow of martini, then smiled and winked. A glow formed in the pit of my stomach. Damn, he was too sexy to be believed—and that's what worried me. I sipped from my glass.

"Sounds like a seduction to me," I replied in a purring voice.

He leaned over and kissed me, his tongue tracing the outline of my lips until I opened them. The glow kindled into a tiny flame licking at my nerves, accelerating my heartbeat and respiration.

He pulled back and bussed the tip of my nose. "Later. Dinner first, and then sorting, with seduction as a reward."

Had he read my mind? I finished my drink, rose, and joined him at the bar, holding my glass out. He smiled a cocky smile and poured, making me want to dump the contents on his head. I didn't like that he read me so well. I changed the subject, and told him about getting tossed from the city council meeting.

"I'm not sure stirring up trouble was a good idea,

although I'd love to have seen you in action," Jason said.

I shrugged. "Just doing my job."

"I talked to Detective Whitten today. Marc's case is at a dead end. He's questioned everybody at the office who may have known Marc and can find no one with a motive."

"Except Brad Holmes and Ken Shay."

"They have alibis. Brad Holmes was home with his wife and Ken Shay was barhopping on South Street."

"Swell—a loyal spouse and a bunch of barflies as witnesses. What do you plan to do now that you've been tossed out of the office?"

He ran a hand over his chin. "I've been gone from my Los Angeles office too long. I can't afford to linger in Port Royale much longer. If something doesn't break by mid-week, I'll have to return."

My heart plummeted to my shoes. Leave? He couldn't be serious. We were just beginning a relationship I wanted to pursue. "But you'll come back, won't you?"

He stared, but I was unable to read the expression on his face. He remained inscrutable, then smiled and traced a finger down my cheek to my mouth. "I may."

His answer pissed me off. It wasn't what I wanted to hear and given his ability to read me, was afraid I'd been transparent as glass with my question. I gulped my drink.

"By the way, I saw an interesting photograph yesterday," I said.

"Oh?"

"It was taken in March of last year. The picture showed Shay and Holmes in a group photo with some city honchos. Guess who also showed up?"

"From the expression on your face and the tone of your voice, I'd have to say me."

"I thought you said you didn't come here."

"I said I didn't come often. In March of last year, I arrived unannounced to attend a board meeting and see Marc. I think there was some kind of political rally being funded by Shay and Holmes. I attended. The picture must have been taken then."

"But you said you said you'd never met any of the city council members."

His brows drew together in a frown and he quaffed the rest of his martini. "Look, Shelley, I attend a lot of political events all over the country. It's good business. I can't be expected to remember every Congressman, Senator, or Mayor I meet at every function. Do you remember everybody you interview? I doubt it."

He spoke in a sharp tone, and I didn't like that he'd turned my question back on me. Before I could snap back a pithy reply, a discreet knock sounded on the door.

I sat on the sofa while the waiter arranged the food service cart in front of the window. When the man left, Jason pulled out the chair and motioned me forward. I sat, still irritated with both him and myself. He leaned over and hugged me from behind, then kissed my cheek.

"If it's any consolation to you, I was here the previous July for a meeting, too." He used a finger to tip my chin up. "I always come back." He dropped a light kiss on my mouth.

That was more or less what I wanted to hear. With my good humor restored, I tackled my salad. Jason opened the champagne. The cork bounced off the ceiling and landed at his feet. Laughing, my doubts faded. Jason *would* return. The damning photo was no longer important.

The succulent lobster practically melted in my mouth and the filet was grilled just the way I liked it. The champagne slid down my throat smooth as silk, the bubbles exploding with taste only a good French wine could achieve. Jason's dessert selection surprised me. I hadn't figured him to indulge in that SoFla tourist favorite, Key Lime Pie. He had requested one large slice and we fed each other. It was the sexiest dessert I'd ever eaten.

Jason poured the last of the champagne. "The strangest thing happened today. Lynnette Palmer stopped by my office asking questions about Marc."

"What kind of questions?"

"Things like, was it true Marc and her secretary, Peggy, were engaged? Did Marc ever talk to me about his job? Did he enjoy working at Shay and Holmes or did he miss being a CPA? Why did he come to S and H in the first place?"

"Not exactly subtle, was she? Did she say why she wanted to know?"

"No, but she looked uncomfortable as hell asking the questions. I covered Peggy by telling her they were just friends who dated occasionally."

"Did you warn Peggy?"

"Yeah, in the break room later. I danced around the rest of Lynnette's queries."

"Maybe she's getting scared."

"Maybe, but she sure left pumping me for information on Marc until the last minute. She should have done that when I first arrived." He finished the champagne and rose from his seat. "I guess it's time to get down to business. Grab a box and open it."

This wasn't the business I wanted to indulge in, but did so anyway while he pushed the service cart into the hall. A distant rumble of thunder told me the hot, humid weather was about to break.

An hour later, we had made progress. A growing stack of clothing spread over the sofa, and Marc's books were piled on the coffee table. Things of a more personal nature like jewelry graced the end table.

"Good grief, a stamp collection," I exclaimed as I opened another box. "I had no idea Marc collected stamps."

"As a kid, he collected everything, but stamps fascinated him. Marlene might like to have it."

I couldn't remember having collected anything as a child, not even Barbie dolls.

A peal of thunder announced the predicted thunderstorms had arrived and a few minutes later the wind driven rain hammered at the windows. It was a typical Florida storm with vivid lightning, cracking thunder, and the rain coming in short hard bursts.

I packed the clothing in a couple of boxes and asked Jason about the books.

"I'll go through them later. Most will go to a second hand bookstore." He picked up the containers I'd filled and carried them to the door. "I'll take these down tomorrow."

He swept up the rings, cufflinks, and tie bars, disappearing with them into the bedroom while I tackled one of the office boxes.

I had barely opened it when a brilliant flash of

lightning followed immediately by the roar of thunder, shook the windows. I emitted a startled yelp. The lights dimmed, blazed, dimmed again, and then winked out. The wind shrieked around the corner of the building and rain pelted the glass like bullets.

"Damn, that was close," Jason said somewhere from the vicinity of the bedroom door.

"It must have struck right outside."

A second later the hotel generators kicked in and the lights popped back on.

"Are you okay?" he asked.

"Fine, just didn't expect it. Wow, it sounds like a hurricane squall line. It should be gone soon. These kinds of storms don't last long."

As we opened and dispensed with boxes of office supplies, the storm moved further inland until all that remained was the gentle patter of a light shower.

I peered into another box. It contained technical manuals and books with such fascinating titles as *The Law and Accounting* and *Offshore Accounts for Everyone*.

Pulling them out, I added them to the pile, and stood to stretch my legs. As I did, my elbow brushed the not so neat tower sending them crashing over into a heap.

I picked up one of the thick paperbound computer manuals. Awkward and heavy, it slipped from my hand. A tissue thin piece of paper floated out from between the pages. I picked it up and stared.

"Jason, look at this. It's one of those cryptograms."

He hurried over and snatched it from my hand. "The first two lines are a message of some sort followed by what looks like a list."

I licked my lips. "You mean like what was on the CD?"

"There are no numbers, just letters."

He took the paper over to the desk and began to jot down possible solutions while I shook the remaining books. Nothing else fluttered out.

I delved into a different box. The first item I saw was a calendar. I glanced at January, but saw nothing of interest other than the name Peggy written on about half the days. I flipped to February. He had marked several days with the words "lunch," "flowers," and "theatre." I assumed they referred to Peggy Wyatt, too. Then my gaze fell on the heavily circled date, February 19th—four days after the murder.

"Jason, what do you make of this?"

He stopped his figuring to look at the calendar. His brow wrinkled. "Maybe he had a date with Peggy."

I shook my head. "No. If they'd had a date, he'd use her name."

"Then I have no idea. Maybe it meant something special to the two of them. I'll ask Peggy the next time I see her." He returned to his puzzle.

"Any luck with the cryptogram?"

"No. I thought I had it figured, but the letters don't match."

The frustration in his voice matched that in his eyes. He didn't like being stymied any more than I did.

"Do you suppose he had a different solution for every line?"

"That's what I'm beginning to think."

My cell rang and seeing the night desk number, answered immediately. "Jackson."

"This is McAfee. You're gonna want to hear this."

"What's up?"

"It's not what's up, but what's coming down. I just heard on the police scanner that windows are popping out of the River Tower Condos like confetti on New Year's Eve."

A chill danced up my spine. "Was anybody hurt?"

"I don't know, but you might want to take a gander."

"Thanks, McAfee." I hung up, turning to Jason. "You're not going to believe this. Windows are blowing out of the River Tower Condos."

He didn't hesitate, but rose and headed for the door. In a scene reminiscent of the night of the Century Condos fire, we sped through the lobby and waited impatiently for my car to be brought down from valet parking.

Police barricades had been set up several blocks away from the condos. I parked and dragged Jason through parking lots and alleys until we skidded to a stop down the street from the huge condo plaza. Satellite trucks from TV stations had parked nearby.

The cops herded the evacuated residents to the front of the restaurant on the corner. We trotted over to mingle. Jason grasped my wrist and pulled me toward the policeman standing by one of the barriers.

"Officer, can you please tell me what's going on? My wife and I were told the building was in danger. We ran down ten flights of stairs and can't get anyone to answer our questions."

Lying or not, his authoritative tone brought results. The policeman tapped his fingers against the bill of his hat. "I'm sorry, sir, but the storm apparently damaged some of the windows."

"But why evacuate?" I asked. "Our windows are intact."

"I think there was also some damage to a few of the balconies. It's better to be safe than sorry. I'm sure you won't be inconvenienced long."

"Look out!" someone cried from behind us.

We jerked our heads upwards to see another plate of glass hurtle to the ground where it shattered with a tremendous bang. Shards flew everywhere and some bystanders screamed.

"Back," the policeman barked. "Everyone move back around the corner."

"Holy shit," I said to Jason as we shuffled with the crowd. "Hurricane resistant glass shouldn't shatter like that. Another corner cut? I wonder what he means by balcony damage."

"Let's find out."

We wandered through the displaced residents until finding a likely couple to interview.

"What's going on? We didn't have any damage," I said to an older man and woman.

"Boy, we sure did," the man said. "We'd just finished dinner when the storm hit. The wind roared and suddenly the window just kind of sucked out. Anything near it went, too. Damnedest thing I've ever seen."

"I'm still shaking," his wife replied.

"You should see my balcony," another woman said. "The sliding glass doors ripped out and took half the balcony railing with it. Tore it right out of the concrete."

"It was a tornado," an elderly man stated. "I'm from the Midwest, and this sounded just like a twister."

"Were very many units damaged?" Jason asked.

"Anything below the twelfth floor looks to be okay. The biggest damage was between the seventeenth and twenty-first floors, although I understand all the windows in the penthouses are gone."

Another giant crash of shattering glass followed by the sound of something heavier falling into the condo plaza had us all ducking. One of the onlookers poked his head around the corner.

"Somebody's balcony just came down," he reported.

I had to see this for myself and pushed my way to the front of the police line. Huge chunks of concrete lay in a pile, the steel railings sticking up like forlorn toothpicks.

Turning my gaze upward, I saw the hole from where the slab had fallen. The sliding doors stood flush with the side of the building. The residents of River Tower Condos would not return home anytime soon.

I wiggled my way back to Jason guiding him to a quiet doorway away from the throng. "I wonder if this will convince the city and the police to look into Shay and Holmes."

"I don't know," he replied. "S and H will call it an act of God or Mother Nature. Someone will also see to it the debris is picked up and dumped fast."

"Why?"

"Neither Shay and Holmes nor certain city officials will want that concrete analyzed, but I'm not sure it will make any difference. I think this may be the beginning of the end. The lawyers are going to have a field day. Let's get out of here."

He hustled me back to the car. My mind spun with

what I'd seen and heard. Already I had my opening paragraph. Under the gleam of a streetlight, I glanced at my watch. It was not yet ten o'clock. I needed to call Cal and have him meet me in the office. With any luck, my story would hit the front page of tomorrow morning's paper.

Once again in the car, we headed back to the hotel.

"You've been awfully quiet," Jason said.

"I'm thinking about my story, which reminds me, I have to call my boss."

I reached for my phone, but before I could dial, it rang.

"Hello?"

"Shelley, it's Cal."

"Cal, I was just going to call. You won't believe what's happened. The storm blew out half the windows at The River Tower Condos and damaged some of the balconies. Can you meet me at the office? I think we can tie in shoddy construction with—"

"Shelley," Cal interrupted in a somber voice.

"What's wrong?"

There was a moment of silence on the other end that caused my heart to thump in slow, heavy beats.

"I just got a call from the police. Doug Elliott's body was pulled out of the Seminole River two hours ago."

Chapter Sixteen

I gripped my phone hard enough to break it. My other hand clutched the steering wheel convulsively causing the car to swerve to the left and cross the double yellow line into oncoming traffic.

"Look out!" Jason grabbed the wheel setting me back on course amid the blare of horns.

I ignored it all, preferring to concentrate on breathing and not passing out.

"Shelley! Shelley, are you there?" Cal yelled in my ear.

"Yes, I'm here. What happened?" My voice shook. I blinked several times to clear my vision and fought to control my pounding heart. I should have pulled over, but the traffic was too heavy. I slowed to a mere twenty miles per hour. Angry drivers leaned on their horns as they passed me.

"I don't have the details yet, but Sorenson's not taking any chances this time. He wants to meet me at the office right now so he can secure Doug's computer and files. And this time he says he's got a warrant."

"Oh, my God, I can't believe this." My voice came out as a croak and my hands trembled.

"What happened?" Jason asked turning in his seat to stare, his hand hovering over the steering wheel.

"Sorenson also asked me to call and tell you he wanted a meeting tomorrow morning at eight o'clock in the office. Come early."

"Cal, was it an accident?"

"I don't know," he replied after a moment of hesitation. "Like I said, I didn't get a whole lot of details—only that they pulled him out of the river."

"Accident? What accident?" Jason hissed.

"But where in the river?"

"Shelley, I told you, I don't know. My guess is Sorenson will clue us in."

My initial shock wore off allowing my mind to function in rational mode again. "Cal, Doug's message! Oh, my God, do you suppose he really *was* on to something?"

"I hope not. He had no idea how to cope."

"What message?" Jason asked, shaking me by the shoulder.

I shot him a look and shook my head.

"Now, you said windows in The River Tower Condos had blown out?" my boss asked.

I gave him the information as I turned into the hotel driveway stopping under the portico.

"Okay, write what you saw and I'll call Slattery to cover now." Cal paused. "I think you should find someplace else to stay tonight, in case Doug wasn't drunk as a coot and just fell into the water."

The thought had crossed my mind, too. An icy chill tickled the back of my neck like a cold feather.

"Don't worry. I will. I'll see you tomorrow morning."

"What the hell is going on?" Jason demanded when I'd hung up.

I jerked open the car door and stumbled out. "Not here. Let's get up to the room."

He followed me through the lobby and into the elevator. I could tell from the look of exasperation on his face he was ready to explode. In the room, he grasped my shoulders, twisting me around.

"Now, what the hell is going on?"

"That was Cal. The police just dragged Doug Elliott's body out of the river."

Jason's expression didn't change, but his hands tightened, his fingers digging into my flesh. "Was it murder?"

"We don't know."

My eyes filled with tears and overflowed into deep, gut-wrenching sobs like on the night of Marc's death. He relaxed his grip and pulled me to his chest.

"Move in with me until this is over or the cops can give you protection."

"I don't know why the hell I'm crying," I replied, gulping. "I hated the son of a bitch."

"You're crying because you're scared. I'm scared, too." He paused, stroking the back of my head with his hand. "There's only one person who's more frightened—the killer."

I sniffed, pulling away. I didn't like losing control and made an effort to regain my composure. I dried my eyes with the back of my hand and sucked in several deep breaths.

"Why would the killer be frightened? So far he's managed to rack up three kills, assuming Doug was murdered, too, and the cops don't have a clue."

Jason steered me toward the sofa, handing me a box of tissues. "I've heard it said the first murder is the hardest. After that it gets easier."

"I can't imagine how killing a human being could

ever be easy," I replied, blowing my nose.

"Me neither, which is why I don't buy into the theory. No, our killer is scared right down to his toes. He thought killing Marc solved the problem, but *his* death only exacerbated things. Too many people know too much. Sooner or later we'll have a name."

Jason had moved to stare out the window. I rose, wadded up the tissue, and tossed it into the wastebasket next to the desk. I saw the sense in what he said, but at the moment was too tired to care.

"Jason, could you leave a message requesting a five-thirty wake up call?"

"Five-thirty? Why?" he asked, turning and crossing to the bar where he poured a small brandy. He held the bottle up to me, raising his eyebrows in an unspoken query.

I shook my head. "I don't even have a toothbrush with me. I have to go home, clean up, and get to the office early. Sorenson has requested my presence."

"All right, but come straight here after work. I'll go with you to pack your things. I'm not taking any more chances. The son of a bitch has already had a couple of cracks at you." He downed the brandy in one swallow.

His words lifted my spirits and I wondered if the non-marrying Jason Mallory was having second thoughts on the subject. I walked over and slipped my arms around his waist, laying my head on his broad chest. The soothing rhythm of his heartbeat banished the last of my tension.

I turned my gaze upward. His lips met mine for a brief, gentle kiss. Oddly enough, at the moment I preferred it to a searing, passion-filled one.

He pulled away, his hands on my shoulders. "I

suggest a good night's sleep. I haven't had one in days."

"Neither have I. I'm exhausted." As though to prove my point, I yawned.

He smiled and kissed me again. "You can have the bathroom first. Go to bed. You'll find T-shirts in the top drawer of the dresser. I'll be in shortly. I have to check my e-mail."

I didn't waste time in the opulent bathroom, but donned the over-sized shirt and crawled under the covers. I was half asleep when Jason came to bed. He rolled over to snuggle against me, his arm clasped around my midsection.

He lightly kissed my cheek. "Good night, Shelley."

I murmured a thank you. This was the man of my dreams—a strong, take charge male who knew when to be gentle.

****

The strident ringing of the telephone jerked me awake. Jason rolled over and answered, then hung up. "It's five-thirty," he said in a sleepy voice.

"Go back to sleep, darling. I'll see you tonight." I kissed his cheek.

"I'll come with you."

"No need. I'm just a few short minutes away and I doubt the killer has my house staked out."

He threw back the sheet. "I think it's best if…"

I kissed him again. "Jason, I'll be fine. Really."

He stared, and then smiled. "All right, but keep your cell handy and dial nine-one-one if you even think something's wrong." He reached out to run his finger down my cheek. "Can't risk losing you."

I drew in a shaky breath. "Don't worry. You won't

lose me. I don't lose easily." I kissed him a third time. "See you later."

The drive home gave me a few minutes to think. Jason didn't want to lose me. Somewhere along the line, I had fallen in love with Jason Mallory. The knowledge sent an old-fashioned chill of delight along my nerves. Goosebumps rose, and I had the most absurd urge to break into a chorus of *Love Me Tender*. Why, I had no idea. I swallowed a giggle, and then sobered. I'd picked a hell of a time to fall in love. Three murders—not for one minute did I believe Doug Elliott's death had been accidental—and two attempted murders of me hung like a dark cloud above our future together.

I drove around the block a couple of times before pulling into my driveway. Nothing suspicious jumped out at me. Still, I hurried inside, checked all the windows and doors before showering, changing clothes, and heading for the office, arriving just a tick before six forty-five. Cal met me at the reception desk.

"Come on. Dump your stuff. We have work to do before Sorenson gets here. Jackson, you really are a bad influence."

"What do you mean?"

"When Sorenson called last night on my cell, he assumed I was home. I wasn't. I was here, doing some last minute editing. I took a page out of your book."

"Such as?"

"Doug took over Bill's office within thirty seconds of hearing he got the job. He brought his computer with him, but he used Bill's, too lazy to set up his own."

"I know. He was prying into Bill's files to see what he could steal and put his byline on."

"I moved Doug's machine back into his old cubicle, grabbed a few of Bill's old files, and shoved them into Doug's file cabinet."

"So Sorenson took Doug's computer that's been disconnected for almost a week, and a bunch of bullshit files Bill never got around to throwing away?"

Cal shrugged and tossed me a shit-eating grin. "Eventually, the cops will find out Doug used Bill's office, but before they do, I want those files you say Doug found. We haven't got much time. Sorenson's due at eight and people will start wandering in soon."

We entered Bill's office. Cal took the desk and credenza drawers while I searched the file cabinets and bookshelves. We came up with a big zero.

"Damn it, where did Doug file them?" Cal said slamming a drawer he'd been through for the third time.

"Don't tell me he filed them in his cubicle and Sorenson got them after all."

"No, I checked last night. Except for the usual stuff, Doug's cabinets and desk were empty. Think, Shelley. Where else could he have hidden them?"

"Hidden them?" I asked, surprised.

"Doug wasn't the strongest battery in the flashlight, but he was smart enough to realize that if Bill hid them, they must be important."

"Maybe he took them home."

"In which case, Sorenson has them. When he left last night, he was headed there."

I looked behind furniture. Cal got down on his hands and knees to inspect the undersides of the desk and credenza.

"Cal, this is useless," I said running my hand behind a bookcase. "Not even Doug would have gone to these lengths. He'd have stashed them someplace with easy access."

"I agree." He checked his watch. "Let's get out of here. I'll be in my office. And don't forget to erase Doug's message."

I did as he ordered. When the first employee appeared for work, I pretended to be busy.

Sorenson and Detective Whitten arrived on time. I was surprised to see the latter. They met briefly with Cal, and then set up shop in the conference room. My desk phone rang.

"Sorenson wants to see you. I told him I'd informed you of Doug's death this morning. Other than that, they know nothing."

I hung up and made my way to the conference room, tapped on the door, and entered.

"Please have a seat, Miss Jackson," Sorenson said.

I eased my way into a chair. This time I was innocent of any skullduggery—well, mostly innocent—and had my nerves under control. Both detectives sat across the table from me wearing grim expressions.

Sorenson began the questioning. "Mr. Randolph tells us he informed you about Doug Elliott's death this morning."

"Yes. I came in early. He was already here and told me." Basically, the truth.

"You don't seem broken up about it," Whitten said.

"I'm not," I replied with a shrug. "I didn't like the guy." Total truth. If they'd wired the chair with a lie detector, I'd pass with flying colors.

"Why not?" Whitten asked.

"He was totally unsuitable for the job. He knew nothing about writing, journalism, or the newspaper business. He only got the position because his aunt owns a huge hunk of stock and is good friends with the owner."

"I hear a lot of resentment in your voice, Miss Jackson," Sorenson said.

"Damned right I was resentful."

"Resentful enough to do something about it?"

I shot him a scornful glance and snorted. "Get real. When did he die?"

"As close as we can figure, night before last. I assume you have an alibi," Whitten said with a smirk.

I crossed my arms over my chest to prevent myself from slapping the snide grin from his face. "I spent the evening at the City Council meeting. Anyone present will tell you I got tossed out on my ear along with a bunch of other people about ten or ten-thirty."

"Coroner says Elliott died closer to one or two in the morning," he said, the smug smile still in place.

"I still didn't do it."

"When was the last time you saw Elliott?" Sorenson asked.

"The afternoon before last around four or four-thirty. He stopped by my cubicle to ask a question."

"What question?"

"I don't remember. I was busy. Cal had given him an assignment, and he asked my advice on how to conduct an interview." A little white lie, but nothing they could disprove.

"Did Doug Elliott know Marc Chambers?" Whitten asked, leaning forward.

"Not to my knowledge."

"How about Jason Mallory?" he persisted.

"Ask Mallory, but I doubt it."

"That's all for now, Miss Jackson. If you think of anything else, please call," Sorenson stated.

"I have a question," I said.

"What's that?"

"How did Doug die?"

"Preliminary coroner's report says he drowned. His blood alcohol level was point one two. That's pretty hammered."

"Are you telling me Doug Elliott got drunk and fell into the water?"

Sorenson stared, his expression grim. "He fell all right, but the back of his head was caved in first."

"With what?"

"Probably a rock, which is most likely now at the bottom of the river. He was alive when he hit the water."

"Or maybe he just fell in and hit his head." Somehow, I didn't see Doug, drunk or not, falling into the river, especially after leaving me such a cryptic voice mail. "Where did it happen?"

"We're not sure."

Whitten threw a glance at Sorenson. My reporter's instincts were on red alert, and the fact I had taken over the interview gave me a surge of satisfaction. "Where did you find the body?"

"We didn't. A couple of snowbirds own a condo on Freehan Avenue. The storm caught them out, so they took shelter under the drawbridge. Elliott's body was wedged between one of the pilings and the seawall."

"It's a wonder nobody saw the body floating down the river during the day. That portion of the river is busy."

Sorenson shrugged. "For all we know that's where

he went in or his body could have been caught on an underwater snag. The storm may have dislodged it."

"Yes, but suppose…"

Whitten cleared his throat and Sorenson took the hint. "Thank you for your time. We'll be in touch."

Both men rose, and I had no choice but to do the same. "How are the investigations going?" I asked taking one last shot. "Are you making any progress?"

"It's a hard nut to crack, but we'll find the killer. Count on it," Whitten said, giving me a hard stare.

I think he still suspected me of Marc's murder even though his threat to match my voice to the 9-1-1 tape hadn't materialized. I nodded and left the room, closing the door behind me. If they suspected Cal had duped them, they hadn't let on.

Back in my cubicle, I called Cal with the details.

"Write up the story about the River Tower Condos and the storm. I'll run it tomorrow. You and Slattery will share the byline. You take over Bill's job."

It was now official. I wanted to cheer, but kept my response muted. "Thanks, but what about Miriam Noble?"

"I've already spoken with her. I convinced her to let me use my judgment in naming a replacement. Now, get busy. I want that story by the time you leave tonight."

I hung up and stared at the aquarium screen saver on my computer screen. I should have been turning cartwheels now that I had the job, but couldn't. It had come at too great a price.

****

I banged out my story and sent it to Cal. In all the excitement, I had forgotten my appointment with

Councilman Jose Cortez. He had a small office in the Port Royale City Hall, but scheduled the interview at his business, Cortez and Company. He and his brothers ran a large lawn maintenance service. I had no problem finding the place and arrived only a few minutes late. His receptionist showed me into his office.

"Miss Jackson, it's a pleasure to meet you," he said with a smile.

"My pleasure, Councilman." I sat, setting up my equipment on his littered desk.

Jose Cortez was in his mid-thirties, and from the picture on the file cabinet behind him, married with four children. He had won election two years ago by a landslide with the perfect combination of Latin good looks and campaign rhetoric straight from the hip.

"Thank you for seeing me, Mr. Cortez."

"Not at all. Would you like something to drink?" He made an attempt to straighten his desk.

"No, thank you. I'm on a tight schedule. Do you mind if I just jump right in?"

"Go ahead. I have a tight schedule, too."

"Shall we begin with development, Mr. Cortez?"

"Not all development is evil, Miss Jackson. Every city needs it in order to thrive, but over-development can kill a local economy if things take a downturn—like a few years ago. Things are looking up, but not to those sky-high levels yet."

"What's your opinion of the development on the Seminole River and the beachfront?"

"Too damned much of it and it's too expensive. Sure, the city gets taxes from the owners, but we also have to provide services. In my opinion, not enough of the taxes are going to supply what's needed."

"Can you explain further?"

Cortez leaned back with his hands clasped behind his head. "Bluntly put, we don't pay our law enforcement, firefighters, or schoolteachers enough. A lot of them can't afford to live here. They should be our first and highest priority, not how much can be socked away in pensions for city workers."

"Is that happening?" I asked. "The mayor denied any such thing."

"It's slowed, but that wasn't always the thinking. It's one of the reasons why I ran for office—that and the fact taxes are rising at an alarming rate. I remember when the housing market took a dump twenty or so years ago. People couldn't sell their homes for what they had in them, so they just let the banks foreclose. It's happening again. And don't even get me started on the insurance rates."

"Which brings me to Shay and Holmes Development and Construction. I looked up your voting record and you've voted against every Shay and Holmes proposal to come before the council. Care to comment?"

"Turn off your recorder. This is off the record and if you print it, I'll call you a liar."

Curious, I did as he asked and licked my lips in anticipation.

"I don't like the way they do business. I met both principals during my campaign. They contributed and I always like to thank a person who sends in a check."

"But?"

"There was something about Brad Holmes I didn't trust. He was smooth and I had the feeling he was sizing me up. I guess if a company is going to invest five grand in a political campaign, they have a right to question me, but the questions weren't about where I stood on anything. They were personal. Did I make a living with the lawn service? Did I have outside investments? Who was my investment counselor? I didn't like it and told him it was none of his damned business."

He stopped and fiddled with a pen. I liked this man. My gut said he was unique—an honest politician.

"Not very subtle for Brad Holmes. What was his reaction?"

"He apologized for offending me and offered to buy lunch. I refused and told him no harm done.

"Then about six months ago, I was at a fundraiser when Kenneth Shay asked me how much it would take to change my mind regarding my no vote on their latest proposal."

"He tried to bribe you?" My voice rose in disbelief. Even for Ken Shay, this was overt.

"I told him to drop dead and if he ever mentioned money again, I'd have him arrested. He backed off real fast, saying he'd meant it as a joke. Since he was drunk at the time, I gave him the benefit of the doubt. Now, I automatically vote against any project headed by Shay and Holmes." He paused and frowned. "Greed is an awful thing. The longer politicians are in office the easier it becomes to look the other way. When I was first elected, Gerald Talman suggested I'd do well if Cortez and Company wanted the contract for all lawn maintenance for the city. I refused. Conflict of interest comes back to bite you in the ass."

I tucked this morsel of information away for a later date. Another interview with this man loomed as soon as I could get to it. For the first time, I'd found a politician I wanted to vote for.

"Did you read any of Bill Mathias's columns concerning bribery and Shay and Holmes?"

"Yes. I started my own investigation into voting patterns. If you want my opinion, I think some of my political colleagues are dirty as hell, and I intend to find out exactly who."

"Mr. Cortez, you sound like a man on a mission. Will I be calling you Mayor Cortez in the near future?"

He grinned, showing even white teeth. "Anything is possible, Miss Jackson." He glanced at his watch. "I'm sorry to rush you, but I have an appointment. Keep me posted on what you find out. Here's my card. E-mail me at the lawn service address."

I took the card and thanked him, promising to keep him informed. His information was dynamite. All I needed was the match.

****

I walked into my cubicle when the phone rang.

"Jackson, come to my office. I have something for you," Cal said.

I wound my way through the cubicle maze, noticing the police presence had left. Cal's office door was closed. I knocked and he barked for me to come in. I did so and closed it behind me.

"What's up?" I asked.

He handed me a manila envelope. "These are Doug's notes. I copied them last night before the cops showed up. See what you can find. They may actually contain a kernel of something important."

I nodded, returned to my office space, and opened the envelope. It contained about a dozen pages of notes, none of which made much sense. Doug's style consisted of numerous exclamation points and heavy underlining of key words like "South," "Shay," and "condos." His spelling was atrocious and his handwriting sloppy. The papers were messy and disorganized. I doubted I'd find anything important or relevant.

I shoved his notes back into the envelope. I had to organize *my* notes on Jose Cortez. Opening the bottom drawer of my desk, I started to drop the package in when I stopped and stared. Several file folders were already there.

A strange chill washed over me and my heart thumped hard. I caught my lower lip between my teeth, glancing around to see if anyone lurked nearby, then pulled out the folders and opened the top one.

A sticky note was attached to the photograph I had identified for Doug. I recognized his sloppy handwriting.

"You and Cal think you're so smart! Well, I know something you don't and when *I'm* finished investigating, you *both* will be singing *my* praises. Take a good look and see what you've missed!! Bring this to my office when *you* see what I did!!!"

What the hell did this mean? I stared at the photo again, but saw nothing—or no one—I hadn't seen before. I turned it over and discovered a second, smaller picture underneath.

The grainy quality made identifying the place it was taken impossible, but the man seated at a table was Kenneth Shay, his hand extending an envelope across the table. The man with him held a drink, partially obscured his face while he reached for the envelope. A payoff? The recipient looked familiar, and I tried to remember where I'd seen him before, but the angle of the photo and the drink defeated me. After a few seconds I gave up. I put the picture aside and opened the second file folder seeking an answer.

It contained a list in Bill's handwriting. I had no idea who the people on the list were until I read the name Ralph Sorrento, head of the office of building inspectors in Port Royale. The last name was Greg Thompson. It had a phone number beside it. On a hunch, I dialed.

"Building inspections, Thompson here."

"Mr. Greg Thompson?"

"Yes. Who's this?"

"Mr. Thompson, my name is Shelley Jackson. I'm a reporter for *The South Florida Standard* and the late Bill Mathias's assistant. I found your name and number while going through his notes. Would you be available for an interview?"

A moment or two of silence greeted my announcement. Could this guy have been Bill's informant—the person who'd sent the first e-mail?

"Oh, God, I thought this was over. Give me five minutes. What's your number? I'll call you back."

I gave him my cell number and hung up half expecting to never hear from him. I was wrong. A few minutes later, he returned the call.

"Mr. Thompson?"

"I couldn't talk where I was. Too many ears."

Traffic noises in the background told me he'd moved outside. "Mr. Thompson, I found your name along with several others in Bill's files. I take it you are his inside man."

"Damn, I thought this went away when he died. What do you want?"

"I want whatever you gave or were going to give my boss." I kept my voice smooth and under control hoping I sounded as experienced as Bill.

"If I do, will you go away and leave me alone?"

"Probably."

I waited while he inhaled and exhaled a couple of times. I could almost smell the combination of cigarette smoke and nervous fear.

"All right, I'll meet you for lunch, but nowhere near downtown, okay? I don't want to take the chance of anyone seeing us together."

I glanced at my watch. It was almost noon. In view of my last encounter with an informant, I chose a busy restaurant in Palmetto Gardens an hour from now.

"This is our first and last meeting, Miss Jackson. After today, I never expect to hear from you again."

He hung up, leaving me wondering what kind of dynamite *he* possessed.

****

I sat in the restaurant sipping iced tea and glancing at my watch every few seconds. Greg Thompson was fifteen minutes late, and I had the horrible suspicion he wouldn't show.

Before I'd left, Cal had copied everything in the folders, including the note left by Doug and the photos. He hadn't been able to identify the second man in the small snapshot either.

"The picture may have been taken with a cell phone. Shay was caught almost full face, but the other guy is only about three-quarters. His hand and the drink are in the way. Still, there is something about him I should recognize," he said.

"Is the envelope a payoff?"

"We have no idea what's in the envelope. For all we know it's a number to Hooker of the Month Club. Can't even be sure it *is* an envelope. Picture's not that good. Take these with you. See if Thompson can ID either of them."

Someone stopped next to the table. I looked up expecting to see the waitress. Instead, I stared into the worried eyes of a man carrying a manila envelope. Without saying a word, he slid into the seat across from me.

"Miss Jackson? Did you come alone?" His gaze darted from side to side.

"Yes. I take it you're Greg Thompson."

He nodded in a jerky fashion, flinching when the waitress asked, "Would you like to order?"

I requested a salad and Thompson a burger. When she left, I said, "What have you got for me?"

He shoved the envelope across the table. "It's the list of names Mathias wanted. I was supposed to meet him the day after he died. I kind of hoped nobody else knew about our arrangement."

"What have you got?" I repeated, opening the envelope.

"Names of people in the building department who have retired in the last couple of years. Some of them are legit retirements, but five or six are younger guys."

I skimmed the list and saw a couple of names from Bill's notes. My late boss had been on the same trail as me. "How did Bill find you?"

"I called him a couple of weeks before he died."

So he wasn't the sender of the first e-mail. "Why?"

Thompson slicked back his hair with a trembling hand. "Look, I'm not proud of this, but I subbed on an inspection for Shay and Holmes one day a couple of years ago. The guy who was supposed to do it was sick."

"What kind of an inspection?"

"Electrical. I had to fail them. The work wasn't up to code. The supervisor asked me back to the construction trailer for coffee and offered me a grand to change my mind. Said he was behind schedule and didn't have time to go through another inspection. Promised to fix the problems."

"Did you take it?"

Thompson shifted his gaze and nodded. "I said no at first, but he kept asking me to give him a break. I finally agreed when he upped the price to three thousand bucks. I needed the money."

"Was that the only time you took money from Shay and Holmes?"

He nodded again. "Yeah. I changed the inspection card to say the project passed. That was the only time I ever inspected one of their properties."

"Who was the inspector supposed to be that day?"

"Bob Hayes."

I scanned the list and found his name third from the end—an early retiree.

"What was the building you passed?" I tried to keep the sneer from my voice. For a few thousand dollars the man had endangered God knows how many people.

He swallowed hard. "The Century Condos."

"The ones that recently burned to the ground?" This time I let the contempt seep into my tone. "Why did you contact Bill?"

"His articles got to me. I saw that wiring. I knew it was bad and would someday come back to haunt me. I thought maybe talking to him would ease my conscience."

"Did it?" I asked with a hint of sarcasm.

"A little, until the fire. When Mathias was killed, I got scared. I put in for early retirement three days ago."

The waitress brought our food. Thompson wolfed down his burger and fries in five minutes flat, then gulped his tea. He belched and tapped his breastbone with his fist. I was amazed he hadn't choked to death.

He wiped his mouth and hands. "I have to get back. I don't expect to hear from you again, and if you try to use my name, I'll deny everything." He slid out of the seat.

"Wait a minute." I showed him the photos. "Do you recognize these men?"

He gazed at the pictures for a few seconds, a brief look of fear crossing his face. "Nope. Never seen them before."

He turned and walked away quickly. He'd lied. I doubt he'd know Ken Shay or the people at the cocktail party—Thompson wasn't that far up in the pecking order. That left the unidentified man.

I stared at the photo. Greg Thompson had just handed me a key. Now I needed to find the lock.

Chapter Seventeen

I followed Jason through the door to his suite, staggering under the weight of my laptop, briefcase, and two duffle bags. Jason dumped a garment bag, another duffle, and a rolling suitcase in the bedroom.

"Did you pack your entire wardrobe?" he asked.

"Smart ass. The rolling case contains most of my notes and Bill's files from the office."

"That's still a lot of clothes."

I didn't answer, but heaved one of the duffles onto the bed. "How long will I be staying here?"

"Can't be too long. I have to get back to L. A. soon."

His words sent my heart down to my toes. He really did plan to leave. I lifted my chin. Rationalization is a wonderful thing. Of course, he had to return. He had a business to run, but he'd be back. I repeated the phrase like a mantra while unpacking, believing it was true or risk terminal depression.

Jason leaned against the dresser, arms folded across his chest watching me. "Want to hear about my day?"

"Was it interesting?"

"Very."

"Make me a martini and order some food. I'll be done here in a minute."

"Your wish is my command, princess," he said

with a grin before exiting.

I hurried to finish my task while Jason ordered. I wanted to tell him about my interviews with Jose Cortez and Greg Thompson.

In the living room, Jason handed me a martini. I gulped, the cold liquor sliding down my throat smooth as silk, its liquid fire calming my frayed nerves. For the first time today, I relaxed.

"So, how *was* your day?" I asked, taking a seat on the sofa.

"I heard from the man who worked for the cleaning service. He's agreed to meet me tomorrow morning for breakfast."

"What did he say? Does he know anything?"

"He refused to talk over the phone, but I think I've found the man Marc used before Peggy came on the scene. He sounded nervous as hell."

"I'd like to sit in on that interview. Do you mind if I come along?"

He shrugged, and then smiled. "I don't care provided you don't tell him you're a reporter. It might scare him off. We'll pretend we're married like when looking at apartments."

"Of course, *dumpling.*"

His grin widened. "There was also an impromptu board meeting called today in the office. They must have been damned nervous to call it with me still in town."

I drained my glass and wiggled it at him asking for a refill. "I take it the main topic of conversation was The River Tower Condos."

"Of course," he said, handing me a fresh drink. "They're covering their asses all the way, blaming the sub-contractors and Mother Nature. Ken Shay suggested firing the supervisors on the project."

"Wouldn't that let the door open for some dangerous testimony down the line?"

"Brad Holmes squashed the idea immediately, saying the supervisors were duped by the subs. Shay shook so badly he could barely hold his coffee cup."

"Probably hung over."

"Not completely. He's scared. I don't think they expected trouble this soon. Holmes appeared calm, but I saw the worry in his eyes. I wouldn't be surprised if both of them are planning a quick move to a Caribbean island with no extradition treaty with the U. S."

"The money is probably already there."

"No doubt. They're covering their asses on the Century Condos, only this time blaming poor maintenance, too." Jason took a long swallow of his second drink. "I also took the opportunity to resign from the board."

The news surprised me. "Why? You could have still nosed around."

"I don't think so. They've politely told me to get lost, remember? Soon, my office will no longer be available. I'm sure that in a few weeks, they'd have asked for my resignation anyway. Besides, they aren't likely to say anything of a suspicious nature in front of me. I've asked too many questions."

The knock on the door signaled the arrival of our dinner. I was hungry enough to eat both meals.

The waiter rolled the cart into the room. Before he left I had the cloches off, inhaling the aromas of roasted chicken in some kind of fragrant sauce, and garlic bread. I pulled up a chair, snatched the silverware, and proceeded to cut off a hunk of meat while Jason opened the wine.

"Hungry?" he asked in a droll tone.

"All I had today was a bagel and a crummy salad. If you don't hurry, I'll eat yours, too."

He laughed, sat, and poured the Chardonnay. "So, how was your day, if you can stop eating long enough to tell me?"

Between bites of meat, salad, and garlic bread, I told him about my interviews.

He sipped his wine. "Sounds like Cortez is politically ambitious."

"He is. He wants Cosworth's job—bad. But Greg Thompson is the real link."

Jason finished his meal and swirled the wine in the glass, a frown on his face. "You know, the person you should try to nail down is the man or woman who schedules the inspections."

"I guess that makes sense, assuming he or she will talk to me."

"Somebody has to schedule the right inspectors for the Shay and Holmes projects. And once the inspector was familiar with the project, the client could e-mail directly to set up a time. So, technically, the scheduler is only involved once."

"So he may not be in on it?"

Jason shrugged. "The right inspector still has to get to the scene."

"I'll get on it tomorrow." I ripped the last piece of garlic bread from the bowl. "I also found Bill's files."

"What files?"

"The ones Doug was digging through, but didn't understand." I finished my food telling him about what

I'd discovered in my desk drawer and the new picture. Gastronomically satiated, I fetched the files and poured another glass of wine while he examined them.

"That's definitely me with Eleanor White." He picked up the smaller photo. "Who's the guy with Shay?"

"I don't know, but when I showed the photo to Thompson he denied recognizing him. He was lying. His eyes got wide and his mouth twitched." I drank some of the Chardonnay. "Suppose we go to South Street tonight and nose around?"

"Why?"

"Doug left a drunken, taunting message on my voicemail night before last insinuating he'd uncovered something vital. From the background noise I'd have to say he was in a bar called The Wild Dog. We could ask some questions and flash the pictures around."

"Miss Jackson, you have just named our night's entertainment."

****

The South Street nightclub district throbs with activity during the weekends, especially after ten o'clock. Since it was not yet eight on a weeknight, we moved easily up and down the street.

Our first stop was The Wild Dog. We ordered beer and sat back to watch the show of waitresses in varying degrees of abbreviated clothing dance on the bar. They gyrated nonstop for twenty minutes only to be replaced by new talent including a few female patrons. The music never ceased and the bar top was scarred with the heel marks of countless cowboy boots.

The waitress brought us another round. I showed her the cell phone picture.

"Do you recognize either one of these men?" I shouted over the music, the stomping, and the encouraging cheers of the mostly male clientele.

"No, can't say that I do."

"How about any of the people in this picture?" I showed her the one taken at the fundraiser.

She shook her head again. "Sorry. You might try the bouncer, Bruno," she said, jerking her chin toward the door. "He sees everybody who enters and has a memory like an elephant."

I left Jason appreciating the dancing waitresses and tackled Bruno—the perfect name for a bouncer. He even looked like a Bruno—tall, beefy, no neck, and arms like fireplugs. I wondered if he'd ever played football or wrestled.

"Excuse me, Bruno?" I asked, sidling next to him.

"Yeah," he acknowledged, cutting his eyes to a new arrival entering the door. He snapped his fingers. "Hey, you! ID."

He matched the driver's licenses to the faces, and then nodded the newcomers through. I took advantage of a lull in the activity to flash the photos at him.

"Ever see any of these people before?" I shoved the cocktail party photo under his nose.

"I've seen the guy on the right several times. Don't know his name." Bruno pointed at Ken Shay.

"How about the others?"

He shrugged, handing the photo back. "It's possible."

I gave him the cell phone picture. "What about this guy, the one on the right?"

"Shitty photo." He stared at it for a few seconds before giving it back. "If my father was in it, I wouldn't recognize him."

I stepped aside as he carded a group of guys wearing University of Miami T-shirts. He nodded them through.

"A couple of nights ago a guy called me from here. His name is Doug Elliott. Ever heard of him?" I asked.

"Nope, but I'm not big on names."

"He stood about five-ten or eleven, kind of a chunky physique, but soft—no exercise. He may have been sporting the remnants of a black eye."

Bruno thought for a second. "Yeah, yeah, I remember him. Fucking weirdo."

"What do you mean?"

"He was drunk when he hit the door, but that's not what caught my eye. He dressed all in black like he was a spy or something—you know, trench coat complete with an Indiana Jones hat pulled low. He ordered and grabbed a waitress's ass. I had to tell him to can it or leave. He got snotty and said I'd be sorry. He was a reporter about to unveil the story of a lifetime. I told him I didn't care if he was Katie Couric, if he didn't keep his hands to himself I'd toss his ass onto the sidewalk."

"What happened then?"

"He strutted to the bar, ordered a beer, and tried to lick one of the dancer's legs. I was halfway across the room ready to collar the son of a bitch when the girl took care of him. Stomped on his hand. He yelled and called her a few names, but settled down." Bruno paused, a furrow wrinkling his brow. "Let me see that big picture again."

I shoved the fundraising photo into his hand.

"You know, this could be one of the guys he met."

He pointed at Shay.

"He met somebody?"

"Yeah. He'd been here about an hour when these two dudes came in and joined him at the bar. They left together a few minutes later, laughing. I heard one say they'd party all night. The last I saw of them, they headed across the street to The Happy Hour."

"Are you sure it was this man?"

"Nope. They both wore baseball caps, and I had better things to do than keep my eye on them." He tapped the image of Ken Shay again with his finger and stared at the photo harder. "The more I think of it, the more certain I am he *was* one of the two."

"Could you swear to it in court?"

"No fucking way, babe."

Elated, I returned to the table and Jason whose gaze was still riveted on the bar. I told him what I'd found out.

"So, he thinks Ken Shay may have met your colleague," he commented. "Hard thing to prove. It's a popular bar, dark, and with lots of people coming and going."

I drained my beer. "And Shay, the party animal, would claim he'd met Doug on previous occasions at several bars and that this was just a chance encounter. Come on, let's go."

Jason shot one last look at the dancer before following me into the street. Our next stop was The Happy Hour. I described Doug and showed the photos to the bartender. He didn't remember three men, but did identify Ken Shay as a quasi-regular.

We tried several other bars learning Ken Shay had visited all over the years, but no one could ID the other men or recall seeing them together two nights ago.

"The last bar where we can place all three of them is The Happy Hour at approximately eleven o'clock," Jason said.

"And according to the cops, that's two to three hours before Doug died. They had to be somewhere along here."

We stood on the corner shouting over the blare of music gushing from a lounge on the corner. A large knot of bar hoppers stumbled out, jostling us off the curb before heading down a side street.

"They seemed in a hurry. What's down that way?"

"A nightclub called The Man Eater. It's pretty good, but it doesn't get rocking until after midnight."

"Three guys—one of them drunk—could sit at a table in a dark nightclub damned near unnoticed for hours," Jason commented with an arched eyebrow.

I didn't hesitate, but grasped his arm and followed the group of noisy tourists.

It was only nine-thirty and The Man Eater had less than a third of the tables full. We chose to belly up to the bar and ordered beers. When the bartender set them in front of us, I went into interrogation mode, showing him the pictures and handing him a penlight I'd fished out of my purse.

"Sorry, but unless they sat at the bar, I wouldn't know them from Adam. Try one of the waitresses." He turned and walked away.

A couple of women in skimpy shorts and tight tank tops stood at the end of the bar. As we approached, one of them set some full glasses on a tray and left.

"Excuse me," I said to the remaining redhead, going into my spiel before flashing the fundraising photo and shining the light on it. I didn't expect the reaction.

"That pervert!" she spat out, pointing a finger at Ken Shay's image. "He comes in here all the time. Whenever one of us passes his table, he tries to cop a feel. And that one leaves a dollar tip no matter how much or what he drinks. Fucking cheapskate." She now pointed to Bennett Russell.

"He's a regular, too?" I asked, glancing at Jason who listened with raised eyebrows.

"I wouldn't call him a regular, but he's in often enough."

"With the pervert?" Jason asked.

"Sometimes. I've also seen him with the other guy on the end," she snapped pointing to Brad Holmes.

"So those three have all been in here at one time or another?" Jason asked.

"Yeah, but mostly the pervert. And he's also been here with *him*," she said with a snarl jabbing her finger at the image of Ron Zimmerman.

"The city manager?" I said. Now this was interesting. "He's a regular?"

"Hell no. He just hassles honest people trying to make a living."

"How?" Jason said.

"My brother had a shop in River Plaza. It was just a little souvenir type place, but shortly after he opened this slimy character shows up demanding protection money."

"Protection? As in mob?" I asked in astonishment.

The waitress snorted. "Look, honey, I'm from Jersey and I know mob when I see it. These clowns aren't half that good. Refuse protection in Jersey and you lose your kneecaps. Here, it was citation after citation after citation for nitpicking shit like gum wrappers on the sidewalk in front of his store. Some guy would come along, toss some trash, and within seconds, along came the ticket writer. It was a politician's way of saying 'pay up.'"

"How do you know Zimmerman was involved?" Jason questioned, draining his beer.

"My brother went to City Hall to bitch to the mayor. He was in the lobby when the dude who tried to shake him down came out of the elevator with another guy. As soon as they passed, he asked a security guard who they were. The guy IDed them as City Manager Zimmerman and his assistant, Frank Delhomme."

"Maybe Delhomme has himself a little sideline," Jason suggested. "One Zimmerman didn't know about."

The woman shook her head and snorted again. "Fat fucking chance. My brother actually met with Zimmerman to complain. Zimmerman thanked him, and the next night on the way to his car, my brother got mugged. The guy told him to pay the grand and forget about getting any help from the city. Hey, Larry," she called out to the bartender. "Get me that magnifying glass—the one you use to check fake IDs."

Larry shoved the magnifier across the bar. The waitress grabbed it, snatched the grainy cell phone photo of the two men out of my hand, and viewed it intensely.

"Picture's not for shit, but yeah, that looks like it could be him—Zimmerman."

"Yo, Lucy! I ain't paying you to chat," a man called out to the girl.

I took the magnifying glass and the snapshot back.

"I'm sorry. We didn't mean to cause trouble. Thanks for your information."

"Hey, no problemo. That's just Murray, the manager. I'm glad I could help."

Jason took out his wallet, extracted a twenty, and handed it to Lucy.

"Thanks, mister. Have a good night." She strolled away to wait on a table. Jason and I gazed through the magnifying glass at the enlarged picture.

"What do you think? Is it Zimmerman?" I asked.

"Hard to tell even with this penlight, but maybe an expert would be able to give a definite answer."

I slipped everything into my purse. "I don't know about you, but I've had enough."

"Me, too." Jason set his empty bottle down and tossed some money on the bar.

Walking back to the car, he said, "The evidence against Zimmerman is shaky to say the least."

"Maybe he thought he'd never get caught. Maybe he's been doing it for so long, he's gotten arrogant and sloppy. And to think Ken Shay had the balls to insist he had nothing to do with the political side of things. He knows plenty of politicians."

On the drive home we passed the now condemned River Tower Condos. Concrete barricades prevented pedestrians from entering the plaza. Already the smaller side street had been cordoned off to traffic. It wouldn't be long before Riverside would meet the same fate. I stopped the car, and we got out to look.

No effort had been made to clear the plaza of the rubble from the previous night. As we gazed upward, several small chunks of concrete hurtled down from the upper floors, hitting the ground with a loud crack. Like a snake, the building was shedding its skin.

The structure reminded me of a face. In the darkness, the upper and lower floors, relatively untouched, resembled jaws, while the middle floors with concrete and balconies missing, brought to mind a gaping, toothless mouth.

I shook my head and shuddered. At least, no deaths had occurred, but it had been a near thing. I glanced at Jason and was startled by the anger on his face.

"As an architect, I'm outraged, but as a board member I'm ashamed."

"Why? You had nothing to do with this."

"Yes, I did. In my eagerness to sit on yet another board, I didn't do my homework on the company."

"But your father sat on the same board," I protested.

"That's right, and he should have been more attentive, too. Brad Holmes managed to nail me in my weak spot—my ego. Another board, another accomplishment, another building block of self-importance." He smacked his fist into his hand. "I should have paid more attention and never have involved Marc. His death is my fault, too."

I took his arm, steering him back to the car. "Jason, you had no idea any of this could happen," I said, driving back to the hotel. "Come on, I'll buy you a nightcap."

In the hotel bar, we ordered brandy and sat at a table in a corner. Jason sipped and brooded, not looking up from the depths of his glass.

"Jason, it's not your fault."

He looked up and smiled crookedly. "Maybe not, but it sure as hell feels like it. It'll be a long time before

I forgive myself."

He bolted the remainder of his brandy, and then reached across the table to trace the line of my jaw with his finger. His gray eyes went dark and my skin tingled at his touch. My heart rate accelerated as did my breathing. A tremendous answering throb from deep inside had me wanting to slither onto his lap right here. I drained my glass and couldn't tell if the heat surging through my body was liquor or passion induced. I ran my foot up his leg.

"Wanna get drunk and fool around?" I murmured in a low, sexy voice.

"Definitely."

We necked in the elevator like a couple of oversexed teenagers, tumbling out when it stopped on the tenth floor and continuing our way down the hall. We paused long enough to unlock the door, and then staggered through the living room, tearing at our clothing until both of us stood naked.

I had dismissed any thoughts of slow, easy sex down in the bar. No, tonight I wanted hot and frantic. I wanted Jason to screw me blind, and I would return the favor.

He kissed and caressed every inch of my body until I shook from need. I cried, begged, and demanded. He plunged inside me and pumped like a man demented. I wrapped my legs around his waist and matched him thrust for thrust.

The burn—oh, my God, the burn. I panted from the heat. My heart slammed in my chest so hard, I feared it would explode, and then didn't give a damn if it did.

The slow ripples of ultimate pleasure pulsed and built. I cried out, writhing, moving my hips faster. My fingernails scored Jason's back. In the dim recesses of my fractured mind, I heard him cry out several times. He spoke no coherent words, only uttering guttural noises. I don't think I had the capacity for rational vocal abilities either. I was deep into gratification.

The heated spring inside me coiled to painful proportions until finally leaping into an eruption. The contractions ripped me from top to bottom. I screamed and dug my nails in deep, grinding my pelvis into his.

Just when I thought I had reached the end to the climax of the century, Jason cried out and made his final lunge. His shaft pulsated. My orgasm renewed, the spasms washing over me again.

He collapsed on top of me, his arms bearing the weight and his breath rasping in my ear. My legs fell limply from his waist. I smoothed my hands down his back and felt a sticky wetness against my palms. I had drawn blood.

Jason moved slightly to allow me breathing room, and I spent several moments trying to suck in enough oxygen to prevent passing out. It was several more minutes before either of us could speak.

He kissed me hard and nuzzled my neck. "I think my back will bear scars forever."

"Sorry. Next time, I'll get on top."

"I wanted to stop the elevator and take you standing up."

"I wouldn't have objected. You're lucky I didn't straddle your lap in the bar downstairs."

"Give me an hour and we'll renegotiate the straddling option," he said with a deep chuckle. "And I expected to sleep tonight."

I laughed and pushed him onto his back, swinging

my leg across his hips. I nibbled on his ears, slowly working my way down his body, savoring every delightful flavor like a gourmet gone wild.

He didn't need a full hour.

Chapter Eighteen

"Did you *have* to agree to an eight o'clock meeting?" I groused, taking a gulp of coffee and trying to focus my bleary eyes.

Two hours of sleep made me cranky. Non-stop sex had put a huge smile on my face. I hate conflicting emotions.

Jason had the audacity to grin. He leaned over and rubbed a knuckle against my cheek before kissing it. I inhaled and savored the scent of his spicy aftershave. If nothing else, he always smelled great.

"Sorry you didn't get your eight hours." He paused, grinning wider. "Okay, I'm not sorry, but what's the loss of a little sleep compared to…well, just compared?"

"Uh-huh."

I yawned, blinked my eyes, and wondered if megadoses of vitamins would help. I'd have to do something if I wanted to keep up with Jason Mallory.

I was still trying to wake up when a man stopped next to our table. He was on the short side, about five-six, and couldn't weigh a hundred and forty pounds dripping wet. I guessed his age at somewhere in the mid-forties, and his chocolate brown face bore a look of worry. His brown eyes scanned the restaurant. He wore a uniform shirt with his name, "Elton," embroidered under an air-conditioning company logo.

"Mr. Williams?" Jason asked. The man nodded. "Please join us. This is my fiancée, Shelley Jackson. Thank you for agreeing to meet me."

"You sure you're not cops?"

"I swear to you, neither Miss Jackson nor myself are from the police."

"Look man, I don't want no trouble. I'm only here because the dude was your brother."

"I understand. Please, tell me about your business relationship with Marc."

The man shot a glance at me. I drained my coffee, remaining silent. This was Jason's interview. The waitress appeared and we ordered breakfast, sausage and eggs for the two of us, and enough calories and cholesterol for Williams to guarantee a short life span.

His rigid posture relaxed when the waitress left, and he began his story.

"I met your brother one night while I was cleaning. He was working late and when I went into the men's lavatory, he followed. He had a proposition for me. If I'd leave an office unlocked for a while, he'd pay me fifty bucks. I got a wife and three kids. Fifty extra dollars sounded like a deal, so I said, sure, why not?"

Which office? Ask him Jason.

"Which office?"

I breathed easier. He was doing great.

Williams shrugged. "Different ones."

"How often did you do it?"

"Once or twice a week. I'd go into his cubicle and he'd tell me which office. I'd clean, leave it unlocked, finish, and then come back to his space. The money would be in an envelope."

"How long did this go on?"

"A couple of months. Then one night he told me he thought he was being watched, and we'd have to make different arrangements."

"Did you?"

"Yeah, he offered me two hundred and fifty bucks if I'd get into the file room, find the files he wanted, and copy them. He left the name of the file and where it was located on a slip of paper in his wastebasket. It only took three of us to clean those offices, so when the vacuums fired up, I'd turn on the copy machine, make the copies, and then return the files from where I got 'em."

"How were you paid? Did Marc leave two hundred and fifty dollars in an envelope?"

Our food arrived, and I fidgeted while it was served. We both knew Marc had paid the man in a dark alley. When the waitress left, I looked at Williams, but he preferred not to answer the question immediately. Instead, he dug into his food, shoveling it in like he'd never get another meal. I glanced at Jason who shrugged and picked up his fork. Suppressing a groan of impatience, I did the same.

Jason gave Williams a few minutes before repeating the question. The man's plate was almost empty. He sopped up egg yolk with a hunk of toast and washed it down with a huge gulp of coffee.

"He didn't work late too often after our new arrangement, so the payoffs were made near the flea market. I live like five minutes away, and I'm familiar with the area. I'd park on the street, meet him in the alley. He'd hand me the envelope, I'd hand him the copies, and I'd go home."

"Weren't you ever curious as to why he was

willing to pay you to do something like that?" I asked, breaking my promise to stay silent.

"Miss, that money bought my kids shoes and put a better grade of hamburger on the dinner table. I didn't much care what the guy's reasons were."

"Why did you quit the cleaning company?" Jason asked, back in control.

Williams shrugged. "I work with machinery. I got laid off and only did the janitorial thing until I could find a better job. I finally did, told him I couldn't help anymore, and that's the last I saw of the man." He paused. "I take it he was the guy found shot in that alley."

"Yes, he was."

"Well, it wasn't the best neighborhood, but honest to God, we never stayed any longer than thirty seconds." He looked at his watch. "Sorry, I gotta get to work. Anything else you need to know?"

"No, thank you, Mr. Williams. You've explained something that's puzzled me since Marc's death. I'm grateful."

"Thanks for breakfast." Williams nodded, pushed back his chair, and walked hurriedly out of the restaurant.

"The alley *was* familiar to Marc. He must have felt safe meeting me there," I said, finishing my meal and draining my coffee cup for the third time.

"How ironic. He felt safe and got killed. If he'd stayed in his house and simply handed the CD to you there, he'd be alive."

"Maybe he didn't want to expose my presence to the people following him."

Jason shook his head. "A simple evening at a

friend's house, you leave with the CD, and no one's the wiser."

"You forget about my profession and my boss. Bill wrote articles, and I worked for him. Perhaps, Marc didn't want to tie me to anything."

Jason shook his head. "A dark alley of all places. Why?"

"Maybe he was getting paranoid and thought it represented secrecy. You know, just before I found his body, I thought about how melodramatic the setting was."

Jason scowled. "Why the hell didn't he mail the damned thing to *me*?"

"Time, maybe? You live in Los Angeles. It would take three or four days for it to get there and longer for you to arrive in Port Royale."

"He could have e-mailed the information and FedExed the CD priority. I certainly would have called demanding an explanation. I think Marc thought too much on this, or perhaps he was too scared to think at all." He sighed, finished his coffee, and settled his gaze on me. "What's on your agenda for today?"

"I have to go into the office for a while. What's on yours?"

"I'm going to pack up things at the office and make the rounds saying goodbye to people. I'd also like to ask Peggy Wyatt to join us for lunch."

"I can help with the packing up if you like."

"You want to watch Brad Holmes and Ken Shay turn purple at your appearance while trying to stay civilized at the same time," he said with a grin.

"Guilty as charged. Once you leave, I will never again be allowed to darken the doorstep."

"Okay. Meet me there at eleven-thirty. And don't forget to pretend you've never met Peggy."

****

I pushed open the doors to the Shay and Holmes office a few minutes early and ambled up to the reception desk. The receptionist gave me the fisheye.

"May I help you?"

"I'm here to see Jason Mallory."

"Your name?"

Her tone made it sound like I was unimportant and not worthy of her attention. I wanted to laugh. She knew damn well who I was.

"Shelly Jackson," I said in a clear voice.

I gazed over my shoulder at the two men in business suits sitting in the waiting area. Their quiet conversation stopped. They looked at me, and then each other with raised eyebrows.

The receptionist snatched the phone and announced me to Jason. I'd won that round.

"Mr. Mallory will be here in a moment," she said, her voice frosty.

She didn't invite me to have a seat. I turned, walked over to a chair, and sat anyway, nodding to the men. They nodded back, but said nothing. The receptionist glared. I guessed I wasn't the most popular person in the room. Jason swung through the glass doors to the offices.

"Shelley, glad you could make it," he said in a loud voice. "Come on back. I have a couple of people I'd like you to meet."

I rose, and he guided me to his soon-to-be-vacated office. I chuckled all the way. I quit when he closed the door, pulled me into his arms, and planted a hard kiss on my mouth. He broke away grinning.

"What did you say to Ms. Bartles? When she called I could feel the icicles in her voice."

"She copped an attitude, so when she asked my name, I said it loud enough for the two men waiting in reception to hear."

"Those are new clients. They were supposed to sign a contract yesterday, but rumor has it they're having second thoughts."

"Pity."

He dropped another kiss on my nose. "I love it when you get sarcastic. Come on, let's go get Peggy. I called her earlier, and she'd love to have lunch with us. Now that she no longer has Marc's laptop, she's more relaxed."

We walked the short distance to the finance department and Lynnette Palmer's office. Peggy looked up smiling at our approach.

"Mr. Mallory, I'm so glad you called. I have a couple to things to file, and then I'll be ready."

"No hurry. Peggy, I'd like you to meet Shelley Jackson. Shelley, this is Peggy Wyatt, Marc's girlfriend."

"It's a pleasure to meet you," I said, holding out my hand. She smiled and shook it. I felt a bit silly, since we'd already met, but went along with the charade.

It was a good thing we did because a man came through the open door at that moment. "Sorry to interrupt, but this will only take a minute." He nodded at us before directing his attention to Peggy. "Peggy, will you please tell Ms. Palmer to have a word with maintenance? IT finished with repairs on my computer, but it was re-installed in the wrong cubicle. I'm in cubicle number six. They put it in number nine. I wasted an entire morning because I thought IT still had it."

"I'll leave a note for her. Sorry you were inconvenienced, Dave."

The man left. Peggy quickly filed several folders in a cabinet behind her desk, then straightened and grabbed her purse.

We walked through the office to the elevators, the eyes of everyone we passed boring into my back. The two men had gone. I hoped they'd told S and H to shove it.

Jason decided on a restaurant not far away that specialized in Cuban cuisine. As we slid into a booth, Peggy said, "I felt a little silly pretending we didn't know each other, but I had to cover my backside just in case."

"I take it Lynnette is not in today," Jason said, accepting the menu from the hostess.

"No. She called in sick—thank goodness. The last few days have been awful what with the fire and the problems at the River Tower Condos. She's turned from incompetent to total bitch incompetent, if you know what I mean."

"I do," I replied. "She's feeling the strain and not handling it well."

"Nobody's handling things well, if you ask me."

"How so?" Jason asked.

"Well, Mr. Shay and Mr. Holmes were in her office yesterday for hours. They ordered lunch in and when Mr. Birdsong joined them, the fur flew."

"They argued?" I said.

"Something awful. I couldn't hear much of what

was being said because the door was closed, but when they finally left, Mr. Holmes looked like a thundercloud and Mr. Shay's face was bright red. I thought he was going to stroke out."

"What about Birdsong and your boss? Were they angry, too?"

"Mr. Birdsong came out a few minutes later looking scared, and when he opened the door I heard Ms. Palmer crying. She came out about a half an hour later saying she didn't feel well and was going home. She'd tried to fix her face, but it was still blotchy."

"I guess these are trying times at Shay and Holmes," I told her.

The waiter appeared and we ordered—*ropa vieja* for Peggy and me, and roasted chicken for Jason with side dishes of black beans and rice, and fried plantains.

"I'm sorry you got involved in all of this," Jason said when the waiter left. "But I have to warn you that Shay and Holmes may not be in business much longer. They're going to get sued every which way to Sunday."

"I suspected as much." She turned her gaze on me. "I heard a lot of people saying you and your paper were to blame, and that S and H may sue for libel *and* defamation of character."

"That doesn't surprise me, but I have a feeling Shay and Holmes will have their hands full explaining their building practices," I replied.

Jason withdrew a folded sheet of paper from his jacket pocket. "Peggy, while I've got you here, could you take a look at this? It's a printout of some information Marc left me. Can you shed any light on the numbers near the end of the sequences?"

Peggy unfolded the paper, spreading it out in front

of her. I recognized it as what I'd come to call "the recipe code." Several minutes passed as she slowly read each sequence with a furrowed brow.

"I have no idea what the letters and numbers at the beginning mean, but I think these four digits might correspond to check numbers. When Marc and I were sleuthing, I recall seeing this number." She pointed to a sequence near the bottom of the page. "I remember it because I had accidentally seen the check on Ms. Palmer's desk earlier in the week. The check number 3795, stuck in my mind because that's my birthday, March 7, 1995. The number 'twenty' at the end could be the amount. The check I saw was for twenty thousand dollars. At the time, I thought it was sloppy to leave a check that large just sitting there for anybody to see."

"Can you remember who it was made out to?" he asked.

"No, I'm sorry. It's been too long. Did you find the copies Marc and I made of the checks? Maybe it's listed there."

"We haven't found the copies yet, but you've been a great help, Peggy. If Shay and Holmes does go under, ask me for a reference. I'll be glad to give it."

Jason took the sheet of numbers back and replaced it in his jacket just as our food arrived.

I leaned over my dish and closed my eyes, inhaling the aroma of spices. My mouth watered. I gave up smelling for tasting, popping a forkful of the spice-laden barbequed beef into my mouth and chewing with reverence. I was in culinary heaven.

We drove Peggy back to the office where she told us good bye and wished us luck with the investigation.

"Will you please let me know when the police find out who killed Marc? I'd rather hear it from one of you than read about it."

"I promise," he said.

Jason got out of the car and opened Peggy's door, then helped her out. He leaned down and lightly kissed her cheek.

"Goodbye, Peggy, and thank you for all you've done. Most of all, thank you for being Marc's friend."

She sniffed and bit her lip. "I'm going to miss him." Her soft voice quavered. Then, she turned and disappeared into the building.

Jason slid back behind the wheel and looked at me. "Well, I am officially no longer connected with Shay and Holmes Development and Construction."

"I thought you had to pack up?"

"That took all of two minutes this morning. An envelope is on the back seat with very little in it."

"So what are you going to do the rest of the day?"

"I was thinking about visiting The River Tower Condos."

"Whatever for?"

"Shay and Holmes built a lot of condos while I sat on the board. They used me to legitimize shoddy construction. With my name on the website, it looks like I condoned their methods. I may end up getting sued in the bargain. My reputation has been damaged, and I'm just plain pissed." He started the car and drove away.

"What are you going to do?"

"I don't know. I'll play it by ear. I want to get a closer look at the concrete."

"What can you tell by just looking at concrete?"

"A lot. I can determine how much cement and aggregate are in it. I can also tell if air bubbles were present. With high rises, someone is supposed to smooth the concrete that's been pumped in, and then under supervision use a vibrating tool to get the air bubbles out. The more air, the less bonding takes place. The less bonding, the less stable. The concrete becomes fragile."

"And if those things are present, what do we do?"

"Take some samples and have a lab analyze them. Then I'll hold a press conference blasting Shay and Holmes to hell and back. Empty your purse."

"What?"

"Empty your purse. I may need a couple of large sized chunks. I don't have anything to carry them in."

I dumped most of my purse paraphernalia onto the floorboards slipping my driver's license, credit cards, and cell phone into my pockets.

Jason pulled into a parking garage a few blocks from the site. We arrived at the condos to find a twelve-foot high, solid wooden fence shielding the property from curious observation.

"How do we get past this?" I asked.

"There has to be an opening somewhere."

He led us down the side street until we found a door. He pushed and walked into the plaza. Several more balconies and concrete had joined those already fallen. The entire building would soon crumble.

I gazed at the structure and gasped. A whole row of balconies had disappeared on what I estimated to be the fourteenth floor. I felt like a voyeur staring into the apartments of people who would never again see their homes. Furniture sat undisturbed and paintings hung on the walls. Draperies stirred in the breeze, billowing out over thin air.

A wave of hot anger slashed through me. Damn! How could Shay and Holmes do this? Was the almighty dollar so important to them that they'd knowingly endanger the lives of hundreds of people? Apparently, it was. I had already formed the opening paragraph of a story when Jason called.

"Shelley, come over here." He examined a large chunk of concrete, a frown on his face.

"What did you find?" I asked.

"Look at this."

He pointed to the raw edge of the chunk. I saw smooth gray cement interspersed with pebbles and lots of hollow spaces.

"Air bubbles?"

"Yep. Some are as big as quarters. Here, put it in your purse."

"Are you kidding? That thing has to weigh forty pounds."

"No way. There are so many air pockets the damned thing is light as a feather. Do I look like I'm straining to hold it?"

I reluctantly unzipped my brand new purse and he dumped the rock inside causing me to slump under the weight. I glared. Light as a feather my ass. I nearly dislocated my shoulder.

Jason picked up another, smaller hunk, looked it over, frowned, and smashed it on the cobblestones. The fragment shattered into a dozen pieces.

"Brittle as hell," he muttered. "If they performed a slump test, I'll eat my hat."

"Slump test? What's that?"

"It determines the mix of concrete. Some of the concrete on every load is poured into a container, left to sit for a while, and then the container is pulled off. If the concrete slumps, then the mixture is thin—too much water. A thin mixture is weak and takes longer to cure."

"What if there's not enough water?"

"Not all the cement will dissolve. It'll look powdery and have no strength." He picked up another piece and broke it with his bare hands. "Piece of crap. It's porous." He found a length of a rusty pipe-like material. "The salt air has damaged the re-bar. No wonder the concrete is detaching. It's popping off like cheap wallpaper."

"Hey, you two!" a voice shouted from near the building. "This is a restricted area. You can't come in here."

A security guard strode toward us. Jason rose and smiled as the man drew near.

"Hello, my name is Jason Mallory. I'm a consultant hired by the builders to do analysis. This is my assistant, Miss Jackson. You've got one hell of a mess here."

The guard removed his cap and wiped his shining bald head free of sweat with a bandana. "Tell me about it. The damned thing's falling apart. I gave notice this morning. I don't want to be anywhere near if it comes down like the World Trade Center. What are you analyzing?"

"The concrete, the steel, anything I can find. When did those balconies descend?" Jason pointed to a pile of twisted metal forty feet away.

"This morning about nine o'clock. Scared the piss outta me. That's when I gave notice."

"Mind if I take a look at it?"

"I don't care, but you should really have a hard hat. Wait here and I'll get a couple from the shed." He trotted toward a small trailer.

"It can't really fall down, can it?" I asked, casting a nervous glance upward.

"It could, but it's not likely."

The guard returned with two hard hats. Jason and I dodged fallen concrete and other debris to inspect one of the balconies.

The jagged metal supports showed where they had ripped from the side of the building. Many of the bolts had pulled out intact while others had sheared off cleanly as though snipped with giant bolt cutters. Unable to help it, every few seconds I looked upward.

"Well?" I asked after he'd inspected everything for several minutes and had taken photos with his cell phone.

"The bolts aren't long enough. Couple that with the inferior concrete, the salt air, and it was just a matter of time," he replied in a disgusted voice. "Come on, I've seen enough."

"What's going on here?" An elderly man holding a box of file folders stood nearby, his eyes narrowed.

"This here is a representative of the builders, Mr. Miller. He's doing analysis," the guard explained.

"You're from those bastards, Shay and Holmes?"

"I'm just the hired help," Jason said. "And you are…?"

"Benny Miller, president of the River Towers condo board." He turned a stern eye to the guard. "As condo president, I'm in charge around here. I should have known the minute he came on the property."

Miller swiveled his head back in our direction. "Let me see some ID."

Jason pulled out his driver's license. "I'm an independent contractor. I thought the building was deserted."

"It is. I came by to get some paperwork from the office. The association's gonna sue those cheap sonsabitches. I don't think you should be here without our lawyer present. You'd better leave."

So far, the association president had ignored me. I took the opportunity to shield my sagging purse by putting my body between the hidden samples and his prying eyes. Down here many condo owners considered their elected board members to be a continual pain in the ass. As such, they were sometimes christened "condo Nazis." Miller looked like he fit the description.

"I understand, but before I go let me ask, have you had any problems before this?"

"Hell, yes. Electrical surges and plumbing issues began within a few months. Lately, windows have broken and I've been getting complaints about loose railings on the balconies and in the stairwells. Make sure you tell Shay and Holmes, we're suing."

"I'll do that."

We turned and hurried toward the door in the fence. Jason had just opened it when a ripping sound came from behind us. We stopped dead in our tracks and whirled. Another hunk of concrete slammed into the ground. Dust billowed and chips flew, a few leaving their mark on my arms. I stood rooted to the spot, my heart pounding. In spite of Jason's reassurances, I couldn't help but visualize the World Trade Center. Miller and the guard sprinted across the plaza for the door. Dust continued to flow across the cobblestones like incoming fog.

I gasped. "Are you sure it won't come down?"

"No, I'm not sure. Everybody out! Now!"

Jason grasped my elbow and hefted the purse from my shoulder. "Come on, Shelley. Run!"

Chapter Nineteen

We ran four blocks until my lungs reminded me I was sadly out of shape.

"Wait!" I bent over panting, hands braced on my trembling knees. Sweat trickled down my temples gluing several strands of hair to my face.

"Give…me a…minute," I said, puffing.

My heart pounded and I had an urge to slide into a heap onto the sidewalk. I sagged. Then a firm hand pulled me upright.

"I think we're all right," Jason said.

I gazed at him silently cursing. The man may have been breathing heavier than usual, but he'd barely broken a sweat and didn't seem in the least bit tired. And all this while hauling my rock-filled purse.

"I jog," he said as though reading my mind.

"I don't care if that building buries me—I can't run another step. Where are the other two?"

"I have no idea, and don't think the building will come down."

"Then why the hell did we run like maniacs?" I straightened glaring.

"Because for just a second, I wasn't sure. Somebody's going to have to implode that building soon. Come on, let's get in the car."

Within minutes I slid into my seat, leaned my head back, and let my breathing return to normal.

Removing the concrete samples from my purse, he laid them on the backseat, and then tossed the bag onto my lap.

"Thanks," he said, starting the car and heading for the exit.

I examined the purse. A little dust on the inside, but it didn't seem to be any the worse for wear. I dumped my discarded stuff back in. "Well, that was fun. What's next?"

"I'm going to take the samples up to a lab in Palm Beach. I called the director this morning. He said he could do it today or tomorrow. I'd also thought I'd stop and see Marlene."

"In that case, drop me at the office. I have a few things I need to do, but first take me to the post office. I want to look at Marc's CD again."

"Why? I printed out most of what was on it. The whole thing is in my hotel room."

"Maybe there's something we missed. Knowing what we now know, perhaps I'll see it in a new light."

The post office wasn't that far away and it only took a couple of minutes to retrieve the CD. Jason let me out in front of the newspaper.

"I may be a while," he warned.

"I'll take a cab back to the hotel."

He nodded and waved, then pulled away. I hurried into the building. In my cubicle, I wrote a quick story on my experience at the condo and sent it to Cal. A few minutes later, he called.

"Nice story, kid, but when are you going to give me something of an investigative nature?"

"I've talked to several people about bribery, the city, and Shay and Holmes, but I want to verify."

"Get the lead out. This thing is rolling. One of the TV stations is running a special report on Monday. I want something with substance for Monday morning."

He hung up, leaving me with a sinking sensation in the pit of my stomach. I really didn't *have* anything new. I pulled Marc's CD from my purse and retreated to Bill's office, locking the door behind me. I closed the blinds, and then turned on the computer, sliding the CD in.

I scanned those damned number and letter sequences a dozen times and still couldn't decipher the letters at the beginning.

Sitting back, I gave my eyes a rest and massaged my forehead. I needed to take a break. Maybe caffeine and a few eye drops would refresh me. I popped the CD out and hid it in the desk drawer, then cautiously opened the door.

It was five o'clock on a Friday night and most of my colleagues had left to get an early start on the weekend. With the exception of a few lingerers, the news room was deserted. I walked into the break room, grabbed a cola out of the fridge, and sat down.

Hell, Jason was probably right and we had gleaned all the information possible from the CD, but I couldn't help wondering why Marc hadn't given the whole kit and caboodle to me. Why just the CD? Of course, he hadn't figured on being murdered, and for all I knew he would have told me everything when I'd shown up.

And what had happened to the research on the consultants? Peggy said he'd finished it. Could the killer have found it? But would Marc have left something that important at the house when he'd gone through so much cloak and dagger bullshit regarding the CD?

I was confusing myself. I drained my soda and twisted my head from side to side rubbing the tension out of my shoulder muscles.

Tired and discouraged, I rose and tossed the can into the recycling bin. I'd give it one more shot before calling it a night.

I reinserted the CD and scrolled through the recipes on my way to the numbers when something I'd not noticed, caught my eye. The title looked strange. It read: MOM'S RECIPES with a year underneath.

Why put a date under a bunch of recipes being used as camouflage? Then a thought jumped into my head. If the first set of numbers in the sequences *were* dates as we suspected, could the year be the starting point?

"Holy shit," I murmured. "Is it all camouflage?"

Maybe the recipes weren't as unimportant as we'd first thought. I slowly clicked my way through and read.

The first was for Basic Bread. The ingredients were what I'd expected—flour, water, yeast in proportions consistent with a loaf of bread.

The next recipe went into great detail on a fruit salad, and the one following gave me some new ideas on spaghetti sauce even though I didn't cook. I read every damned recipe, but found nothing enlightening.

No one has ever accused me of not being persistent, so I read them again. I was halfway through when I stopped. Something didn't make sense. Recipes are usually grouped together by category like appetizers, soups, and desserts. But these jumbled together in no particular order. Of course as camouflage, Marc would have been in a hurry and not care about groupings.

I leaned back, gazing at the computer screen with the ingredients for pineapple upside down cake staring back at me. Maybe my date idea was wrong.

"Face it, Jackson, you're stumped."

I glanced at my watch. It was nearly six o'clock and I'd had a long day. I was about to eject the CD when something odd in the ingredient list caught my eye. The first letters of the words "flour" and "cake" were capitalized.

Curious, I scrolled through more and discovered a pattern. For all I knew, Marc had been a lousy typist. I returned to the beginning and made a list. By the time I finished, I had eighty letters. On a hunch, I arranged them horizontally and realized what Marc had done. He had embedded a cryptogram in the recipes.

"Marc, you brilliant stinker." I called Jason. "Where are you?"

"On my way back. I'm almost to Boca Raton. Why?"

"You're not going to believe this, but I think I may have solved the puzzle." I told him what I thought I'd discovered.

"Traffic's a bitch, but I should be there in an hour. Are you still at the paper?"

"Yes, in Bill's office."

I hung up and turned my attention back to the cryptogram. I forgot about being tired and plunged in trying to decipher the code.

****

A rap on the door broke my concentration. I rose and opened up for Jason.

"Let me see it," he said, brushing past me.

"I've been trying to match the letters. I counted and found the letter 'r' appeared the most, so I assigned it as the letter 'e'. Beyond that, I'm lost. There are no breaks, so I don't know how many words there are or their lengths."

Jason sat staring at the jumble of papers covered with my attempts on the desk. He studied them silently for a few minutes.

"I'd say you're probably right about 'r' being 'e'. Let's see what else I can find." He swiveled toward the computer and scrolled through the recipes, stopping at every capital letter. "If we assume the first set of numbers in each sequence is a date, then I think the year listed is the starting point. And there *are* breaks between the capital letters."

"Where?" I asked, leaning over his shoulder.

"Look, the first recipe has five capitals. The next has none. The third has four and the fourth none. I'll bet no capital letter in a recipe signifies a break. Let's try it."

He arranged the letters into groups until they resembled a sentence.

"That's it," I murmured. "There's a pizza place not far from here that delivers. Shall I order?"

"By all means."

I slipped away to call, leaving him to work on the code. Giving him space, I returned to my cubicle, read my e-mails, and got current on my voice mails. It was no easy task. I was burning with impatience and curiosity. When finished I gathered forks, plates, napkins, and a couple of cokes from the break room, taking them to Bill's office. Jason didn't look up and rather than disturb him, I left to wait by the elevators for the delivery man.

I smelled the tantalizing aromas of pepperoni, garlic, and onions a floor away. By the time the elevator doors opened, my mouth watered. I paid, tipped the guy, and resisted the urge to wolf down a piece in route to the office.

"Food's here," I announced, setting the hot cardboard box on the desk. "How's it going?"

Jason turned toward me and grabbed a slice, sliding it onto a paper plate.

"I think I have about a third of it."

I bit into the pizza. The spicy pepperoni blended with the mellow mozzarella, and the mild sauce didn't overwhelm the other ingredients.

"Is what you've got so far making sense?" I asked through a mouthful of crispy thin crust.

"It will if I can unlock a few more letters."

"Can I help?"

"Here's what I have so far. See if you can read something I can't," he replied, shoving a sheet of paper my way.

Jason gobbled three pieces of pizza and downed his coke, then turned back to the computer, while I tried to make headway with the code. I finally gave up.

I finished off another slice and cleaned up, putting the remains of the pizza into the break room refrigerator.

I returned just in time to hear Jason shout, "Yes!"

"Did you do it?"

He turned to grin and slapped the sheet of paper in front of him on the desk.

I hurried to his side and read: "*Check file room.*

Back of second drawer fourth cabinet from left. Also bottom desk drawer nineteen."

"Oh, my God," I breathed. I threw my arms around his neck. "You did it!"

"Now, all we have to do is figure out what he meant. The file room part is easy, but I don't know what he's talking about with the last sentence."

"Bottom desk drawer nineteen. The nineteenth desk somewhere? The nineteenth folder or piece of paper?"

"I have no idea."

The number nineteen hovered along the fringes of my memory. I straightened and closed my eyes focusing. I concentrated and remembered a big number nineteen with a circle around it. Where had I seen it?

"The calendar," I said.

"What calendar?"

"Remember the calendar we found in Marc's things? It had the number nineteen circled. We thought it may have been for a date with Peggy."

"Okay, but nineteen what? How does the nineteenth of February correlate to this nineteen? Marc was dead by then."

I thought hard trying to put the pieces together. They had to fit. "Jason? Marc wouldn't risk putting an important piece of information where it could be easily found."

"Of course not," he said with a hint of impatience in his voice. "The file room is used for old contracts and project notes. It would take forever to search through them all, so I can see why Marc hid something there."

"Then this desk drawer nineteen is most likely in

one of the offices."

A snippet of conversation heard earlier in the day wiggled into my memory. I rushed back to my office and rummaged in my purse for the slip of paper with Peggy Wyatt's home phone number on it.

Jason followed. "What's on your mind?"

I dialed and waited, praying Peggy hadn't gone out. Finally she answered.

"Peggy, this is Shelley. I have a question. Remember today when a man came in to complain about a computer being in the wrong spot?"

"Sure. Why?"

"What did he mean by the cubicle numbers being wrong?"

"Oh, well, the cubicles are numbered. That way if we have to dismantle everything for a hurricane, the equipment gets back to right person. It's easier than taping a name on the equipment. People come and go, but computers are forever. Why?"

"Peggy, what was Marc's cubicle number?" I looked at Jason who watched with a tense expression on his face.

"Number twenty."

"Twenty, huh? And number nineteen is next to it. Is that the cubicle where he left his laptop?"

"Yes, it was empty. Twenty-one is also vacant. It's an end unit used for storage."

"Peggy, I can't explain right now, but promise I'll call you later."

I hung up, gazing at Jason who smiled and nodded. "Cubicle number nineteen. Right next door and available. Why would anyone search a desk in a cubicle no one used?" He gave me a hard kiss. "And you said you weren't any good at puzzles."

I kissed him back. "You broke the code. What do we do now?"

Why even ask? I knew exactly what we'd do.

"Go to Shay and Holmes and take a look in the file room and desk, of course."

I retrieved the CD from Bill's office and locked the door. We dashed down the stairwell to the garage. In less than an hour, we'd have the answers, and maybe the name of the murderer.

****

"Wait a minute," I said as Jason wheeled into the parking garage in the Shay and Holmes office building. "How will we get in? Today was your last day. Didn't you have to turn in your keys?"

"Yes, but I have Marc's. The police found them in his townhouse and returned them to me. I forgot about them. They're in my briefcase, which is still in the trunk."

We parked and rode the elevator up to the Shay and Holmes floor. The reception area was lit by a small light over the desk. I peered through the glass and detected no signs of anyone present. Jason used the key and we slid in. My heart rate accelerated, and I fought a tendency to hold my breath. The place after hours gave me the creeps. A red dot on a camera in the corner above the reception desk glowed.

"We're going to be on film," I said in a hushed voice.

"So what?" Jason said with a shrug. "In a few hours all pertinent information will be in police hands."

"We're still not supposed to be here. Have we tripped an alarm?"

"Possibly. I don't know the security code, but I used a key. It's not like breaking and entering. If someone shows up, I'll just say I forgot something and came to get it."

His words didn't help my anxiety level. I had no idea who Jason's someone might be, but sure as hell didn't want to meet them. The skin on my scalp prickled. I couldn't shake this premonition that all was not right.

"Come on, let's get this over with," I whispered.

"The file room is down this hallway."

He bore left flipping on the light. We passed several doors, turned right down another corridor before stopping. A plastic plaque attached next to the door read File Room. The door was unlocked.

"Is the door normally unlocked?"

He shrugged, pocketing the key ring. "Nothing sensitive would be stored here."

Jason flipped on the light. The room was about twenty-five feet square. File cabinets four drawers high ran along all of the walls with another grouping in the center of the room. Shelves containing boxes stacked almost to the ceiling rose above the cabinets.

"Holy shit, what is all this?" I asked, still speaking in a low tone.

"Records," Jason replied in a normal voice.

"But why? Haven't these people ever heard of electronic storage?"

"They have both, but you're right. Most of this should be stored in a facility or put on CDs. A fire would wipe out everything. I guess Tim Shay and Bob Holmes liked having the hard copy around. Could be the new management doesn't use this room anymore."

"Which file cabinet did Marc mean?"

Jason paused, his brow furrowed. "Good question."

He turned to his left, opened the second drawer in the fourth cabinet, and reached into the back, pulling out a file labeled, Palm Beach City Hall, 1984.

"Not this one," he said, replacing it and moving on.

The fourth cabinet on the next wall was so crammed with files another sheet of paper wouldn't fit. Jason didn't bother looking.

"Hold on," Jason said. "We're going about this in the wrong way. What's the first thing you saw when you walked through the door?"

"The cabinets in the middle of the room. They're two deep with boxes stacked on top."

"Exactly. And there are five in each row."

He turned and walked to the fourth cabinet on the right as we had entered the room. Pulling out the second drawer as far as it would go, we peered inside. It was two-thirds full. Jason reached behind the metal partition holding the files upright. With a grin he extracted an unlabeled folder that had been lying flat and opened it.

"We have lift-off," he murmured.

"What is it?" I peeked over his shoulder, eager for a firsthand look.

"It's his research into the consulting companies Shay and Holmes paid."

"Who's Dynamic Consulting in Lake Barton?"

"It says here the president is listed as James Harrison and the vice-president is…" he paused to smile at me. "Mary Anne *Shay* Harrison."

"Shay?"

"Uh-huh. Marc did his homework. He's got notes

at the bottom of each entry. Mary Anne is Ken Shay's youngest sister."

"Look at this name," I said, pointing at Blaze Consulting. "The president is listed as Jennifer H. Hamilton. 'H' for Holmes?"

"Yes, although Marc doesn't say what the relationship is. Maybe he didn't know."

"Actually, she's Brad's father's second cousin," a voice from behind us said.

I whirled, staring at a disheveled and white-faced Lynnette Palmer standing in the doorway. Ken Shay and Brad Holmes looked over her shoulder from the hall. All bore hard, angry expressions with the exception of Shay. He just looked scared.

Jason immediately yanked me behind him, and a second later I saw why. Lynnette held a big, nasty-looking gun in her hand.

I know nothing about guns, but the little I did know told me this was not the thirty-eight revolver that killed Marc and Bill. No, I stared down the business end of a semi-automatic.

Trembling, I grasped the back of Jason's shirt, clenching the material in my fists. My breath had become lost somewhere in my throat and my heart hammered away so fast my vision blurred around the edges.

"Don't be an idiot, Lynnette," Jason said. "Put the gun down. We're unarmed."

"Not quite. You have knowledge. Ken, go get the car and bring it around to the garage elevator."

"Lyn, it's over. Grab their cell phones and lock them in here. We can be on a plane to the islands in an hour," he urged.

"They know too damned much. Chambers was nosing around. I think he may have discovered our account numbers. I've worked too hard to have it all end now."

"Lyn, don't do anything else stupid. You've already…" Shay put a hand on her shoulder.

She shook it off. "I said get the fucking car. They have to disappear."

I stifled a ragged sob. We were dead. It was only a matter of when.

"Lyn…" Shay tried again.

"Now, goddamn it! Or do you want to become a statistic, too? We don't need you to run this company." She advanced into the room.

"Ken, for once in your life do as you're told. She's right," Brad said, following Lynnette. He also pulled a small gun from his pocket.

Shay swallowed and backed off. "Right. Give me a few minutes."

He left us alone with Bradley Holmes, Lynnette Palmer, and the guns.

"You killed Marc."

Jason spoke the words in a quiet tone, but I recognized the underlying rage. My grip tightened in the absurd fantasy I could stop any actions he might take.

Lynnette shrugged. "I didn't want to. I didn't mean to. It just happened. I'd been suspicious of him for several months. I hired a private investigator to tail him. Unfortunately, he didn't see or talk to anyone of importance."

"What made you suspicious?" I asked, my voice barely above a whisper.

"One of the other accountants was working late one night when Chambers left his cubicle. He must have thought he was alone, because he didn't minimize the screen. The accountant saw he was into files he had no business seeing. He ducked into a neighboring cubicle and watched your brother burn the information onto a CD. He came to me the next day. That's when I started watching him."

"How did you know Marc would be in the alley?" I persisted.

"I didn't. After the private investigator turned up zilch, I decided to do a little surveillance of my own. I started following him. I was parked down the street when he left his place. I thought midnight a strange hour to be going somewhere, so I followed. I parked around the corner and watched him go into the alley. I thought for a moment he was making a drug buy except there was nobody else around."

"So you followed him," Jason said.

His hands gripped the open file we'd been reading so hard, his knuckles turned white. His back muscles tensed beneath my hands, and in the confines of the small room he'd never get any closer to the woman than another step.

"Yeah. I demanded he give me everything he copied. He pretended not to know what I was talking about. I pulled the revolver just to scare him, and he lunged at my gun hand."

Lynnette curled her lip and tightened her grip on the gun. I wanted to scream, but couldn't. My vocal chords refused to work, and I wasn't sure my lungs would release the air necessary. My legs trembled so badly, I had no idea why I still stood. A trickle of sweat crept down my spine, making me shiver.

"Are you trying to tell me it was an accident?" Jason demanded, his voice rising with disbelief.

"The gun went off. The next thing I knew I'd popped him two more times. I searched, but couldn't find a CD or even anything on paper. So I grabbed his keys and took off for his place."

"But you didn't find anything, did you?" I whispered.

"Not a damned thing."

"I'll bet my appearance shook you up," Jason said.

Brad Holmes spoke, cutting off Lynnette's words. "We had no idea Chambers was your brother. We decided to let you stay to keep an eye on you."

I swallowed to moisten my throat. "Why Bill?"

"When his story hit the newsstands, we thought Chambers had given him the info," Holmes said. "When no files or CD's showed up at the townhouse, I thought maybe Mathias had them. Lynnette called Mathias and lured him to the park with the promise of information. When Mathias showed I shot him."

"You didn't even talk to him, did you?" I asked.

"Hell, no. I took his cell and wallet to make it look like a mugging. Then I threw the phone and Lyn's gun into the river. I grabbed his keys, but couldn't find anything at his place either. Never got a chance to snoop in his office."

Shay reappeared in the doorway. "The car's in place right by the elevators. Brad, Lyn, for the last time—we don't have to do this. Let's just lock them up and get the hell out of here."

Holmes turned to Shay, contempt on his face. "Shut up, you whining, drunken wimp. You manage to screw up everything you touch. We'll take them out Alligator Alley, shoot them, and let the gators do the rest."

Nausea rolled in my stomach. As a reporter, I'd seen photos of victims who'd ended up in the Everglades. Semi-eaten and badly decomposed bodies were not a pretty sight.

Shay glanced at us, and then back to Lynnette and Holmes. His face had gone pasty white and his hands trembled. I wondered if he suspected there might be three victims for the gators.

I'd often heard it said that in times of imminent, violent death, a person will do anything to prolong his demise. I realized it was true. For reasons I couldn't understand, I wanted to keep him talking as long as possible.

"And Doug Elliott?"

"That fucking moron had the balls to call Ron Zimmerman and say he had proof Zimmerman was taking bribes. He demanded a meeting in a bar on South Street. Said if he got an exclusive story, he'd withhold publication until Ron could get out of town."

My gaze shifted to a heavily sweating Ken Shay. "You delivered the bribes. Did it ever occur to you, your partner was setting you up as the fall guy?"

Lynnette answered, scorn dripping from her voice. "Of course he didn't. Ken isn't that bright."

Shay shot a frightened glance toward Bradley Holmes, a pleading look in his eyes.

"You both showed up that night, got Elliott drunk, and killed him," Jason finished.

"I had nothing to do with his death. Brad told me to get lost," Shay interjected.

Holmes shrugged. "After Ken left, I slipped Elliott a mickey. He never noticed when we headed for the river."

"What was his proof? He must have shown it to you." The reporter in me had to know these things.

"He said he had some kind of picture of Ken handing Ron an envelope in The Happy Hour."

"What kind of proof is that? There could have been anything in that envelope," Jason declared.

I marveled at how normal his voice sounded—steady with no hint of fear, although he must have been scared, too.

"That's what I said, but oh, no, you had to go and produce another body," Lynnette said. The gun trembled in her hand and sweat stained the underarms of her blouse. Lines grooved down her gray face reminding me of a granite carving.

"Yeah, but I told you, we couldn't take the chance," Holmes replied.

"And you ran me into the canal."

Holmes shrugged. "I hired some gangbanger to steal a car and do it. Knew you had become a problem when you talked to Sharon Ireland."

"You had someone following me."

"You talked to a lot of people. Wanted to see who. I also sent a message to that pious Dave Brooks."

"You won't get away with this." My voice shook.

"Sure, we will. Count on it. The company's done for and in a couple of hours my money and I will be on a nice Caribbean island with no extradition treaty with the U. S." Holmes looked at his watch. "I'm afraid it's time to go. Give the file to Ken and walk out—slowly."

Shay circled around behind us and snatched the

folder from Jason's hands, then shoved me in the back.

"Do as he says, Miss Jackson. You, too, Mallory."

I wondered if I could create a diversion, giving Jason a chance to tackle Bradley Holmes. Could I handle Lynnette Palmer and her gun? In a scuffle, Shay would bolt like a scared rabbit. Lynnette stepped aside into the hallway letting us pass, and then grabbed me, grinding the gun into the small of my back. Homes did the same with Jason.

"Don't try anything silly. If you do, the reporter buys one. Just head straight out the doors to the elevators," she ordered.

Shay fell in behind us. Didn't he realize his cousin and his partner found him a liability? This close, I smelled the fear on him—a strange combination of sweat, scotch, and a nauseating cologne.

My death wouldn't cause any wrinkles in the universe, but Jason's would make international headlines. We entered the reception lobby.

"Drop the gun!"

The voice came from behind the desk and scared the crap out of me. I cried out. Lynnette Palmer jerked and whirled. Jason jumped, wrenching me from her grip, threw me to the ground, and covered my body with his.

A shot rang out. More followed, and deafening gunfire echoed in the room. Someone cried out in pain. The glass doors shattered. Wall paneling splintered. The explosions went on forever.

Then silence, almost as scary as the shots, descended. The stench of gunpowder clogged my nostrils and burned my throat. Combined with Jason's weight pinning me to the floor, I found breathing difficult.

Finally, he rolled off. "Are you all right?"

"Yeah," I croaked. "I think so."

Ken Shay was sprawled face down a few feet away. He lifted his head and looked around with a terrified expression, the file still clenched in his hand. Bradley Holmes writhed and sobbed on the floor, his hand clutching his shoulder. Blood oozed between his fingers.

An unmoving Lynnette Palmer stared at the ceiling with sightless eyes, the gun still clutched in her hand. She'd taken numerous shots to the chest.

Police officers poured from behind the desk and out of the conference room. Jason helped me to my feet and oddly enough, I shook harder now than I had earlier. Sorenson slapped handcuffs on Shay and pulled him upright. Whitten stood nearby, gun drawn, to cover.

"Thanks for calling, Mr. Shay. You did the right thing."

"I had to. It was time. The killing had to stop."

Kenneth Shay, bon vivant and man about town, hung his head and cried.

Chapter Twenty

It was after two in the morning before the police released us. The truth had come out about me finding Marc's body and making the 9-1-1 call. Jason and I also confessed to being the culprits in searching Bill's office.

Sorenson and Whitten were not happy with our interference, and I expected they'd have liked to toss both of us into a cell along with Shay. Bradley Holmes was in the hospital recovering from his wound. Two cops kept a vigil outside his door.

Whitten delivered a stern lecture on the sins of hindering an investigation in an acid tinged tone. "Miss Jackson, the next time you find a body, call the police. If you uncover information from a computer, file cabinet, or an investigation, remember who's in charge. And don't give me any of that first amendment crap."

It took a pinch from Jason to make me go into my contrite routine. "Let's hope none of that happens again."

When the dust had settled from the shooting, I'd called Cal. Once released, I met him at the office and wrote while he edited. We were too late for the Saturday edition, but Sunday morning would see the story from my point of view. Cal rewarded me with three days off. Whoopee. Three stinking days? I was almost gator bait and I'm given three days? Oh well, considering the alternative, I'd make do.

Meanwhile, back at the police station, Kenneth Shay sang his heart out. The whole mess had started when his father, Tim Shay, died. The company was making money, but not enough for Ken. He had expensive tastes and an ego that wouldn't quit. He loved being Mr. Executive. Unfortunately, he wasn't Mr. Businessman. When the business began to lose money, he talked Holmes into cutting corners to staunch the hemorrhaging. The building inspectors called them on it.

The next logical step had been to bribe the inspectors. That's where Lynnette Palmer and Dennis Birdsong came into play. They needed the right people in the right positions to pull off any kind of scam. So, out with the old, and in with the incompetent and greedy. It worked for a while in Palmetto Gardens and Sunshine Beach, but they needed to streamline the game.

Shay admitted he was amazed at how quickly his partner and cousin took to crime. Bradley Holmes had always worked the public relations angle and had a close relationship with several city councilmen, some of whom didn't mind getting dirty. Holmes sniffed them out. Sub-standard projects were built, and then sold at huge profits. The city used Shay and Holmes for government construction whenever possible—with certain council members receiving kickbacks funneled through dummy consulting firms, all owned by S and H relatives, at least on paper.

Shay and Holmes had it down to a science until Jason was elected to the board, asking questions and making requests.

But Bill's article had shocked the partners. His information was too accurate for simple research. Holmes suspected the leak had come from the city, and according to Shay, conducted several meetings with city officials on the payroll. When the accountant informed on Marc, the two realized they had a major internal problem and mistakenly pegged him as Bill's source. Lynnette Palmer, trying to be a team player, botched the whole thing by killing him.

Neither man thought much about Jason until he showed up for Marc's funeral. His relationship to Marc scared the crap out of them.

Shay swore he had no idea who killed Marc and Bill, until the end. He and Holmes were dining out when a call from the security company interrupted them. Informed the cameras caught a man and a woman entering with a key, but not disarming the alarm system, sent the two scrambling back to the offices. Holmes alerted Lynnette who agreed to meet them there. It was during the ride that Bradley Holmes confessed to multiple murders, and Lynnette's role in the first.

When it became obvious Jason and I were destined for the same fate, Shay caved. If he went to prison, he didn't want it to be for accessory to murder. Instead of getting the car, he'd gone to his office and called the cops.

In his confession, Shay named Bennett Russell, Gerald Talman, Eleanor White, and Ron Zimmerman as his co-conspirators. He named the man who scheduled building inspections as in on the scheme. He also gave up his co-workers. Dennis Birdsong and two accountants, including the one who'd fingered Marc, were rousted out of bed and arrested, too. Holmes had lawyered up, refusing to talk.

We knew Peggy had sent one of the e-mails to Bill, but never discovered the other sender. I suspected it was someone who had either seen or heard something suspicious, but didn't want to be identified as a whistleblower. Jason and I still had no answers for Marc's behavior.

"My guess is he was scared to death and not thinking straight. In his mind, mailing the CD to himself and giving you the key as back-up made perfect sense."

I'd shivered remembering the alley. "And he did try to call you earlier that evening. Whatever instructions he was going to give me died with him. I can only assume he wanted me to get the CD to you and the information on it to Bill."

"Like I said, he was scared to death."

That was early Saturday morning. I now sat at my kitchen table enjoying a cup of coffee and reading my article in the Sunday *Standard*—my ordeal emblazoned in bold headlines on the front page.

Reporter Cracks Bribery-Murder Case by Shelley Jackson.

"By Shelley Jackson," I murmured out loud.

A shiver of self-satisfaction vibrated through me. I'd waited a long time to see my byline on a front page story. I glanced at the clock—almost noon. Was it too early to start checking my e-mail and voice messages for congratulations? I felt like a crusader saving the city from evil, and the thought of all that praise coming my way left me a trifle breathless.

My cell phone rang. It was Jason. I'd not spoken to

him much since I moved back home. I'd returned yesterday afternoon disappointed he'd not tried to dissuade me from leaving.

"Hi, dumpling," I teasingly answered. His deep rumbling chuckle in my ear sent a wave of warmth surging from head to toe.

"I just finished reading the paper. You did a great job. I hear the mayor is calling a press conference later."

"He should. The city council is decimated."

"One of the local TV stations just broke in to say the scheduler's body was found in his car in the parking lot at a mall. He committed suicide."

"Really?" I asked, wondering if I should check it out, and then remembered I had a couple of days off. Cal would send Slattery.

"Sorry I haven't called, but I spent most of yesterday on the phone to L. A."

"Don't worry about it. I've been writing follow up stories. I went to bed at nine o'clock and didn't wake up for twelve hours. I am, however, well-rested and free as a bird today. Want to come over and watch the press conference? Afterwards, we can…talk."

I put a lot of meaning into that last word. The ironic thing was I did want to talk—about us. I planned admitting I loved him. Before I went to bed last night, I'd even mapped out how to solve the problem of a coast to coast romance. A new office in South Florida would make a great place to transfer the company headquarters.

Daddy would want me to have a bang up wedding, of course, and as long as Jason didn't object, I saw no reason not to indulge him. A strapless white gown with

Mother's pearls would look elegant. I even visualized my attendants wearing autumn colors.

"Shelley, are you there?"

Jason's voice brought me out of my fantasy. "Oh, yes, sorry. I was thinking. What did you say?"

"I said I'd like to talk to you, too. The press conference is scheduled for three o'clock. I'll come by a few minutes early."

"Wonderful. I'll be waiting."

I hung up heaving a deep sigh. He wanted to talk? To confess how much he loved me? I drained my coffee cup and jumped to my feet. Today was going to be the best day of my life.

****

Jason arrived fifteen minutes early. I opened the door and gazed into the eyes of a relaxed, smiling man. In his hand, he held a single red rose.

"A reward to one of the most fascinating women I've ever met," he said, extending his arm.

I took the rose and buried my nose in its slightly opened petals, inhaling the sweet, heady scent.

"Come on in. You look rested."

"Now that Marc's killer is dead and the whole story out, I can sleep again."

I laid the rose on the hall table and led him into the living room. "Have a seat. Can I get you some coffee?"

"No thanks." He sat down in the corner of the sofa. "Have you spoken to Detective Sorenson in the last twenty-four hours?"

"No, why?"

"He took the information from the cryptogram and checked out the bottom drawer of the desk. It contained a hard copy of a list of names. A CD was taped underneath the drawer."

"A list? What kind of list?"

"Marc had filled in the blank spaces on those codes. We were right about the dates, account numbers, check amounts, and the year being the starting point. The letters in front of the account numbers referred to specific banks in the Caribbean. The letters before the dates were Marc's code for the criminals."

"He called Gerald Talman Wicked Knight—WK. Eleanor White—BOW—stood for Bitch on Wheels, and Bennett Russell had the distinction be being referred to as Fearless Leader."

It figured Marc would be a *Rocky and Bullwinkle* fan. "FL. What about Zimmerman and the building inspector?"

"The building inspector wasn't listed, but Zimmerman was AD, as in Adolph."

"Adolph Hitler?"

Jason shrugged. "Why not. It turns out he's been running extortion for close to the entire twenty years he's been City Manager."

"And the Mayor? Was he in on any of it?"

"Not that we know of. Cosworth and Zimmerman were close friends and political buddies, but apparently not close enough to share the goodies." Jason shot a look at me. "I called Peggy first thing yesterday morning and gave her the news."

"Oh, good. I was so wrapped up in writing, I forgot all about her. How did she take it?"

"She was shocked, but not overly surprised. I guess the events of the last week or so made her suspicious that someone from Shay and Holmes had killed Marc. She just didn't suspect her boss and the CEO." He picked up the remote and turned on the TV. "I like Peggy. She was in love with my brother and would have made a good wife."

He settled back crossing his legs, his attention on the screen. Without knowing why, I took his last sentence as a mild rebuke.

Before I could question him, the TV station interrupted regular programming with breaking news. An empty podium standing in a large room appeared onscreen. In the background voices babbled. A TV reporter stepped in front of the camera.

"Good afternoon. This is Tom Resnick with Channel 8 News. We are in the press room of City Hall awaiting the mayor and what's left of the city council for a press conference. This weekend's stunning events have slammed the residents of Port Royale with shock and disbelief. Council members Bennett Russell, Gerald Talman, and Eleanor White, along with City Manager Ron Zimmerman, were arrested late Friday night in connection with a bribery scandal involving well-known entrepreneurs, Shay and Holmes Development and Construction Company.

"Kenneth Shay, the Chief Operating Officer, is also under arrest, as is Bradley Holmes, the CEO. The Chief Financial Officer, Lynnette Palmer, was shot to death by police in the Shay and Holmes offices. She, Mr. Shay, and Mr. Holmes were attempting to kidnap at gunpoint a member of the Shay and Holmes board of directors, renowned architect Jason Mallory, and *South Florida Standard* reporter, Shelley Jackson. When ordered to drop the weapon, Ms. Palmer opened fire, dying in the ensuing gun battle.

"In a statement to police, Mr. Shay said that Ms.

Palmer confessed to the murder of Marc Chambers, an accountant at Shay and Holmes, and that his partner, Bradley Holmes, was responsible for the deaths of investigative reporter, Bill Mathias, and reporter Douglas Elliott."

A door opened behind the podium. The mayor, Jose Cortez, and Anne Hodges, along with several others filed out. The mayor walked up to the bristling microphones adorning the stand, while the rest flanked him a few feet behind.

"We're about to begin." The TV announcer stepped out of camera range.

Mayor Cosworth looked as if he hadn't slept in weeks. His normally jovial face was grim and no amount of make-up could hide the deeply grooved lines in his forehead or those running from nose to mouth. He'd aged ten years since I'd last seen him. The sheet of paper in his hand shook. I'd heard that lawsuits being filed against Shay and Holmes and the city had already hit lawyers' offices.

The mayor cleared his throat. "Ladies and gentlemen of the press, I want to thank you for attending. As you know, the city of Port Royale is deeply saddened by the actions of some of its council members and the city manager. People I have known and worked with for many years are accused of bribery, defiling their oaths to serve the community, and shredding the confidence of the citizens. For this I truly and humbly apologize. Late yesterday, I asked for and received the resignations of Gerald Talman, Russell Bennett, and Eleanor White along with that of City Manager Ron Zimmerman. I then notified the Governor asking him to appoint replacements as soon as possible."

His shaking hand reached for the glass of water on the stand and he sipped before continuing.

"Ron Zimmerman was my friend and confidant for many years, and while I had no knowledge of what was occurring, as your mayor, I should have been more vigilant. Therefore, it is with deep sorrow that I tender my resignation effective as soon as the Governor replies to my request."

He gestured with his hand to the people behind him. "To my left is Councilman Jose Cortez. I've asked that he be appointed as interim mayor. Next to him are Grace DeWine, John Graham, and Harold Shipley. I suggested them to replace Bennett Russell, Eleanor White, and Gerald Talman on the city council. On my right, is Councilwoman Anne Hodges whom I hope will be your Vice-Mayor. Beside her is Raul Martinez, the man I asked to take Councilman Cortez's place. On the end is Miguel Cruz who will step up from his position as Assistant City attorney to fill the vacancy left by Mr. Zimmerman."

Cosworth sipped again from the glass. In a matter of hours, his entire political world had collapsed.

"Because of my close association with those arrested, I want no hint of impropriety to arise regarding their appointments. As stated earlier, I have been in contact with the governor and he has agreed a special election should be held as soon as possible. We will announce details when they are available.

"All construction performed by Shay and Holmes Construction and Development in the past six years will be re-inspected. Anything found to be substandard will be dealt with by the city. Mr. James Collier will take over the reins as head of the building department.

"I have been your mayor for over twenty years. I like to think I accomplished some constructive good for the people of the city, but feel I have let you down when it counted the most. For that I am grievously sorry and most ashamed."

A close up camera shot showed the tears in his eyes. For the first time in my life, I felt sorry for a politician.

"I know you all have questions, but at the moment I have no answers. I cannot comment on an ongoing police investigation, and my heart is too sore to comment on anything else. Thank you for attending."

He turned abruptly and walked through the door followed by the others. Shouted questions bombarded their backs. The TV reporter returned on-camera.

"Here is yet another shock with Mayor Cosworth's decision to resign. The selection of Jose Cortez as interim mayor will be popular. He has been…"

Jason clicked the TV off. "Do you think Cortez will run for Mayor?" he asked.

"Without a doubt. He's young, charismatic, and ambitious as hell. Ten years from now he'll be Governor or Senator Cortez."

I rose from the sofa. Now was the time to drop my bomb. "Jason, we need to talk. There's something I have to tell you."

He also stood, smiled, and ran a knuckle down my cheek, then feathered a light kiss in its wake.

"I know. I want to tell you something, too, but ladies first."

I pulled back from his kiss looking him in the eye. I'd never said this to a man before and wasn't sure of the correct protocol. I plunged in anyway.

"Jason Mallory, I love you." I held my breath awaiting his reaction.

He smiled and raised an eyebrow. "Do you, my dear?"

"Very much," I assured him. "So much so that I'm beginning to think in terms of marriage. Does that scare you?"

He rose and pulled me up with him. "Right down to my socks."

His failure to repeat those three little words caused my heart to constrict. "Do...do you love me?" I didn't like the hesitant tone of my voice.

"I haven't really thought about it. I love being with you. You can carry on a sensible conversation and being a reporter, you've learned how to listen—an art a lot of people lack. But marriage—I don't see it. I think I told you that a long time ago."

My heart no longer constricted. Instead it plummeted straight down to the floor. I gaped at him as my gaze swept his face hoping to see something other than the pitying expression he wore.

"But...but I love you," I cried, wondering if he hadn't heard correctly.

"Shelley, think about it. We'd devour each other like cannibals. Within two years we'd be reduced to bones. You claim you love me, but the simple fact is I'm the first man you couldn't control."

"What are you talking about?"

"You say you're looking for a nice guy, but you dump every nice guy you've ever known."

"I don't dump them. Things just never worked out," I protested still in the dark as to what he meant.

"Take Marc. He was a nice guy. Did you ever realize that everything you two did together, every place you went, was something you liked? You enjoy South Street, the beachfront, and Riverside. Marc preferred dinner in a quiet, out-of-the-way restaurant. He loved the symphony, the opera, and a good play."

I stared, confused and at a loss for words. "I…I didn't know that."

"You never took the time to find out. You did what you wanted to do, and because he was a nice guy, Marc went along with it. It placed you in control. And the minute you were in control, you lost interest in, and respect for, the nice guy."

"That's not true!"

"Yes, it is." He stopped and ran his hand through his hair. "Suppose I did say I loved you. Suppose we did get married. Where would we live?"

"I haven't worked it all out yet, but we can solve any problem that faces us."

"You just got Bill's job. Would you be willing to chuck it all and move to L. A. where the reporters are plentiful and highly competitive? Could you start at the bottom after having been on top? Or do you expect me to close up my offices in California and move here—something I'm not willing to do."

"But I read you were considering opening an office in South Florida."

He shook his head. "Shelley, you're a reporter. Do you believe everything you read? I am expanding, but not in South Florida. Texas is much more tax friendly to business than California. I've also been in active negotiations to acquire a construction company in Singapore to cover my far eastern sites. In fact, I have to leave for the airport in a few minutes. By this time tomorrow I'll be on my way there. My company's just been hired to build a sixty-story office building. Sorry, but I have no intention of moving here. Will you consider moving to Los Angeles or Texas?"

I brushed a hand across my forehead. "Why do I have to make the sacrifice? We can work something out." His logic irked me, and I floundered for an argument strong enough to convince him I was right.

"A coast to coast marriage? I don't think so."

"But we're so good together," I cried. "We have to at least try."

He shook his head, the pity growing stronger in his eyes. "You're the last person I'd expect to confuse fantastic sex with love. Maybe I do love you, Shelley, but right now it's just not enough. At the moment, I'm still raw with guilt about Marc. And I was too angry at his murder to grieve. I need time. I need space. And I need to concentrate on my business. Let's give it a few months. Three months from today one of us will call and the other will be happy to answer the phone. But my guess is one, or both of us, will forget to punch in those numbers."

"That's not true!"

He leaned over and pinched my chin between his thumb and forefinger, lifting my face. His lips lightly brushed mine.

"Yes, it is. I know it, and so do you."

He walked to the door and opened it, then turned to face me one last time. I half expected to hear the words, "Frankly, my dear, I don't give a damn."

"Goodbye, Shelley. Who knows? I could be wrong. A part of me hopes I am."

He smiled and stepped through the doorway. The door closed with a soft, but very final click. His footsteps disappeared down the sidewalk. A car door slammed and an engine turned over. A second later, he pulled away.

I stumbled into the living room, sinking onto the sofa. My chin quivered, and I clamped my teeth down hard on my lower lip as though the physical pain could alleviate the emotional. It did no good. Tears trickled down my cheeks.

"No, he's wrong," I said out loud. "He's wrong about everything."

I didn't break up with Marc because I lost respect. The chemistry between us had been wrong. I ignored the fact I hadn't cared enough about Marc to call when I knew he was upset about something. Did that mean I'd lost respect for him? *No, not possible.*

Jason was the man of my dreams, my future. I had to get him back.

"You'll see, Jason. I will call. Forget three months. I'll call next week, just to say hello, and the week after that. I'll call every week until you agree we're right for each other."

I wiped my eyes and face with the hem of my shirt and raised my chin. I refused to let him walk away like Rhett Butler.

My cell phone rang. I leapt to my feet and ran into the kitchen. Jason! It had to be Jason calling to say he'd made a mistake—that he was coming back, that we'd straighten out any problems about who lived and worked where. An east coast office of Mallory Architectural could be lucrative and a boon to his career. Maybe he'd realized it. If not, I knew I could convince him *my* logic was the one to follow.

I fumbled for the phone looking eagerly at the incoming ID. My shoulders slumped. It was Cal.

"Hello, Cal," I answered with no enthusiasm.

"Jackson, where are you?"

"At home, why?" I sniffed and reached for a tissue from a box on the counter, blotting my cheeks.

"I just got a call from Everett Weiland."

"The environmentalist who chains himself to every tree and lives out in the middle of the Everglades? What did he want?"

I tossed the tissue into the trash and sat at my kitchen table. Many people considered Everett Weiland to be a dedicated conservationist. Just as many considered him a nut case.

"He claims someone is dumping toxic chemicals into the 'Glades, killing fish and wildlife."

I sniffed again. "The sugar industry has been accused of doing that for years. What makes this any different?"

"Weiland says he knows who's doing it and has pictures to prove it. He also refuses to go to any government agency. Claims they're in the pocket of big business—including the chemical companies. He's in town for another couple of hours and agreed to meet you at a little bar called Ralphie's on Juniper Avenue. It's across from the cemetery."

"Cal, I can't. Not right now. Send someone else." I had to concentrate on wooing Jason back. He was my priority at the moment.

"Jackson, I'm not asking you. I'm telling you to go meet him. This is the kind of story that makes the careers of reporters *and* editors. Did I tell you the wire services have picked up your latest on the bribery scandal? The *New York Times* called for crissakes."

I straightened my spine. "You're kidding."

"I don't kid. They may use excerpts from your piece on one of the inside pages. It's the kind of thing a mid-market reporter dreams of. American News Network also called."

I visualized my name as a byline in the *New York Times* and being interviewed by John Claymore, their top reporter. I had the potential to be the next Bob Woodward. A rush of adrenaline surged through me. Then Jason's face flashed through my mind.

"Cal, I've got a personal problem at the moment and…"

"There are no personal problems when it comes to news reporting, Jackson. Those who hesitate lose. I don't intend to lose. Now, that's Ralphie's on Juniper across from the cemetery. Got it?"

I wavered. I'd give Jason a few days without me, and then call. In the meantime, it wouldn't hurt to see what this environmentalist had to say.

"I'll find it."

"This could be big, Jackson. Don't blow it."

He hung up. I slipped a new disc into my recorder and jammed it into my purse, then changed clothes. Grabbing my car keys, I stopped in front of the foyer mirror to run a brush through my hair and smoothed color on my lips.

My nerves hummed with excitement and anticipation. The Everglades and its environmental protection were of national interest. The front row in the White House briefing room swam in front of my eyes. I smiled at my reflection.

Then, my gaze fell on the red rose Jason had given me. I picked it up and held the fragrant bloom under my nose, inhaling the intoxicating perfume.

"I'll call, Jason. I promise."

I laid it on the table, turned and ran out of the house to keep my appointment with Everett Weiland.

A word from the author...

I was born in Indianapolis, Indiana, but lived for many years in Memphis, Tennessee which I now consider home. I have two adult children and seven grandchildren. At present, I reside in Ft.Lauderdale, Florida with my husband, Bruce.

I've been a serious writer since 2002 and belong to Romance Writers of America, River City Romance Writers, and the Florida chapter of Mystery Writers of America.

I love writing and hope readers enjoy the journey along with me.

~*~

Other Suzanne Rossi titles
available from The Wild Rose Press, Inc.

ALONG CAME QUINN
ALL IN THE FAMILY
A TANGLED WEB
NEARLY DEPARTED
HEAR NO EVIL
THE REUNION
DEADLY INHERITANCE
DEATH IS THE PITS
THROUGH MY EYES
A NOVEL DEATH

Thank you for purchasing
this publication of The Wild Rose Press, Inc.

If you enjoyed the story, we would appreciate your
letting others know by leaving a review.

For other wonderful stories,
please visit our on-line bookstore at
www.thewildrosepress.com.

For questions or more information
contact us at
info@thewildrosepress.com.

The Wild Rose Press, Inc.
www.thewildrosepress.com

Stay current with The Wild Rose Press, Inc.

Like us on Facebook

https://www.facebook.com/TheWildRosePress

And Follow us on Twitter
https://twitter.com/WildRosePress